To Joan
and
in memory of my father
Des O'Sullivan (1929–2000)

I have already died all deaths,
And I am going to die all deaths again.
Die the death of the wood in the tree,
Die the stone death in the mountain,
Earth death in the sand,
Leaf death in the crackling summer grass
And the poor bloody human death.

'All Deaths', HERMANN HESSE

AUTHOR'S NOTE

This is a work of fiction. Though based on many factual events, a certain licence is taken with historical detail and timing. The surnames of actual participants in these events have been changed. The personalities and motivations of all the characters are purely fictional. No offence is intended to any relatives of the people upon whom these characters are based.

*T*he sheep, sheared and skinned, hangs by fettered hind legs from the ash tree in the farmyard. Its inner layer of tissue is stretched opaquely over the sculpted musculature. Blood drips from the clubbed head and stains the few clumps of wool that have not been gathered up from below. A last spiritless kick sends the naked form swinging lightly. The movement sets off the dogs again, encouraging each other to ever wilder claims from their rude, low-slung kennel. Inside the farmhouse, a man breaks open a potato. The steam from the flowery pulp rises and renews the film of sweat on his face. He picks out a strand of wool from the starched innards with bloodied fingers.

When the boy, home from school, his son, bolts into the yard, the hanging sheep is a dizzy red blur to him after the running. Then it is a pair of eyes following his more hesitant progress. Only when he reaches the half-door of the farmhouse and looks back does the stripped animal become a sore, a peeled scab all across the boy's flesh. He retreats from the yard into the kitchen, tripping back-wards on the step.

'Where did we get the sheep, Da?'

The man rolls the hot mush in his mouth around the words.

'Ask me no questions and I'll tell you no lies. You're late. I was waiting on you to finish the sheep.'

The boy wonders what tortures remained for the raw pendulum of dead meat in the yard.

'I had to carry a box home for Mary White. The Master said to.'

'Couldn't she carry her own box home? What was in it?'

The boy shrugs, edges away towards the stairs leading up out of the kitchen. His father, splitting another potato, has yet to look up *at him. The boy is hungry but the need to escape is stronger. Stronger even than the ache in his arms and legs that has already begun; his mother's starved, greyhound face and the big cow's belly under the bedclothes awaiting him.*

'What kind are you that you wouldn't look at what you were carrying? Where you going now?'

'Up to see Mammy.'

His father lowers his spoon and pushes back his stool.

'Come on. It'll be dark in no time and we won't be able to see our noses. Bring the bucket.'

There are a few knobs of timber in the bucket for the unlit fire. The boy tips them out on the hearth and from one, a twisted knot drops out. It is the clenched shape of his mother's hand gripping the bed sheet. He hurries from the kitchen, where the little light that has leaked inwards is already leaving.

Half-buried stones on the yard shine from the earlier rain in silted whorls of mud. The red-black stain spreads outwards. He has never felt so fearful of the howling dogs. The makeshift kennel walls rattle too loosely under the strain of their assaults. His father steadies the suspended sheep with one hand. In the other, he holds a long knife and the boy understands. He looks at the sheep's underside. It is the baby inside her that sucks the life out of his mother. His stomach sickens.

'Why do the sheep have to be hanging up in the air, Da? Why's it off up there, Da?'

His father traces a line along the underbelly with the blunt end of the knife.

'To keep the rats off. Stick the bucket in there under him.'

The boy obeys, crouching forward with an eye to the knife above him that presses close to bursting. A redbreast flitters down magically before him as if from the dead sheep's mouth and the boy becomes momentarily lost in the darting and halting of its playful search. Then, he is startled by a crack, a splintering of timber from the kennels. He tries to clamber away but falls over the bucket and, heavily, against his father's legs. The knife, his father's only prop now, passes through the slick of membrane and slides all the way down the underbelly, releasing a flood of blood over the boy. The dogs – a black, a brindle and a white – bully each other madly out through the gaps in the exploding kennel. The redbreast veers upwards and away. The boy flees.

'Don't run!'

The dogs rush by his father, taking him like a corner. Out in the next field, the boy wades against the cross-flow of earthen drills, tripping on peaks, stumbling in hollows. The dogs are more sure-footed and are upon him before he makes the far ditch. He coils himself up blindly, hedgehog-tight, but teeth sink into his bare legs, into the arms protecting his head and neck, and through the shirt on his back. He tries to scream, to cry out that the blood is not his, but he cannot, and, besides, it is too late because his own blood is one now with the dead sheep's. He is already surrendering to them when a paw claws its way into his mouth and he bites hard, the gristle of sinews and sharp nails splitting between his teeth.

His father rushes in, wielding a timber lath from the broken kennel. He thrashes the dogs, cutting weals into their gaunt-ribbed flanks, beating them away from the boy. Yelping vaingloriously, the dogs scatter and gather a little way off. The boy's body is aflame with pain.

'Kill 'em, Da! They nearly killed me.'

His father looks down at him, thinking. He doesn't come near. He looks at the dogs. The startled black ovals of their eyes are averted from him.

'You only got a few scratches and you wouldn'ta got 'em if you didn't run. You were lucky you weren't ate alive, boy.'

His father slopes away, the dogs preceding him, their long narrow heads lowered almost to the ground. One is limping badly. The white. The boy tastes the foul, indigestible bone of defeat.

This is the dog he chooses to avenge himself upon.

A shrapnel of crows exploded from the trees and hedgerows and filled a wild dark acre of sky above the plain of fields stretching towards the town. The song he'd been humming absent-mindedly as he locked his dogs in the lean-to shed forgot itself. Slowly, respectfully, the dead bell pealed. Last thing a fellow expected to hear at seven in the morning.

Sergeant Tom Enright hated Tipperary but, dead bell or not, he was glad to be back there. A week of leave in Listowel's cold and damp had set winter creeping unseasonably through his bones. The bark and howl of his greyhounds were easier to listen to than Mary's constant pleading – *You'll be shot, Tom, and what then?* – and the child's screeching – *Can you not shut him up, Mary?* He whipped the stick he'd been stripping against the kennel door, letting fear insinuate itself within and the noise became a whimpering.

Above him, the lowering grey continued to make of itself a more distant milkiness. The hills, a mere shade less pale than the sky, had begun to form themselves. Across a field spiked with clusters of reed, two worn paths wider than a cart trail meandered. Dog-runs. Fragments of small animal bone, ceramic, brittle, glistened with milky light. Stray balls of rabbit fur, like thistledown, stirred in the wet grass.

He flexed the stiffness out of his muscles, and the hangover, clutching at the base of his brain, yielded its grip a little. The breath he drew in seemed enormous and to fill even the scarred hollow at the right side of his chest. Bloody Hun bastards. His boot cracked against the frail door to quieten the latest whines from inside.

Dense early summer foliage obscured his view of the town so that only the nesting place of the dead bell was clearly visible with his good eye. The limestone cathedral tower reminded him again of one he'd seen from Funchal harbour on a grey morning before the colours of Madeira started up, of red-tiled roofs, the flame of bignonia vines. The tic, a snapping stretch of the neck where once he'd shipped a hawker's ice pick in Hong Kong, rippled through him and the machine of his body tightened up. He didn't need the miracles of bleeding statues or Mary's prayers to survive, to grow stronger. The morning was enough for him, and the dogs and Tipperary and the rough-and-tumble of whatever new twist the dead bell marked in the fight with the rebels. Pot-luck shooters, the lot of them. Seven bullets they'd needed to set the dead bell ringing for Constable Finnegan, the man he'd come to replace. Shot down in front of the wife before the most of them took to the hills.

He kicked the shed door again because the dogs had gone too quiet. He savoured their confused response. Muted, dissipated howls, frail-pitched weakness strangling them in their darkness. Foley, his doggyman, was nowhere to be seen. Sometimes he wondered if the fellow ever came near the place, the dogs always seemed so hungry.

Lighting a cigarette, Enright walked towards the car parked at the timber gate. The coughing didn't last long and what he spat out into the grass was clear as pine resin. He began to turn the mud-encrusted crank of the Ford Touring car but weary pistons protested the four-hour trip from Listowel. He caught his own reflection, sky-wrapped in the windscreen. Out in a sweat already. He tried again but the crank shot back and skinned his knuckles. He kicked the radiator grille, denting the neat aluminium symmetry a little more. No let-up in the dead bell. He took the Webley Mark VI revolver from inside his bottle-green Royal Irish Constabulary tunic and eased the catch back. The rough, indented grip scratched into his palm as he held the gun ready in his trench-coat pocket and set off for the town.

Fuck it, he told himself, only another mile.

Beyond the flat green excess of countryside, the Lady's Well Road descended steeply into the market town and became Pike Street. Each entrance road to the town was possessed of the same declivity as though the weight of buildings, paving, packed-earth streets and people had pressed downwards over time making a crater of the place.

As he looked down from the summit of Pike Street he felt again that sinking of the stomach he'd had on his first day in town, provoked in him by the District Inspector's initial misgivings. Always the same, all his life. The misgivings of others. Below the clock tower down the Limerick docks at fifteen years of age, and Dempsey the skipper with the wilted whiskers below a boozy nose. *Not even in a boat on the Feale?* Or signing up for the 29th Battalion in Vancouver, the Medical Officer, McDermott, Scots-sceptical and repeating . . . *Declares that he is not subject to fits of any description?* Even the Army Land Grant official, *Debility – you ready for thirty acres of grief, Lieutenant?* Shouldn't have been surprised when DI Johnstone had challenged him too. Six weeks' training in the Phoenix Park depot and not a mention of Mary's younger brother, Jimmy. Then, even while his palm was still warm from the welcoming handshake, *Can we depend on you, Constable?*

Enright hadn't known then that Johnstone was an ex-Irish Guard, though he might have guessed from the ramrod bearing and the supercilious lock-fastness of the jaw. A rum lot, those buggers. Came across them over in France, shaving when there was scarcely enough water to drink and polishing their boots before they lobbed them down in the muck. But Enright had faced Johnstone down – *And why wouldn't you?* – thinking he'd let him work for his sir or ask for it. *Our Barracks in Listowel think your brother-in-law may be a rebel and it seems he owns the cottage you and your wife live in.*

Enright went hurriedly by the high boundary wall of Dr Brady's house at the end of Pike Street, and with a shiver, as he always did. The place might have been a wing of the Balfour Military Sanatorium over in British Columbia, with its pitch-dipped beams latticed across white walls stained by the green rain from pines alongside. Pike Street widened out on to the more prosperous Cathedral Street, with its superior, more solid class of two- and three-storey buildings. On the far side of the street the dead bell above the Romanesque cathedral pealed its last.

My wife's people have no time for me nor have I for them, and as for the cottage, that's an arrangement between my wife and her brother. His reply had been greeted by mirthless laughter and a grin thin as a crack in an eggshell. *By God, I think I may have found the scarecrow I needed, now that we've scattered the rebels into the hills.*

Enright soon learned that John Carty, Sinn Féin town councillor and general muck-stirrer, hadn't been at home when the black gang called at midnight a week after Finnegan's murder. The blacked-up minstrels, two RIC men from Dovea Barracks and an Auxiliary officer, took his younger brother Liam instead. Out on the Holycross Road, they put a few bullets in his skull and hung a placard round his neck. SPIES AND TRAITORS BEWARE – BY ORDER OF IRA. Finnegan's murder avenged, the two Dovea boys and the Auxie were moved to safer waters up west.

Beyond the river bridge that divided the town, Enright entered the unusually wide plaza that was Main Street. Among the handful of shopkeepers unlocking timber shutters, shawlies out hunting for scraps and men heading to work, there wasn't one he'd ask for whom the dead bell had been ringing. It was always better to pretend to know everything, he thought sourly, like the God they cowered beneath. Each one in turn hoved well clear of him in deference to the reputation earned in dispatching fifteen men to one or other far incarceration, while more than a few others had felt the lash in a dark lane after curfew or worse than the lash in the holding cell below the barracks.

Enright crossed the intersection of Main Street with the long, chestnut-lined mall comprising the red-brick townhouses of merchants, solicitors and uppity clerks. A mere three months in the barracks and already a sergeant and running the show, he'd raided the workshed behind a furniture store down there and smashed up their underground Republican Court. Three more heroes for the detention camps and a good battering for a send-off. *There's only one law in here, Charlie boy, and I make it up as I go along.* A hardy bugger that Charlie Dooley, though. Have to watch his back if that rebel court clerk ever got out.

Neither the recollected glory days nor the absence of blood on the streets offered much sustenance as he wound his way along the narrow, meandering curve of Friary Street. His stomach ached with a hunger that the brain might easily have taken for trepidation if a fellow wasn't careful. Every disparate, bothersome thing seemed to have found a common purpose as yet unknown to him. Sinn Féin's overwhelming victory in the elections; the encroachment of the rebels ever closer to town; the shooting of Sir Arthur Vicars outside Listowel that should have had nothing to do with his grip on this Tipperary town but somehow had; the persistent shivers and stiffness in him at odds with the season; Mary's deepening disaffection. The dead bell.

The barracks stood unimpressively among the ranks of shops and houses fronting Friary Street. A squat two-storey block, the manure of past mart days caked its rough grey dash up to the ground-floor windowsills. Thrown stones and the occasional bullet hole from before Enright's time had left their pockmarks. Caged windows and the blind-seeming slit in the weighty door irritated him each time he turned into the street. Even a mug like Gabriel Jack back in BC knew that climbing into a hole didn't make you safe. Safety was out in the open, where you stood half a chance of being the hunter not the hunted. Mary ought to know that, instead of imploring him to lie low in the barracks. She'd listened to that half-bred Okanagan often enough.

The echo of Enright's hobnailed boots passed uninterrupted along the valley of closed doors and curtained windows. Only once, on the morning after the first miracle at the bleeding statue in Templemore, had he seen the street so deserted at this hour. Buck savages, he thought, no better than the Redskins or the Chinamen or the juju boys over in the Congo. He banged out his signature on the heavy barracks door; a knock, a pause, then two quick ones. The slit opened upon a pair of youthful, unfamiliar eyes bobbing uncertainly in the slice of light. He knew the eyes of all the men, fear in the most of them. He'd studied them often enough, tested them in his distrust. The perplexed bovine stare of Head Constable Gallagher. The Scot, Baldwin's dull inscrutability. An Ulster accent emerged, light-weight and panicky.

'What do you want?'

A sense of anonymity oppressed Enright and he raged against it, fighting back the foolish thought that he'd returned to the wrong place.

'Open the door or I'll . . .'

The eyes floated away into the well of darkness. Muffled words were exchanged inside. He pulled out his revolver, stood with his back clamped to the door.

'Open the damn door!'

The same terrified young eyes reappeared. Of course. The new man. The air Enright pulled into his lungs from the enclosed street tasted rancid and smelled worse; a foul admixture of yesterday's stewed gruel and last night's damp sleep escaping from the cracked doors and ill-fitting windows of Monk's Lane, a forbidding tunnel of decay opposite the barracks. Four weeks they'd waited on a replacement for Phelan, the latest deserter, and this was what they got.

'Listen, boy, I'm your Sergeant. Now, pull the bolts like a good lad.'

As the door eased inwards, the metallic rumble of heavy engines skirting the top of the railway bridge drowned out the young constable's apologies. Papenfus and the Auxies motoring in from their borrowed mansion at Castle Bennett. Five, six faces worried in Enright's direction from behind the barracks counter. Gallagher, grey-haired and anxious, stood ridiculously to attention as he addressed the phone.

'Two miles outside the town, Mr Johnstone. On the Templemore Road.'

Relieved to know that his grip on the town remained intact, Enright's temper improved. He looked enquiringly at the others as they buttoned up tunics, fiddled incompetently with the breeches of Lee Enfields. One shook his head despairingly, another eyed Enright contemptuously. One old, the other useless. Keane, all paunchy and soft too around the shoulders. Harvey, the Tan, whose accent he could never make out, sleep-faced and ragged. And here, beside him, another hopeless case, he supposed.

The young fellow was taller than Enright by a few inches, six foot, maybe six one, but stick-thin and too delicate a face, all long lashes and skeletal cheeks. Enright elbowed the new man's loose-fitting sleeve. The clash of sharp bone hurt both of them.

'What's going on?'

'An ambush, Sergeant. Two dead. Two of our boys from Clonore Barracks.'

Paddy Kinahan was getting bolder still. Ran the rebel show in these parts but remained no more than a face in a photograph to Enright, though he saw that big-chinned scowl become a smile now and a laughing wrinkle spread across the gravestone slab of high forehead. Stopped a train outside town a month back and robbed the post. Blew a bridge last week that shook Enright out of his sleep in the barracks, thinking he was back in France, it was so near.

At the counter, Gallagher acted out an absurdly confused pantomime of saluting and replacing the phone in its cradle. Outside, the traffic of Auxies, joined now by the main body of Tans, began to roar to a halt. The only decent stand the Head

Constable had ever taken was to insist there wasn't room in the barracks to accommodate more than a handful of those Tan layabouts; jailbirds and con men all. On seeing Enright, Gallagher's expression changed from nervy obsequiousness to relief. The door shook under the rain of blows from outside. The whiplash in the voice of Captain Papenfus found its echo in Enright's gruff command to the new recruit.

'Get the door . . . What's your name?'

'Timmoney, sir. Edward.'

A fist-like tautness of body and a busy stride made up for the Auxie captain's lack of inches. His Glengarry cap clung precariously to the thick, shaven head. He held his temper in check with a similar precariousness. The sound of Papenfus drumming on the barracks counter with his stubby fingers distracted the Head Constable as he spoke. Already flustered with a grief that melted the waters of his eyes, Gallagher floundered pitifully.

The South African, Enright knew, had earned a detachment similar to his own. They had both kicked off the provincial clay from their boots but the stocky Boer had walked away from privilege, not, as in Enright's case, from a swampy farm outside Listowel that would never be his anyway and a shebeen in Tea Lane that he lost because his aunt took a husband at forty-five and broke her promise. Papenfus had survived the slaughter of his battalion at the Somme, not far from Pozières where Enright, out digging a jumping-off trench with the Canadians, copped a flesh wound in the right thigh from a Bergmann hail that mowed down half a dozen men around him. After the war he'd ended up in Edinburgh, an unlikely medical student until he enlisted in the Auxiliary Force. A year of rough raiding later and he still went unscathed. Lucky. But getting hit, left, right and centre and surviving, as Enright himself had done, that was more than luck. He didn't try to name the quality. What mattered was that he knew he possessed it and that it was something more substantial than the Boer's bullet-dodging luck. A hell of a lot more than the two dead men had out on the Templemore Road. And what, he demanded of Gallagher, was the idea of a two-man patrol in the first place?

'It wasn't a patrol, Tom. They were cycling over to see the bleeding statue, God help them. I suppose they thought they'd be safe going out at five in the morning and they had a lift back fixed up in a Tan lorry.'

Constable Baldwin muttered some incomprehensible impre-cation. Queer sort of a fish, Enright often thought. Something uncanny about him with the evening-shadow gauntness always on his cheeks and the unexcitable but flinty temperament, the same when he was beating some fellow to a pulp as when he sat down to chow.

'One of them had a sick wife. I suppose he was going over to pray for a miracle or something.'

'Ag, this people? Can't they see this *vrot* statue for the trick it is?'

Gallagher ignored the Boer ostentatiously.

'We've to bring the bodies in here to the barracks, Tom. This is gone beyond the beyonds. Fourteen policemen murdered around the country yesterday. Where is it all going to end?'

Papenfus slapped the counter with his open palm. The con-ference was over.

'Come on, Tom, we're wasting time here. Now-now.'

Enright's liking for Papenfus wasn't unconditional. Whenever the Boer's innate sense of superiority was directed at him, he blanched.

'Go easy, Pap. We'll find nothing only bodies out there now anyway.' Skirting the Auxie officer's offended glare, he called to the new constable. 'Timmory. You come with me in the Captain's lorry. And Baldwin, you go in the Whippet.'

Baldwin never quite acknowledged Enright's orders but invariably followed them as he did now with a sigh implying their inadequacy.

'Timmoney, sir.'

The tone was helpful, forgiving. There'd be a deal of fun to be had with this gawky young lad yet. Enright turned to Gallagher.

'The Ford's banjaxed out at Lady's Well. Will you get someone to pick it up . . . sir.'

'You're abusing that car, Tom. Anyone would think you owned it.'

An old complaint upon which Gallagher fell back whenever his authority stood exposed for the illusion it had become.

'I'm making damn good use of it. Somebody might as well.'

A scrum of Auxies and newly arrived Tans gathered at the doorway. Cock-of-the-walk NCO's, the Auxies; pipe-smoking, leather-gaitered, their gun holsters conspicuously displayed. Enright was left unfazed by their swagger, having seen how the British army worked in France and knowing these were just the shop-boys who'd replaced the dead roll of hapless public schoolboys. The Canadian Expeditionary Force had been no democracy either and his own promotion from the ranks a mere expedient too, but at least there had been little of the kow-towing he'd seen the Tommies at.

'Tom. A word before you go.' Gallagher's was the mien of a beggar. He drew Enright away to a quiet corner of the teeming front office. 'The new fellow, Tom, keep an eye on him. He's a decent lad but he's after having a hard time of it.'

'Where was he stationed?'

'Not that kind of a hard time. He was in a seminary three years and came out. I'd say he's a bit tormented, God help him.'

Torment? Enright thought. The failed priest didn't know the half of it yet.

'And, Tom, don't be led by that Papenfus fellow. I have it on good authority he was in on those murder gangs below in Cork and we don't want a repeat of what happened here after Constable Finnegan. I won't stand for it, no matter what Johnstone says. We're policemen not . . . '

'Anti-murder gangs, I believe they call themselves. But you know me, sir, I won't be led nor driven.'

On the street outside, a searing odour of burnt oil emanated from the Crossley Tender as it thrummed at the head of a line of three lorries and a Rolls Royce Whippet armoured car whose Vickers gun, mounted in the turret, pointed towards the Templemore Road. Then, above all the raised voices and clatter of boots, Enright heard the yelp of a familiar voice from across the street, nasal and grating.

'Serg'nt, Serg'nt. The fellow's here. The lad they sent after you.'

Danny Egan, ex-soldier and vagrant, his mind and half of his face torn asunder in the war, pondered the problem of the black leather glove in one hand and the ragged, beltless trousers held up with the other.

Enright climbed into the cab of the lorry beside Papenfus. He watched Danny put the glove in his mouth and, holding up the trousers with both hands now, make his way across from the entrance to Monk's Lane and seeming deliberately to set his shabby plimsolls into each cake of horse manure as though they were stepping stones at a river crossing.

Danny's speech came through what remained of his nose and, with what remained of his brain, he obsessed. Imagining himself a district inspector, he went from barracks to barracks and, in most, they let him leaf through the Guard's Diary and the Occurrences Book. Then he'd scribble indecipherably into his own tattered red notebook. When he was all done, they'd fill his billycan with tea and send him away with a jam sandwich. No one knew where Danny came from and Danny himself couldn't remember. Funerals were his other obsession. No one died in town or within a twenty-mile radius without his hovering among the bereaved and walking, small but erect, before the final procession to the cemetery, where he crouched as close to the open grave as the indignant relatives allowed, assuring them that their loved ones were in *a better place entirely*.

A plaintive whine came from behind the glove in the ex-soldier's mouth as Timmoney gawked from the lorry. His pale, pitying face angered Enright.

'Did you never see a gom before? Try looking in the mirror, son.'

Before them, the Crossley Tender began to trundle away from the gutter. Papenfus raced the engine and was about to swerve out on to the street but Danny Egan blocked the way.

'Call him off, would you? One of our sentries almost shot that daft bugger the other night. Sneaking around in the dark. What the hell's his game, hey?'

'Probably just looking for a place to sleep.'

At the open window by Papenfus, Danny whisked the glove from his mouth and waved it at Enright.

'This is one of his! He dropped it above at the railway station. A big, tall lad in a black leather coat. I'd say it's him, Serg'nt. Black hat an' all.'

'Where is he now?'

Enright's whisper was playfully conspiratorial.

'He's down the town.'

'Well Jesus, man, follow him. And report back to me this evening.'

Enright banged his fist on the dash as Papenfus fumed and Timmoney gaped and the Crossley Tender had almost reached the top of the street. Then Papenfus slammed the engine into gear and they shot forward. Enright laughed. Glad to be back.

Beyond the last thatched row of hovels on Pudding Lane, they emerged on to the open road sloping out of town. Over the low wall to his right Enright saw a nun walking along a path in the convent grounds. A magpie for Christ. Pity there weren't two. One for sorrow, two for joy. As a young girl in the Bedford school, Mary had announced angelically to the class-room her intention of becoming a nun. She wasn't the only one but somehow her piety seemed more fitting than that of Annie O'Connor who was too simple-minded or of Kitty Flynn who was too plain. And there was still too much of the nun about Mary; a sinking of the spirit in her presence, an irritated sense of never coming up to scratch in those holy eyes.

'Down in Cork, we went into the *koppies* after these buggers, Tom.'

Enright nodded, listened inattentively to the Boer's fantastical descriptions of chases and summary executions he'd been in on down south. He'd heard the boasts before. *Had some* RIC *men down there knew what had to be done and served up the Shinners on a plate for us.* The insinuation hadn't rattled him then and it wouldn't now. He'd given Papenfus his answer. *And what happened to you lot in Cork, Pap? Seventeen Auxies down in one go at Kilmichael.* But they'd both forgotten the slights when they were sober again. Another thing he liked about the Boer.

Still, it had been easy to come up with an answer back then, when they hadn't had a shot fired at them in town since his arrival. A different game now though with Kinahan and his mob getting so cocky. These men from Clonore Barracks weren't Enright's responsibility but they wore the same green uniform as he did and their bodies lay, not down in Cork or over in Limerick or below in the wilder south of the county, but a few miles out the road. Let this pass and they'd be swarming all over the town next.

Mary would, no doubt, be beside herself when she heard of the ambush. Might even write though she swore she wouldn't ever again after he'd slapped the child because she wouldn't stay in bed and ignore the wailing. The same old thing anyway, even if she did write. *Will you at least think about us, Tom, before you get dragged in so deep you can't get out?* She had a trick for saying things like that. The ugliness of tears would evaporate, and all soft and beguiling, she would touch his face or his arm or whatever bare part of him she could find. *Will you?*

'We're not jumping in bald-headed like bloody Bantus, Pap. We'll hunt them nice and easy like old – '

'Spare me the Chief Quinisco stories.'

On the other side of Enright, the young constable looked as though he was praying to be assumed into heaven or any damn place that wasn't the cab of a lorry on its way to pick up a couple of dead bodies. Gabriel Jack's stories of the Okanagan ancient had proved the perfect rejoinder to the Auxies' blundering ways that so often got them cornered. *A buck savage wouldn't hunt like you lot do, Pap.* Chief Quinisco hunted alone, armed only with a knife. Following for days until the bear stopped, sick with fear and running, he'd look in the eyes to see if they'd really given up or if there was some trick left in there. Smile a while after that and act all foolish and innocent like it was a game, ha, ha, then drop the hands before a mad rush at the big furry monster of a thing and, while it hugged him, he'd whip out the knife and slice it open.

'Time to hunt those devils down, Tom.'

Papenfus brought to mind Danny Egan out pursuing demons in black leather coats. Some weeks before, Enright had sent the ex-soldier on a wild-goose chase just to get him out of the barracks. *Would you go up to the railway station and keep an eye out for a fellow for me, Danny?* Filling in the Crimes ledger, Enright hadn't looked up, hadn't bothered to think when the ex-soldier asked for a description. *Oh, a dark lad, Danny. A big tall lad they sent after me. Armed to the teeth he is.* He hadn't noticed Danny slide away from the front counter and out on to the street but he heard the plimsolls squelching on the wet footpath, like a rat running along a trench.

The air inside the cab had become warm and torpid; the high ditches of hawthorn and elder all around them, an enclosure. Suddenly, the windscreen was peppered with the buckshot of heavy rain. Enright imagined the bulbous drops smashing against the faces of the dead men.

At the brow of Knoxtown Bridge, they waited and took stock. The narrow road ran straight down for fifty yards to the ambush site and, just beyond, lost itself for a while in a winding tunnel of vegetation. Then, silvery with rain, it opened out again for a stretch before disappearing over the next bridge, half a mile off. The darker clouds had sneaked away to empty out on the town three miles behind them. The aftermath of rain contrived a light so precise that the dead men's faces, even at that distance, were clearly visible to Enright. They lay within a few feet of each other among pools of blood that were shadows painted too thickly. Oddly, and Papenfus confirmed this with his opera glasses, three bicycles, rather than two, lay abandoned and askew about them. Enright surveyed the fields below, surreptitiously covering his bad eye as Papenfus speculated.

'Maybe there were three of them? Maybe Gallagher got it arse-wise?'

A slick of trodden grass bisected the field rising away to the right from where the dead policemen lay. A bit of height there to fire down from. But the trail didn't seem to lead any further than the single cow emerging now from the cover of an old oak in the corner of the field. Enright listened. Birds celebrated loudly the passing of the rain and the gunshots, and returned to the young in their nests among the high trees. A few, bolder and blacker, swooped down to consider the carrion on the rough road iron. The lone beast's complaint, loud and bleak, reached the bridge and its persistence convinced Enright that the rebels had gone.

Away at the next bridge, a convoy inched along the roadway. A few lorry loads of Northamptonshires over from Templemore. He wiped away the tear that had squeezed itself through his clenched eye. The flash of a hand grenade at Commotion Trench a year after Pozières had done for it. Ended up in No. 13 Canadian General Hospital on the Sussex coast. How could a fellow have any luck in a place with a number like that? *The tear duct, is that all, sure I never cry anyway!* The doctor, a neat and pitiless Québecois, dropped the eye-patch in a bin. *You will now, Lieutenant.* Another lavender-scented Frenchy like Mary's brother-in-law, Toussaint Martin, over in Chicago.

A disturbance to the rear released Enright from the memory. With Timmoney alongside him, he hurried down after Papenfus to the bottom of the bridge where the Crossley Tender and the armoured car and lorries idled. A few bleary-eyed Tans leaned against the cut-stone walls on either side, aiming rifles at their phantoms. More pot-luck shooters. The rest of the men had moved back and Enright saw that they surrounded an open twelve-seater charabanc. He recognised the driver, all twenty stone of him and none of it muscle.

Jim Donegan ran the garage beside the barracks and, in Foley's estimation, would sell his own mother for a bent shilling and use her head for a hammer. Had some laugh the day he caught Donegan in his shed up there in the hills with the petrol the rebels were supposed to have stolen from him. As if those boys would let him spread a story like that and not been in on it too. Two tanker loads inside and a broken-down British Petroleum lorry his mechanic couldn't fix. Like all greedy men, Donegan didn't know when to draw back. But Enright did. Let him off on a promise. Not long after, the fellow served him up a rebel, the last one he'd bagged before things quietened down in the town. Thady Griffin from Pudding Lane, caught with a couple of IRA memoranda in his sock on his way to Sunday Mass to pass them on to some other Shinner whose name Enright tried but failed to beat out of him. He'd let the garage man steal a third tanker of petrol last month on the strength of that.

Behind Donegan, faces petrified by the exposed journey from town peered out from beneath shawls or hats or flat caps. Pilgrims off to the bleeding statue, Enright supposed, from the crooked shapes of them. A sorry-looking lot, ugly with age or sickness or both. Only one among them carried no weight of misery in her expression. A woman, in her fifties perhaps, small and hunchbacked and too grey for her age but well enough dressed, the high collar of her coat lined with fur.

'How're the dogs going, Sergeant?' Donegan filched a cigarette from inside the tepee of his oilskin cape and proffered another to Enright, an honest crook sharing the spoils. 'Half this crowd'll be dead before I get 'em over to the statue in Templemore. Will we get through, do you think?'

Enright cut off the man's palaver with a dismissive shake of the head.

Circling the charabanc for a second time, Papenfus lighted upon the hunchbacked woman. His fellow Auxies quietened down, colluding in the threatening silence. She looked back at Papenfus, undisturbed, it seemed, by the revolver propped playfully on the charabanc rail before her.

'What kind of miracle are you praying for, ma'am? A husband?'

The woman adjusted her collar, then her gloves. Slowly, finger by finger.

'I never pray for myself. I pray for anyone and everyone who needs my prayers. Today, I'll pray for you.'

Her fellow passengers sank horrified into their seats at the thought of what her defiance might mean for them. Enright smiled. The same mad imagination that allowed them to believe in miracles, now clearly offered visions of roadside slaughter. Papenfus stood back from the charabanc and raised his Luger. A flutter of moans swept through the passengers.

'Everybody down and make it bloody snappy.'

The driver tried Enright again with a mimed appeal. Enright ignored him, consumed as he was by the spectacle of the hunched woman. Papenfus offered no assistance as the woman began to negotiate awkwardly the drop from the running board to the ground. Drawing closer, Enright thought she might fall and couldn't decide whether or not he should help her. When he spoke to Papenfus, it was to put the dilemma away and the disgust at her vulnerability now that her face was turned from them in her struggle.

'Send them up the road, Pap. They'll cover us off while we pick up the pieces.'

Like a crab crawling down a rock, Enright reflected, the woman gained a sudden stealth and eased herself downwards. He felt as though he held a hammer in his hand. But she reached the ground and his fist opened out and slipped furtively into his pocket.

There was a whore that shape in Barcelona, in a brothel stinking of phenol. Sacred Bleeding Hearts all over the walls and a Victrola scratching out the same tango over and over and the women coaxing. *Puedo ayudarte, marinero?* La Cheposa. A fellow went with her too. Marshall, the old goat he met up with while on the beach in Hong Kong and followed from boat to boat for a few years, learning every trick and mistake in the book from him. La Cheposa, black silk chemise and high-heeled shoes. *I know, Tommy lad, but they're all of a piece when they're lying flat in the dark.* Marshall blamed her for the dose that put a stop to his wild roving, as if he could have known, there had been so many.

The woman passed between Enright and Papenfus, disregarding them both. La Cheposa, Enright repeated silently and shivered. How was a fellow ever to warm up at all in a country cold as this? The heat of battle might do the trick, he thought. Long as it didn't turn to fever. Or worse.

The blind, the lame and the old led them down towards the dead. One bandy-legged elder, bowling along the tilted deck of the road's incline, slipped and was dragged up by a young Cockney Tan who might have been his grandson with the same livery slum face. Alongside Enright, Jim Donegan slowed up wheezily for breath. The big man's oilskin cape smelled like a wet day in a trench. The self-pity in his obsequious whisper seemed an offence to the dead men lying on the road up ahead.

'I had a tip-off from a lad in the BP office above in Dublin, Sergeant. He said they're doing their own investigating 'cause they got no joy from the polis.'

Leading the procession, the hunchbacked woman had taken out a rosary beads and counted out milestones of prayer. How was it, Enright wondered, that the most botched up and battered of creations made the most fervent believers?

'I gave you Thady Griffin on a plate, Sergeant. You said you'd keep the BP crowd off my back.'

'You were well paid for Griffin. Another tanker of petrol. What more do you want?'

The big, dimpled hand clutching his sleeve and dragging him to a halt infuriated Enright. He chopped it away and pushed the garage man against the low stone wall.

'You promised you'd protect me. That's all I'm saying.'

'And I did. But not any more. Not unless you give me something on Paddy Kinahan. You know him better than anyone. Aren't you dealing petrol with him?'

Funny how even the craftiest of crooks could give themselves away with the slightest of delays in the eyes swimming up from some inner calculation.

'I didn't meet the man since he ran out of town after Finnegan was shot.'

'Well, you can protect yourself from BP then. And from Kinahan too. Wouldn't it be unfortunate if he found out who betrayed Griffin?'

The cow Enright had seen earlier shoved its dung-caked bulk against the wall and peered out over in dumb wonder. Nearing the bodies, Enright felt the old relief of survival, of walking among the dead and hearing his own breath and the thump of his heart and, all around, the noise of continuing that the dead couldn't hear, and human voices small in the vast arena of the exploded world. Timmoney's voice came, hushed and surprised.

'The other bike. It's a ladies' bike.'

Papenfus choreographed the reluctant honour guard of pilgrims into place about the fallen policemen. The whites of a blind man's eyes drifted skywards, as if to parody the unseeing whites of the dead men's eyes. One, balding, his thick moustache wet with blood and rain, had taken it in the chest. A dark clotted soup oozed from the tear across his shirt front. The other leaked grey brain slush from a divet where his ear used to be. From over by the ditch, Papenfus called to Enright. Whatever it was he held in his upraised hand, Enright couldn't see through the moisture filling his bad eye.

'Bloody tripwire. Strung from the tree here, neck high.'

The Boer flung the wire into the ditch and its thin metallic recoil sang as it slashed at the undergrowth.

Squatting between the dead men, Enright retrieved the handguns they hadn't had the clarity of mind or, perhaps, the time to draw. He found a thick missal in the pocket of the moustachioed man's greatcoat and some cigarettes. Coins, a few scraps of paper and a letter were all the other man carried. 'The pain is a bit better these days', and at the bottom of the single page, 'Your loving wife, Breda'. A reply not yet posted, 'Don't worry over me.' Read a hundred of them in his time. Love letters from the Front too bloodied to pass on to the widow; postcards from home for dead men.

He pocketed the cigarettes as he browsed through the hand-written notes. A mess list, an address in County Limerick but no name, a verse in progress. 'The days are long, the nights are longer/But every hour our love gets stronger.' *Gets* crossed out for *grows*, *grows* for *blooms*, and *blooms* hatched out too. No wonder the fellow couldn't make up his mind to draw his gun. He passed the effects to Timmoney, whose hands shook as he took possession of them. Respectfully. Soft white hands that didn't belong at the end of a uniform sleeve.

Up at the bend of the road, two of the Northamptonshires crawled into view, surveyed the scene and stood up sheepishly. They beckoned to the rear and waited on their column.

'Hey! Tom!'

Papenfus stood in the shallow trench of dyke along by the roadside hedge. A group of Auxies and Tans, handguns drawn, rushed to his side. The pilgrims broke ranks and retreated into a huddle, leaving the bent woman to stand alone.

Half-hidden in the tangle of long grass and whitethorn shoots at the feet of Papenfus, Enright saw the third body. A raised skirt, pale shapely legs, the purpling pearls of toenails on one naked foot. He stepped down into the dyke and knelt by the body. The brown dyke-water seeped instantly through the green serge of his trousers. One raised knee exposed a fringe of dark pubic hair beneath the soiled underclothes. He lowered the skirt as Papenfus, gingerly keeping his distance, drew back with his stick the veil of vegetation covering the face. The breath swept out of Enright's weaker lung. The stick fell from Papenfus's grasp and he sank back onto the bank of the low dyke. The audience of Auxies and Tans turned away. A Tan officer screamed at his men to bring up another stretcher, then answered a muttered reply.

'Right, well, strap some bloody planks together then. And hurry that lot back to the motor.'

Mud sucked at Enright's shins and knees as he raised himself to sit beside Papenfus. The ambush site was a melee with the advancing Northamptonshires joining the rest, all of them wandering about urgently but to no apparent purpose. Enright lit one of the dead man's cigarettes and passed another to Papenfus. The smoke cut into his right lung but he stopped himself from coughing aloud. They couldn't look at the young woman except to glance while they inhaled. They talked to fill the silence spreading out from her.

'The Tan boys'll break a few windows in town tonight, Pap.'

'Lot of bloody good broken glass will do.'

'No harm in giving them a few strokes of the lash.'

'It's not enough, Tom.'

Enright yawned. He felt a lazy shiver of anticipation spread through him.

'I've a few men who'll blacken up and do the business, Tom, but we need someone to point us in the right direction.'

'What am I, some class of a native guide, is it? You're not in Zululand now.'

'You know the territory.'

'The town's my territory. Anyway, you saw the order we got after the Sack of Balbriggan. No more reprisals.'

'So, you're following orders now, hey? What about France and those stories you tell me. That all just talk? Time I talked to some of the Clonore crew. What's left of them.'

'They can't be trusted. How do you think the rebels knew those idiots were cycling over to the statue this morning? And, Pap, don't step on my fucking corns.'

Enright wished the Tans would come and remove this woman from his sight so that he could think straight. He looked at her again. The grass by her face stirred about on the breeze as though she breathed lightly in sleep. The head might have belonged to a different body such was the impossible side-ways angle of the neck. A delicate necklace of red droplets marked the alabaster throat. Above the high forehead freckled with spats of mud, a fine tracery of unloosed curls softened the edges of her tightly drawn back hair that was jet black as an Okanagan's. The profile, however unnaturally displayed, was a thing of perfection.

'Hey? Can you hear that lot up there in the *koppies* laughing at us, Tom? So what's your decision? You with us?'

There were no decisions, Enright thought, not in the heat of battle nor in the heat of life, only instincts, good or bad, right or wrong. He assented with a shrug, as though Mary, eighty miles away in Listowel, might hear if he spoke the word. He hadn't felt this tense surge of release, of preparedness, for years. Not since the day the RMS *Missambie* docked at Bologne and he was one of the few among those Canadian volunteers who'd ever set foot in France before, even if it was only to sample the wine and the bouillabaisse and the *putains* in Marseilles. One of the very few too who'd ever killed anything more than a wolver-ine or a bear.

'Who do we hit, Tom?'

'We'll see. There's a man owes me a favour.' Enright slid down into the dyke again, let his boots sink into the viscous bed. Never killed a woman, never would, no matter what. How could a fellow live with a dead girl haunting him? 'I'd better see if she has any papers on her.'

Below the hobnailed noise of soldiers returning to the lorries at both ends of the road, their rage stalled in repetitive curses, Enright heard the low murmuring of the well-dressed hunchback, who gazed sadly at the young girl's twisted form. He contained his anger, not wanting, though he recognised the foolishness of the thought, to disturb the girl and because he wanted his touch to be as soft as his numbed hands allowed.

Fingers brushing lightly about her, Enright tried the pockets of a jacket soaked with rain and dyke water and too flimsy for this indifferent summer weather. Smoke rose from the cigarette dangling at the corner of his mouth and stung his eye. He began to unbutton her jacket. The damp blouse clung opaquely to her skin; the nipples like two small wine stains on a linen table-cloth. Then the small breasts seemed almost imperceptibly to rise. He blamed the haze of cigarette smoke until a moan arose from her and sent him careening back and he shouted at the praying woman above so as to catch his breath.

'Get the hell back to the charabanc.'

Papenfus stood up from the bank of the dyke and bustled the woman away but Enright saw the wonder that transformed the plainness of her features. He knew what she was thinking. A miracle.

'She wasn't dead in the first place. Now, clear off.'

Soon would be, though. Easy to confirm that if he had waited for her eyes to open because he knew that dying look well enough, that grey veil of sadness disappearing away into a dull marbled nothingness. But a few Tans arrived at last with two planks held together by a short strut studded with rusted nails that had been bent double in hammered haste. He left her to them when she began to scream.

Walking back towards the bridge, he found Donegan puking by the roadside. Mortal fear, Enright supposed. Saw men throw up the last scraps they'd ever eat on this earth because of it. Damn near spilled his own guts in that shell hole up in front of Commotion Trench with Clancy, the mad Clare boy.

'God help us, Sergeant, the poor little thing.'

'Just think, Donegan. That could be you one of these fine days.'

Donegan's flushed and sweat-beaded face no longer sought pity. The bitterness of humiliation hollowed out his voice.

'I'll have something fairly definite for you. Soonish. I'll do the best I can.'

'Very definite. Very soon. Will I show you why?'

The stupidly inquisitive cow had poked its head again over the wall near Enright. He took out the Webley from inside his tunic and raising it, moved in on the unsuspecting beast. He felt a silence gather behind him, sensed the eyes fixed on his back. There was no going back though his actions had already become less spontaneous and his hand trembled from the weight of the gun. Just a matter of getting used to it all over again. From five or six yards, he fired a shot into the side of the cow's head. It went down heavily into the oblivion below the hedge, shaking the road iron under his feet. Easy enough to do, really. Donegan began to retch once more and when the big man dropped to his knees, Enright felt the road iron shake again. Pity there wasn't a rebel to plug on the roadside now that he'd started. Or a cottage in view to let a few shots off into. He felt the greyhound's frustration at being reined back in the slipping shed but knew the hare would eventually scamper into view. With a little help from Donegan. And if they didn't get Paddy Kinahan or some of his crew, there were plenty of targets in the town even if they were small fry.

Larry Healy, Sinn Féin councillor and publican. Clem Shanahan over at the gasworks. Johnny Dooley, whose family ran the local picture house and brother of the brave Charlie, whose toothy grin Enright had reduced to a gritty rubble. Fellow might have kept his front teeth if he hadn't maddened him with smart-aleck threats. *You'll leave the town at the head of a small procession, Enright.* For the moment, he'd drag those townies into the holding cell and make them believe he had no intention of going after their friends in the hills.

As Enright overtook the stretcher-bearers and their pitiful cargo, he looked out across the fields. Easy enough country compared to the wilds up in the Kootenays, full of bears and every vicious bastard of an animal known to man, where you'd lose a trail if you blinked a teary eye and your life if you blinked the good one. A blind man could hunt here. No point in trying to explain a thing like that to Mary. *Don't write so, Mary, I never asked you to in the first place.*

The last time a man spat in Enright's face was at the Santa Anna Cabaret in Manila. Himself and Marshall resplendent in newly purchased pineapple silk shirts, fresh from winning a packet of dollars betting on the cockfights. *How come you never bet on the white, Tommy lad?* Marshall wasn't himself at all and Enright didn't yet know why, though the little Fluke with the American twang behind the bar guessed. *No drink, buddy, your friend got the pox bad.* The bar counter too deep, Enright swung and missed. When the fellow spat, all hell broke loose but the jazz band played on, and to the braying rhythm of 'Jackass Blues', he stomped the barman's face to a pulp.

Clem Shanahan was a disappointed man. In his late thirties now, he'd once been a leading light in local republican circles. Then the talking and posturing, at which he'd been so adept, stopped. Shanahan was swept aside by the younger men. Paddy Kinahan, it was rumoured, became the particular focus of his resentment though he remained a rebel, if a marginal one. A spare dog at a coursing meeting who wouldn't get a run if every last dog was hobbled. Still, pulling him in on occasions such as this served a double purpose; a warning to the townspeople who still imagined Shanahan mattered in the movement and a bum steer to convince Kinahan that the police knew little of the workings of his crew.

The holding cell in the barracks basement smelled of the sewer pipes that passed behind walls sweating a sheen of urine. Mushrooms, the raw white of exposed bones, sprouted in moist corners. Enright pulled his trench coat tighter over his shoulders but found no greater warmth. He tried one last pricking of the fellow's conscience.

'Is it worth it, Clem? Killing and maiming the innocent for the sake of a republic?'

Thick-lipped and docile though physically sturdy, the fellow's mild lisp was, by contrast, oddly girlish.

'Her blood is on your hands too, Enright.'

Shanahan spat and Enright put him on the floor with a straight right to the jaw and wiped the spittle from his own face with the same fist. The steel toe-cap of his boot found Shanahan's stomach, crotch, spine and forehead. Whatever pleasure he'd taken in the assault fell to unease and when Baldwin took to the task of leathering the fellow more severely still, Enright realised that Shanahan was deliberately leaving himself open to every blow when any fool knew to roll himself in a ball. *One hand on your head and the other on your lad.* Marshall's advice back in the dockwalloping days.

'That'll do, Baldwin. And you, Shanahan, you're on my list. You lads fire one shot in town and you're for the cemetery.'

Baldwin aimed a few final blows at Shanahan so as not to appear too amenable to orders, Enright supposed. He wondered if the fellow invited the beating because he'd never left the holding cell with any real credentials. Open cuts, livid lacerations, trophies to show off in a late-night public house and reclaim some of his former status among the rebels. Or perhaps it was a matter of disproving the lisping effeminacy. Saw plenty of that too. Toussaint Martin mouthing off in his prissy accent about the battle for Vimy Ridge that Enright had missed out on, the *real* Canadian show that won the war where all the Frenchy had done was drive a kitchen wagon behind the lines.

'Send in Timmoney with a mop and pail. And throw this lad out on the street.'

Larry Healy, a long lanky fellow with a deadpan defiance behind the high colour of his cheeks, displayed his usual air of mild indifference. Even the crimson-dyed water in Timmoney's pail bothered the young constable more than it bothered the Shinner publican. He'd married a girl almost half his age a few months before and now she was expecting their child. Always the first stick Enright used to prod him with.

'Did you find out who mounted your wife yet, Larry?'

Too familiar a jibe by now, it left the barkeeper unperturbed.

'What did she make of the young girl your pals crippled out the road? Young enough to be your daughter she was, Larry, just like your missus.'

Healy had an inner stillness that Enright had seen in men before but not in many.

Captain Big Toe Holland of the 29th Battalion was one. The philosophy teacher who'd saved Enright's life near Courcelette. Scuttling back with Clancy and a couple of other lads from C Company after a rush on a German block, the sky falling down on top of them as they ran, ducked, ran until Enright hit smack into a Hun with the head of a butcher on him and his Lee Enfield jammed. Then Holland, out of nowhere. *Hit the deck, Enright.* Blew the head clean off the shoulders. Down in an abandoned enemy dugout later and Holland still as a statue as Enright and Clancy tried to figure a way out of the maze of trenches with more tributaries out of them than the Yangtze Kiang. And what did Captain Big Toe think? *Right now, I'm thinking that the proponents of the Manichaean fallacy might well be disabused after a day at Courcelette.*

Same with Healy. Sitting in the holding cell but cocooned in an aura of easeful remoteness. And Healy was having the same calming effect on Enright as Big Toe had back then, or perhaps it was the tiredness scraping at his eyes, the good and the bad. A torpid silence gathered in which he reflected on the incongruousness of having been saved by a man who only hours later blew his own head off. Pulled the trigger with his big toe. Left a long letter to his wife and a lot of good that was to her. *You never write long letters, Tom.* Couldn't even find his own words to write, quoting Hun philosophers instead. *The world is indifferent beyond measure, without purposes and consideration.*

Behind Healy, Constable Baldwin waited for the signal to start the beating. Timmoney mopped up the last of Shanahan's blood and shrank from the room. Never thanked Captain Big Toe for saving his life, Enright recalled. He'd tried hard to bring himself to do it but couldn't get beyond feeling demeaned because he owed his continuing existence to another man. He couldn't explain to Baldwin that he'd decided to spare Larry Healy by way of belated apology to a dead philosopher. In any case, all he wanted was to go upstairs to his room for a few shots from the bottle of Jameson he'd brought back from Listowel but not before executing a few feints in his hunting strategy. A message for Larry Healy to dispatch to Kinahan.

'Weren't you lucky now those men weren't from our barracks, that were shot? Will I tell you why, Larry boy? Because Paddy Kinahan and his column might be safe up there in the hills but they haven't me chasing them. I've my own beat to look after. But you townies aren't safe and if any of my men here in town get as much as a scratch, it'll be an eye for an eye. We have a list and you're on it. Will you tell that to the boys when they're in your shebeen skulling pints?'

Enright was less displeased than he pretended when Baldwin told him that Johnny Dooley was away in Dublin searching out parts for a broken projector at his family's cinema.

'We wired the hotel. Bin there two nights, the bugger.'

'Fair enough. We've made our point anyway.'

The Scot seemed to divine too precisely the extent of Enright's fatigue and resorted to grim sarcasm.

'What's your game, Sergeant? Lettin' 'em away soft so they'll think there's no sauce left in your bottle?'

'No. An old Irish game, Baldwin. Sending the fool further, they call it.'

He hated when the phrases arising unbidden in him were his father's. The king of fools.

Somewhere between the end of the third Jameson and the beginning of the fifth or sixth, there occurred a moment of true serenity in Enright. Too briefly, he was on a train passing through Midwest plains on his way down to the cousin in New York, the panic of his escape from Canada and the guilt of abandoning Mary mellowing to forgetfulness. Pat Joe's address in his wallet – 96–10 Northern Boulevard, 9952 Corona, Long Island, New York City. *Never heard of no Enright here.* Often thought he should have got out back there somewhere and started afresh in that vast sea with corn for an element instead of dreaded waters. On the straw-filled mattress in his barracks room he was a fretful passenger once more in a carriage loud with relentless chatter.

They live among the shadows, Sergeant, and our job is to make those shadows hold real terrors for them. Johnstone had employed almost exactly the same formulation when he'd introduced him to the task ahead a year earlier as when he'd waylaid him outside the holding cell an hour before. A man acting a part, Enright had always thought and wondered what lay beneath. *Do whatever you have to do, carte blanche, eh?* That declaration had seemed familiar too. Made a fellow's skin crawl, did Johnstone. The rigid posture, the practised lines delivered without emotion, the palpable cold emanating from his pale, almost translucent skin.

Enright shivered. His heart raced and his legs and arms felt as leaden as ever they had done in the late winter hours. He pulled himself up by the windowsill alongside the bed, and slipped the Jameson bottle inside his tunic. The creaking boards under his feet sneered at the weight in himself he wanted to forget.

As he descended the stairs, Enright welcomed a lightness into his head, played along with the sway of it. Outside the day-room door he waited and heard the brush of a heavy page like a sigh. The Bible, he supposed, or a book of blooming poems. He silenced his own sniggering with a finger to the lips, a wink to the unlit space about him.

His nostrils flared in the stench of death, a rotted undergrowth disturbed, as he entered the room. He went straight for his cigarettes. Timmoney sat on the long bench at the other side of the room, his face one with the insipid pallor of walls that had forgotten what colour they were meant to be. The book he'd been reading lay open beside him. Pages fluttered as though a ghostly hand searched out where it had long ago left off the story, to die. Against the wall to Enright's left, two tall coffin lids stood, pitched towards a descent. The astringent cut of sulphur from the struck match seared through the fug he could no longer hold his breath from.

'Timothy, I thought you could do with a belt of whiskey. A sad old sight, eh?'

Tiredness, dread and tears had left dark circles under the young constable's eyes.

'Timmoney, sir. Horrible.'

'Horrible? Not at all, boy. I'll tell you horrible. I was wounded one time over in France, Pozières it was, and they were carrying me on a stretcher over to have the leg fixed up. And we passed an outhouse with the door flung open that was filled to the ceiling with the rotten bits they cut off of lads. Arms, feet, hands, legs in a great big bloody heap with the steam rising off it like you flung a grenade into a whorehouse or an asylum. A charnel house. *Un calvario*, the Spanish call it. A philosophy teacher told me that. Un fucking calvario is right.'

From behind the glass-framed door of a cupboard, Enright took down a pair of white china cups reserved for important visitors to the barracks. He poured a brimful for himself, a half cup for Timmoney. As he closed the cupboard door, the dead men floated into view on the glass. His own reflection and Timmoney's seemed no less pale than those of the two men lying side by side in the coffins that filled the broad table.

'You were in the war, Sergeant?'

'I was. Myself and a gormless young lad from Clare called Clancy volunteered. Off our ruddy chumps we were and we thousands of miles away from it in Canada.'

'I wouldn't say that. I'd say it was right brave of you.'

Timmoney's commendation felt too cloying.

'Here, throw this back, boy. It'll put hairs on your chest.'

'Keep it for yourself, sir.'

'Go on, weren't you practising with the wine for the last three years.'

Timmoney darkened in Enright's shadow. His secret too offhandedly out, leaving him downcast, diminished. He took the cup.

'Go on, boy, it'll settle your Johnny-jitters.'

The white cup shook in Timmoney's white hand, the whiskey swirled and lapped. One snowed-in night on the thirty-acre plot the Canadian army gave him outside Nelson, Enright inveigled whiskey into Mary to help her stop thinking about the child they lost. Stop himself thinking too. His surprise at her capacity for Gabriel Jack's rotgut had soured him. Often thought that was the night the second child was made. Out of his whiskey-blinded desperation and her oblivion.

'Have you a woman?'

A cow's-lick of black hair fell over Timmoney's eyes and he left it there to hide behind. He held the china cup in two hands now, a chalice.

'Did you never have a bit of jig-a-jig, boy?'

Timmoney drank, his gullet struggling to contain the burn of whiskey. He floundered on the hard bench but a swift abandon of gulps from the cup steadied him and when he looked up at Enright, he showed a pulpit face; condemning, superior. Enright bristled. Did they teach them that look in the seminary or did some fellows suck it out of their mother's milk? His own son had it too, in the moment between feeling the sting of a slap and the caterwauling.

'Don't give me that sanctimonious gawk, boy.'

'Show some respect for the dead, would you?'

Timmoney stood up, shaky but defiant.

'I've a good mind to break your jaw, Timmoney.'

'You remembered my name.'

Disarmed by the young constable's artless expression, Enright laughed and pushed him back onto the bench. He sat down a little way off from Timmoney. The pages of the book between them on the bench had come to rest. He couldn't remember exactly when he'd last read a book. Not since he'd killed that Hong Kong huckster, at any rate. A story about a white dog or wolf or something. A tall tale. He laughed again. Timmoney's glance over the rim of the cup he sipped from was glassy and unfocused.

'What are you reading?'

'*Moby Dick.*'

Looking across from the low bench, Enright saw only the peaks of the dead men's noses over the edge of the coffins. Ridiculous Punch-and-Judy noses on them. Imagined this of all his dead. Imagined the same of his mother and the tiny, puce brother she'd died giving birth to, a doll set aside so that she could sleep forever.

'The one about the whale?'

'Aye. I'm always reading about the sea.'

'I was on the boats myself for a while. Saw the world, as they say. Well, the edges of it, anyway.'

'Did you really?'

'The edges of it is right. Could've taken one of those pony carriages with the pink and yellow curtains up the Rock of Gibraltar. Or gone the ten miles from Piraeus to the Parthenon in Athens. Or the train ride in from Port Said to the Pyramids and the Sphinx. Never bothered. Riddle me that.'

'Were you long at sea?'

'Signed on at fifteen. Messboy on an old tramp steamer plying over and back to Liverpool. The *Beckstone*. After that, for a long stretch I went everywhere until I damn near died out on the brine and gave Canada a go.'

'I never went anywhere.'

'You're only a pup yet. It's all before you. For what it's worth.'

Timmoney's head fell around in loose circles, rounding up the stray and bleary thoughts. The long-lashed eyelids fluttered in their struggle to keep apart. Enright thought about shaking him awake, pouring another whiskey or two into him but felt too comfortable, slumped against the wall and sinking, so that he no longer had to look at those preposterous noses and their great, cave-like nostrils.

Time bore him softly along then for a while. Timmoney slept and Enright wallowed in drunken recollection of Mary White dressed in white, the day before he went to Limerick to catch the *Beckstone*. He had cycled out to Bedford from the aunt's pub in Listowel for a last look at the farm. Blushed when he saw her, back from her boarding school, for the night lusts of which she was the sole object, and would have cycled on, had she not called out to him, skittish in the heat and fullness of the summer's day. *I heard you're going away to sea, Tom. Aren't you going to say goodbye?* Squeezing on the brake with the same hand that stoked his desires in the night. Then she'd searched with butterfly hands along the roadside hedge. A good patch for wild strawberries, halfway between his father's five acres and the Whites' sixty-five. He had wanted to tell her that he was being driven away, that he didn't want to go, that he was afraid. *I'll pray for you, Tom; I might even write.*

Four years later, sick with a dose in Penang, Enright wrote the first letter. He was off the tramp steamers with their capricious itineraries by then and gave her the postal dates for the rest of that trip. Never imagined that she'd write back, but she had. Words were all they saw of each other until Canada. Hers, flowing over page after page, telling what seemed like everything of herself and keeping him warm at three bells of a dogwatch among wild Cape Horn greybeards and cool in the swelter of Indian Ocean nights. His, trapped in one or two pages but at least not pretending to bare every last corner of his soul.

A distant banging and shouting addled his brain into wakefulness. His stomach turned in the putrid day-room air. His spine uncoupled itself painfully from the wall. He punched Timmoney's arm and the china cup shot from the young constable's hand and smashed itself to pieces on the bare floorboards. Timmoney gaped at the last of the spinning shards, at the dead men, at Enright.

'Go out and see what that racket's about.'

Timmoney raised himself and, stumbling forward, took a blow to the hip from the corner of the death-laden table. The men shivered in their coffins and he careered away to the door, letting in a welcome relief of cold air, and Enright recognised the pleas for admittance as Danny Egan's.

'Tell Keane to let him in.'

He poured himself another Jameson, lit another cigarette. A gob of whiskeyed, smoky phlegm rose in his throat and he spat it out onto the slivers of china. No red bloom or toxic yellow in it. Constable Keane's objections, drifting sparely from the front door, bore the queer disembodied quality of sleep talk or the last words of the dying. The scrape of cigarette smoke caught Enright's bad eye.

A high, unwashed odour reached into the day room before its bearer did. Danny carried the war in his every pore and yet remembered nothing. That was a kind of luck too.

'I'll report to Serg'nt Enright. No one else.'

The face, left five years before to heal itself all wrongly, appeared at the door.

'Danny. You're working late tonight.'

Danny stood goggle-eyed, his intended revelations forgotten in the presence of the corpses. He shook hands briefly but firmly with Timmoney, then with Enright; an extra clasp with the second hand for the sergeant. Harder hands than Enright had imagined, a calloused knot in the palm of the right. At the door Timmoney waited, equally awestruck, and seeking from Enright some sign as to what he should do with this mad vagrant whose hands dared now to alight upon the foreheads of the dead.

'Well, what do you make of them, Danny?'

The ex-soldier's ravaged profile hovered, raw-edged with cold, in over the moustachioed man's face. He blew a breath on the eye lumps and watched intently for some response.

'They're in a better place entirely, God bless them.'

'I thought they might be but you never know these days with the bleeding statue and all these miracles.'

The spastic snap of Enright's neck when he saw Timmoney's scandalised expression brought the girl's twisted neck painfully to mind.

'Where was your God today, boy?'

Moving back from the table, Danny unintentionally blocked off Enright's view of the lanky young constable but, in any case, the dead men distracted him. He saw in their expressions, though he didn't quite understand why, that they must have known their killers. A hint of relief there, was that it? A nervous cast, almost a smile, on the blue lips of the older man. *Ah, lads, we're all Irishmen, aren't we?* But of course they knew. Hadn't they been stationed up in Clonore Barracks for years, right in the middle of Kinahan's territory? They'd have known him from a child.

He sensed now that both Timmoney and the ex-soldier watched him closely and with concern. Impossible to get nicely drunk twice in the one night. Second time around there was this strangeness, this febrile life pulsating in everything around him, even in things that were only things, dead objects.

'The worst thing about a war, even this bloody skirmish with the Shinners, is getting hit and not knowing who shot you dead. Christ almighty, if I'm ever shot and I don't know who done it, I'll . . .'

'What difference would it make? Wouldn't you be dead one way or the other?'

'Couldn't you curse the bugger with a look, Danny, damn his living nights? Ah, to hell with it. What were you doing out at Castle Bennett the other night? I heard you nearly got yourself shot, you clown.'

'I was looking for something I lost.'

'What in God's name have you to lose?'

Danny gazed perplexedly at Enright's face as though he might find his answer there. Then he considered the corpses again. He shrugged.

'I don't know. There's something belonging to me out that road somewhere.'

'For Christ's sake, mind yourself, will you? So, what has you breaking down the door to see me?'

'The man in the black leather coat, Serg'nt, I followed him like you told me to. But it's not you he's after. He was looking for Jim Donegan.'

The BP investigator Gallagher had spoken of, no doubt. Enright began to feel clear-headed again.

'He was asking all over, even asked a girl he bumped into. She was coming out of Molloy's with a parcel. You know the young one who plays the piano at the pictures? One of the Dooleys. A good ten minutes he was talking to her. But I don't think he found Donegan 'cause he's gone back to Dublin on the train.'

'Dooley? Isn't she a sister of those Shinners? Johnny and Charlie the Toothless?'

Danny cocked the bad side of his face at Enright.

'Should I follow her too, Serg'nt?'

'Go way out of that. You're too old to be chasing after young ones.'

'I'm not that old, am I?'

Enright laughed and slung an arm over Danny's shoulder like a man rescued from drowning, drunk with fresh life. He drew the repulsive face towards his chest, breathed in the damp, trench stink of the fool's flesh.

'What would I do without you, Danny? The only sane man in Tipperary. Barring myself.'

Bedford,
Listowel

Dear Tom,

I am three weeks waiting to see would you write first. I
should know better. The day I heard about the two policemen shot near you, I had to go into the barracks in Listowel
to ask were you one of them. I wrote you a letter that night
but I held on to it because it didn't occur to you to let me
know you were safe and because of the way you hit Jerry
when you got drunk here the last time. You might as well
have hit me and I told you about that in Canada the time
Gabriel Jack disappeared. I won't let my child be struck no
more than myself. Once, Mister Enright, but never again. I
wasn't reared that way and I won't rear any of mine that way.

I know that you are under a very great strain at the present
but ever since we came over home there's no rhyme nor
reason to your actions. First, the mad drinking every night
of the week and drinks on the house for every Tom, Dick
and Harry in the pub. Then you volunteer for the IRA down
here and get your back up when they won't have you and
join the other side. Where's the sense in that? Standing
against the same lads you were buying pints for? If you
were only trying to get away from me and Jerry, you'd
be back on the boats. But there's more to it than that.

I used to think the worst thing a woman could expect
from a man is the kind of glad eye for the women that my

sister has to put up with from Toussaint over in Chicago but it's far worse to have a man with a glad eye for trouble and danger. Most of the time you might as well not be here at all even when you do come, with your thoughts always in another place or time and none for me.

All you tried was one place for a job here and I know that Vicars gave short shrift to your officer papers over at Kilmorna and insulted your father's memory. I am not saying you should take something back-breaking, like you seem to think. What I am saying is we could try Dublin or another big town like Galway, which I hear is nice enough. This is not what I wanted to come home to, worry and stories of your carry-on up there in Tipperary. I get it easy enough compared to some things I hear about the wives of the police but every day is harder. A certain lady of our acquaintance spat on the footpath beside me yesterday in John Street. I could give you the name but I know what you might do. Me, I can mind myself, but what friend can Jerry hope to have in this place when he gets bigger? Do you ever think of that or about the future at all?

What I would like to know is, where is the man in the sanatorium I went halfway around the world to find. I threw away a comfortable life for you and what do I get? A borrowed cottage on the side of the road and a visit from the King every so often. Is it any wonder that I was cold to you that night? Anyway, what am I supposed to do with Jerry when he cries inconveniently, lock him out in the shed? As for you, you wouldn't even shave before you came to bed, like I asked you to. Am I supposed to enjoy having the face cut off me, or the smell of whiskey sickening me, for that matter?

Even as I write I can see the foolishness of my pleading but it is this or silence and I won't be silenced by any man. I am in your hands, Tom Enright, and I am afraid. You say they are all only pot-luck shooters but there are very

many of them and only one of you. In your letter from
Balfour three years of eternity ago, you said such nice things
about me and such terrible things about war. What has
swayed the balance against me?

I remain yours,
Mary

In the bright moonlight, the gouged peak of Devil's Bit Mountain stood clearly visible above them, an inverted arch, a passage to the stars. Night frost dusted the rising fields. The crisp air fined the lines of every living and dead thing and, all across, sounds carried like secrets. A sheen of sparkled slate marked out Donegan's shed in its tree-cloaked grove. On the road below, Enright waited with Timmoney and Baldwin.

As they settled into position, the girl was on Enright's mind again; her prone image would not be banished nor her goddess face nor the absurd notion that she had, after all, as the bent woman had imagined, been raised from the dead. Helen Peters had survived, though she was paralysed from the neck down. A servant-girl of twenty-one from outside Cashel, she'd been a chambermaid at Castle Bennett House. When old Sebastian Bennett, Catholic but resolutely Unionist, had left and let the Auxies take the mansion for a base, the girl found employment in a boarding house for old and indigent ladies near the town. Enright couldn't understand how he'd never noticed a girl of such conspicuous beauty on the streets whose secrets he prided himself on knowing so well. On the morning of the ambush she'd been cycling over to Templemore to visit the statue. Was she, he wondered, simply curious or just another Holy Mary? Was she sick maybe, or a sinner? And if a sinner, what was her sin? Or had she merely gone to show herself off in the crowd, looking for a husband or a boy?

'Someone's coming down the field.'

Timmoney's urgent whisper shook Enright from his speculations. He recognised Donegan's lumbering walk and the cagey squat of the head on thick shoulders. For weeks now, ever since the killings, he'd been haunting the garage man's nights. Sometimes he'd bang on the back door of the house on New Street until the fellow answered and beckoned him in with his big man's heavy whisper like a gust of wind sucking at a sail. *Jesus, the whole town'll hear you, Sergeant.* On brighter nights, Enright tossed stones at his bedroom window and stood below, a ghostly reminder. *If you don't come up with the goods soon, Donegan, I'll be letting Paddy Kinahan in on our little secret.* The man promised and promised, until Enright told him he didn't believe in promises. Then he tried tears, until Enright told him he didn't believe in tears either.

'What's going on, Sergeant?'

'Ask me no questions and I'll tell you no lies, Timmoney.'

Donegan stopped in the middle of the field, his arms hanging out thickly from the bulk of his torso like a bear's.

'Are you on your own, Donegan?'

''Course I am.'

'Because I'm not. We'll talk in the shed, out of the cold.'

The Webley primed in his trench-coat pocket, Enright approached the grove ahead, the moon-white walls of the shed. Night trees were never quite trees to Enright after Mametz Wood and knowing what the shells could reduce them to, eerie stalagmites under a moon. The high branches of trees waving up out of the Panama Canal water too, skeletal, drowning. Donegan trailed breathlessly behind as Enright entered the grove and waited by the big door, whose bottom timbers had been splintered by rain and rats.

A column of light slid inwards and Enright saw at once that the petrol lorry had been removed. Donegan sat heavily against a workbench, knocked over a can and went fumbling to the ground after it.

'Where's the lorry you fecked off BP?'

'We sorted out all that business.'

Donegan reached up and grasped the vice-grips clamped to

the bench, to lift himself by. The tips of his fingers hung between the heavy side-bits and as he climbed he saw that Enright watched the screw.

'What d'ye mean, sorted out?'

'They sent out a lad to track me down and he said he'd fix the lorry and see me right with BP if I filled back a tanker load into her, to keep them happy. Some mechanic though. He lifted the bonnet and had it fixed in ten minutes. Wish I had a lad like that to run the garage for me.'

'A lad in a black leather coat?'

Up from his crouch and dizzied by the effort, the heavy man nodded.

'Why didn't you tell me this all the nights I called on you? What's his name?'

'Mick Cullinane.'

'And what did he make out of the deal?'

'Not a brass farthing and I offered him plenty. Said not to insult him, taking him for a cheat.'

'No one does anything for nothing.'

Donegan's wistful expression suggested a hankering after an honesty he never had.

'He didn't ask for a thing. And I got a letter from BP saying they're leaving me the contract.'

'I can still hang you, Donegan. One word from me to Kinahan and you're a dead man.'

'All I gave you and you still treat me like dirt.'

Funny how even the very lowest of men craved dignity. Until the local sergeant came out to the farm about the sheep hanging from the ash tree in the yard, young Tom thought the story of the Enright family's treachery back in the Whiteboy days baseless. His father's plea of mitigation crushed him. *You're after me for a lousy sheep and my great-grandfather over at Kilmorna served up a rebel to ye.* Then Joby Enright told Sergeant Larkin that the sheep was a scabby old carcass riddled with fluke he'd found on the side of the road. The blood haunting the boy's dreams became a poison to him and he imagined worms gnawing at his intestines. He felt Larkin's disgust again in this petrol-stinking shed, his aversion to a lesser being.

'What do you have for me?'

Pangs of conscience or painful calculations, Enright couldn't be sure which, unfolded on Donegan's face like a series of masks donned and discarded, one more ugly than the next. He seemed to forage after some justification for his act of betrayal and played with the vice-grips as though he intended punishing himself once Enright had left.

'They had no right to go hurting that young one. Such a terrible waste.'

'You knew her, did you?'

'I used be doing business with Sebastian Bennett and she often served me tea out there. They'd no right to go stringing a wire across the road if they weren't going to keep a proper eye on it.'

Enright began to feel that the cold was greater inside the shed than out, like the icicle-strewn sleeping porch at the Balfour San. *Which of us do you want to kill, Doc, me or the bloody bug that's biting me?* The dew-damp of the field had soaked through to his socks.

'Spit it out, Donegan.'

A heavy sigh marked the end of the battle playing itself out in Donegan's mind, as it ended all battles. He spoke in a hesitant staccato like a man up and down out of the water for breath.

'The Dwyers. From up there behind Clonore. D'ye know them?'

'Yeah. We shipped Eamon away to Ballykinlar Camp a few months back.'

'Well, his brother Martin and the cousin. He's Dwyer too. Red Johnny. Neighbours of Kinahan's. They're out gunning with him. Well, anyway. Red Johnny's sister's getting married soon. So they're having a bit of a hooley. A kind of a secret wedding party before the real one. Next week. Next Tuesday night.'

'And?'

'There'll be a fair scattering of the boys down for that. Even Kinahan maybe. There's a good chance they might be staying in their own homes for the night. After the few pints and all. Red Johnny 'specially. His grandmother's dying. He'll want to see her, I'd say. And his wife. He didn't see her for months, I believe.'

When he got back to the roadside, Enright couldn't conceal his delight.

'You got something, then.'

'All I wanted, Baldwin, and more.'

The dour Scotsman allowed himself a smile and Enright wondered why he wanted so badly to tell Timmoney what was in the offing, knowing well you couldn't tell a fellow stuffed to the gills with qualms a thing like that. Couldn't wait to see the sceptical look wiped off Pap's face though. Make the bugger wait a few more days before telling him. For the laugh. Papenfus would do the same to him. That was what kept men going, knocking a bit of fun out of each other, while the rest of them cried manic, cowardly tears in their shell-hole bivouacs.

After Enright's perfunctory inspection, the seven-man patrol marched out of the barracks yard and, in a diamond formation, went along Friary Street towards the town square. The chill he'd picked up at Donegan's shed showed no sign of abating even after three days. At Gallagher's morning lecture he'd felt certain that everyone in the room could hear the whistle of his wheezing chest. Even on a good morning, these talks seemed like a waste of time and to bear no relation to the reality beyond the barrack walls. But Gallagher insisted that they continue, worked away on them each night like a priest preparing a sermon. Today, he had droned on about the Food and Drugs Act. Watered-down whiskey and dodgy food cans.

All through the lecture, Enright had kept his arms folded because he was afraid that if he let his hands free on the desk before him, they would betray his feverishness. Only Timmoney noticed his discomfort or, more likely, was the only one naïve enough to mention it. *You're a bit under the weather.* An inexplicable delay had occurred in Enright, between the desire to jump to his feet and the act itself. Then it became more than a delay and he fumed. *I wonder when the priest turns water into wine on the altar, would that be an offence under the Food and Drugs Act, boy?*

Back in the barracks, having seen the patrol on its way, Enright went into the scullery and brewed himself some strong tea. That would bring the sweat out, once and for all. *A-drinking whiskey all the night/And China tea all day.* Picked that up on the boats, those first trips, a messboy, a peggy to able seamen and firemen and lower. *Piss, boiler water, billage,* they called the brew he brought from the galley. And always tepid, spit-warm or plain bloody cold, they complained, though the spillage burned blisters through his trousers and the pot handle welded itself to the flesh of his palms.

Enright filled his tin mug and carried it to the day room to consider his wife's letter again. He took the envelope from inside his tunic, drew out the sheets of notepaper and spread them on the desk alongside the single blank one that awaited his answer. Her letters, during his years at sea, he would read over and over so that they were consigned to memory within hours. At night he recited them like prayers, in place of prayers eventually. This letter he had read but once, so infuriated was he by having his secrets or those she knew of exposed in a letter that could have ended up anywhere.

His offer to join the local rebels, he'd already told her, had been made in the throes of the three-week drinking binge after his return from Canada, when he'd been provoked by the big talk of small men. He'd listened to their impassioned but vague proclamations, their tearful tales of injustice, their late-night descent into imagined heroics. Then, one night, he could take no more. He suggested they follow him over to Kilmorna and shoot Sir Arthur Vicars, the careless ex-Keeper of the Irish Crown Jewels. Enright had more reason than any of them to kill him after having had the door slammed in his face up there. Pulled out the Colt Peacemaker he'd brought back from Canada. Gabriel Jack's. *Wouldn't be the first man I put away with this beauty.* Their old guff ended then and he'd changed his mind about shooting Vicars because Mary would certainly have been told that he was the instigator. All the same to Vicars now anyway. Shot dead behind his burning pile by the local heroes. And Jimmy White among them? The same Jimmy who had come to the cottage with the local brigade's answer to Enright's offer to join them. *They won't have you, Tom. They make out you're too wild, that you'd get us all killed.* All apologies, the young fellow had been after that but Enright was having none of it. *They won't have me 'cause they still think we gave the Whiteboy away a hundred years ago.* Then, not knowing what else to say, Jimmy spat out Mary's secret by way of a ham-fisted compliment. *I'm glad she found you, Tom. I thought she'd never be right again after Martin Fuller died.*

Enright had remembered a little pale weed of a fellow with red hair and studious expression who must have been at least ten years older than Mary. The thought of it sickened him though he'd never been able to ask her about Fuller. Even yet, sixteen months later, she hadn't mentioned the late lamented son of the solicitor she worked for all those years she was writing the long letters. He wondered why he hadn't burned the whole bundle long ago as he tried now to compose a suitably terse reply to her latest.

Her mention of the sanatorium too, even putting a name on it, was unforgivable. He'd had enough trouble trying to talk his way around the reference to *debility* in his Certificate of Service at the RIC recruitment office. In spite of a chest half-poisoned with the chlorine gas from that time in Maroc and blown in by the grenade at Commotion Trench, he was no consumptive. They'd tested his spittle often enough in the sanatorium. Fit as any man he ever met. Even Gabriel Jack, who could walk thirty-five miles in a day and who took Mary in with his half-bred talk of guiding spirits and easy-going ways that were only an excuse for being trampled over by whites and Redskins alike and pretending not to care. That was real debility. Had her fooled up to the eyeballs with his wild songs and the smiling glint in his eye, like an ember on a sod of turf, when all he wanted was what any colour of a man wanted from a woman pretty as that. *How the hell do I know where he's gone, Mary? He's half a savage and that's what they do, wander off.*

He wrote her name, and then:

> I will be home for a short while in two or three weeks' time. In the meantime, I trust that you not write me things that are better not written down.
>
> Tom.

Awash with sweat, he sank back in his chair and closed his eyes. Drained, he felt none the less at peace, until he saw Papenfus standing before him and couldn't remember hearing him enter the day room. The Boer looked away quickly as though hiding some conclusion. Enright felt off kilter with the day and everything in it, Papenfus included. From the Auxie officer's demeanour, the usual dash was absent.

'You look a bloody mess, Tom.'

'Touch of a cold. You're not looking too chipper yourself, Pap. What's up?'

Papenfus pulled over a chair and sat but couldn't make himself comfortable. He took out his cigarettes and chucked one across the desk at Enright.

'Ag, there's talk of peace. Serious talk. We're donnered, Tom.'

'If I'd a penny for every rumour of peace I heard these last few months, I'd have the vault in the Munster and Leinster Bank filled to the brim.'

'I've been talking to a chap, a friend of mine from Edinburgh. Been posted to Dublin Castle and he says there's a big push on to get a truce going. Can you imagine it? Kinahan and his *vrot* rabble walking around the town like bloody heroes.'

'Not when we're finished with them, they won't.' Enright clenched his neck to subdue the spasm there. When he leaned forward he felt like the judge with the black cap on his head he'd once had nightmares about. 'I've good news for you, Pap. What are you doing next Tuesday night?'

'Salus hon-o-or virtus quo-o-que.'

Enright's voice rang out clearly above the racket of the car engine and the wind whistling through a small crack at the far edge of the windscreen like a guy rope in a gale. He was off to see the dogs at Lady's Well, Timmoney at his side. If it hadn't been for the hymns, standing guard on the cathedral steps while the barracks' breast-beaters attended Sunday morning Mass would have been intolerable. And the music. God or no God, he felt sometimes a vast sense of uplift as the sound swelled from the great fluted pipes of the organ inside. Timmoney strained to make himself heard and his high-pitched shout, seeming hysterical, disturbed Enright though the words themselves were lost.

'What?'

He slowed the car to lessen the noise. His cramped neck anticipated trouble.

'There was another suicide yesterday.'

'What?'

'Another policeman. Up in Monasterevan Barracks this time. That's seven of us this year, at least.'

'What do you mean, *at least?*'

Enright glanced across at the young penitent, who stared bleakly at the road ahead through the straggled ends of his black forelock, his knees high to his front in the restricted space.

'The barracks accidents. They can't all be accidents.'

'Cowards and madmen, the lot of them.'

'There's only so much a man can take, being despised like this. The way they look at you, even in the cathedral.'

'No harm in being hated. You know where you stand when they hate you. When they start ignoring you, then you're really in trouble.'

Not a whit of respect had he gleaned for himself those first years on the boats, long after the days of potwalloping and the slopping out for other men had passed. But after he killed the Chink huckster that all changed. Had to lie low a while, get himself new identification papers, but Marshall saw to that and was always good for dark hints at Enright's new reputation every boat they signed on to. Wanted him at their side then, if the knives came out in the fetid dark of an Algiers alley or a Naples whorehouse. Behind all the back-slapping and free rounds, he knew they hated him because he was stronger, and even if he wasn't stronger, he was more vicious and men felt that kind of inferiority like a cancer in the belly.

'I can't get that girl out of my mind, Sergeant. And the child. Murdered before it was even born.'

The bad side of Enright's chest tightened.

'She was pregnant?'

'Five or six months gone, I heard.'

'When are you ever going to shut up about that young one? Bloody unnatural, if you ask me. This is what happens when they lock you away from the women, son.'

There was no relief to be had from the contractions in his neck until he pulled the car into the verge by the field gate at Lady's Well.

'Are you coming in?'

The young constable brought out a book from inside his tunic and opened it.

'I don't like dogs. I'll have a wee read.'

'Keep at those books, son, and you won't be long turning into a barracks accident yourself.'

The yelp of running dogs lifted Enright's spirits again. There was nothing like a dog in full flight to make a fellow feel what it might be like to be truly free. Their sheer power and the grace of speed over bulk in them. He saw Foley and Danny Egan over by the shed and ambled towards them.

Danny sometimes slept in the loft of the dog shed though Enright couldn't for the life of him figure out how a fellow could get a decent kip with the hungry dogs below baying for blood. He lit up a cigarette and watched the quartet of greyhounds at play as he coughed.

The black took most of his attention, as always. Arrow Valley Puca, named for the ghostly black dog of legend. Elegantly up on tiptoes for all its sinewed spread, the bends of the rear legs angled to perfection. He held out great hopes for the dog though whenever he saw it, he couldn't help thinking of the white he'd rejected from the same litter over in Cashel against Foley's advice. Even had a name in his head for it – Arrow Valley Snow – and often wondered who'd bought the dog and where it was now. But today the black had that aura of invincibility about it. Well within itself as it sprinted alongside the blue and the pair of brindles, it turned on a sixpence to leave the lot of them blocking each other clumsily off from a quick change of direction. Foley knew Enright's preference.

'He's looking good, Sergeant. We'll collect silver with that one yet.'

'And if we don't, I'll know who to blame. How come I never see you out here?'

A wary laugh rose from Foley's wiry, bow-legged frame.

'Well, there's a coincidence for you. I never see you out here either.'

Sixty if he was a day, Foley lived in a cottage nearby with his wife and eleven children. *We're still trying for the even dozen* was his wicked-winking boast. He trained dogs for six or seven men and, though far from the breadline, dressed as raggedly as Danny did. Or as Danny usually dressed, for today he was resplendent. The tweed trousers, patched but passable; the woollen jumper obviously new, its musky smell doing valiant battle with his unwashed body odour.

'You've the cut of a gentleman about you today, Danny. Where did you come across the style?'

Tearful gratitude softened the better half of Danny's face and won out briefly over the raw dropsy of the rest.

'The nuns knit the jumper for me. Pure saints they are.'

Foley eyed the new outfit with jealous derision.

'And you fecked the trousers off a corpse, I suppose.'

'I did not, Foley, I got them out at Castle Bennett last year but I didn't wear them until the arse fell out of my old ones last week.'

Helen Peters came to mind again. In spite of himself, Enright had to know more about the crippled servant girl.

'Did you know the young one who got caught up in the ambush, Danny?'

'She'd do anything for you that girl, give you her last copper. A face like an angel and a flirty twinkle in her eye too. Not for the likes of me, of course.'

Enright watched Danny grin and shrug off the thought or the instinct or whatever it was. He walked away. His dogs gathered round him; mouths opening into red-raw depths, tongues hanging drool, glassy eyes staring blankly. The old farmyard panic seized him momentarily but the snap of his neck banished it. He shooed the dogs away and kicked out a threatening foot at the grass as Foley protested.

'They're hungry, Sergeant, but not hungry enough to eat a sour Kerryman.'

'Well, feed them, so.'

Danny hadn't finished darkening Enright's day. Scuttling up alongside him, his dew-soaked plimsolls sliding and unbalancing him on the damp grass, he grabbed Enright's arm for support.

'I got wicked drunk last night, Sergeant.'

'No harm in that, Danny.'

The vagrant whispered out of the mangled half of his face.

'But, you see, I was supposed to call up to you, to tell you something.'

'Tell me what?'

Enright felt weighed down by Danny's grasp but couldn't bring himself to shoo him away as he'd done the dogs.

'That fellow in black, he was in town again yesterday. Only he was wearing a brown suit.'

A curious thought bothered Enright. He'd invented a ghost for Danny to chase and now it wouldn't stay away. He wondered if there was more to this BP man than Donegan claimed. No mere coincidence after all that he'd been talking to the rebel Dooleys' sister outside Molloy's Hardware? Hauling himself into the car alongside Timmoney, who crouched over his book like a praying mantis, he made one last laughing stab at rescuing the day.

'D'ye know what we'll do, Timmoney? We'll drive over to Templemore and take a gander at the bleeding statue. What d'ye say? Maybe I'll be converted.'

'I don't know. Wouldn't it be a wee bit dangerous driving over there in the car? Just the two of us, like?'

'A joke, boy. Can you not remember what it's like to laugh?'

On board the RMS *Missambie*, crossing from Canada with the 29th and the other battalions, they'd hit straight into a North Atlantic squall and Enright knew he'd gone back on the sea too soon. The ship slammed into the solid pit of roiling waves and took it green across the bows on the upsurge. While the waves tossed bile from other men's stomachs, Enright struggled to expel the memories of Marshall's appalling end and the ensuing panic that had driven him, half-crazy, from the sea. Young Clancy had done the best he could because Enright had once told him the whole sordid story. *It'll pass, Tom, it passed before.* Spent the whole trip down below not to have to look at the water. Shaking and flapping and yellow as a quarantine flag. No porthole, nothing to breathe but his own foul, suffocating breath and, nearby, the engine thrumming in his guts, night, noon and morning.

Those days and nights he spent on his barracks mattress after the chill he'd picked up at Donegan's shed, his memory of that voyage had more than once become too visceral. Timmoney was solicitous with hot toddies and offers of books to read. *Just leave the whiskey and get us something to spit into, will you?* Gallagher appeared occasionally at the door but never stepped in. *Nothing worse than a summer cold, Tom.* Enright detected a measure of relief in the Head Constable's show of benevolence; a father's gratitude at his wild child laid low a while. There wasn't the energy to be angry with either man because the coughing drained all of that out of him.

Only with Papenfus did he raise his voice. *What damn good are you capable to on Tuesday night, Tom, in this condition?* They'd have to go ahead without him, the Boer insisted – Baldwin, himself, and a couple of his Auxies. *I told you I'll be all right, Pap, now get out of here and let me sleep.* But he slept only fitfully, waking out of troubling dreams into a restiveness that clung to minor irritations and would not let go; itches scratched until they became wounds. The mysterious BP man; the servant girl; another letter from Mary, a short one.

He sent Timmoney to find out what he could about the stranger and his most recent visit to town. The enquiries yielded little or nothing. The fellow had arrived from Dublin on the Saturday morning train, stayed overnight in the Railway Hotel near the barracks, and gone back Sunday evening on the last train. A wire to BP revealed that the visit wasn't related to Cullinane's work.

'So what did Cullinane do between Saturday morning and Sunday night, Timmoney?'

'He can't be a rebel, he's too open. All he did was go to the pictures.'

'He came down all the way from Dublin to go to the pictures?'

'And Mass. Same one we went to.'

Enright wondered how, while guarding the cathedral doors, he could have missed the stranger and felt more agitated still. Only later did he remember that the Dooleys' sister played piano at the picture house and that Cullinane had spoken to her his first time in town. Cullinane's movements might be unguarded but Enright couldn't get the fellow out of his mind.

Then there was Helen Peters. If Papenfus hadn't insisted on a doctor, Enright might have forgotten her a little longer. He was sure he'd discouraged the Auxie captain sufficiently, until he woke late in the evening of the second day to find a hand clamped to his forehead and a knuckle banging the hollow side of his bared chest. He had pushed the hands away and covered himself before he saw Dr Brady above him. A big-framed man, still solid enough in spite of the thinning grey hair and the vellum skin, his years among the sick and the dead seemed not to have diminished his composure.

'Have you trouble breathing, Sergeant?'

'Wouldn't you, if you took a grenade in the chest?'

The cheerful ones were just as bad as any of them. That fellow in the 3rd General Hospital at Wandsworth Common, two months after the grenade, nodding as though in agreement as Enright spoke. *Not that I don't want to, mind, but I'm in no fit state to go back yet, Doctor.* Then an orderly had interrupted them and while the two men whispered outside the office door, Enright read the verdict at the end of the page on the desk. *He is now much improved. For disposal please, J. Herbert Parsons.*

'Were you ever tested for TB, Sergeant?'

The doctor's question was marginally less patient than the first, which pleased Enright.

'I was, a hundred and one times, and I haven't it. What I have is bronchitis after the chlorine gas.'

'I'll send one of your men down to Devlin's for some camphor and Sloane's Liniment to rub in. And Moore's Cough Syrup. Strong stuff but you can't beat it.'

Enright remembered that Brady worked up at the Union Workhouse and Infirmary where the crippled girl had been taken.

'That young one from the ambush. Is there any hope for her?'

'I'm afraid things have taken a turn for the worse there. We put her in the old laundry room at first because she was hysterical for days. Now there's not a sound out of her but she won't be moved to a ward. What can we do only grant her what might be her last wish?' The doctor pondered the mysteries of the sky outside the barred and dusty window. 'If it wasn't for that little hunchbacked lady calling on her, she'd have nobody.'

'The woman she worked for?'

'No. No connection at all. I believe she's a Birr woman, a sister of May Dooley's. The picture hall Dooleys.'

'The rebel Dooleys.'

Lying perfectly still, Enright imagined what it was like to feel no sensation in the legs, the arms, the hands, and imagined too well. He made quick fists below the bedcovers to dispel the momentary but convincing pretence.

'She's a decent woman. She's convinced the girl's a miracle child. Who knows but that she may be right.'

'Not much of a fucking miracle.'

'Speaking of miracles. I've never seen so many scars on a man. Must have had God at your side, what?'

Enright turned to the wall to hide his leaking eye, in case the horse-doctor started poking at that too.

'Fifty-one, Doc, one short of a pack and no jokers. I wonder has He any scars?'

On the third morning, Timmoney came with the medicines

and a letter from Mary. He offered to rub the liniment on Enright's aching chest.

'Go way and leave me alone. I might as well be rubbing holy water on it, for all the good that stuff'll do.'

But when Timmoney left, he tried the liniment. The burn of it helped, offering an alternative discomfort that was easier to bear because it was on the surface of his flesh and not hidden where it could be anything his idle mind imagined it to be. He drank from the cough bottle and though he gagged on the nauseating taste of ether, not throwing up felt like the first victory won in his recovery.

How many days had he spent vomiting up every last trace of the ether in him and in how many hospitals had he held his breath against its pervasiveness? More than any man deserved in a handful of lifetimes, that was for sure. Bagthorpe, King's Canadian Red Cross, Essondale, Woodcote Park, Camiers, Wandsworth Common, Hastings, Balfour. Dressing stations, military hospitals, general hospitals, convalescent hospitals, sanatoriums and worse. He'd long ago sworn never to see the inside of another one. He told himself he was feeling better and itched to go after Red Johnny Dwyer and the cousin, Martin. And Kinahan with his big block of jaw and the eyes like cigarette burns on the photograph paper.

Then he read Mary's latest letter, dismissing it and yet stupidly disappointed at its brevity. He stared down the questions until they became mere scratchings on a scrap of paper. A man lived and fought on if he had the heart to, after what he'd been through and what he'd done, and if he was meant to. What was it about women that they had to make more of it, make a song and dance of something that came to nothing, in the end, but the difference between a good dog and a bad dog? Plodding along or sprinting flat out, and bugger-all worth thinking about in between. Running until you drop. And you weren't the slipper, the dog nor the hare but all three together. The Holy fucking Trinity. Every child, his own included, had to learn that before he went out into the world. No spirit out of some drunken Okanagan dream to guide him. Nothing. Nobody. Only his own nature that he was born with, that he'd die with.

Bedford,
Listowel

Tom,

If you are interested at all in knowing it, your son is very
sick. I have a terrible feeling this is something very serious.
Could he have the Enrights' bad chest, I wonder, because he
wheezes worse than you most of the time? I don't understand
why you don't care about him. How can there be anything
more important than a child to be a father to and show him
the way in the world?

You minded me so carefully before the baby we lost and
even before Jerry that it is beyond me why you hit him.
Why shouldn't he cry if he's sick? Hasn't he every right to
when he can't yet talk to tell us what's wrong with him? If
anything happens to Jerry, I will have nothing.

Do you remember when we used to write to each other?
All those far places. I used to go down to the library and
find them on the map and then find things to read about
them. You made my world a bigger place than Listowel and
I thought I might have a better life than the thankless
drudgery of my mother and her mother. You let me dream
and now you won't even let me sleep, not that I do anyway
with Jerry so sick.

You won't give up your pride for love of me and that is a
terrible thing to say after all our years together, even those
we didn't spend together. Myself, on the other hand, I would

give up nearly anything for you, for all the good it is doing
me. At least my sister is living under the same roof as
Toussaint, as bad as he is for the women. All his old Frenchy
talk is a lie and I always knew it but you don't talk at all and
sometimes I think that silence is a worse lie.

Will you please start talking to me, Tom? You're further
away from me now than you ever were those four years in
the war when you suddenly stopped writing to me, or over
in Canada when you were getting more tired by the day and
wouldn't listen to me and punished me for something I had
no hand, act nor part in, which is your own wounds and
your restless spirit. You are still trying to do too much and
still courting danger. You are like a boy that way with no
sense for all your experience.

Look at yourself up there in Tipperary, Tom. Alone when
you have no need to be. Fighting when you have no need
to be. There is more to life than proving yourself in war and
strife. Those are your very own words in the letter you sent
from Balfour, which I so often read in hope. Are you ever
going to give yourself and the rest of us some peace?

Mary

An hour before he was to meet Papenfus for the night raid on Clonore, Enright stretched himself out on his mattress, the damp side turned over and forgotten. Though not tired, he couldn't stop himself from yawning and every yawn provoked a rage of twinges in his neck. Same thing in the crouch those minutes before zero hour and the up and over and maybe down for all of eternity. Yet, the last thing he expected was that he might sleep. Or dream.

He walked along the Templemore Road and the pitch of the descent from Knoxtown Bridge was steeper than it should have been. In his hands he carried a box wrapped in brown paper, big and bulky as his kit box but curiously light. He was a boy and Mary White had grown. Dressed in white, she walked ahead of him swishing a slender hawthorn stick and decapitating dandelions along the grassy verge. From within the hedge came the brush and crackling skulk of some animal stalking them of which she seemed to be unaware. *What's in the box, Mary? Why have I to carry it?* Some of the dandelion heads remained attached to the stems that were bowed and broken. The split shoots oozed a milky froth. *Ask me no questions and I'll tell you no lies.* She swung the stick once again, sending a dandelion head sailing away up in the air, where it exploded silently in a snowfall of feathery seeds. *You can carry itself, so, if you won't tell me what's in it.* He thrust the box into her arms and began to run towards the bend in the road. *Ah, Tom, it's too heavy for me.* The animal, invisible in the hedge alongside, kept pace with him and he wasn't sure if it was his own heartbeat or the beast's he felt inside him. *There's nothing in the box, Tom, and it's not even mine, it's Martin Fuller's.* He knew that he mustn't look back at her as he shouted. *Fuller's only a little weed and, anyway, he's dead.* He turned the bend only to find another, a younger Mary White standing before him, the box in her motherly embrace. Terrified, he jumped into the ditch though he knew the stalking beast would devour him and woke just as its teeth were about to sink into his flesh.

Enright knew at once by the quality of the darkness in his room that he was late for Papenfus. There wasn't time to waste on lighting the Aladdin lamp. He pulled out his kit box from under the bed and found, by touch, what he needed to bring. The tin of black boot polish, the Colt Peacemaker. He went along the dark upper landing to the room Baldwin shared with Timmoney and a few of the Tan boys. Gallagher snored loudly as Enright passed by his door. There was a light-headed sense of confidence in moving about so freely while other men lay, weighed down by sleep. Like ghosts might feel, if ghosts existed. But he didn't float as ethereally as he'd imagined because Baldwin arrived at the door just as Enright was about to ease it inwards. Taken by surprise, Enright dropped the polish tin. The noise sent ripples of fluttering through the suddenly amplified breathing of the sleeping men in the rooms off the landing. He couldn't yet see the Scotsman's face but imagined the look there of impassive contempt he usually reserved for the more callow of his fellow constables.

'Get that bloody tin for me, Baldwin, will you?'

Baldwin found his wily way through the extremes of obeying and disobeying.

'Leave it. I've enough for the pair of us.'

A strong, bracing odour of carbolic soap filled the landing and Enright saw that Baldwin had dressed up in his suit and tie. His usually unkempt hair was greased back and his face glowed ruddily from washing and towelling. Enright himself hadn't shaved all day and his bleary eyes needed dowsing but there wasn't time.

They met up on a back road near the Auxiliaries' quarters at Castle Bennett House. The place might have been burned down long since if it hadn't been for the military presence there. Not that Enright cared. An eye for an eye, a big house for a cottage was fair enough. Half the pleasure in ordering the torch for a rebel's home was the prospect of seeing some mansion tumble in the flames, like Vicars's house below in Kilmorna. Served him right. *An NCO, young man, is not an officer in my book nor is a son of Joby Enright likely to be a gentleman.* Wouldn't have shot the daft bugger like the Listowel boys had done all the same, ten, fifteen men to one, he supposed.

'Christ, Tom, you're cutting it fine.'

'The old Johnny-jitters getting to you, are they, Pap?'

Their spirits improved as they blackened each other's faces. Even Baldwin allowed himself a smile when one of the Auxies inhaled a blob of polish and took a fit of retching and laughing all at once. Eyes jammed tight, Enright ignored the burn on his cheeks as Baldwin applied the finishing touches to his eyelids and remembered other nights of disguise. The raiding party he went out on at Maroc when they'd lost three good young lads. Out with five, back with two, himself and Clancy. Fourteen days' Special Absence for their trouble. That night they used mud for their faces and there was plenty of it. All those whoring weeks back in Amiens he seemed to have been spitting the little pebbly grains out of his mouth, no matter how much he drank. And there were the nights out on the fall hunt with Gabriel Jack in Arrow Valley. *Goddam moon-face, we gotta fix you up, take the shine off you.* The red-rust dust of a Ponderosa pine bark was his mask back then. Daubed it on himself that last night with the son-of-a-bitch half-breed. *Look more like an Okanagan than I do now, Thomas.*

Since the fever had ended, Enright had pored over the Ordnance Survey map. Every turn of their road had etched itself in his mind and every location – Kinahan's farmhouse, the cottages of Red Johnny and Martin Dwyer – firmly fixed.

Half an hour, forty minutes at most, would take them to the
Widow's Cross, where they'd leave the car. From there, five
minutes across the fields to Kinahans'. Another ten to Red
Johnny's and back to the car for the short drive to Martin
Dwyer's.

Papenfus took the wheel of the Bennetts' petrol blue Lancia,
Enright alongside him.

'We want no shots fired out in the open, Pap, or they'll be
heard all over the parish and we'll lose the lot of them.'

In the back seat with the other Auxie, black-faced Baldwin
grinned.

'Did ye get that, Captain? Frigging black man calling the
shots. What d'ye make o' that?'

Enright banged his palms together in a thunderclap, burning
with exhilaration.

'Grease your sea boots, lads. We're heading into rough waters!'

The stealthy approach was the same each time. Boots and
trouser legs dampening in wet fields; the vicious fingering from
thorny hedges; irritations that would have their release. The
four of them, fanning out to front and rear of the buildings,
Enright and Papenfus taking turns to smash in doors; boot, fist,
shoulder, whatever it took. Once inside, the same screams of
young and old and the same shadows from the torches, epileptic,
scuttling along the walls like gigantic but insubstantial lizards.
Then the search through the rooms and the perfervid hope
that he'd hit the jackpot before Pap or Baldwin did. Only at
Kinahans' was their man not at home.

Papenfus, screaming in a falsetto Enright thought ludicrous
and disappointing, found two young fellows in a bedroom off
the parlour; one about eighteen, the other in his early twenties.

'Keep those bloody hands where I can see them.'

At first Enright was sure the older one was Paddy Kinahan
though they both claimed to be his brothers and not the man
himself. They pushed the pair through the fancy parlour, where
Enright swept his gun hand across the ornate sideboard and

sent a pile of china plates and a couple of ceramic dog statuettes crashing to the floor. Out in the kitchen, the mother's appeals were unrelenting as her half-dressed sons stumbled into view.

'Paddy's not here! Paddy's not here!'

The father, tall and grey-haired, tried hard to shame the intruders with a silent show of dignity. Papenfus ordered the two brothers to face the wall and raise their arms above their heads. When they looked into the torch light as they turned, Enright now felt certain that neither one was Paddy Kinahan. He'd looked at the photograph on the file often enough. Neither one had quite the same chiselled edge to the big square jaw nor the promontory brows like tufts of grass on a cliff edge. He couldn't convince himself that this was a mere trick of the present jumpy light or of the camera or his memory. Then, the father broke his silence and Enright knew that Kinahan had eluded them.

'You'll never catch Paddy. He's too smart for the likes of you guttersnipes.'

Enright cracked the butt of his Colt into the man's jaw and sent him back against the heavy kitchen table. The table screeched loudly as it slid across the flagged floor and a jutting corner of the scrubbed pine top caught Papenfus in the crotch, doubling him over. In the confusion, the Kinahan brothers made a break for the door. Baldwin got a shot off and there was a loud groan but they kept on running, slamming the door shut behind them. Enright yelled at the Scot, aping the guttural mountainy accent of Kinahan senior as best he could.

'Don't fire outside. It's not our man.'

Papenfus had recovered himself sufficiently to start kicking at the grey-haired man on the floor, blaming him for the blow he'd taken and for the young men's escape. His studded boot soles knocked sparks from the flagstone like fireflies in the flittering light. The man's wife clawed at Papenfus, stripping streaks from his blackened face.

The rest of the night went more smoothly, except that running up the open stair ladder from Red Johnny's kitchen,

Enright felt a boyhood pang and the woman he found there had the look of death on her too. The wide eyes in her skull-like face lit up with astonishment and he wondered if she imagined her time was up and the devil come to take her. Her little cry was an infant's vague appeal. He got back down just as Baldwin discovered Red Johnny making from his bed in a room off the kitchen. Small and wiry, the red-haired rebel stood paralysed by the torchlight like a lamped rabbit.

'Have I time for a prayer?'

A pool of urine trickled out from between his bare feet.

'Had our boys? Or the young one? Where's Kinahan?'

'Hail Mary, full of grace, the Lord is with thee . . .'

Enright slid past Baldwin, took aim and shot the young man in the face. The beam of light tracked the rebel's convulsive fall back on to the bed and Enright went closer, quick breath seething through his clenched teeth. He put the Colt to the pulp of Red Johnny's temple and fired again. The eyes took a few seconds to realise they were dead. Then they clouded over. The gun felt wild and hungry in his hand and he wanted to shoot into the eyes too but Baldwin grabbed his shoulder. The smell of blood and cordite was the smell of France, of chaos, and unsteadied him.

He pushed through the pair of keening sisters in the kitchen and took a strange delight in the brush of their breasts as they struck out at him. One of them, Red Johnny's wife, he supposed, held a baby, its face awash with tears and snot, its breathing gagged and hysterical. She screamed a curse on him.

'You shot my Johnny! That you may roast in hell, you animal!'

To hell with her widow's curse, he thought. More old *ráiméis* and jigger-pokery.

A bent old man stood by the door, a rolling spastic tremor in his right hand like a man trying to light a match in a hurry. His eyes betrayed a realisation of powerlessness that bore a pitiful finality. Words were almost on Enright's lips to speak but he hauled them back and went out into a mucky yard that was hopping mad with hens and a couple of throaty ducks. *Everyone gets old and useless.* But not everyone. Not Red Johnny. Nor his cousin Martin.

They rustled him up from a kitchen settle bed and it took three of them to beat the fight out of him.

'Don't shoot me in the house. How'll they live in here if you do that?'

Papenfus laid claim to the skinny youth upon whom the reality of rebellion seemed now to be sadly dawning. Fending off the apoplectic parents and the memory of the widow's curse, Enright watched Martin Dwyer closely. Though he'd seen it a hundred times before in France, there was something hugely compelling about seeing a boy become a man and die in the space of a short few minutes. Like Clancy up in front of Commotion Trench though this fellow showed no signs of madness in between. *Why did we come over here at all, Tom, are we mad after all?*

'It's all right, Ma, don't be afraid. I'm not. All right, Da?'

They quietly gave up their desperate attempts to get past Enright for a last living touch of their son. Parents and child, their eyes were for each other only.

Papenfus pushed him along but there was a firmness in the fellow that would concede not even a hint of a stumble as he stepped across the packed earth kitchen floor for the last time. Beside Enright, the parents knelt and when they began to mutter incoherently, he thought they were begging him to spare their son. But they weren't talking to him. They were talking to their God.

He followed Papenfus and the rebel to the porch of the cottage. Dwyer reached for a trench coat that hung there, a makeshift brown serge belt on its waist, but sharing in a glance at Enright an almost amused sense of the absurdity of the act, he lowered his hand. A dead man's cast-off coat was a strange thing. Enright remembered finding Captain Big Toe's hanging on a nail in the dugout and putting it on, the brief struggle with superstition before necessity won out.

When Enright spoke, he made no attempt to disguise his voice.

'Tell us where Kinahan is and we'll let you off.'

Papenfus stepped forward.

'He's not yours to free, Enright.'

'Shut the fuck up, Pap. Where's Kinahan, son.'

'What kind of a man do you take me for? This field over here. It's not ours yet. Shoot me there.'

Papenfus grabbed the fellow's nightshirt and tried in vain to turn him around before they reached the gate into the field. Even with the Webley clamped to the back of his head, the rebel's progress was unstoppable. There wasn't a man alive who'd ship a bullet for Enright and the knowledge depleted him. Not a one. Not the Boer for sure.

'Let him into the field, Pap.'

Papenfus cursed him but lowered the gun and let Dwyer open the gate with the practised casualness of an ordinary act.

'No tricks now.'

Enright knew the young fellow wasn't going to run. Turning to face them, Martin Dwyer looked from Enright to Papenfus as though choosing between them. His gaze fixed itself finally on Enright.

'I know you. You're the Kerry sergeant from the town. But I don't know the other lad.'

Papenfus ordered him to kneel and Enright sensed the odd reversal of calm and high nervousness in the two men.

'I won't kneel before any man. Who is he, Sergeant?'

'Shut your fucking mouth.'

Enright wasn't sure which of them Papenfus addressed. Sheer bad luck, he thought. If they'd got Kinahan, they probably wouldn't have bothered with this young lad. If anyone deserved to know the answer to the last big mystery, it was Martin Dwyer. Enright saw the Webley rising out of the dark into the torchlight and was about to tell him but the young man spoke first.

'There's a girl . . . would you give her a message . . . would you tell her I'm sorry for . . . ' Then the shot went off. The rebel took a step back, grimaced and stared down at his suddenly bloodied chest. Papenfus stumbled back, jerked himself forward again, dodged with exaggerated craftiness to the young fellow's side like he was going to pickpocket him. The second shot, aimed to the head but hitting instead the neck, put Martin Dwyer to his knees.

'. . . tell her I'm sorry I . . .'

The rebel gurgled bloodily and the frenetic Boer fired again.

'Jesus, forgive me my . . .'

After the third shot and the slump and sideways fall, Dwyer's fingers clawed into the soft earth as though to commence the digging of his own grave.

They stopped the Lancia at a river bridge, two miles from town. They scaled the low stone wall and went slipping and stumbling down to the river's edge. Though little more than a stream, the brown, boggy waters tumbled noisily and spared them the effort of conversation. With some rags they'd brought along, they helped each other remove the black polish from their faces and the ice-cold water felt good on Enright's enflamed cheeks. The light of morning began to form all around them. Pale at first across the grey-vaulted sky but then a burnished gold suggested itself and from the distant hills they'd left behind them, a deep red sun began to rise and push the blanket of cloud up from the horizon. *Red sky at morning, a sailor's warning.* Enright's hands, raised out of the water again, were the colour of Ponderosa pine dust. The young widow's curse troubled him inordinately.

Closer to town, a tabby cat walking along the convent grounds wall paused in mid-stride as the Lancia went past. Pity it wasn't black, Enright thought. Then, his unease attached itself to an unexpected and disturbing conviction. He was sure that his sick child had died in the night and the visceral intensity of his panic tangled his innards into painful knots. *If anything happens to Jerry, I will have nothing.*

Timmoney stood framed in the lighted doorway of the day room when Enright and Baldwin entered by the back of the barracks.

'Did you get any of them?'

It felt strange to hear someone speak softly again after the loud exchanges that still rang in his ears. Funny, he thought, how when the whisper of the sea returned after a storm there had been this sense too that it had been there all along, only that he'd let himself become distracted by the bluster of wind and high waves. Baldwin, still churlish at his marginal involvement in the executions, pushed roughly past the young constable.

'Ge'outa my road.'

Enright knew he'd be better off lying down but, quite certain there would be no rest for him, he went by Timmoney and into the scullery to make some tea.

'Go way to bed, Timmoney. What you don't know won't harm you.'

The kettle began to boil up on the stove. Timmoney loitered, a thoughtful look on his face as though he were composing a sermon on vengeance being God's prerogative and pondering which biblical quotations to employ. Enright loaded the pot with a fistful of tea leaves and filled it to the brim with scalding water. The rising steam burned his face and left an irritating tingle. He poured himself a mug, went to the dresser in the day room and spiked the tea with a few shots of whiskey. The desultory light diminished everything. Only now did he notice that the smell of the dead policemen hadn't gone away after all these weeks.

Timmoney joined him, placing the matching blue-and-cream striped mug alongside his on the table. Enright studied the leaves floating on his bog-watery tea.

'Why didn't you bring me along?'

Too surprised to deliver the dismissive answer he felt the question deserved, Enright remained silent.

'They deserve hell for what they done.'

'Someone has to put them there first, son. Would you?'

'I don't know . . . but it's a war and most of these fellows never get caught and . . .'

Timmoney's inner debate went underground again, leaving Enright oddly disappointed, but its hasty re-emergence infuriated him.

'I think it's the girl, really. And the wee child in her. That's what really rankles. The innocents. The Slaughter of the Innocents.'

'And the men's lives mean nothing?'

'It's just that the girl is so pretty and – '

Enright slammed his mug down on the table, the hot spill over his hand bothering him only vaguely as he grabbed a fistful of Timmoney's shirt.

'Listen, boy, it's nothing to do with the girl or her child. It's a matter of not backing off, is what it is. Not letting them think you haven't the stomach to hold your ground. And that's why I didn't bring you, sunshine, because you'll never have the stomach for anything only sitting on your arse and thinking and reading old muck that some fool made up because he never lived a real honest-to-God life of his own.' He pushed the young constable away. 'Jesus Christ, Timmoney, did they send you down to Tipperary especially to annoy me or what?'

Beneath his dishevelled forelock, Timmoney was like a boy peering out from a hiding place at some half-understood unpleasantness. Enright's hands would not rest easy. He clenched and unclenched them and watched the bloodless skin of his palms embedded with dark tracks of polish. He held his mug with both hands to warm them. The whiskeyed tea offered no relief as it passed through the twist in his gut.

'Fuck it. Everything. Fuck it.'

Slaughter of the Innocents was right. His own child dead, he was sure of it now, like their first child and his blue-lipped doll-brother and the girl's child too. He cursed himself for having spoken his unease aloud.

'Danny Egan called after you went out, Sergeant.'

Enright wondered if the bad side of the ex-soldier's face burned like his own did now. Damn polish. Bit of muck would do if there had to be a next time. Or a dab of coal dust like they used for that shellback ritual when a boat crossed the International Date Line and had so terrified him once. Or a neckerchief over his nose like the time he helped put out the forest fire near Nelson and they walked around the streets for two weeks after, talking to each other through the muffle of cotton under a sky so dark a dirty dusk all day that they almost forgot what Kootenay Lake down below and Morning Mountain and Toad Mountain up behind looked like.

'He says this fellow Cullinane is back in town.'

Enright sensed the thrill of release, of a diversion however foolish.

'Where is he lodging?'

'He booked into Hayes' Hotel this time.'

The day-room door opened. Enright hadn't heard Constable Keane's approach and wondered if he'd been outside listening. He looked as if he'd just woken and still bore that early morning mask of collapse in the middle-aged.

'Did I hear the kettle, lads?'

In an hour or two, when the news came in from the hills, the portly Keane would be putting two and two together and whispering the result to the rebels. As if they'd have to be told. They knew who had been sitting on them in the town so it wouldn't take them long to figure out, Enright thought, who was shitting on them in the hills.

'Ye're up and about early. Are ye coming back in or going out?'

Enright stood up and tapped Timmoney's shoulder.

'We're going out, Keane. We've a man to meet in the Hayes' Hotel before he hops off back up to Dublin with himself.'

The town roused itself from its repose as Enright and Timmoney walked towards Main Street. From the houses fronting the street, ordinary morning sounds emerged so distended as to seem accidental and purposeless. The voices of men complained of one thing or another and it was all the same complaint. Women answered with a sour dispiritedness. Enright felt the icy balm of the breeze on his cheeks, inhaled deeply to know relief from the tightness on the bad side of his chest.

Out in the wide spaces of Main Street, working men in caps and scarves trudged along to O'Meara's Mill and Grainstore, to Coady's Coalyard and Duffy's Gasworks, to Maher's Knackery and Thompson's Cattle Yard; yesterday's dust and smells still on them. An ass covered in raw sores and dragging a low cart followed Jack Dan Shittyfoot, who scraped up yesterday's horse manure from the street to sell at one and six a load.

Enright reflected on how the new Sinn Féin-dominated council had decided to change the street names to something more patriotic. Some rebel priest got himself elected chairman of a committee and dredged up the names of dead heroes. Pike Street became Kickham Street, Quarry Street was renamed Mitchel Street. A couple of ancient Gaelic names were retrieved for good measure – Slievenamon, Garravicleheen – though there were probably no more than a handful of these Midlands townies who could speak a word of the language. Enright's mother being a Dingle woman, he had forgotten more of it than they'd ever know. *Tomáisín bán a cheann,* she'd called him for the blond hair of his childhood, before she fell silent.

'Thank Christ, we don't have to go breaking our backs like those lads.'

'What else can they do? Haven't they a living to make? We shouldn't be out walking after what happened last night.'

'Only place to hide is out in the open, son. Would you go breaking your back for a pittance then?'

The bleary-eyed young constable looked wistfully away to the clock on the cathedral tower.

'I won't have to. I'm going to head away foreign one of these days.'

'Still reading those old fairy tales of the sea, are you?'

'They're not all fairy tales. There's a fellow called Conrad writes them and he was a sailor himself.'

They turned up the narrow alley beside Hayes' Hotel. A colony of feral cats scattered before them. Not an untainted black among them.

'The Polish fellow?'

'Aye. He has some great stories. For the likes of me that's never gone anywhere, there's a lot to learn in them of life and such.'

'Stories aren't life, son, only throwing a shape on things.'

One of Mary's letters reached him in Port Stanley after he and Marshall found an old hack of a sailing ship heading out of Hong Kong to Chile for guano, because the old-timer knew how to pick up some fake identification papers on the way. Hell of a cold spot and he shivered even to think of it and the unearthly crack of ice floes all through the night like the crust of the world snapping apart. *I'm after reading three books of Joseph Conrad out of the library and I sometimes imagine you the man he's writing about with your wandering spirit.* Found a Conrad book months later in a Seaman's Mission in Helsinki. *Lord Jim.* Spent an afternoon trying to read a bit of it but got fed up waiting for the fellow who was supposed to be telling the story to get on with it.

'What kind of men are in those books anyway?'

At the back door of the hotel, the smell of frying food from inside set his stomach rumbling.

'I don't know. Men fighting the odds, I suppose.'

'You need to read something that'll cheer you up.'

Enright rapped on the door with his knuckles. The timber felt warm and steam rose from the gap at the base. A small, wizened man opened the door impatiently, the crystallised pus of sleep lay scabrous at the corners of his eyes. A blast of heat from the kitchen seared across Enright's face and he turned to catch a cool breath before he went in. The man retreated, his filthy shirt-tail hanging out.

'*Monsieur le chef.* There's a Cullinane staying here. Which room is he in?'

'How would I know? Ask out the front.'

The man busied himself with a frying pan and a few steaming pots on a cooker so encrusted with dirt it looked like some barnacled thing dredged from the sea floor. Enright reached into the pan and lifted out a slice of sizzling black pudding with his fingers. He tossed it about on the palm of his hand before taking a bite.

'*Merveilleux, mon vieux.*'

Enright heard Toussaint Martin in his own exaggerated intonation, the absurd grandiosity in that chicken coop of a restaurant kitchen in Chicago. *L'homme qui a peur de l'amour, Thomas, il a peur de soi-même, n'est ce pas?* Thumb-ass, he pronounced the name. Dumb ass.

Out in the front lobby, they found a young girl of no more than fourteen fetching glasses from a cabinet behind the desk. Short and heavy, her white apron hissed crisply with starch and she smelled soapy fresh. The glasses tinkled together in her trembling hands when she saw the uniformed pair. Another Helen Peters, Enright thought, with the wire waiting on the road for her.

'We're looking for a Mr Cullinane. What room is he?'

'He's the gentleman adin in the dining room, sir.'

'Good girl yourself.'

Looking towards the dining-room door, he caught a glimpse of himself in the long mirror on a coat-stand alongside. Still unshaven and with the blotches angry on his cheeks, he was like a man back from a night pinned down in a no-man's-land. Felt that way too, the mad urgency of battle persisting inside. Drawing closer to the dining room and watching his own advance, he realised he was beginning to look more and more like his father. Except for the eyes; his father's habitually lowered or sneaking glances up from below. Might have been a half-decent cut of a man if he'd ever looked the world in the face and hadn't always given the impression that he had something to hide or hide from. Through the glass panels of the door, Enright saw that Cullinane was alone in the dining room.

'I'll wait here. I'm out on my feet.'

'What were you at all night, Timmoney? With a woman, were you?'

Cullinane sat with his back to the door by a window overlooking Main Street. Hardly a sharp dealer then since sharp dealers always faced a door. And Enright realised too that the fellow must have seen them pass by the window a few minutes before. The BP man didn't turn or look up from his newspaper and Enright found himself growing irritable again. He laid a hand on Cullinane's shoulder. There was no tautening of the muscles only a slackening, a shrugging off as though to protect the well-tailored charcoal grey suit. The lack of wariness suggested that he was expecting someone. Someone he didn't particularly like. Donegan, no doubt. Enright sat down opposite him.

'Mr Cullinane. You're an early bird, aren't you?'

Constrained within his expensive suit, the neat grey-and-black striped tie tightly knotted on the crisp white collar, big hands reaching out of starched cuffs, the sallow-skinned man reminded Enright of one of those prospectors made good he'd seen over in BC living out the dream that kept them going through those days when all the gold they chiselled out was nothing but the peacock ore of fool's gold. Younger than those fellows though, younger than himself. Twenty-five, twenty-six maybe.

'You're Sergeant Enright.'

More surprised by the Kerry accent than by the fact that the stranger knew his name, Enright bristled.

'What part of Kerry are you from, Cullinane?'

'Blennerville, outside Tralee. And yourself?'

Enright looked at his own hands, the polish still lining the creases. He moved a plate and rested his elbows on the linen tablecloth. There was no great mystery to the fellow's knowing who he was. Chances were Donegan had warned Cullinane about him.

'What has you sneaking around the town again? More business with Mr Donegan, have you?'

Cullinane's eyes betrayed him. His hand went to his lips, wiping the moisture from both corners. Behind Enright, the door from the kitchen creaked open and he swung round instinctively. The pink-cheeked girl from the desk came through, a plate of food in one hand, a teapot in the other. The sepia-flowered carpet might have been a mire, so haltingly did she approach, and having deposited her load, she fled before Cullinane could thank her.

'I'm not here on business, Sergeant.'

'So why are you here?'

'I came down to meet someone, to see someone.'

'And who might that be?'

Cullinane forked a sausage, bit off a piece and considered his answer. Enright took some black pudding from the fellow's plate but didn't bother with a fork.

'A girl.'

The fried blood mush in Enright's mouth sickened him because the girl that came to mind was Helen Peters and the inexplicable question followed of how they'd got the child out of her paralysed body. He swallowed and felt nauseous.

'You're annoying me now, Cullinane. If there's a girl, what's her bloody name?'

'It's nobody's business who – '

Enright jumped to his feet and Cullinane struggled upwards to face him. They were almost of the same height and equally broad-shouldered but Enright could tell by the unguarded stance that Cullinane wasn't in the habit of fighting. He punched the BP man in the face, knocking him back down on to his chair. His heart skipped a beat and winded him.

'Get up, Cullinane, and defend yourself.'

Cullinane had noticed the grease stain from Enright's fingers on his shirt front and worked at it disdainfully. A faint trace of scarlet coloured his cheekbones.

'I'm not fool enough to hit a uniform. And I'll have to live in this town. The girl's name is Bridie Dooley.'

The rebel Dooleys' sister. More to Cullinane after all, Enright thought.

'You're moving down here to Tipperary?'

'I'm leaving British Petroleum at the end of the week. Jim Donegan asked me to run the garage for him.'

Enright sat down to rest his aching leg muscles.

'By the look of you, you're doing mighty well out of BP. So why would you be coming down to these backwoods to get your hands dirty in a tumbledown garage for half nothing? Or did BP give you the boot, maybe? Were you up to no good, Cullinane?'

'I won't give them the pleasure of firing me. They don't trust me because I'm Irish. If I was there the rest of my life, I wouldn't be promoted any higher. Anyway, I've had enough of the road. I prefer working on engines. I'll be happier at that.'

'I'm Irish myself and I don't trust you either.'

Pushing aside his plate, Cullinane sat back in his chair and stroked his clean-shaven chin, holding Enright's stare, though not belligerently.

'It's like this, Sergeant. I know I'm taking a cut in the money but I'll be away from BP and I'll be near Bridie. That's all I want. I've no other reasons for being here. None. That's the truth.'

A cool customer, Enright thought, spinning his romantic yarn. Uprooting his whole life for a girl he'd seen, what, three or four times? A fancy Dan like this one? Only a woman would do the like of that. Like Mary. And that was nothing but some kind of a jumble of loss and pity and wanting to get out of Listowel and aching to see the world of her books that didn't exist anywhere outside of her imagination. And Martin Fuller's. Herself and Cullinane would get along the finest. *You will not give up your pride for the love of me.*

'I'll be watching you, Cullinane. You're on my list now, boy. You and her Shinner brother Johnny. I won't be long knocking a few teeth out of that gob of yours like I did Charlie's. See what Bridie'll make of you then.'

Enright took a last sausage from the discarded plate and left Cullinane looking nonplussed behind him. But his appetite had gone, his stomach felt queasy, his face on fire. The screaming widow's curse would not let itself be forgotten and her face was there every time he blinked the itch from his eyes. Lack of sleep was all, he knew the feeling well enough. Days and nights trapped under fire. Courcelette. Commotion Trench. Nun's Alley. Or lying beside Mary after Gabriel Jack had gone. *And now you won't let me sleep, not that I do anyway with Jerry so sick.* He tossed the sausage on a table by the door.

The sight of Timmoney sitting exhaustedly on a soft chair in the lobby, his eyes drooping sleepily, made him want to fall down. He kicked Timmoney's boot and the sudden lurch, like a dead man kicked impossibly alive, seemed to draw the words out of Enright unbidden.

'I've to go down to Listowel. The child is . . .'

He pressed a thumb and forefinger into his eyes, pushed them all the way back until they hurt and when his hand fell to his side, he savoured a moment or two of blissful, starry-blind relief.

When Mary White came to Balfour sanatorium, Enright hadn't recognised her at first. Nurses, doctors, the other men, floated respectfully by, vast and remote as the statue of de Lesseps pointing the way into the Suez Canal or that gigantic carving of the Daibutsu in Kobe. His eyes didn't bother to follow them any more. He had given up the ghost and lay as silently as his mother had done in her last days, knowing as surely as she did that something had already died inside that was not worth living after, though unlike her, he could not have said what that thing was.

The last time he'd spoken was to dictate a letter for Mary. The nurse wept as she wrote. *The only reason I am sorry to die is that I didn't see you for so long and I never will now.* A year later, after he'd driven her away, he found that she had left the cigar box filled with his letters. Alone in the cabin, he read the letter he'd written from his Balfour deathbed, those words that she kept throwing at him like cold water dowsing him out of his despair on the Nelson plot. *I always seemed to be making life harder for myself when I should have taken it easy and life wouldn't have been so hard on me.* The florid copperplate lettering so unlike his own scrimped hand that he wondered if the nurse had made the half of it up. *I found nothing in this world but death and misery except for you.* Thought about burning the lot, letters, cigar box and all, but because they were all he had left of her, he kept them.

On days like this one, the noise of the long drive from Tipperary still thrumming in his brain as he sat five minutes in the Ford outside the cottage, the letter always lay between them; the measure against which he would inevitably fail in Mary's presence and the little weed Martin Fuller's absence.

There was no stir about the cottage, no vestige of death. No carts or carriages, no neighbours scurrying in through the high, careless thickets of bramble with bread wrapped in muslin and sympathy. It seemed to Enright that he should have been able to sense whether or not Mary was inside, but he couldn't. He felt as if he'd fallen asleep in one place and woken up in another. Like poor Clancy waking alongside him in the no-man's-land crater up in front of Commotion Trench. *I'm off to do the milking.* Standing up and walking towards the Hun lines, with Enright trying to clutch at his legs, and for all his screaming, Clancy wouldn't let himself remember where he really was or where he was going or why. *I'll pretend to be your brother, so, Clancy. I'll pretend to be anyone you want!*

He got out of the car, slammed the door noisily. His legs felt as rubbery as an old sea dog's.

'Mary!'

No one heard him. Funny how a fellow could know that from the hollow way his voice rang back into his head, a scout sent out and coming back with nothing. The kitchen, darkened by the thick web of bramble outside the window, was prim and tidy, as she always kept it. Little lacy bits and pieces and chequered gingham curtains and the delph glistening on the dresser. Even the shack outside Nelson looked like a half-decent home under her busy hands though he'd deliberately drag the dirt in with him so she'd know what it was like to labour without end, as he did in that godforsaken place with its ranks of thick plane trees that kept coming at him no matter how hard he slogged. No danger the army would give him a decent bit of land up above Quesnel or somewhere. Scorched alive in the sun, slipping and sliding when the rain made a soup of the loamy soil, and icy ruts twisting his ankles in the winter before the snow came and sent him inside. All for thirty lousy acres that were supposed to pay for the scars and the wheezing in his hammered-in chest. *Nobody owns nothing, Thomas, only the white man's fool enough to think he owns a goddam thing 'cept for his songs and such.*

He went straight into the bedroom, threw off his coat and boots and got in under the eiderdown. He found Mary's scent in the depths of the pillow and slept, but not for long and was woken by a shadow falling across him. His scalp tingled and the sweat of his sleep frosted his spine. Under the covers, his hand moved stealthily to the Colt.

Jimmy White leaned against the jamb of the door and Enright wondered how long he'd been there. Long enough to shoot him if he had a mind to, he supposed, if he was carrying a gun.

'You should be more careful, Tom. Couldn't you have brought the car around the back?'

Jimmy was nineteen years old and above the lean, boyish face had the same fair hair as Mary. When they'd first come back from Canada, he'd been the only one who'd listened credulously to Enright's stories. But he was hearing different stories this past while and it showed. His brother-in-law's disappointment was a matter of indifference to Enright though he wondered now whether the news from Clonore, when it reached Listowel, might make man enough of him to try putting the widow's weeds on his sister.

'I'm always careful, Jimmy. Where's Mary?'

'Gone into the doctor with Jerry.'

'Is he all right?'

'We thought it might be the 'flu. But he's over it, thank God, whatever it was.' A look of soft pleading took the edge from Jimmy's accusatory tone. The same old White trick, letting you think they were giving in when they were only starting on you. 'She's in a bad state worrying about you up there in Tipperary, Tom.'

'We had all this out before. I've no more to say about it.'

'She's getting no end of abuse on the street. And I'm getting it off the lads.'

'Would these be the same lads who gunned down Vicars and shot DI Sullivan in front of his child in Listowel? And plugged that old fisheries inspector in the back of the head?'

'It's a war and they were on the wrong side. So are you, Tom.'

Enright sat up in the bed and drew out the Colt.

'You and your mates wouldn't know a real war if it pissed on your leg, boy. And you can tell your pals, if they want to come after me, I'll be waiting for them. As for you, you'd be better employed warning off those bastards that are spitting at her. She's your sister, Jimmy, you should be minding her.'

The presence of the gun had little effect on Jimmy's determination to have his say.

'I am minding her. But you're her husband and you're no help to her, only making enemies for yourself up in Tipperary as if you haven't enough of them down here.'

'Will I have to be watching my back with you too?'

Once, when he was in Yokahama, he took it into his head to buy a kimono from a hawker for Mary. The only white one he could find, it came with black trimmings. Inside, he'd wrapped a fancy pearl-handled penknife with a half dozen blades and a corkscrew in it for Jimmy. Only after he'd sent off the kimono did the smart-ass bosun on the *Stavelock* tell him, and everyone else who cared to listen and laugh, that white with the black *odi* was the kimono of mourning. Got a letter back from young Jimmy, tucked in between the folds of Mary's. *When I'm big I'm going to do all the things you do.*

'I can't make you out, Tom. Fighting to let the likes of Vicars keep our country off us and he ran you when you looked for a job over there.'

'If you fellows ever got hold of Vicars's place, would you give me a few acres of it or anyone else, barring the few farmers among you? I know a land-grab when I see it, son. Rebellion, my arse.'

'It's a terrible shame Martin Fuller died. He was a grand quiet man. All he wanted was his books.'

'And Mary.'

'She'd have had a decent life with him.'

'Get out before I break your jaw with a box, Jimmy.'

'You can't come and go as you please, Tom. Not any more. I'm not warning you, only telling you.'

Enright's second waking was to the half-light of evening and the sound of Mary's voice making two singing notes and a question of his name.

'To-om?'

Back in Balfour, he'd watched as if from a great depth, the trembling lips of a pretty stranger force themselves into a smile. She'd worn a green felt cap that dipped alluringly over one eye. The short-cropped blonde hair revealed a long, cream-skinned neck. Then she spoke and it was by her voice, still fifteen and belonging on a summery lane, that he had recognised her. He'd tried to speak and found that his silence wasn't the voluntary withdrawal he'd imagined it to be. The shallow breaths coming out of his imploded chest gave him no purchase on even the least of words. The desire to speak to her was the strongest desire he had felt in months, perhaps in years. He knew at once that the strength would come. For days he'd planned what he might say to her and there was so much that sometimes he became impatient with himself for losing track of it all, as he lost track of her news from Listowel and her laughing wonder at the New World. But when the time came, he was too shy or afraid to repeat at any length the words of love and gratitude and grief he had compiled, and Mary withdrew into shyness or fear too, so that even now, after two years of marriage, there was a distance for them to travel towards each other each time they met, on a road above which Martin Fuller lay in ambush.

'To-om?'

Enright slipped the gun under his pillow, swept back the eiderdown and swung his feet to the floor. He felt better and his head was clear as he leaned down to get his boots on.

'I'm in the bedroom.'

He looked up from his boots and she was there, the sleeping child on one hip, the other hip curved out with that casual grace he knew turned the eyes of men as it had of schoolboys. Since Canada, she had let her hair grow back to its younger length, and despite the slight greying of her creamy complexion, her face, smaller within the careless tresses, still checked his breath on first sight.

'Well, Tom.'

'Well, Mary.'

'I didn't expect you.'

'I was worried.'

'I get in a panic.'

'I don't blame you.'

Sometimes it worked like this. He hoped it would do so today. He looked at the child. Red-faced, wet about the mouth, it drooled in slumber. He envied its peacefulness, its closeness to Mary. He began to lace the second boot, taking his time so he wouldn't have to stand up too soon and be like a fool not knowing what to do next. He longed to hold her.

'He looks fine now.'

'He does. Handsome like his daddy, aren't you, Jerry?'

'He got the looks from the Whites.'

'He has your eyes, hasn't he? That nice blue.'

Mary drew closer but remained just out of reach at the end of the bed. He stretched his arms, worked the stiffness out of his back and neck, and stood up. She went around to the other side of the bed and set the child there. Raising the pillow, she placed it alongside her son to keep him from rolling. Enright did the same with the pillow on his side. He sneaked the gun along under the pillow, making a big deal of puffing up the feathers.

'Are you hungry, Tom?'

Arms folded, she was edging around the bed, a self-conscious stroll, and peering in at the child like it was a river below a bridge. Enright let go of the gun but the oily smell of it was on his hands and the rest of him stank like a butcher's stall. She was behind him now and he hoped that no trace of the polish remained on him.

'Famished. I'll have a wash first. And a shave. Would you shove on the kettle?'

'Are you staying long?'

'I can't. I'm not supposed to be here at all. I only sneaked away.'

At the bedroom door she halted and Enright thought the argument was about to recommence. She swung lightly round in the dancing way she sometimes still had that made even the dowdiest of work skirts seem a diaphanous thing.

'I didn't think you'd come, Tom. I'm always glad when you surprise me nicely.'

Outside at the rain barrel behind the cottage, Enright stripped down to the waist and invigorated by the cool evening air, began to torture himself with the icy water until it became a pleasure and the last of the dry buzz around his brain dissipated. He looked out across the easeful north Kerry glens, with their soft greens, a scattering here and there of somnolent sheep and slow cattle. Thirty acres of that might have compensated him for the battering he took in France. Maybe. Thirty acres of that and he might never have fallen down on the job nor been persuaded to seek some temporary release with Gabriel Jack amid that infinity of monumental crags clothed in dark trees that lay beyond Nelson. He found instead that trouble had followed him as it always did.

The trip had been the half-breed's idea. The acres of plane trees crowding in on Enright's resolve, he'd become angry and uncoordinated with fatigue. Then, one sweltering afternoon, Mary and Gabe laughing and swapping songs on the verandah, he fell like one of those broad-leafed trees; heavily, hopelessly because a tree knows if it can't stand up it's no more than a lump of lumber. *You're shaking it rough, Thomas; why don't we cut loose o' this place a coupla days?* Mary pitched in then, squeezing water out of a piece of flannel or maybe it was his sweat, he couldn't tell. *You should, Tom.* Would have thrown a punch at the half-breed, only he knew there was nothing left in his fist but the ache of the axe.

Down river, the heat was a ringing in his ears and a layer of invisible clothing that couldn't be peeled off. But there were shallow-water streams to lie belly-up in, ink-blue pines to shelter under and the grouse drumming among them like the mysterious reverberations from a West African jungle and the half-breed's piss-yellow rotgut filled their tongues with bullshit all night and drove them crazier by the day. *Fifteen years on the lam, Gabe, and never had a friend that didn't go and die on me.* And Gabriel Jack whimpering like a baby. *I ain't one thing nor the other, Thomas. Deal me worse than the goddam Chinamen they do, 'specially Fritzy Bildheim.* Crying each other's praises, they were. *Who's Fritzy Bildheim when he's at home?* Tears yellow as the rotgut streaming down the leathery face. *Orchard guy, outside Penticton, raped my sister couple o' years back.* Enright cried too, though he didn't know why. *What d'ye say we go and shoot the bugger, Gabe?* But drunk as he was, Gabe was having none of it. *If I can't do it, it don't deserve to be done.*

Enright splashed the memory away, cleaning and tormenting himself with the rainwater. A granite sky closed heavily over the low fields. He towelled himself dry and dressed quickly in the failing light.

In front of the fire in the open hearth, he shaved; a small mirror propped up on the high beam of the mantelpiece, a ceramic bowl filled with warm water in a cubbyhole below. The heat played pleasurably across his cold flesh as the smell of boiling stew warmed his insides. Mary floated in and out of view in the mirror and they measured each other in the ever-lengthening hold of their reflected glances, and the longing in him was sweet because its satisfaction seemed assured. She sang softly as she worked. He couldn't remember when he'd last heard her sing but the song was all the more welcome for that.

For love is pleasing and love is teasing
And love is a pleasure when first it's new.
'Not *pleasure*, Mary, *treasure*.'
He laughed and she laughed too and finished out the song
instead of the old, *What do the words matter anyway, at least I'm
not afraid to sing, like some.* Then she talked and talked, carefully but careful also not to make it seem so. The child woke
but cried only briefly before she snatched him up.

When he'd finished shaving and sat down to eat, he was
aware of the child watching him with curiosity at first, but
soon indifferently from the security of its mother's shoulder.
Enright tried a tentative, apologetic smile. The child ducked
away but soon sneaked a surprisingly bright-eyed and open
look. He could not believe that his own eyes were as beautiful
a blue as the child's.

All through the meal the talkative peace reigned, Enright
himself breaking into effusiveness on the subject of his dogs.
But the child grew restless again and three cups of tea alone,
while Mary tried to coax him into sleep, sent Enright back to
that hunting trip with Gabriel Jack.

Three days walking they were when they came on the trapped
wolverine. Ugliest, sourest bastard of an animal Enright ever
saw. The Glutton they called it, the Skunk Bear. A dark, dirty
brown, long-haired thing, halfway between a bear and a
weasel, it made a couple of vicious drives at them but the trap
on its hairy-soled paw pulled it back and drew the kind of
abandoned howls he hadn't heard since France. *Skunk Bear's
the evil spirit, Thomas, bad sumix.*

Then Gabriel Jack told how the young Okanagan men went
out into the wilds to find their guardian spirit and couldn't
come back until they dreamed a grizzly bear or a coyote or a
rattlesnake, or maybe the blue jay Gabe imagined himself to be,
that gave a man the power to find people who'd been drowned
or otherwise lost. *Ain't afraid o' nothing, the wolverine, and his
belly ain't never full enough. You dream that son-of-a-bitch, you*

*spend your days hunting something that ain't there and getting
mad as hell 'cos you can't find it.* Enright had laughed, but
uneasily, because the Okanagan might just have described the
hungover feeling of irritation and angry longing that bothered
him after the days and nights of rotgut. *You don't believe in that
old shite, do you?* But Gabriel Jack gestured towards where
they'd come from. *Don't matter if I believe it or I don't. You can't
see Toad Mountain from here but it's still there, ain't it?*

When Gabe whipped out the Colt Peacemaker, Enright
stepped back, thinking wildly that the Okanagan had tricked
him into the wilderness to shoot him and take Mary. But he
fired at the wolverine. And missed. *You gotta help me get Fritzy,
Thomas, I can't shoot straight for shit.* After he floored Gabe for
scaring him he had the fellow shooting straight as a die before
they got back to Nelson. Or thought he had.

'Jerry's down for the night now, Tom. I've the coach bed
fixed up for us.'

She pulled back the curtain on the long alcove by the hearth.

Tenderness embarrassed Enright. He negotiated it awkwardly,
at best lumbering across it.

'C'mere, Mary love.'

His breath wouldn't come as he waited to see what would
become of her questioning expression.

A smile.

'No. You come here.'

A few hours later, Enright slipped quietly out of the coach
bed so as not to wake his wife. He hadn't slept and they hadn't
made love. *Just hold me for a while first, Tom.* The pleasurable
familiarity of her skin under his hands failed to arouse him.
Too damn weary and there'd be a price anyway, he thought,
for whatever satisfaction he might have got. Softly, she'd ask
promises of him in return and even if he'd wanted to make
promises, the time was well past for keeping them. He was left
with an emptiness, a vague discomfort around the crotch and
the darkness pressed too close, seething with its dead.

He brought his clothes to the bedroom and dressed, leaving the boots until he would go outside. He felt around under the pillow at the sleeping child's side for the gun but it wasn't there. His eyes, grown used to the dark, soon caught sight of its oily slick on the sideboard alongside a little stack of books and the cigar box where Mary kept his letters. Cause enough for a row at any other time, she'd let the matter pass unmentioned. All out to rope him back in, he thought, make him give up again. *What's the point in killing yourself over a few acres of trees when you could get a good desk job after being an officer in the Canadian army?* He wondered what kind of a life it would have turned out if he and Gabriel Jack hadn't gone after Fritzy Bildheim. But life was all ifs. If he hadn't gone to sea; if he hadn't gone to war; if he hadn't come back to Ireland. If he hadn't been pushed out of it in the first place by his mad aunt and her lover, fat Paudie, the sailor-boy.

The books on the sideboard reminded him of Martin Fuller again. He imagined them chatting in the half-dark of the solicitor's office about Conrad and whoever the hell else.

The child made small, dream noises. Fair hair, slicked with perspiration to a delicate coxcomb, rose and fell above the throbbing scalp. Jerry. After Mary's father. Wouldn't call a dog after his own father though it had been Mary's first suggestion. Martin, she'd wanted to call the dead child. Spent a long winter's night in the Nelson shack carving that name onto a little wooden cross and listening in terror lest her soft breath cease at the end of a sleeping sigh.

He tried to imagine this second child in years to come. A twelve-year-old helping his father in a farmyard or a cottage garden or a town yard. At fifteen with some girl on a summer road. On land or sea, behind a desk or an altar or a gun at twenty-one. Who would he look like? Jimmy White? Or like Enright himself, darker? Funny how his son would never know that his father stood above him this night, a ghostly presence. He left the bedroom.

The kitchen was a new darkness to get used to and, making his way towards the bed, he knocked over a chair but caught it before it fell. Mary stirred and he felt sure she'd been awake all along.

'Are you off already?'

'Have to make it back for parade.'

He began to put his boots on in the dark.

'Tom?'

He didn't answer.

'Are you not going to kiss me goodbye?'

He went to where the voice had come from, found a shape that warmed to substance under his hands. He kissed her and as he drew away she held on to him briefly and then let go. The silver of a look touched him.

'I know it was only pretend the way we were today. But we have to pretend so we can know what it could be like. How does a woman become a wife or a man her husband only by playing the part until it comes naturally?'

He didn't allow himself to remonstrate with her, ask from which book she got that notion or if she'd got it from Fuller. He remembered young Clancy's last mad stab at pretending. Pretending he wasn't in hell. Pretending he hadn't seen or heard that foul answer from the Hun corpse's mouth.

'I don't want to lose you, Tom.'

'You won't.'

'I went a long way to find you. I did everything I could.'

He stood up, ready to flee. What if they were to pack up that very night, he wondered, go down to Queenstown and wait on the next boat out? That way she might never have to hear about the reprisals in Clonore. Why not? Why not carry another secret off with him to hide from her?

'Wherever you want to go when it's all over, we'll go there. I promise. As far away as you like.'

The starched linen pillow subsided beneath her like a sigh.

Enright arrived back in Tipperary with the sun's first bright stirrings. The emerald sparkle through roadside hedges lifted his spirits. Real flying-fish weather. The Ford swept through the vivid air, peppering dry ditches with a hail of loose stones, and he felt elated at the thought of what balm the summer might yet bring to his bones. Closer to town, he kept to the main road rather than cutting over to check on his dogs at Lady's Well so that he'd be in the barracks early. He was racing back out to Lady's Well within the hour though not before Gallagher had waylaid him.

The Head Constable's room always brought to mind those fusty little offices of white men along the West African coast or over in the Far East. Ship chandlers, agents, port sanitary officers. Windowless holes or shuttered tight against the blaze. And the men themselves, a tremble in the hand, a voice sick and tired of listening to itself bounce off bamboo walls but trying hard to convince the visitor of his sanity, his worth.

Enright knew that Gallagher's initial attack was a mere preliminary, an attempt to work up the courage to say what was actually on his mind. He'd long ago learned how to fend Gallagher off. Let him rant on, say nothing and wait for the precise point when his real purpose emerged to deflate him with an innocent, preferably offended, riposte.

'. . . And on top of scooting off to Listowel without a by-your-leave, you take the motor car. Did it not occur to you that it might be wanted here? And another thing. Even when you're here, you're ducking in and out so much I can't find you half the time . . .'

The arguments with Mary had fine-tuned the hurt expression he now allowed to form across his lips, the waters of his eyes.

Though he resisted at first, Gallagher was soon affected. He became hesitant.

'. . . I mean to say, is it any wonder I might be . . . you know, suspicious . . . you weren't out in Clonore the other night, were you, Tom?'

'I went down to Listowel because the child took ill and Mary was beside herself with worry.'

'I'm sorry, Tom . . . only I told Johnstone, I told him if any of our men was in on that . . . that escapade, I'd hand in my resignation on the spot and there'd be consequences. Serious consequences. I'm not without influence in . . . in certain places. Is your son all right?'

'He's over the worst of it.'

Five minutes later, as he brewed himself some tea in the day-room scullery, a gloating Constable Keane came with the bad news.

'I think you better go out to Lady's Well, Sergeant.'

His first thought had been for Danny Egan. After that, he'd felt too angry, too cheated and, when he got to the field and saw the charred timbers of the fallen shed, too sickened to think. No human remains, just those of a dog. Burnt meat, though some of the colour and build persisted in the shape melded to the scorched wood. The black. Arrow Valley Puca. Foley was there, crying great big snotty tears and wiping them off on his sleeve.

'What kind of devil would go firing petrol over a dog and burn him?' He handed Enright a torn square of cardboard strung with bailing twine. 'I just found this behind the shed. They must've forgot to tie it on the gate. Or somebody came on them maybe.'

ENRIGHT IS THE NEXT DOG FOR HELL, it read. He threw the message in among the smoking stumps and watched it darken and blacken and failing to catch fire. At least, he thought, the whole damn town hadn't got to see this warning and his authority been undermined even further.

'Keep this message to yourself, Foley. Where's the rest of the dogs?'

'I have 'em in the yard. They let the other ones out before they set the shed alight. They knew the good one.'

The petrol-reeking smoke wafting towards him set both of Enright's eyes streaming and he felt the smouldering heat redden his face. He drew back but the warm sun kept the heat on him.

'They'll pay dear for this.'

As he strode across towards the Ford, his rage fixed itself upon Johnny Dooley, who'd escaped the last round-up of detainees. Johnny I hardly knew you, it would be after he'd finished with him. From the small island of smoky gloom in the long sunny field, Foley cried out.

'Any old coward could kill a dog. He might be vicious but a dog's as innocent as a Jaysus child, in the heel o' the hunt.'

The Stella Cinema was a far cry from the picture palaces of Vancouver or Chicago or New York, with their gilt and red plush and the great holds of their orchestra pits and the classy vaudeville turns between shows. Little more than a hayshed, in truth. Johnny Dooley wasn't in the makeshift timber ticket booth as Enright had hoped, but he found a biscuit tin filled with coins there and guessed the fellow couldn't be too far away. Through a gap in the back door of the hall proper, Enright discerned Bridie Dooley's silver-lit profile as she thrashed out a loud piano chase to match the dash of horses across a dusty creek on the screen. Cullinane was there too, tall in his seat up the front, gaping at her.

The audience stared rapt and pathetic at the screen, at worlds he himself had felt and tasted and walked in. And, he thought, they could never truly imagine another country, another continent, because the real difference was in the smell, the heat, the colours, the quality of the street noise and like Canada, the chastening scale of the landscape, none of which the shades of grey above them could convey.

He stepped back out into the lobby, whose walls ran with green damp like a dungeon's. As he did so, Dooley emerged from a door to the rear of the ticket box. Short and jug-eared, Dooley had the cocky slink of a small man high in his own estimation. After a flicker of nervousness, the fellow's expression settled back into one of contempt.

'It's ninepence downstairs. One and six for the balcony.'

'Is that right? Well, we have seats below in the cells and we don't charge a penny for them.'

'I know nothing about your dog, Enright.'

Behind the glassed-in front of the ticket booth, Dooley buzzed around bluebottle-busy as he fidgeted with the coins in the biscuit box and the rolls of pink and green tickets. Enright opened the door and caught Dooley by the neck. He squeezed hard and pressed his thumb into the Adam's apple. With the free hand, he dug a few coins from the biscuit tin and tightened his fist around them. A tip from Marshall in his dockwalloping days. *Always put a penny in your punch, Tommy lad.* Dooley swung a wild right and caught the hollow side of Enright's chest with a blow of spear-like sharpness. In return, the struggling rebel got four knuckles and threepence worth of fist in the jaw. Enright dragged his prey out of the ticket box and outside into the lane leading to Friary Street, where Timmoney stood guard. Small-knuckled fists beat at his arm as Dooley fought for breath. He let go and as Dooley battled to get air down his constricted windpipe again, Enright punched him in the stomach and a surge of vomit cleared the passage once and for all.

A blade of pain sliced through Enright's chest and he leaned briefly against the lane wall but raised himself away from Timmoney's concerned look.

'Are you all right?'

'I'll be grand once I'm finished with this little bastard.'

He aimed another kick at the prone body. The ribs gave in with a satisfying crack of small bone.

Enright let Timmoney take most of the weight as they carried the young Shinner back to the barracks. In the holding cell, they propped him on a chair. Then Baldwin sidled in. Like a bloody gundog that fellow, Enright thought. Smell blood through a twelve inch thick wall, he would.

'Do what you like to me. You got nothing out of my brother and you'll get nothing out of me.'

The gap between Johnny Dooley's defiant declarations and the physical evidence had become preposterous. Trembling volcanically, he rocked himself back and forth like a Musselman at prayer, all the while holding his ribs together in a pained self-embrace.

'Sure, how could he talk with a mouthful of broken teeth?'

Propped at a corner of the table between Enright and his garrulous victim, Baldwin sniggered and lit himself a cigarette. He blew the smoke at Dooley. Over by the heavy metal door of the holding cell, stained with rust or perhaps long-spilt blood, Timmoney stood. It seemed to Enright that the young constable wanted to join in but didn't yet have the stomach for it.

'Wait until Cathal and the rest of the boys are out. We'll see who'll be sniggering then. There'll be no place in our country for the likes of you once the struggle is over.'

The fellow hadn't a clue, Enright thought, couldn't keep his mouth shut.

'So Charlie is calling himself Cathal now? Trying to make a real Irish man of himself, is it? And hardly a word of the Gaelic between the lot of you, only the old codology you learned in your language clubs. And I suppose you're Seán now and not just little flap-eared Johnny?'

'Yes, my name is . . . *Seán is ainm dom.*'

'Will we have our little chat in Gaelic, so?' He laid on the Kerry *blas*, thick and fast. '*An bhféadairis, a Johnny a' chaca a chroí, cen sort breillice a dhfadh ainmhí bocht saonta chun báis, díreach cun díoltas a imirt air a mháistir? Agus tánn tu casta leis an nGaoluinn, an bfhuil? Éist a theallaire mar do chuirfinnse Gaoluinn síar tríot agus aníar tríot agus suas trí pholl do thóna.*'

Dooley lowered his uncomprehending eyes.

'I didn't think so. Have we a hammer, Constable Timmoney?'

'I'll find one.'

Timmoney looked as though he was steeling himself to use the hammer and not just fling it on the table like an unexploded grenade as Enright intended.

He let the quiet fester around Dooley's mind for a while then and weariness settled in irresistibly around his own. He would sleep tonight and the sooner the better. He almost regretted having asked for the hammer because the effort of wielding even its spectre seemed beyond him.

Ten minutes earlier, a canine howl from Dooley after he'd shipped Baldwin's boot in his groin had triggered an idea in Enright's mind that made the loss of Arrow Valley Puca more bearable. Now he saw the new dog, the white he'd passed up from the Cashel litter, race along the Lady's Well field and he felt content just to watch it and not worry for now precisely how he'd find it. Foley would know.

Timmoney returned with the hammer and his grim calm suggested he'd left his qualms outside.

'His sister is outside. With that Cullinane fellow. They want to talk to you.'

Dooley forgot about the hammer and his damaged ribs for a moment.

'What's he doing here? I don't want that fellow standing up for me.'

'You don't like Mr Fancy Dan Cullinane, so? Why's that?'

'He's not wanted in our family. He has a fool made out of Bridie. Only after the one thing and he'll be gone once he gets it.'

'If he has any sense, he will. I'll let you have a chat with Constable Timmoney here.'

Timmoney took Enright's place and laid the hammer on the table like a neophyte prince setting aside his crozier.

As he passed by Baldwin, Enright whispered sidelong.

'Don't let him use the hammer or we'll never have the blood cleaned up before Gallagher gets back.'

For once, the Scot deigned to laugh at a joke of Enright's though he hadn't entirely meant it as one.

Out at the front counter he found Constable Keane, his cap too small for the pumpkin head and lodged ridiculously at the pole, talking to Bridie Dooley and her Don Juan in hushed, reassuring tones that ended abruptly when Enright arrived. He dismissed the pot-bellied constable with a sour look.

The girl was younger and plainer in full face than she had appeared in profile. Yet, in spite of the almost blunt nose and the forehead that was a little too high, there remained a definite attractiveness about her that seemed to reside in her eyes, which were mistily myopic and vulnerable. A girl, he somehow felt, who might easily be blinded by the blandishments of a sweet-talker.

'Can I help you, miss?'

Cullinane's arm lay protectively across her shoulder though his face betrayed a nervous discomfort and, perhaps, second thoughts about what he'd landed himself in for with the Dooley clan. Dropping everything for love: his big job with British Petroleum; the city life for small town strictures. Only thing that fellow would drop for love, Enright thought, was his trousers.

'Bridie would like to know when she can expect to see her brother.'

'I wasn't talking to you, Cullinane. Miss Dooley?'

Enright felt foolishly disappointed that she seemed so afraid and despising of him, her eyes slipping and sliding from contact with his, though it was hardly surprising after what he'd done to Charlie Dooley some months before.

'My brother wouldn't do a thing like that.'

Her voice was not what he'd imagined it might be like. A tone or two deeper than girlish and, in spite of her trepidation, unexpectedly formal. Enright didn't know quite what to make of her, except that he didn't take the instant dislike to her that he'd expected to.

'A thing like what, Miss Dooley?'

'The dog, she means.'

'Would you mind letting the lady speak for herself, Mr. Cullinane? Or do you want another dose of what I gave you the last time?'

Bridie Dooley looked at her paramour. Enright savoured the comedown in the dark eyes promising an explanation that hadn't yet come to him.

'You were saying, Miss Dooley?'

At a bar counter in Panama once, Enright sat with a couple of lads off the *Torrence*. Down a winding street, high, latticed windows above the royal poinciana trees and the red and gold fire of their flowers. In a smoky cabaret, strident with brassy jazz, wondering where to head next, at two in the morning. A couple sat over in the corner; a mulatto girl too free with her hands to bother much about her defences, the ragged topography of her face mellowing as Enright drank and ogled. Then a big black guy crashed in the door, took the cigarette from his mouth and stubbed it out on the blonde's face. Marshall slammed the fellow to the floor with a fist to the back of the neck. And what did the blonde do? Met Marshall on the pole with a beer bottle.

When Bridie Dooley turned her attention to Enright again, he saw a more measured expression of that protective admonition. What made a woman blind herself to a fellow's faults like that? An unwillingness, he wondered, to have her mistaken choice made public, even after she'd admitted it to herself? Like Mary?

'We're respectable people, Sergeant. We might be for Ireland but we're not for this kind of barbarity. And Mr Cullinane feels the same way. Will you be letting my brother go soon?'

Enright leaned closer to her, excluding Cullinane.

'Since you ask so nicely and I know I can trust you to keep Johnny on the straight and narrow, I'll let him out to you in a few minutes.'

She offered him the reward of a brief smile.

Back in the basement cell, Enright found Dooley lying on the flagged floor, a new cut opened over his left eye. The hammer was nowhere to be seen but Timmoney sat opposite, pale and puce-lipped in his righteousness.

'Jesus, Timmoney, you're a dark horse, right enough.'

'I gave him the fist not the hammer.'

Enright grabbed a hold of Dooley's collar and lifted him to his feet. The little squeals of agony annoyed him and he stuck an elbow into the fellow's ribs. Dooley's legs buckled but Enright held him up, denying him the comfort of the floor.

'I never went near your dog. Or the girl.'

'I asked him about her. Who the father of the child was.'

'What the hell are you playing at, Timmoney?'

'Could be anybody, he says. Called her a tramp.'

Enright found a new strength from somewhere, though his chest ached and his neck felt like it was clamped in a vice-grip. He slammed Dooley against the wall.

'What do you mean, a tramp?'

'Old bachelors, married men even. All she wanted was up in the world and the sooner the better.'

'You know an awful lot about her, don't you, Johnny? How come that is?'

'The whole town knows the kind she is. A servant girl with notions, trying to latch on to some old fellow with more money than sense and carrying on with every Tom, Dick and Harry.'

'Such as? Give me names, Dooley.'

'I don't know for sure. I'm only saying what I heard. Danny Egan even, someone said. When he had a few shillings in his pocket.'

In a moment of blank confusion, Enright's grip loosened and Dooley hit the floor. The very idea was absurd and yet he'd already put Danny and the girl together in a rough embrace she couldn't possibly have acquiesced to.

'Clean him up, Timmoney, and throw him out of here.'

'But we can get more out of him. His aunt's the girl's only visitor. Why?'

'Let him off to hell out of it, will you? And forget about that girl.'

He made himself think about the new dog as Timmoney washed Dooley's face, which lolled uselessly about like a corpse's. Arrow Valley Snow. Put Foley on the case and find out who had the dog now. And he'd take it, steal it, commandeer it . . . What was that other word he was trying to think of? With a bit of luck, the owner would be a Shinner and the pleasure of walking away with the white all the greater.

Washed clean, Dooley's face seemed to glisten with a hopefulness that begged puncturing but Enright satisfied himself with a small denting of the fellow's pride.

'Mr Cullinane convinced me to let you off, Dooley. Make sure you thank him now, won't you, like a good lad. And listen, son, I'll find out who burned my dog and I'll do the same to them. And if anyone else makes a move on me or my dogs or my men, you, Larry and Clem are for the high road.'

The metal door opened and Baldwin stuck his face in, black mischief written all over it.

'Gallagher's back. With the DI. They want a chat, Sergeant.'

'Tell them I'm gone out. Come on, Timmoney. And get rid of this clown, Baldwin.'

The Scot fixed his lazy grin on Enright and let it linger a while before slouching over to do what he was told. It occurred to Enright that Baldwin was the kind who'd kill a man for less than a sour look. Then again, Baldwin probably thought the same way about him.

Out in the barracks yard, Enright sat into the Ford that had taken five aggravating minutes to wind up, every second of which he'd expected Gallagher to appear with a solemn summons to the DI's presence. The thought of Johnstone's dank mushroom flesh added to the shivers already coursing through him.

'This isn't a good idea, going about in the night. With things as they are.'

'Stay in the barracks if you want, Timmoney, but I won't hide in a hole.'

'Where are we going?'

'I don't know yet. Did you see Danny Egan today at all?'

'It's a filthy lie, sir, what Dooley said about the girl.'

'Maybe so, but I'd like to hear what Danny has to say about it. And if Dooley's lying, I'll take him out a dark road and cut his prospects off.'

He felt Timmoney's stare burning into his side face, grating on his nerves. He knew the kind of stare it was without having to look. The kind Danny got when fellows, used to the ugliness, tried to discern if he was quite so monstrous beneath.

'We'll try the workhouse. They give him a bed there sometimes when he's not too drunk.'

Where the crippled girl lay, he thought.

'Are you coming or not, Timmoney?'

In the dense, starless dark, the cut grey limestone of the Union Workhouse and Infirmary retained an odd luminescence, like those shapes etched on the retina when some bedazzlement closed the eyes. Along the two-storey façade no lights shone. As Enright steered the Ford in by the back gate and up past the kitchen garden, he felt the old dread return. *Do you want the young lad ending up in the workhouse, Joby?*

Sergeant Larkin had waited a few days after the funeral before he called again. The father's answering shrug lodged in young Enright's throat like a globule of lumpen black bread. The sheep still hung in the yard but the slime of its second skin had gone hard and smooth and the bluebottles had made a home of it. Back at Gun-Mahony's estate, two cattle lay cut and left bleeding to death from the jugular. *Why don't you ask the O'Keefes over there in Kilmorna that'd feck the shirt off a corpse's back?* Bluebottles all over young Tom's face that he gave up swishing away. *Da didn't cut them cattle, Sergeant, I done it.* The two men looked down at him, disbelieving. The sergeant's hand patting the boy's bowl-cut thatch, then blocking the father's slap from the boy's face.

Enright cursed himself for not having thrown on a coat over his uniform. His teeth chattered as he glanced jealously at Timmoney, who seemed immune to the cold and whose eyes held the bright longing of a fellow looking into a fire.

'Johnny Dooley is the father of that child. All that filthy talk was a lie. He reddened up whenever I mentioned her name, and why is his aunt the only caller?'

'What the hell does it matter who the father was?'

Shoulder-height and tiny, the window of the old laundry room faced north, so that whatever light crept inwards even on the brightest day must have been minimal. Enright stared at the small opening, from which no light crept outwards either. Timmoney fixed his tunic front, slid a hand nervously back along his black hair that had the blue tint of gun metal in it.

Some twenty yards away, the bars of the front railings seemed to hum, strummed by the breeze. Further off, high, invisible trees betrayed a mild agitation. Enright looked in the window, Timmoney crowding behind him, and saw nothing at first. Then a small pale disc formed, a ray fish in deep dark waters under a moon. The face began to take shape as if by Enright's will alone. The slender lines of the eyebrows, the bud of her mouth, a faint glistening of teeth. Then, his senses alert to every stir, he was sure he saw the lips move. He pressed his forehead to the cold glass, listening hard. All he heard was the shuffle of feet up by the railings. He turned, thinking Timmoney had retreated, but the young constable stood directly behind him. He caught a quick glint from over by the railings and wrestled Timmoney to the ground with him as the first shot slammed into the wall of Helen Peters's mausoleum and ricocheted away in among the potato drills of the kitchen garden. The second shot hit the slates above the outhouse before Enright had time to reach for his gun. His chest tightened, the cold he felt had nothing to do with the night air. He had forgotten to bring either the Colt or the Webley. Timmoney made to move but he pressed him back down. No sign of a gun in the young fellow's fist either. If those boys kept their heads out there, he thought, he and Timmoney were for the high road. Serve them right if they copped it, gawking in at a poor crippled girl like that.

A sound, a tiny tap of metal on metal. The gun sliding through the bars of the railings, he imagined. Then the air around them was rent asunder by the screams of Helen Peters from her bed, the clatter of feet running away on the road outside, and Timmoney repeating like a rosary prayer, 'You saved my life, Tom, you saved my life.'

'She saved us.'

He stood up and brushed the clay from his uniform, his flesh still hard from the fear, the back of his neck tingling with relief.

'Stick close to me, Clancy, my luck is starting to rub off on you.'

He knew he should go inside and calm the girl after what she'd done for them. A miracle of sorts, he supposed. But lights flashed on in the workhouse and a few braver souls ventured out and he left her to them.

'I'm not Clancy, I'm Timmoney.'

'God Almighty murdering bastards.'

He'd be all right, he thought; he'd be able to move in a minute. But he didn't move. Saw Gabriel Jack fold up like this after they killed Fritzy Bildheim. Scrawny little fellow, Fritzy, stepping out onto the porch of his clapboard mansion, taking a leak over into the rhododendrons, wobbly drunk, laughing through his fishy gums. *Gimme the gun, so*, and Enright snatched the Peacemaker from the half-breed and Fritzy was already down in the pink flowers with a hole in his forehead before Gabriel Jack got to tell Enright why he didn't want to kill the orchard-keeper after all, that it wasn't his sister was raped but his mother twenty-five years before. *You mean to tell me you had me kill your father?*

Enright sat up straight, letting the world in on him again. At the other side of the day-room table Gallagher meditated sadly while Johnstone, all rigged out in a black dinner suit, played with his fob-watch. Funny how the mind worked, the worm in the muck of memory knowing well where it was going all the time. Johnny Dooley, a father too, maybe, if Timmoney had it right. Larry Healy with the pregnant wife. The bachelor boy Shanahan. Never be Pa, Da or Daddy to anyone, any of them,

after tonight. A stone in a graveyard, at best, for a drunken son
to piss against, like he'd done once for no better reason than
a mad notion that the insult might drag Da out of the grave
and stand up for himself, even if it was only as a ghost to his
wailing son.

Enright wondered if they'd taken Danny from the shed out
at Lady's Well before they burned the place down and Arrow
Valley Puca along with it. Had they been perhaps surprised to
find him there and shot him to protect their identities? Or had
they come for Danny and the burning been a malicious after-
thought? Gallagher's voice was barely audible.

'We have to keep the men in the barracks tonight, Inspector.
Let the military out to Ballytarsna for the body. Feelings are
running too high in here. Danny was . . . you could say he was
one of our own.'

Straightening his bow tie as though impatient to return to
his dinner party, Johnstone nodded his assent. Gallagher's relief
was short-lived.

'Apart from Sergeant Enright, of course. We'll want a report
from the scene.'

On his feet, his colour high and a panic of regret at his
impetuousness already emasculating him, Gallagher found some
faltering words of protest.

'It isn't fair to ask the sergeant. He was the closest Danny had
to a friend. Isn't that right, Tom?'

The District Inspector wasn't happy with his hair, his bow
tie, his predicament. His hands fixed the first two and he
looked to his sergeant to fix the last. Gallagher too pleaded
silently. In the spaces between the two, Enright found a large
portrait of King George V to stare at. Another grey-whiskered,
sad-eyed moron, he thought.

'You only have to look at the state of the man, Mr Johnstone.
The shock . . .'

'Sergeant Enright and myself have seen a damn sight worse
nights than this. Now sit bloody down.'

The sincerity of Johnstone's outburst surprised all three of them. Maybe the fellow was half-human after all, Enright thought, maybe he was hiding nothing behind his rote phrases and his indifference towards his men than the same filthy sights and sounds that all of them carried home from France.

Too old for the recalcitrance he persisted with, Gallagher seemed merely eccentric and his objections inept, ineffectual.

'I won't be ignored like this. I've policed this town a long time and I know the people and I like to think that . . . that I'm trusted by . . . by some at least to do the right – '

'Sit down, Mr Gallagher, or would you prefer to write that letter of resignation after all? I'll have no difficulty in accepting it, I can tell you.'

The Head Constable had never in all his years of service, Enright supposed, disobeyed an order. Even now, the effort defeated him. In the silent desperation that had become his natural state, he retreated from the day room.

'Better get along, Sergeant, and do what needs to be done, eh?'

All that was missing was a pan of water for the DI to wash his hands of the consequences. When Enright stood up, he felt dizzy but not uncomfortably so. A gun in his hand and a target would balance him out. And a drop of Jameson.

Johnstone didn't give a damn about Danny Egan any more than he gave a damn about his own men. Just another score to settle. Or have someone else settle on his behalf.

'Enjoy the rest of the party, sir. You better hurry now. The wife'll be waiting for you.'

Johnstone's expression was not that of a man offended but, strangely, that of a thief apprehended.

'My wife is in Galway, Sergeant. She's dying. I'd rather you not mention her again.'

Outside the day room, the barracks seethed with mutinous whisperings and raised voices called to order by the white-flag wavers, Keane their spokesman. Enright found the two groups squaring off like a bunch of barroom brawlers at the muscle-flexing, muttering stage. He ignored the middle-aged waverers and the blaming scowls they directed towards him and addressed the others, Baldwin among them though not with them. Never with anyone that fellow.

'I'm mad as hell too, lads, but you'll have your day.'

'So, sit on our cage, is it?'

Ow kedge. Harvey's polyglot accent mystified Enright again, offered distraction from imaginings of Danny's execution. Half Cockney and half something else that put him in mind of Arabic but couldn't be, since the fellow was as pale as a Scandanavian.

'Where the hell were you born, Harvey? You're no Cockney like it says on your file.'

'I don't know.'

'You're an orphan so?'

'No, I'm from nowhere in particular. That's the truth.'

'I'm watching you, Harvey, if that's your real name. Now, son, no one breaks out tonight or they'll have me to answer to.'

The muttering died down though Enright guessed that a punch or two might be exchanged in the barracks before the night was out.

'Constable Baldwin. We're going to Ballytarsna.'

Keane sat erect, trying to make himself less portly behind the cover of his acolytes and steeling himself for a pronouncement.

'There'd be no corpse out there if it wasn't for you and your Auxie pals, Enright.'

'Nor any rebel ones in Clonore either. As if you give a tinker's curse about Danny Egan . . .' He stopped himself because his heart was skipping wildly. 'Watch your back, Keane, I know your game. You might be safe from Kinahan but don't count your chickens with me.'

Up in his room, Enright took the kit box from under the bed and opened it. The Colt lay wrapped in an oilcloth on his neatly folded suit; the Webley was a paperweight holding down Mary's letters. He couldn't remember putting the guns in the box or what distraction had led him to forget them before he'd gone to the workhouse. Could've copped it out there and it'd all be over now. He'd be laid out below in the day room with a Punch-and-Judy face on him and the news travelling down to Listowel. And then? What the hell did it matter to him what happened then? A sadness passing as surely as the assiduous tending of his grave would. He armed himself with the two guns.

'I'm coming with you.'

Enright swung round, the pair of guns instinctively cocked.

'Jesus, Timmoney, don't sneak up on a man like that. You're not going anywhere. Johnstone's orders.'

'You saved my life.'

Fanatical and troubled, the fellow was like a tossed coin and God only knew, Enright thought, which side he'd fall on. Saved plenty, keeping himself and his men out of harm's way by ignoring half-assed orders. Got fourteen, seven and three days' Confinement to Barracks for his trouble. Bastards even docked his pay. Never went out of his way like Captain Big Toe to save anyone though, except maybe for Clancy that he minded like a son, for all the good it did. Never made a medal. Not one. Not the Military Cross, the Meritorious Service Medal. Not the Distinguished Service Medal nor even a lousy Military Medal. Nothing. But who ever won a war trying to make a medal or stopping another man's bullet? Even his best mate's, when he'd be dead next day anyway. He reached in under his suit in the kit box for the Jameson, sucked long and hard at it.

'The girl's screams saved the both of us.'

'Danny was a good man in his own way. He didn't deserve to be murdered. He never did anyone any harm.'

Enright pocketed the guns, closed the kit box and kicked it back under the bed. He threw on the trench coat he used as an extra blanket of late, to be cast off during the night depending on whether he had the shivers or the sweats.

'Danny's some kind of a saint now, is he, Timmoney? And when he was alive, you thought he was a circus freak.'

'That's another reason I should go. Can I have a wee drop of that?'

Enright handed him the bottle. There wasn't much whiskey left. Enough to make a young lad wild but not so cock-eyed that he couldn't hold a gun straight.

'I'm not going out to Ballytarsna, Timmoney.'

'I've a fair notion where you're headed for.'

Enright put the two guns in his trench-coat pockets. You couldn't save a fellow from himself anyway. Not Clancy. *Good luck so, Tom.* Like an ordinary day's goodbye. Not Gabriel Jack. *No need for you to go running, Thomas. I set you to it, I aim to take what's coming.*

'Suit yourself, son. Only don't shit on the wicket.'

The forecourt of Castle Bennett seethed with Auxiliaries readying themselves to raid the Ballytarsna area as Enright arrived. Men ran to and fro as if the stones underfoot were grapes and they were trying to stomp out a drink strong enough to fuel their vengefulness. He wandered among them looking for Papenfus. On the fan of granite steps leading into the house, where every light blazed in a big, angry wakefulness, he found one of Pap's crew who'd come to Clonore with him.

'Where's the captain?'

'Flipped his lid, hasn't he.'

Tall and wiry, the Auxie already had the suggestion of a stoop in his mid-twenties and Enright saw the tumble of fallen heroes in his eyes like a question.

'He's what?'

'Try the chapel.'

'There's a chapel in the house?'

'Turn left inside the front door. It's straight ahead.'

'I need a few men to blacken up and come into town. Are you with me?'

The Auxie shrugged but silently assented.

'Give me a minute to muster up Pap.'

He mounted the steps lightly, pushing the Auxie officer's dispiritedness from his mind. Fellows like Pap didn't *flip*, he thought, though it was hard to avoid the memory of the Boer hopping around Martin Dwyer like a wasp that couldn't get its arse straight to deliver a sting.

Inside, the house was all mica-flecked marble and richly carved dark timbers. He hurried along the passage to his left that began with white marble tiles silencing the stamp of his boots but ended in kettledrum timber that drowned the faint whine from a phonograph inside the locked door of the chapel.

'Papenfus! It's me. It's Tom!'

No answer except that the orchestra sped up momentarily, staggered and sped on as though following the baton of a conductor with a bad twitch. Like his own, his neck straining to get out of the noose of his tunic collar. Only now, as he leaned against the door, did he become aware of the breathlessness that tightened his chest after the sprint along the passage. A carved oak saint pressed its hard little body against Enright's spine.

'For Christ's sake, Pap, let me in. We've work to do.'

A slow, halting drumbeat of footsteps resounded from inside. The music had lapsed into a tentative equilibrium. The complications of the door lock seemed to confound Papenfus for so long a time that Enright was on the point of giving up on him.

At last, the door swung inward on the scarlet-lit chapel but too quickly for Papenfus, who tottered and fell at the release. His shaven head hit the floorboards like a dumb-bell and set the grille of the little gate to the altar jangling out of tune with the phonograph music that was halfway towards giving up. Enright recognised the melody even in its death throes. 'After the Ball', that Mary used to sing. *After the day is through, Mary, not done.* In an alcove to the left of the altar, a statue of the Blessed Virgin lowered its eyes embarrassedly.

Papenfus smiled up at him from the floor, settling into his newfound perspective, enjoying it. His face in the light from the red altar lamp was a bruised fruit; dark under the eyes, hollows in the cheeks that Enright hadn't noticed before. He offered the Boer his hand. Then he forced it on him, dragged him to his feet and got him to a pew. The phonograph attempted a scratchy but effective imitation of silence. Papenfus was having trouble sitting up but didn't seem to mind. Everything amused him; the floor, the horn of the phonograph, the carved panelling on the walls, the altar, Enright's face.

'Howzit, mate! Twitching Tom. The men christened you Twitching Tom, did you know that? Tommy the Twitcher. Tom Twitch.'

Enright gave up trying to hold Papenfus upright. The Boer's head rolled forward but he stayed on the pew. When he spoke again, it was as though he addressed an invisible coterie in Enright's absence.

'Sourest bugger I ever met. Hates his own worse than we do. Why is that, Tom?'

'I'm not one of them no more than you're a damn Zulu, Pap.'

Enright wanted to knock him flat but it would have been too easy.

'Why're you always crying, Tom? Why do you always look like a man at a funeral?'

'You're wasting my time, Pap, you're drunk.'

Papenfus steadied himself and the joke was beginning to elude him.

'Ag, it's over, Tom, it's all politicking now. No place for a soldier.'

'It's over for Danny but not for the bastards who shot him.'

'Christ's sake, Tom, they did the man a favour. What kind of life did he have?'

Easy or not, Enright clattered the Boer and sent him thudding on to the floor. Papenfus landed absurdly in a seated position and, unsurprised, stared at Enright, seeming already to have forgotten the punch.

'Why would you want to stay in the firing line when the HQ mob are grazing with the rebels?'

'You lost your nerve, Pap. I saw you lose it out in that field up at Clonore, if you ever had any. Run away if you want.'

'The only thing I ever ran away from was my old man's bull-whip. After that, everything I did was a spit in his eye. He fought Kitchener in Mafeking and I fought on Kitchener's side in France. But that young fellow I shot, that was my Uncle Ryk I never met. Nineteen-years-old, strafed by the British at Paardeberg. Made me wonder if I was spitting in my own eye all those years.'

'Call it what you like, Pap, but you're chicken.'

The Boer's laughter filled the chapel; soaring up and down, it found low harmonies with the timbers of the floor, high ones with the glass of the altar lamp and the grille of the altar gate.

'You try so hard. Christ, it's pitiful. Bluff and bluster, nerves of steel and all that *vrot* . . . Look at yourself, Tom, you've got a face palsied stiff from trying to hold yourself together.'

But Enright was already walking away, angry fit to burst. Just as he wanted to be, just as he needed to be this next hour. So loudly did his boots batter the floorboards that he didn't hear the catch of Papenfus's gun being released.

'Hey?'

Enright glanced back and the Luger wavered in and out of line with his chest.

'Bang, bang! Fall down, you daft bugger, you're supposed to be dead.'

Killing Shanahan was easy. He lived alone half a mile outside the town in a roadside cottage with a big, wide, boggy field to the rear and not a tree for a couple of hundred yards to hide behind if a fellow got that far. Shanahan didn't. Off he went, haring it through the bulrushes, four of them after him, and it would have been funny if Enright's legs hadn't felt so heavy and he the slowest of the chasing pack for all his efforts. Baldwin led, his slick black hair flapping like a loose hatch cover in a storm. He ran straight as a die and let the rebel do the fancy dodging from the bullets that weren't yet flying except in his panicking brain.

The mudpack on Enright's face dried even as he sprinted and fell off like scabs, leaving an itch he didn't dare scratch. When the first shot rang out, followed by a piercing cry from Shanahan whose run became a one-legged joke of a hop, Enright gave up the chase, saved himself for the remaining targets. Dooley especially. Four more shots rang out from the far corner of the field and he wondered if Timmoney had fired one. Then the three hunters jogged back towards him, not a face on any of them because of the black polish; shadows, weighty and upright as men.

'Very generous with the ammunition, Baldwin. You'd think you were paying for it yourself.'

Fiddling with the Webley, Timmoney avoided his glance. Hard to tell what he was hiding, guilt or cowardice.

'I kep' shooting to stop his gabbing, ken?'

'What'd he say?'

Baldwin laughed as he worked his hair back with both hands, his flat cap under his arm.

'Thought it was you was pluggin' him. "The IRA don't want me, Enright," he says. "I don't care if I live or die any more." Said any man was entitled to one blunder.'

'What blunder? Did you not ask him?'

In correcting the Scot, Timmoney was a boy out to impress his schoolmaster. Earnest, precise and irritating.

'What he said was, "I could live to a hundred and Kinahan wouldn't give me another chance to redeem myself, as if he never made a mistake himself in the heat of the moment." I told you not to fire, Baldwin. I said to wait for the sergeant.'

'Shut your gawb, sonny, you didn'ae get one frigging shot off.'

'The gun jammed. Or maybe I . . . I never used one before. Not for real. But I tried. I did. I might as well have fired.'

Head bowed, Timmoney seemed to blame the Webley for the loss of his eternal soul. Enright grabbed the gun from the young penitent. It hadn't jammed but he put on a show for Baldwin none the less, though he knew the Scot wouldn't believe him.

'The catch, you dummy, the . . . Christ, Shanahan's mistake, pound to a penny it was the tripwire business. Do you never think, Baldwin? He's the one should've been watching the trip-wire when the girl cycled into it.'

'So? He's paid for it now, hasn't he?'

Enright felt cheated. He blamed the trigger-happy Scot, but knowing that his own body had let him down left him weaker still. Baldwin seemed to observe his every thought and find each one more amusing than the one before.

Back in town at ten minutes to one, they parked the Ford at the Friary Street entrance to Main Street and changed into plimsolls. They slipped down the street so close to the shuttered shops and pubs and the Munster and Leinster Bank that they might have been slithering along the walls. At the lane beside Larry Healy's pub, Enright gestured at Timmoney and the Auxie to take the back door. The two went lightly along, crawled the few feet beneath a side window and went crouching on into the dark well of the lane. He gave them a minute to get in position and then led the way past the front door of the pub to a second door alongside, painted the same dull green.

Even on the street, Enright got the same after-hours whiff of stale smoke and fly-blown dregs he'd breathed in for years after they'd taken his father away because of the slaughtered cattle. *Sure, it'll only be for a while, he'll be out before you know it.* Aunt Kate, gap-toothed and filthy and cunning. *But who'll mind the dogs and the land?* And he hadn't understood the joke it was to her and Paudie and his pals at the counter, spluttering through dribbles of porter. *Land, ha ha! Swamp, hee hee! They grow rice in better, abroad in China!* His face burned under the mud as it had done back then. *But the dogs?* He gave Timmoney and the other lad at the back door another few seconds. *What dogs, sure the dogs was took for compensation after the cattle were cut, barring the white they couldn't find.*

Enright kicked at Larry Healy's door and heard an echoing splintering of timbers from behind the pub. They took turns at shouldering the door but the bolts inside held. A nervous, yellow light flickered in the fanlight above the door. Then he heard the Auxie's voice from inside.

'Where's Healy?'

A woman screamed.

'Larry's gone to Dublin!'

An older woman joined in.

'On the evening train, ask anyone above at the railway station and they'll tell you!'

Beside Enright, Baldwin grinned like a minstrel.

Bolts slid back; three, four but not enough of them for Larry Healy. The door opened. The Auxie with the stoop pinned Healy's pregnant wife back against the wall with one hand and held the door she was kicking out at with the other. Timmoney legged it up the stairs, moving so fast in the urgent fluttering of light he seemed to glide and trench coat flapping loud as a No. 1 Cape Horn canvas in a blow, reached the first landing. As he tried to decide whether to go left or right, a door opened directly in front of the young constable.

Larry Healy really did look like a man stepping on a train. Coat-collar turned up, hat brim down over the eyes, a cloth bag in his hand. His unperturbedness enraged Timmoney. He hit Healy with an uppercut. Not a bad shot either and it took all the publican's stubbornness and a firm grip on the door to stay upright. The women were impressed too and their wails went up a notch.

'I know who you are, son. You're the failed priest from Tyrone.'

'Shut you're gawb.'

Timmoney sounded more gutter Gorbals than Baldwin himself and all the black polish on a shoeshine stand couldn't hide the Scot's annoyance. Healy's collarless shirt ripped at the left shoulder seam as Timmoney grabbed a hold of it and dragged him forward. The gun, Enright's Webley, kept reminding the young constable of its presence, swaying over and back like a pendulum. He pushed Healy towards the stairs. The barkeeper grabbed the banister for support and Enright, at the foot of the stairs, holding on to the lower end, felt the shiver in the timber. Larry Healy spoke his last words.

'There's no need to push, son. God forgive you for – '

Timmoney raised the Webley but before he could fire, Healy wheeled away to avoid the shot and fell out into the air where there were no steps to decline his fall. His legs tried for purchase anyway and pantomime bicycling he went until the deadweight of his head pulled him down and hit the steps. Something cracked, nothing loud or survivable as a femur or such; something vital, and all of them there knew it. In the hiatus from the screaming and scuffling they watched the remainder of Healy's fall; disappointed, anguished, amused, the usual gamut of reactions to a failed circus act. Enright stepped aside and the blood-soaked head, face up, hopped on the hallway tiles like a punctured ball. Once, twice, almost three times.

Then the young woman's screech had Enright clutching at his ears. He pointed to a door at the foot of the stairs and gestured to the Auxie and Baldwin to take the women in there, out of the way. They struggled but were easily tamed with Baldwin's open hand. Timmoney shouted from the top of the stairs, forgetting his Glaswegian accent as he stood, not knowing what to do next, waiting to be told.

'Don't hit them!'

Baldwin slapped the older of the two women across the back of the head for good measure and hit her again when he saw

Enright look at him disgustedly.

The eyes were the only things moving on the body stretched out on the sloping rack of the stairs. Slack as a dead man, the neck or the spine gone. Like Helen Peters. Enright's leg muscles ached with the onset of cramp. His arms too. The Peacemaker wouldn't let itself be lifted.

'Can you stir, Healy?'

The eyes surveying the end of a world had no interest in Enright. The door, its paint gone yellow after years of cream from the first white, and from behind which Healy's wife called more softly now – 'Lar, Lar, you should've gone when they told you to' – took all his attention. Was he trying to sketch her on the blank surface of the door, as Enright had once summoned up Mary, all those dying or crazed nights? Was he willing the door between them open? Or thinking as Enright had done, what bloody good he'd be to any woman in this state or as a father to any child, only a slobbering burden on everyone around him? Enright went down on one knee beside the barkeeper as Timmoney began his descent from the landing, his shadow thrown back up into the heights of the landing above, enormous.

'Say a prayer, Larry.'

He thought that, at any moment, Healy's would become the shoot-me eyes of fellows welded to barbed-wire or with too many bits of them missing to go on or gone mad with some trouble that burrowed so deep inside them they thought the whole damn world could see it. Instead, the eyes cursed Enright.

'I've been damned a thousand times, Larry, and I'm still here.'

Getting the nozzle of the Colt over and in behind Healy's left ear was the hardest part and at the same time not so hard really. All in the head, all this heaviness, this fragility stoked by the women's keening. Another widow, another curse on him. Shot lads in the din of hell, whizzbangs, coal-boxes, Jack Johnsons deafening him; the loudest human roar nothing but the whimper of a dummy in a crowd. He tasted the blood in his mouth, warm, sickening, before the trigger was even halfway back. It was the taste of Nature's explosive collapse, of disembowelment.

Running back up Main Street, Enright might have been carrying a full pack, so slowly did he move, sea-legs on him worse than two months off dry land and hot as that hell off Alexandretta. The *Enselaar* it was. A suffocating desert blow from the east, the whip of sand across his face. The engines all shot and Marshall all clapped out, his penis big and black as a Bobby's baton oozing and the same yellow ooze out of his mouth. *A man died on board the other day, Mary, of a terrible poison, a good old mate of mine.* Last letter he wrote her for four years until he was dying again in Balfour, because he couldn't write lest he poison her or, later, lest he terrify her with his madness. *The lad's the last thing to go, Tommy lad.* A joke the time Marshall told him that, the old skirt-chaser. But the old goat was right.

Enright stopped for breath and looked around the street. Curtains moved but no lights shone and no surge of avengers streamed out to brave the guns. The same shower of gutless bastards who'd get scuttered at Larry Healy's wake, he supposed, follow the hearse and weep and gnash and fill the valley with tears.

He felt sure he was going to fall down right there on the street but he kept on talking to himself. That was what a fellow had to do, keep talking to himself, reminding himself that he wasn't part of all that was exploding, burning, collapsing all around him. He remembered what Captain Big Toe had said one time as they passed through Fricourt, was it? A place so far gone it could never be a town again. That some irreversible moment came amid all the battering and clattering; the fall of one last building, one last brick, maybe even one last pebble. *A moment,* said the fool with the trigger-happy big toe, *like the one that passed through a man and brought him with it into eternity.*

He sat back onto the windowsill of Molloy's Hardware and rested against the long shutters, certain they had left him behind and gone on to Dooley's. His insides seemed poisoned, his head huge, his face swollen, rotten. He clawed at the damp mixture of mud and Healy's blood that had spurted onto his face. If they saw him downed, he thought, they'd sneak out of their hovels and batter him to a pulp. First one, tentatively. Then a few, kick and run, kick and run. Then the whole damn town, kicking, running. The skyline of Main Street was the gap-toothed smile of a whore, of a mad bitch of an aunt.

Like an underwater current, an irresistible surge passed through his stomach and across his brain and flung him on the footpath. Three times he emerged from a timeless dark. Once, he was sure he saw Larry Healy, the head split open but the face alive. Then it was Gallagher in mufti he imagined on the far side of the street running like a younger man. Next thing he knew, Timmoney knelt beside him, holding his head up out of the water or whatever slime was drowning him, gurgles coming out of his mouth instead of the words that forgot themselves as soon as they'd occurred to him. His eyes drooped shut and the bright spinning stardust he saw below him was impossible and wrong. Then Mary White appeared, dressed in white, and he was back in Balfour San. *Hold my head, Mary, until I wake up or I don't.* Mary singing him softly back to life. *Wand'ring the dear dead days beyond recall. Not wand'ring, Mary, once in.*

Lying on his barracks mattress, Enright seemed to be up in the swaying gallants under too bright a sun. A vague awareness stirred in him of being surrounded by black faces when his eyes had risked the blaze of light moments before. Briefly, he was a terrified pollywog again set upon by King Neptune and his Royal Barbers determined to drag and bully him through the initiation ritual. *I crossed the bloody Date Line twice already!*

Amid strange whisperings he felt the balm of something damp touch his cheeks, his forehead. He recognised Timmoney's voice.

'We'll have to bring the doctor.'

'He's covered in blood, for Christ's sake. How're you gonny explain that, your holiness?'

Baldwin, spiky as ever. Start a row in an empty room, that fellow. Watch him though, don't turn your back on him, Tommy lad. Enright smiled to himself. He knew he could open his eyes now if he wanted to.

'I'm washing it off the best I can.'

'He won't thank ye for calling a doctor. He's buggered. Seen plenty like him that fell asunder whenever there's a bit of action.'

The light was less raw when Enright sat slowly up. With a hand whose trembling he couldn't quite master, he knuckled his eyelids apart.

'No doctor, Timmoney. And Baldwin? I'll lay odds I'll out-live you, boy.'

Baldwin shrugged. Enright would have preferred an argument that might have brought him raging back to his senses. Instead, he was seized by an overwhelming despondency that dragged him back down on the pillow.

Timmoney came towards him with a bloodied rag that was like something from the insides of a dead beast and he pushed it weakly away.

'Did ye get Johnny Dooley?'

'We were too busy scraping you off the street, remember?'

'Leave him be, Baldwin. If it wasn't for him, we wouldn't have got any of them.'

Enright turned his face to the wall, astonished and ashamed to be on the verge of tears.

Bedford,
Listowel

Dear Tom,

You're not long gone and I am up at the kitchen table
because I can't sleep. You didn't sleep either and you needed
to worse than me. No sooner am I over Jerry's sickness than
I see the weight falling off you again. You are pushing yourself too hard, Tom, and the worst thing is I can't open my
mouth to you because I'm getting afraid of you again, like
in Canada when just because you got tired, you started
imagining horrible things about me and Gabriel Jack. You
think you know everything that's happening around you and
that you're always right but you're not. I don't know how you
can be a policeman because you can't see what's under your
nose, you can't add one and one and get two, only some
other strange number of your own reckoning.

I said about pretending what a normal life is like but I can't
pretend any more. I go round the place pretending everyone
isn't talking behind my back. I pretend the spits and jeers
don't hurt me. I pretend the stories Jimmy tells me now about
your rough carry-on up there aren't true, that you're maybe
even in on the killing of men in their beds, and I tell him
about your promise in the letter you sent from the Balfour. I
pretend that you care about Jerry even a little bit. I'm nearly
more worn out from pretending than from living. I don't even
bother reading any more because that's just pretend too.

I might be a fool but it's very simple to my eyes. If you really loved me, not to speak of wanting the best for Jerry, you would give up the policing and come to us. You would not think that anything was worth fighting for, only him and me.

Mags won't put up with Toussaint's philandering much longer. I got a letter from her the other day and she said she found him with a young one in the kitchen of the restaurant and she won't have it. I very much think that she is going to leave him in the lurch and she is right to, even though it is a sacrament she's leaving. She worked hard the last five years to make a go of that restaurant with him and this is the thanks she gets. Not that I am thanked for going a thousand miles to you and you won't come eighty for me, only offer an empty promise that we can go away when the trouble is over. I know you are a very proud man and that your pride has often been sorely tested but I also know that the longer you continue up there, the less there will be to be proud of.

It was strange, the two of us lying here in the dark and yet miles away from each other. I was just waiting for you to say something, not even anything important or about the way things are gone with us. Of course, you didn't but I didn't either and it is sad but the truth is that such is the way we are now.

Everyone says there is going to be a truce – after that, what excuse have you for staying on in the police? What excuse will you have then for ignoring us? I very much think that Jimmy is right when he says you will find one.

Remember the time when you were young and I found you up the hills? Remember the blood I got on my white dress and I didn't pretend to mind? I mind now, Tom. If I was young again, I don't know would I be such a saintly little nun of a one making a martyr of myself without the sense to know there would be no end to it.

Love,
Mary

For days on end Enright lingered listlessly in bed or sat slumped against the wall on the day-room bench until the darkness prompted him to make the wearying climb to his quarters again. He had no taste for whiskey, not even for a soft Scotch, though Timmoney was there at every hand's turn bearing yet another bottle. The occasional pang of hunger brought with it the nauseating image of Danny Egan's unclaimed corpse, rotting away in the workhouse morgue, and of Helen Peters, a few doors away, trapped in the sickening pall.

He became convinced that the doldrums would pass when they found Danny's relatives or, if there were none, at least discovered where he was from. And yet, he had neither the will nor the energy to help in the task. He watched, he listened, he held his head in his hands. Nothing moved him. Not even the changing mood of the barracks from the fraught aftermath of the rebel funerals to the barely contained jubilation of the time-servers as reports of an impending truce gained a substance that failed to convince Enright. Too many scores left unsettled, he reckoned, too many mysteries unsolved. On both sides.

Timmoney and the few others who felt betrayed by the Government's rumoured capitulation to the rebels seemed ignorant of this reality and he was in no mood to enlighten them. He viewed the spectacle of their comings and goings with such utter detachment that he felt all but invisible. Whether they scowled or leered or worried at him, he felt the same indifference. When he read the *Tipperary Sentinel*'s account of the killings of the previous week, this sense of apartness merely confirmed itself.

Danny, as was to be expected from the local nationalist rag, merited a few spare lines tucked away at the bottom of an inside page.

SHOCKING DISCOVERY
The body of an ex-soldier has been recovered by police at Ballytarsna. Further details were not available at time of going to press. The matter is under investigation.

No mention of the boghole he fell into after the single shot to the back of his head, of the placard tied around his neck – SPIES AND TRAITORS BEWARE – or of Danny's harmlessness. And there was no investigation, not from the off, and with a truce expected daily, it had simply become injudicious. Not that it mattered a damn. They'd be well scattered by now, Paddy Kinahan or who-ever he'd put on the job. No suggestion in the newspaper either of any connection with the deaths of Shanahan and Healy, no link of justification. Instead, a report on the town killings, as high on melodrama and wronged innocence as any dime novel and as far from the truth. *Blood marked the passage with its deadly script.* Another poet in the wrong job, Enright thought, though it was true that the hallway had been smeared with blood. Healy's blood too, but it had come from Timmoney's coat as he stumbled away from the aftershock of the pub owner's exploding head. In consequence the young fellow was drinking like a fish these days, going from a swagger one minute, to a hunched penitence the next. In-between times, he was all over Enright like a mother or a wife or a whorehouse hostess. *You have to eat, Tom. You'll waste away, Tom. Just a wee drop, Tom.*
Enright skimmed through the newspaper's editorial amusedly.

This weekend will probably witness a welcome ending to the destruction of life and property – a factor of incalculable help in promoting and God-speeding the

blessed work of the Peacemakers who meet today in
our Capitol for the second time.

He smiled to himself at the unintended reference to his Colt.
But he kept the best laugh until last. The story that exercised
the town's imagination at least as much as the murders and the
truce did. A story that shamed and bewildered believers, inside
and out of the barracks, and gave the non-believers something
to gloat over.

Enright had observed the whispers and the jeers all week as
the mystery of the bleeding statue in Templemore unravelled
in farce, and wondered now what the local newshounds had
made of it. Nothing. He allowed himself a chuckle as he sat
alone in the day room and went through each page of the rag
once again. Not a whisper of young John Walshe's unmasking,
of the red ink vial secreted in his cuff that brought the blood
to the statue when he touched it, of the tidy sum of donations
pocketed, or of his overnight disappearance. The only trace of
the story was the discreet removal of the usual advertisement
offering photos of the blessed Walshe at a shilling a go.

Gallagher, a believer in both God and Government, went
about punch-drunk, smiling stupidly like a man concussed, his
world turned upside down but oddly better. Timmoney was
nonplussed by the godless universe dawning upon him and
offering, at once, an escape from guilt and a bleak meaning-
lessness. Or so it seemed to Enright as he lay low without the
interest to say, I told you so. Timmoney wasn't the worst of
them anyway. Not by a long shot. Especially now that he'd
been blooded. And he'd need the young fellow when he was
back on his feet and, truce or no truce, tormenting the rebels
again. As if to confirm Enright's faith in him, it was Timmoney
who led them to Danny's true identity and dragged him out of
his week-long torpor.

Three in the afternoon and Enright lay on his bed, staring out
by the window grille at a grubby blue sky. The airless room felt

sultry but tolerably so. He had been reading Mary's letter again or reading between the lines the unsubtle hint about Mags and her philandering husband when Timmoney looked in on him.

'I've an idea how we might find Danny's people, Tom. I just came down from the dead house and I wonder . . . Do you remember when he shook hands with us the night the corpses were laid out in the day room?'

All Enright remembered from that night were the Punch-and-Judy noses and too much Jameson swilling around in his veins and unbalancing him. Timmoney stabbed a finger into his right hand.

'Danny had a thick callus on his palm, tough as a nut, and there was something familiar about that but I couldn't think what until this morning. So I went up to the dead house to see was it true.'

'See was what true?'

'He was a chippie. Or maybe a stonemason.'

'Danny Egan?'

'I know, but when I was in the seminary a couple of boys came to set them there carved panels in the new chapel. Some of us students helped to carry the stuff in with them and we talked a while and then shook hands. You know, like you do. And afterwards, I remembered about the welt they both had in the palm. Very noticeable it was and especially when there were two fellows with it. So one of our lads told me these wood carvers, they get the callus from working the mallet and stone-masons the same.'

Enright sat up on the bed and the glimpse he caught of the sky outside seemed brighter than before. Within hours, Timmoney's speculations brought results. Danny's father was being escorted from Drumshallee, a village outside of Athlone, up in the Midlands. In the morning, Danny would find a rest-ing place, at last. Timmoney wanted Enright to join him in a celebratory swig from the bottle of Jameson before they'd go up to the dead house to pay their last respects. Enright refused on both counts. He thought he might sleep right through the night for a change. Viewing the corpse, smelling that rot all over again would ruin whatever chance he had of a restful night.

As he drifted off to sleep, he thought that maybe a truce wasn't such a bad idea after all. Give him a chance to get back into shape and more time to spend with the dogs until he came right. The new white especially. Arrow Valley Snow. Might even go over to Roscrea tomorrow and see if the word that had come from Foley about the dog's location proved reliable. More time to spend with Mary too in a truce, he thought, less for her to be fretting over for a while. A lull too might draw the snakes out of the grass. Paddy Kinahan. And Johnny Dooley, who, he was relieved to hear, had slipped away to hide in the hills after the bruising he'd got in the holding cell and wouldn't have been home even if Enright hadn't collapsed on Main Street that killing night.

Enright woke before seven, all fired up in the roseate morning light. No time to think, no need to. Everything seemed to have been decided as he slept. He was going to Danny Egan's funeral and, on the way back, would make a diversion to Roscrea for the dog. He dressed quickly. His bone-hard cock pushed out against the scrabble of his fingers as he buttoned his trousers. A ravenous hunger stirred in him.

He plunged down the stairwell in his socks; boots in one hand, the Colt Peacemaker in the other as he stuffed it inside his tunic, where it filled out the concave side of his chest. He stumbled into the day room with one boot on and bending, on the move, to get into the other. Baldwin sat there somnolent, dejected. His dank hair hung down over his ears and a straggle of fringe covered his forehead down to the eyebrows. The day room stank of cheap whiskey, the bottle on the table held but a quarter inch of the yellow stuff.

'On the tear, are you, Baldwin?'

The Scot displayed none of his usual wilful cussedness as he addressed the whiskey bottle.

'My old man just died.'

Respectfully, Enright left the tying of his bootlaces though the delay irritated him.

'Ma gutted him with a frigging bread knife.'

Enright didn't know what to say. He was startled and yet unsurprised at what came out from under the stone Baldwin had lifted from his life.

'I should'a killed the bastard long ago. Saved her the trouble.'

The unlikely sympathy Enright had begun to feel for the Scot evaporated and he went towards the scullery door to whip up a quick brew and butter a few thick slabs of bread.

'Stood a head over him and I still did'nae have the guts to do him. Cut the throats of Huns twice his size but could'na do him. What'ye make o' that?'

'A man doesn't kill his father, does he? I'm off to Danny's funeral. I'm running late.'

Baldwin looked at him quizzically.

'Why would you want to go to there?'

'The man deserves a decent send-off. There'll be no one there only the family.'

Same thing if he copped it himself, he knew. Mary. The child. Maybe not even the child. He cursed Baldwin silently for stirring up the old, unsettling mystery of his own mother's funeral and the more unsettling one still of his father and the mystery of the dead cattle in Gun-Mahony's field that hastened his end.

'You'd no come to mine, Enright.'

'What would I be doing going over to Scotland to see them shove you in a hole?'

Baldwin shrugged a tired full stop to a conversation that should never have been started. Enright did without the tea, cut himself a heel of bread and went outside to find the Ford. He checked that the bottle of whiskey, wrapped in an oily rag, was still under the driver's seat. He didn't touch a drop until Birr an hour and a half later and that was just to get himself back to where he'd been when he woke without a troubling thought in his head. But Birr bothered him unreasonably when he remembered that Dooley's hunchbacked aunt came from the town.

The Jameson helped again somewhere the far side of Athlone, a few miles from Danny's village and the hole in the ground they had ready for him. He was hitting the road in spots, getting forty-five miles an hour out of the Ford, flying over hump-backed bridges, driving into the dazzle between trees and taking bright-blinded chances on the lie of the road ahead; and laughing through the wind-loosed tears in his bad eye.

Drumshallee graveyard was devoid of trees, a field more naked than mere grass, for all its bleached gravestones and Celtic crosses scabby with pale yellow lichen and bird droppings. Enright preferred it that way, the bare finality of it all. No leaves to fool the living with the false ghostliness of their voices. Crashing along loudly by the pebbled pathway, he was unsteadied by the inexplicably loose boots. He looked down at his feet. The bootlaces were still undone and a chuckle burst forth from him as he knelt to tie them. At the far end of the graveyard, a small group had gathered. In that wide unshaded space, the sun's heat proved unrelenting. The heavy serge and the hurrying left him bathed in sweat. Damn good way to get sober again though he wished he could find a tap to dip his head under, but the murmur of prayers had already started up ahead and there was nothing for it but more hurry.

Fourteen or fifteen people eyed the sky or their feet or some place within the mid-distance of themselves. Enright counted nine police uniforms and one military, an officer. He wondered who the others might be. Parents probably; a few siblings or more distant relatives. Drawing closer, he noted the two black-veiled women; one old and crouched, the other young and erect. Danny's mother and sister, no doubt. And the priest, of course, small and rotund and going through a chore. Enright stumbled as he misjudged the gradient from the path to the grass verge just twenty yards from Danny's grave. Faces turned still mouthing prayers, took stock of the intruder as he straightened his shoulders, and dismissed him. All but one. An RIC man. A sergeant like himself but spruced up and suspicious of the bedraggled intruder.

Enright went in among the constables, who regarded him no less suspiciously. What did they think he was? An impostor? The worst lunatic in Ireland wouldn't pretend to be an RIC man. Except for Danny Egan, whose daft notebook inside Enright's tunic pressed against the Colt, Mary's letter slipped in between the pages. *Mags won't put up with Toussaint's philandering much longer.*

The coffin was no better than a discarded gun crate; a thing of borrowed timbers, unplaned and flaking away at the split ends, a pauper's box that the weight of clay would burst open like a fist in a kettledrum. Some bloody send-off. Hardly a one there that didn't look like they had something better to be doing. Not a tear. Not one, until the breeze across the open field smarted Enright's bad eye. When he wiped it off with the back of his hand, he sensed that the misgivings directed at him had ebbed. He felt himself to be the object of mere curiosity now, a diversion from the insect-drone of prayer.

Across the gap of the grave, the family group stood as though in opposition to the phalanx of uniforms. The mother's expression wavered between resigned sadness and a smile. A memory perhaps, or relief at her son's deliverance from his wounded mortality. The sister's veil was more darkly opaque, the lips, visible below the veil, lightly closed, not pained. Eyes narrowed to the sun, Enright divined a resemblance to Danny in the sickly, grey-haired man standing between the women. Staring into the grave, the man fidgeted with a rosary beads as though counting how many days he had left before his own end came.

When the prayers came to a staggered, uncoordinated end, the older woman went slowly down on one knee, took a handful from the mound of clay and stood again waiting for the box to be lowered. At the priest's silent bidding, the constables around Enright moved into place; one to each end of the three canvas straps, looping the spool round their wrists and testing the slack, used to the work.

Enright stepped forward and tapped the constable nearest him on the back.

'I'll take this one.'

The constable looked beyond Enright at his own sergeant. He turned dismissively then from Enright, who locked his hand round the constable's upper arm.

'He was a mate of mine, Constable. Do me a favour and scoot.'

Pale with resentment, the constable handed over the canvas strap and returned to consult with his sergeant. Enright was so distracted by their mutterings that when the plank was slipped from under the coffin at his end, he felt himself in danger of being dragged down into the hole with Danny. He got his grip back but the weight remained immense. From the snide looks of the other strappers, he knew what the game was. They were letting him bear the brunt of the load, the coffin dipping in his direction. He glared at them, his nostrils wide with the strain and the hammering in his chest as Danny went down. Never saw Clancy buried or Gabriel Jack, and Marshall's grave was the Indian Ocean, stitched into a canvas and weighed down with a few splice bars, sinking without trace, and he couldn't remember his mother's funeral, not a cry or a prayer or a tear of it. He'd wondered often enough if he'd even been there, but never could bring himself to ask anyone.

Enright felt his end of the coffin touch the floor of the grave and he let go of the canvas strap so that the constable at the other end fell onto the mound of clay behind. Enright shot him a snarl of a smile as the local sergeant came to his side.

'Who are you? What d'ye mean ordering my men around?'

'I knew the man in the box.'

'You might have tidied yourself up a bit.'

The sergeant preened himself for comparison as the clay from the old woman's fist pattered along the timber below.

'Down in Tipperary, we don't have time to be admiring ourselves in the mirror. Now, if you don't mind, I'll go pay my respects.'

The constables had begun to dig into the mound of clay. A slow drumbeat of earthen clods slammed the coffin and Enright steered well clear of the hole. He tried to think of something kind to say to the relatives. Danny's own oft-spoken words occurred to him, *He's in a better place entirely.* He wished he could just tell them straight out how he'd avenged Danny's murder, let them know the price the rebels had been made to pay.

The young woman's black-gloved hand raised itself mechanically when he stood before her. Beneath the veil she was a plain-looking girl, her nose broad and manly, her down-swept eyes set too close together. There was no grasp in her hold and the cold leather made her seem still more detached.

'Sorry for your troubles, miss.'

'Missus. Thank you.'

He moved confusedly on, muttering the same sentiment to each of the others, and made his way back around the grave, not looking in.

All that was to be heard from the depths now was the skittering clatter of clay upon clay, more and more muted as the grave filled up. Enright watched Danny's sister and speculated. A widow so young, he wondered, or married to a Shinner too despising of her brother to show up? He knew it would be best to leave then and avoid the censorious sergeant and his minions but the earlier haste had left him lazy and the sun cast a drowsy spell over him. He leaned against a tombstone to take the weight from his aching legs.

The white-cassocked priest went among the relatives with hands of solace that hovered, never quite touching flesh or even the cloth on their backs. Then, after Enright had turned disgustedly away only briefly, he imagined, the priest seemed mysteriously to have vanished. Not a glimpse of his ghostly garb was to be seen flittering through the standing stones. All around him, constables kicked clay from their boots, banged clay from shovels, rubbed clay from trouser legs and bantered but quietly out of respect for the next-of-kin, who moved off almost surreptitiously, as if they might, at any moment, be called back. The pristine sergeant loomed above Enright, blocking the sun, darkening the mood of the place.

'You're a damn disgrace to the uniform. What'll the poor wife make of us now?'

'Whose wife?'

'The man we were burying. Are you sure you're at the right funeral?'

Enright laughed suddenly. He held the sergeant's arm apologetically. The day had assumed an airy, disconnected quality.

'Jesus, Sergeant, I thought I was at the funeral of a man shot below in . . . Danny. Danny Egan.'

'You are. Or you were. I think you better go back home now.'

'Tipperary isn't home, I'm a Kerryman, but that's not really home either . . .'

When Enright detached himself from the tombstone and stood, the turning deck of the world unbalanced him slightly. Danny had a wife? And what the hell was she doing, letting him wander around the country in that state? Johnny Dooley's suggestion that Danny might have fathered Helen Peters's unborn child seemed less fatuous now. He tried to distract himself from the images that raised themselves.

'What's your name? I'm Enright . . . Did I tell you that already?'

'Bohan.'

Something familiar about the accent, he thought, someone he was reminded of.

'Did they have any children, Danny and the missus? Any child they might have left at home for the funeral, like?'

'No children, no. Now I'll have to insist that you leave, Sergeant Enright. Or there'll be consequences.'

Blustering loudly to make up for the trees that weren't there and the wind that wasn't blowing through them, Enright scattered his vile thoughts.

'That's a Clare accent, am I right? I knew a lad from Clare when I was over fighting in France. Clancy. Went mad again and got blown to smithereens stepping up into a no-man's-land pretending he was off to do the milking.'

The three black-clad figures neared the front gate of the cemetery, the women floating in their long blackness, the old man hobbling lumbago-stiff between them.

'The grandest lad, though. A real pal. From outside Kilrush, do you know it? I got out of a sick bed to come up here, that's why I'm a bit rough-looking.'

The sergeant stared at him blankly, his anger undone. Better get away from here, Enright told himself, before the fellow started feeling sorry for him. He moved off, every part of him aquiver with rushing and pushing forward though he made himself walk. The party of three had left the graveyard and he didn't know which direction they'd taken out on the road. He began to run, serge and bulk tugging him back, jittery legs too loose at the knees.

At the gate, breathless, he spotted them turning a bend to the right. Released from the obligations of a graveyard to tarry, be processional, they moved more quickly. Enright unbuttoned his tunic, took off his cap and tossed both into the car. In shirt and braces he felt better and the breeze he stirred as he ran cooled him. At the turn of the road, he called out.

'Mrs Egan! Mrs Egan!'

The two women halted, looked back and then quizzed each other silently. The old man limped along, oblivious. Pulling in breaths so big and wheezy he was seeing more stars with each one, Enright walked the last twenty yards of road metal that was flat as a deck in a calm but felt like an incline. He couldn't remember why he had run after them. A mistake but it was too late to turn back. Because he couldn't locate the young woman's eyes beneath the veil, he felt exposed and her silence irritated him. He parroted on, filling the void.

'I used try to mind Danny a bit and feed him when he needed . . . He used to sleep sometimes in a shed I had . . . But I couldn't mind him every minute of the day with the way things are gone, could I?'

'He's in a better place entirely, sir.'

He wanted to ask her if that was a phrase of his she remembered, or just a thing people in these parts said of the dead. And, suddenly, a dozen furious questions came to him and began to dribble out because he could no longer contain himself.

'Could you tell me why, missus, did you let him off wandering? Could you not keep him out of harm's way? Have you no notion of what it's like down in Tipperary these times?'

The young woman raised her veil to reveal an expression of forbearance, a shirt-sleeved drunk on a lane holding no terrors for her.

'Whoever I have to answer to, it's not to you, sir.'

'I know, I'm sorry. But listen, what kind of a fellow was he? That's all I want to know really.'

'He had a very nice disposition. That's a lovely thing in a man. And rare, I may tell you.'

She began to walk away and Enright took a step after her but the older woman blocked his path. She raised neither her veil nor her head and he could only guess whether or not she was looking up at him. Her voice came thin and ancient and he couldn't help but defer to it.

'I thank you, sir, for taking the trouble to come all the way from Tipperary for my son's funeral. Annie done her best. She was only a girl of eighteen when she lost him five years ago.'

'But wasn't she his wife? And weren't you here too? Couldn't you have kept him?'

'They left him standing at our front gate, sir, off the back of an army lorry. He didn't have an iota where he was or who we were. All he done was turn around and walk off down the lane. So we brought him back and we kept bringing him back until we seen there was no use in it. Off he went on us, looking for something he lost, he says. And do you know what? He was happier than any of us because we knew what we lost and he didn't. He always wanted to be a policeman when he was a child and when he forgot everything else, even his trade, he must have remembered that. Isn't life cruel, sir, the way it makes fools of us all in the end?'

Enright felt all the rush and bother subside in him. The woman's weak, confounded questioning that sought no answer, it seemed to him, but solace in the song of her own voice, provoked an inner stillness that made him suddenly aware of the singing chatter of thrushes and the thick perfume of elderberry in the spray of their white flowering and the verdant expanse all around him and the sky, cornflower blue above.

'What can we do only battle on, missus? Was he good at the carpentry?'

'Any man with a pair of hands on him could be a carpenter. Danny was only a few months away from being a master craftsman like his father but off he went to France. Nothing in his head going over only cathedrals. Chartres and Reims, that he wanted to see the inside of. Won't you mind yourself now, sir, on your way home?'

He stood in the road and watched until all three had receded from view. Forty-five miles, the long way back by Roscrea. At least there might be the dog for company on the last leg of the journey.

Requisition. That was the word he'd been trying to think of since he'd first hatched the plan. Not beg, borrow or steal, but requisition the dog. A military word and a good one. A soldier could take what he wanted to survive, to lift his spirit, to battle on. In a real war, the cottage on the outskirts of Roscrea would have had little to offer that was worth requisitioning. An open larder in the dun kitchen revealed a slab of shrivelled bacon, a chunk of bread coated with green mould; the horse-manure reek of bad tobacco; a toothless wife, he reflected sourly, the wrong side of sixty and hair on her like a wet badger. Out in the yard by the side of the cottage, the dogs kicked up a racket and Enright recognised the hunger in their howls. The man of the house had long since been reduced to papery skin over bent bone.

'You're what?'

'I'm requisitioning the white dog. I'll give you a fair price. Three guineas, say?'

''Tis worth five and it'll win more. Anyway, I've no notion of selling.'

'I'm taking the dog by order of the IRA. Are you with us or against us?'

The old fellow eyed Enright cagily from the far side of the kitchen. His wife tucked herself in behind him and urged him on to defiance with a whistling, toothless whisper.

'You're wearing a policeman's trousers.'

'I'm in disguise. I shot the man who used to wear these.'

He rooted in his pocket for the money, counted it out with his fingers in there. Then, for the laugh, he whipped out his hand in a flash, the index finger pointing like the barrel of a gun. The woman screamed and then seeing her imagination had run away with her, ducked sheepishly in behind her terrified husband again. A pound to a penny she'd been among the throng down in Templemore groping at the bleeding statue. The husband too. That look in his eyes that wanted to be dead and gone from this miserable existence but afraid to die. Enright turned in disgust from them.

Outside, Arrow Valley Snow took the lead on his neck without protest and followed Enright to the Ford. Even the dog, Enright guessed, knew it was going *to a better place entirely.*

A kind of silent pandemonium reigned in the barracks when Enright arrived back there in the late afternoon. Men scurried around to no seeming purpose, stony-faced and preoccupied. Out by the back passage to the day room, Keane made him none the wiser, merely offered the usual filthy look and hurried on. He went in to the day room and found Gallagher slouched at the table, his fingers counting out the beads of a rosary, his lips jabbering in prayer.

'What's going on around here?'

The Head Constable's expression was pained to a pinch, the big eyebrows turned down to a frown and spiky wild.

'No sooner had we word of the Truce agreed and then . . . then this, God help us. This is what happens when you go too far into blood, Enright. When you lose respect for other men's lives, you don't be long losing it for your own.'

Ice gripped the bad side of Enright's chest. The pulse throbbed in his throat as if it were some living thing that wouldn't be swallowed. Gallagher's head went down again like a man who preferred drowning to living in a world that was too crude and ugly.

'A young man hanging himself from the rafters. It's the devil's work. I warned DI Johnstone. I warned you all.'

Enright told himself not to run as he left Gallagher to his lamentations. This was what came of fellows thinking there was a God up there watching their every move. And what had Timmoney done? Healy's fall an accident that didn't matter a damn because Enright was going to shoot the bugger one way or the other and Baldwin it was who'd shot Shanahan in the field.

At the top of the stairs he wondered why he was about to put himself through the sight of the dead man when he'd spared himself from seeing Danny's ugly, melted death mask. He heard Marshall's warning voice – *Don't look at my lad, whatever you do, don't look at my lad*. Heard once how a hanged man's lad stiffened up bigger than it ever did in life and Marshall's had been bad enough to put a man off it for months, for years.

A few feet from the door of Timmoney's room, a sob exploded from Enright unbidden. He coughed loud and long to cover himself. *You saved my life, Tom.* He couldn't remember Timmoney's Christian name as he drew a breath as big as his battered lungs allowed and stepped into the open doorway.

Baldwin hung from the ceiling, swaying with a bony creak. The thin rope embedded in his neck, a neat encircling kink in the flesh. Below him, Timmoney lay facing the wall, trembling and foetal on one of the beds. Enright couldn't bring himself to cross the threshold of the room that was guarded by the hanged man's pop-eyed, swollen leer. The grossly protruding tongue reminded him of those mad flaring masks he'd seen in Ceylon or was it somewhere in Africa, the Congo maybe?

'What are you doing in there, Timmoney? Why isn't he cut down?'

Timmoney sat up, clamping his back to the wall as though to avoid the bare, thick-veined, swinging feet that were already marbling to stiffness.

'They're waiting on the doctor. What am I going to do, Tom? I'm going to hell like Baldwin, God have mercy on my soul.'

'This is the closest you'll ever get to hell, boy. So, come out of it.'

Timmoney raised his eyes and flinched at Baldwin's grotesque sneer.

'I can't. I can't walk past him. I'll never be able to, all my life.'

One basket case hanging out of the ceiling, another mortifying himself with the sight was more than a fellow could take. Launching himself into the death room, Enright caught Timmoney by the scruff of the neck and dragged him out onto the corridor, slamming the door shut behind him.

'I've blood on my hands. I'm tainted, Tom.'

'Get that old jiggery-pokery out of your head, boy, or I'll beat it out of you, do you hear? All you done was fight back same as any half-decent man would.'

Enright resisted the temptation to kick out at the squatting constable as he'd done to Clancy's mangled remains when the firing stopped and the stretcher parties roamed no-man's-land, throwing bits of fellows together to make a half-dozen corpses out of a score of dead men.

'Christ's sake, Timmoney, I thought you were dead and this is the thanks I get. Bloody wailing and snivelling.' Enright slid down by the wall to a crouch. His knees pressed into and relieved the soreness in his chest and held in the panic that was rising in him. He rocked back and forward, rocking the breath out of himself in wheezy sighs. 'I should never have brought you along. I should've known better than piling more torment on the likes of you.'

'It's my own doing, Tom, not yours.'

How could a fellow be so forgiving, Enright thought? What was the point of it? How could you survive on it? Gabe hadn't. *You was just the gun in my hand, Thomas.* Clancy hadn't. *I came out of Essondale of my own free will, Tom, you didn't force me.*

'Look it . . . what's your name?'

'Timmoney.'

'No, your first name.'

'Edward. But they call me Ned at home.'

'Look it, Ned. This uniform we're wearing, it's a red rag to a bull for these Shinners. So what do we do? Wait to be gored or catch the bull by the horns?'

'But killing . . . Thou shalt not kill.'

'The spider kills the fly. Your bloody God wiped out Sodom and Gomorrah, didn't he? Men, women and children. Didn't matter a damn to him.'

'But he was God and a spider is an insect.'

Funny, Enright thought, how two people could be talking and it still feel like silence. Same thing with Mary sometimes. Often.

'And what are we, only a bit of both? What made you join the police, Ned? You're no more a bloody policeman than I am.'

'I let my family down right bad when I came out of the seminary. I was trying to make up for it some way. Trying to prove I could stick some bloody thing out and make them proud of me again.'

'You want to forget the relations or you'll never have a minute's peace. Get away out of here and see a bit of the world.'

'I put in for the Palestine Police. If I don't get it, I'll go away to America or the sea or somewhere. Did you never think of going back to the sea?'

'A fellow'd want to be in the whole of his health for that game, Ned. Go and settle somewhere. The sea'll only make an old man of you before your time or drive you to the loony bin.'

'But it has to be better than this hell-hole. Do you not miss it at all, Tom?'

It seemed to Enright that he was doing for Timmoney what he had refused to do for Clancy; distract him from the horror with some pretence of normal conversation.

'Sometimes I miss the colours. And the heat. Jesus, I could do with a few months of the sun now. Even thinking of it, I get the old feeling of striding up from some port into a Sailortown I was never in before. Nobody knows you and you've no ties, no one to spend the few dollars in your pockets on only yourself. That's a damn good feeling, Ned, in a warm place. But it's a doldrums of a life between ports. All hard slog, a job of work, nothing else. Time runs slow out on the waters. Then you land and look in a mirror in some bar or brothel and you wonder who the clapped-out old bugger looking back at you is.'

They sat for a long time, listening to the scurry of feet below, the occasional creak of the weighted rope on the rafter of the death room.

After he'd requisitioned the dog in Roscrea, Enright had driven a few miles out the road and stopped for a celebratory drink. Found Danny's notebook on the floor beside the bottle and studied it as he drank. Page after page filled with long spidery trails of black ink or blue and no meaning to any of it except to fill up as many pages as Danny could, as many days as he was allowed before the blank pages took over. The glass of the windscreen had exaggerated the sun's heat, suggesting that the summer might yet warm his bones, and slowly, deliciously, little pin-prick tingles of optimism had spread across his skin.

'Of all people, Tom, I'd never have imagined Baldwin would do such a thing. I used to wonder if the man even had a soul, because, sure as God, he'd no conscience. Why would the likes of him kill himself?'

'Who knows? The ground has only to crack open the once under a man and every step he takes after that he's thinking he might fall into a hole.'

In the lugubrious light of the barracks landing there was no sunny consolation to be had. Enright bit his fingernails distractedly. Bit and spat, bit and spat, until there was nothing left to him but to start into the flesh alongside the serrated cuticles.

*T*he boy waits in the field until he is sure his father has tied up the dogs in the yard. Blood has dried to a crust on his face, along his arms and on his legs. He feels the ticklish rawness of it across his skin. A cold wind blusters fitfully like the fluttering in his windpipe. Sometimes the flap of the torn shirt on his back is so wild he almost topples over. His legs are fragile, sapless stalks, rooted only lightly in the earth. His retreating father's gruff complaints are answered by the merest whimpers from the dogs. Then there is silence. The boy closes his eyes and falls into a welcoming darkness. His small body rolls into the trench between clay-peaked drills.

When he wakes, the day is so searingly bright as to suggest, at first, that the sun has broken through the grey. But there is no sun. He picks himself up. He does not attempt to dust himself off because he is too young to know that he can or should. He walks slowly across the drilled field. His legs are heavy and he must pull them high not to be caught by the trip-up mounds. Each pull is like the wrenching loose of thistle clumps from among the potato drills, scratched limbs prickly with pain.

He thinks that if he can get past his father, wherever his father is in the silence up ahead, and if he can drag himself up those stairs and place himself before his mother with his wounds, that she will raise herself up. He imagines this as he approaches the yard. Her knuckled hands loosed, softly escaped across his cheeks, through his hair, her arms binding him to her, words pouring from her like tears.

There is no gateway from the field into the yard, only a wide gap in the autumn-crinkled hedge. He stands there, watches the dogs *that are tethered to the trunk of a great oak alongside the ash tree from which the flayed sheep hangs. He stares at the white. The white knows though it pretends only a passing glance. The boy waits. When the dog's next passing glance comes, the boy is smiling. The dog is finally taken in by his forgiving shrug. Then the screaming starts in the farmhouse.*

His first thought is that his mother is dead because the screams, though indecipherable, are certainly his father's. From the boy's throat, a moan rises and joining itself to the wish not to hear, not to think or know, it gathers enough substance to cry out, almost enough to set the uneasy dogs howling too but the sudden clarity that his father's voice gains in a more profound octave stifles the boy's lamentation.

'In the name of Christ, girl, can you not make some stir of an effort and not be lying there like a corpse?'

The dogs know better than to bark. Even the wind relents as the boy waits to hear more though the cold does not. He looks away from the house to the lesser evil of the head hanging below the meat. The sheep's eyes wide open and seeing nothing. It is difficult to imagine the world all around him gone but the boy tries hard to feel what it might be like to be nowhere. All he achieves is a blurring of focus in which the dark fleshy socket of the sheep's mouth seems to stir as his father shouts again.

'Wouldn't we all love to lie down quiet and die? Wouldn't it be an ease to us all not to have to put up with this curse of a world? Will you answer me, girl? How'm I supposed to do everything and you melded to the bed? Mind the land, mind the dogs, mind the young lad . . . Take the holy eye off you. Don't be giving me that, as well as everything else.'

His mother is not dead but, in an instant, the relief he feels is undone. His mother's voice is only briefly strange to him after its long absence from his ears. The familiar range and tone of it is there but bent to a music that repels him.

'Leave me alone. All I want is to die, it's the least I deserve.'

His father shouts something incomprehensible and weak. His mother answers at the top of a voice that is stronger than ever it was in the boy's life.

'The child is dead. I told you not to. I warned you I'm too old. Useless and old! Didn't I lose three already?'

His mother is not dead. She can speak after all, though not to the boy. He goes to where the sheep hangs, avoiding its eyes. The knife with the scarlet blade is on the ground below as he expects. He sneaks it into his trouser pocket when the dogs are looking self-consciously away, embarrassed for him.

The white seems glad to be untied from the oak tree and willing enough to suffer the leash through the gap into the field and on across to the next field and the next. The argument turned one-sided again, his father's voice, blustering defeatedly, dissolves in the distance the boy puts between himself and the farmhouse. Out here he has strayed into other men's fields, frightens other men's sheep, evokes the curiosity of other men's herds. The dog is not limping and he wonders if he has chosen the right one but he cannot decide so he goes on until, much later, he reaches a field by the road and next to Gun-Mahony's landscaped front pastures.

He knows this place well, the stream shallow in its deep trench beneath a long canopy of hedging. From these shadowed depths he has heard the thunk and tinkle and laughter of tennis parties and felt an uplifting light-headedness, a dreaming of nothing in particular, a giddy, secret knowingness. Today, as he tugs the reluctant white down into the culvert after him, he hears above the whispering stream only the lowing of Gun-Mahony's cattle and feels the hard sliver of knife against his thigh, pressing its purpose upon him.

He ties the leash to an elderberry stump in the thicket above him and rests against the hidden bank. Pebbles of clay slide from around him and he watches the ripples breaking into each other on the surface of the water. He tries to follow one ripple and then another and another to their expanding end but this proves impossible. The white complains with a low nasal growl.

After a while, they seem both to have forgotten what it is that has brought them there. The cattle in the next field have fallen *silent. There is no sound but the brushing of their hooves through the long grass, sweeping ever closer, ever further away. It is hard to tell the difference until much later and closer to dusk that is almost a darkness in the boy's hiding place, and the pace and proximity of the brushing sounds tell that someone is hurrying not through Gun-Mahony's pastures but through the field behind the boy. He peers out.*

The field slopes upwards from the ditch and along the crest a young girl in a white dress floats. By her blonde ringlets he recognises Mary White. The dog looks out too and barks to be held back from a similar freedom to hers. The girl pauses, turns. She begins to walk towards them. The boy unsheathes the knife from his pocket and the white leaps away from a memory. Mary White pauses again a little way off and the boy imagines his own eyes, big and bright as a lamped rabbit's. He cannot stop himself from looking at her. He remembers her telling the Master at school that she is going to be a nun. Her eyes are holy even as they are frightened. The cattle start up again, too many of them, all sounding the same brute alarm. He wants to kill them. He wants to kill everything.

'What happened to you, Tom? All the blood?'

Only now does he notice that she is holding the box he carried home from school for her. A long time ago.

In the first weeks of the Truce no one knew anything for certain except, it seemed to Enright, that he should leave town and the sooner the better. With enough Jameson on board, he imagined that Mary had set an unlikely conspiracy in motion. Most nights, he and Timmoney had more than enough to drink and he saw her writing letter after letter. Dear Mr Donegan. Dear Mr Cullinane. Dear Captain Papenfus. Dear Head Constable Gallagher. Dear Mr Doggyman Foley. Dear bloody everybody but himself. Not a line from her since the Truce.

In the chorus of self-interested voices telling Enright to go, Jim Donegan's was the loudest of all.

'You want to keep the dogs behind my garage?'

Jim Donegan's office, a stone shed in what had once been a stable yard, stank thickly of oil and sharply of petrol fumes. The walls glistened with sweaty slug trails. A cladding of cobwebs, darkly permanent, filled the higher spaces. Donegan sat in a large armchair that was soggy with black garage-damp. A debris of paper scraps and open ledgers, with pages like distressed metal sheets, covered a rough-hewn tabletop.

Donegan repeated Enright's assertion as though it were a request. He tried to smile but the muscles buried in his heavy jowls twitched and pulled the smile apart. Enright's Jameson hangover was bad enough, but every day felt spoilt and sour to him now, hangover or not. A week into the Truce and the atmosphere on the streets had already changed. An airy optimism prevailed and the young, as always, were the first to take advantage. That very morning, he and Timmoney down the Watery Mall following up a complaint about young fellows

breaking the globes of the streetlamps there, had found five or
six shoeless waifs on the river bank behind the low mall wall.
Their spokesman defiantly insisted there was no police any
more – *me mudder said, until we get our own.* Clattered the
little pup across the ear. *Go home and tell your oul' one you got
a slap off the ghost of a policeman, so.*

'The dogs'll be safer here where I can keep an eye on them
from next door.'

'But, Tom, greyhounds need room or they'll go mad in the
night, howling. And the rebels'll be wondering why I let you
keep the dogs here.'

Perched on the rickety table, Enright paid little attention to
Donegan's complaints. The earlier incident still irritated him.
Until we get our own. The rumours had already begun to filter
down from the Midlands of trench-coated rebels daring in
broad daylight to patrol the streets, the RIC hiding in the barracks until they were gone and then taking their turn. Enright
was determined not to let that happen in his town. Nor let
their shady Republican Courts back into action again either,
with their cowboy law. At least in those Midland towns, he
thought, the rebels had begun to show their snouts. Not here.
Not a whisper of Kinahan or any of his go-boys. Johnny
Dooley still on the lam too since the night Enright battered
him. *Much as we'd like to, Tom, we can't touch them when they
start appearing back.* Gallagher's warning had a pretence of
exasperation. But a dark night, one to one, who was to know?

In the yard beyond the open door, Cullinane tinkered with
the engine of a smart, dark green car. Under the tan dungarees
streaked with a black finger-wipe or two, he wore a spotless
white shirt and brown tie. His flat cap, a tawny tweed, was a
cut above garage wear.

'Does that lad always dress up like a dog's dinner for work?
He looks more like a bank clerk than a mechanic.'

Today, everything about the world seemed to strain
Donegan's credibility.

'Tidiest man I ever met. He washes his hands after every job.'

Enright leaned down from the table towards Donegan. The big armchair trundled back unsteadily along the cobbled floor like the wheelchair they'd put Enright in over in Balfour, before he got up and walked to meet Mary in the sleeping porch the day of his ham-fisted marriage proposal. *Will we tie the knot, Mary, before the rope frays?*

'That fellow is too honest for his own good. I can't even let him price a job or I'd be gone broke in a week.'

'Is he a Shinner, do you think?'

'Not at all. He had a brother in the police below in West Cork. But he left the force and he's gone away foreign.'

No wonder Johnny Dooley had such an aversion to Cullinane. An RIC man in the family would be some dose for a patriot to swallow.

'Sensible man, if you ask me, Cullinane's brother. You'd be better off out of here too, Sergeant.'

Enright stood up from the makeshift desk and strolled across to the open door. Cullinane hadn't once looked in the direction of Donegan's office. Forget him, Enright told himself, he didn't matter. But ignored by the mechanic, it felt like he himself was the one who didn't matter any more. Whatever light was left in the shed when he closed the door seemed to be absorbed by the round suet-face at the desk, accentuating its liverishness. Donegan tried a busy, diversionary scrabble among the papers before him. Enright picked up Donegan by the loose cheek.

'Wouldn't it be grand and handy for you if I high-tailed it out of here?'

'I'm only saying you'd be safer away out of here, that's all. Everything that happened in the town since you came, you're getting the blame for it. Kinahan's awful cut up over Larry Healy. They were very close.'

Donegan's terrified self-pity sickened Enright and he released his grip on the jowls that were slithery with spittle. Saw the same wet wallowing in his father when his aunt brought him into Tralee jail. *Three bloody years, I'll never come out of here alive, will I?* Sensing that his father's tears were for himself and had nothing to do with him, the boy had kept his strange secret and not asked the question that haunted his nights. *Did you really cut the cattle, Da?*

'I'm only telling you what people are saying, Sergeant.'

Enright wiped his hands disgustedly along his trousers. The same the world over these small-time crooked merchants. Every port crawled with them. Heads down like Donegan's when you caught them out, feigning shame or fear to mask the greed that moved them, but the brain busy all the while calculating the price of release.

'I'm not finished here by a long shot and you're not finished helping me.'

'But what can I do for you now?'

'For a start, you can keep an ear to the ground for fellows boasting about their heroics.'

'Do you honestly think anyone's going to boast about shooting a gom in the back of the head or crippling a young one?'

'I know who crippled her but I want to know who made her pregnant.'

Crouched low over his desk, the big man shook his head, though not in refusal.

'Why? What does it matter to you who the father was? Sure, it could be anybody. She was a pretty little thing, Sergeant, but she knew it and she'd do anything to rope in some foolish old widower or bachelor.'

'You're a bachelor yourself, aren't you, Donegan?'

'I am, but I'm no fool and those Shinner boys aren't either. Listen, Sergeant, there's some things a fellow can't find out. That's just the way of the world. It doesn't always add up, does it?'

He held two handfuls of paper scraps aloft as if to prove his point and Enright smiled at the Tipperary Daibutsu's risible venture into philosophy.

'And I want to know who burned my dog. I'll haunt those buggers and you along with them until I get the answers.'

Out in the cobbled yard, Enright stepped across rainbow-slicked puddles of oil to where Cullinane immersed himself in the bowels of a motor engine. He watched closely to see if his presence brought a shake to the big-knuckled hands but noticed only their strength amid the snares of rubber and metal. Marshall had once tried to make an engineer of Enright aboard the *Torrence*, Manchester to Port Said. Fireman lost a hand freeing up a piston and the old goat persuaded him to go down below with the black gang. *What the hell kind of work can a deck man do ashore apart from stevedoring, but get yourself fireman's papers, Tommy lad, work up to engineer and you got yourself a trade.* Couldn't make sense of the big lump of an engine and never made it beyond coal-passer.

'Why didn't you tell me your brother was a policeman?'

Cullinane straightened up and, taking an oily rag from the pocket of his dungarees, wiped his hands with a slow thoroughness.

'I wasn't hiding anything. I thought you'd know, I suppose.'

'Was he a closet rebel or just another gutless coward afraid he'd get shot? Where's he hiding himself anyway?'

'He went to America. He did the sensible thing, I think.'

'You think so, do you? And I suppose you think I should run away too, do you?'

Cullinane stepped back and raised his palms defensively though his eyes stayed neutral.

'That's your own business, Sergeant.'

'Damn right it is.' Enright swallowed back a few worrying skips of breathlessness that left him feeling faint. He steadied himself with a hand on the door of the motor car. 'For your information, Cullinane, I've been everywhere from Canada to China and I don't care for any of it.'

He lifted his feet carefully as he walked away because the cobblestones might easily catch a fellow off-guard and some fool he'd have looked then. He put the shortness of breath down to the smokes and the Jameson, but come that evening he and Timmoney didn't drink any less than on the previous one.

Then a couple of days later, Papenfus offered his advice. Enright thought the Boer had already shipped out, so that he imagined this was a return rather than a farewell. Not that it made much difference to the mood of Enright's day anyway. He'd just spent ten minutes yelling at two constables he'd sent to look into the robbery at the railway station of a box of tools and a couple of shovels because he'd been too busy filling out Monthly Report forms for Gallagher to go up there himself. The pair had let themselves get a silent run-around that could only mean the robbery was the work of the rebels and no one dared answer their questions. He wrote up the constables' report himself, declaring the incident a breach of the Truce. The first. At last. See what Gallagher made of that, with a face on him these days like all his troubles were over and he about to be assumed into heaven as a bonus. He couldn't wait to see who the rebels would put up as Area Liaison Officer under the Truce arrangement. He hoped it would be Kinahan but doubted it.

On his way to spoil Gallagher's day with the report, he met Papenfus in the corridor near the day room. The Boer's nut-brown skin healthily flushed, he was back to his old blustering self again as he peeled off his leather gloves and offered a hand.

'Howzit? Came to apologise for that night at Castle Bennett before I go. Damn well deserved that *klap*. No hard feelings, Tom, eh?'

Enright kept his hands to himself.

'Where you running off to?'

'Back over to Edinburgh. I believe I may try medicine again.'

'Better get the shake out of your hand then or you'll do more damage than you ever did in a uniform.'

'Ag, Tom, why stay? Nothing left to chase here but your tail.'

The narrow corridor offered no way past Papenfus if Enright was to get to the Head Constable's office. He walked deliberately towards the Auxie officer. Papenfus held his ground until Enright was almost upon him but the forced swagger had already left his compact bearing. Enright passed him by.

'Tom, you don't belong in this country any more. Believe me, I know what it's like to come home after years on the trek. You tell your folks, your friends, about the wonders of the wide world and it's a bloody personal insult.'

'Vamoose, Pap.'

'You've seen more of the world than any man I ever met. For Christ's sake, if you can't find somewhere to go, who the hell can? And you've got a woman who's crossed an ocean to be with you. And a son. Can't you see you've got everything a man could want?'

Enright blamed the mention of Mary for the sudden sweep of loneliness he felt. The handle of Gallagher's door occurred to his fist as though out of darkness. He got himself inside the Head Constable's office but Gallagher wasn't there. He waited for Papenfus to pass along the corridor. Damn fool Boer, he thought, to imagine a killer could become a healer.

Gallagher was nowhere to be found until later that evening and, vacillating as ever, he played down the railway station incident.

'Tom, there's young lads queuing up to join the rebels these times and Kinahan's probably letting them prove themselves by stealing a few shovels and the like. Isn't it keeping them from doing worse?'

August became a long doldrum of a month. Warm, though nothing like the heat Enright had known in his days of wandering. Not nearly hot enough to roast the chill that persisted in his bones or the portentous inner quaking that had never altogether relented since the night of his collapse. Evenings on Main Street, and especially those early night hours beyond the old curfew hour of nine o'clock, took on the dimensions of a celebratory outdoorness. Naples came to mind, but without the colours or the careless extroversion. The Galeria on Via Roma. Darkly beautiful women and simmering men strolling or drinking coffee and liqueurs; policemen dressed up to the nines like vaudeville generals, all gold braid and epaulettes; the brightly coloured spokes and rims of street-cart wheels. Yet, music and laughter and a heightening of spirits there was. Fellows sitting on shop windowsills playing fiddles or melodeons; girls dancing impromptu polkas; bare-foot children running wild along the dusty packed-earth streets. Enright himself, whenever he walked among them, felt like he was walking through another man's dream, seeming to inspire not even a second look, and there were brief moments when he almost allowed himself to forget that he was certainly being watched and forget who he was watching out for. Kinahan, Dooley and their pals, now parading around in puttees and trench coats pretending to be policemen.

One balmy evening he stood just beyond a small crowd who'd gathered to hear an old fellow, in out of the bogs from the rough, cracked-leathery cut of him, play jigs on a concertina. His mother's instrument, the concertina. She played with the same wistful detachment she brought to kneading dough on the kitchen table or scrubbing clothes on the washboard. The old fellow displayed a similar though happier self-absorption as he winked a greeting at the latest listener to join the circle, even swapped words mid-tune. Another evening, a nervy and rest-less Timmoney at his side this time – *That fellow over there is watching us, Tom, I'd swear it* – he stopped outside Moloney's pub and listened to a last verse and chorus of 'The Kerry Dances'. The young man's lilting tenor voice, too chirpily effeminate but clear and true, loosened the grip of agitation on his mind for a good hour after. Let the song sing away in him until all the words were retrieved from memory as they walked down the Main Street, across the Watery Mall and up to Friary Street.

Back at the barracks, the song stayed outside the back door and all he was left with, on that and every other evening, was Mary's continuing silence, Timmoney's swinging moods, and more Jameson. Most mornings if it hadn't been for the dogs, in their first weeks of training for the coursing season, he'd have stayed in the straw.

'The white's flying it. And the others'll be grand once they settle in the garage.'

Foley was clearly relieved to have the dogs off his hands during the night hours. Arrow Valley Snow had taken to the confinement in Donegan's yard well enough, not being used to much better up at the cottage in Roscrea, but the others never stopped yelping.

'They'd want to start settling soon or the whole street'll be up in arms over the racket.'

The two men stood by the gutted shed at Lady's Well that still smelled of smoke and petrol, watching the dogs rip to red-stringed shreds the leashed hare they'd been chasing all the long, warm afternoon. Sharp-fanged and furious, they punished the hare for the frustrations they'd endured at Foley's hands as he brought them time after time to the moment of the kill and then denied it them. He honed down their instincts for food and revenge and running to the one instinct for which neither he nor Enright had a precise name.

'Is he as good as the black?'

'Not yet but he will be and better. He was wicked stiff. That fellow in Roscrea wasn't walking him half enough.'

Enright kicked a heel into the dry earth.

'Are you sure the ground's not too hard for him? Should we find a softer field?'

Foley stepped gingerly away from Enright's side to find the safety from which to object to the slight.

'The whole country's dried up. What'ye want me to do? Piss all over the field before they start running or what?'

Then he stepped further away as though he needed an even greater no-man's-land between them for whatever he was preparing to say next. Enright's cigarette hand stayed at his lips, the smoke hovering dangerously close to his bad eye. Foley sucked on his own cigarette for courage.

'Is there any point in it at all, Sergeant?'

'In what?'

'Me. Training your dogs. For October, like. October's a long way off.' Foley pumped himself up, primed the well of words stuck somewhere between his chest and the stub of cigarette clamped between his teeth. 'I'd say things might be very different by October, Sergeant. I'd nearly put money on the whole business being sorted out.'

'Would you now?'

No further succour to be had from the cigarette, Foley spat it out. Such was the silence in the field that Enright could hear the hiss of the stub in the grass. Down at the centre of the field, the dogs had separated, each to enjoy its share of the sundered hare. The white had the best part of a torso; the others fed on scraps of legs and ears.

'And I suppose you'd be advising me to be on my way, would you now?'

'If I was in your boots, Sergeant, I'd be gone so fast you wouldn't even remember I was here in the first place.'

Enright picked up a charred lath from the ruins of the shed and advanced on Foley.

'There's no call for that now, Sergeant.'

The doggyman's voice rang so shrilly he might have been attempting to sing. Even the dogs looked briefly away from their meat to see what shape of an animal made such a noise and what shape of an animal caused it to cry out.

Enright tossed the lath aside.

'And if I was in your boots, Foley, I'd buy myself a new pair.'

The general indolence in the barracks through the weeks that followed hadn't extended to the Head Constable. Unlike those who'd remained enervated by their conviction that the Government had betrayed them or by mere war-weariness, he had come to regard the Truce as an opportunity to redeem the force's honour. *We've a chance now, lads, to be proper policemen again and we'll show that crowd in Dublin Castle we haven't lost our sense of decency and duty, even if they have.* When the word came in about the stolen car, Enright couldn't wait to get into Gallagher's office and see the thick moustache and the big spiky eyebrows droop once again in despair. He swept into the paper-musty room, feigning a gravity that was at odds with the high excitement he felt.

'A spot of bother out in Barnane, sir. The rector's car stolen – by order of the IRA.'

He slapped the scrap of paper, delivered a few minutes earlier by the rector's gardener, on Gallagher's desk.

> The motor car, property of Rev. Andrew Thimson, is hereby requisitioned and will be returned as soon as possible in mint condition – By Order of the IRA.

'Requisitioned, what?'

Struck again by the odd recurrence of that word which had taken so long to come to him as he'd planned to grab Arrow Valley Snow, Enright saw slab-faced Paddy Kinahan struggling for inspiration and coming up with the same term he himself had found. His heart thumped too hard against his chest and he told himself to sit down and did.

'The rector won't be driving that car any more, sir.'

Gallagher turned over to the blank side of the paper, seeming to examine it as closely as the front.

'It's a clear breach, sir. No ifs or buts about it.'

To Enright's surprise, Gallagher gathered himself quickly. There was no further protest, only a thoughtful interlude during which the Head Constable's eyes, damp with age, darted everywhere but on Enright, as though following the logic of a many-sided argument. Enright was unsettled by the sense of his presence having been forgotten.

'You're right. We can't overlook this. A proper gentleman the Reverend Thimson is too. What kind of guttersnipes are they at all?'

'You'll pass the report on to DI Johnstone then?'

'No, I'm acting DI for a while. Mr Johnstone's gone up to Galway. His wife died and the truth is . . . well, it seems he fell apart entirely. You think you know a man, eh? He might be gone a fair while, I believe.'

The description of the insouciant ex-Irish Guard's grief perturbed Enright further. When he looked at Gallagher, he didn't like what he saw. A confidence at once smug and self-effacing. A fellow with a whip, making out he wasn't going to use it, Enright thought.

'Sit down a minute, Sergeant, we didn't have a decent chat in ages.'

Gallagher brought the flats of his hands together as if in prayer and rested his chin on the steeple of fingers. Enright's neck veered towards a spasm.

'Timmoney doesn't look a well man to me. Is he drinking a lot, do you think?'

'He takes the odd drop but his work is the finest.'

'Trying to keep up with those Tan lads, I suppose? What's bothering him?'

'God.'

Gallagher was offended at the perceived facetiousness but it was true. While sober, the young constable seethed with a fraught despair. *I can't close my eyes, Tom, but Baldwin's swinging there in front of me.* Only in whiskey or the prospect of it did trust in his God's mercy return. *I suppose there's men that done worse and were forgiven, isn't there, Tom?*

'I'm sending him up home to Tyrone for a few weeks on sick leave. See if that'll straighten him out. He has his whole life in front of him and I've no intention of letting him ruin it in my barracks. I care about my men. They're the only family I have.'

Enright stirred uncomfortably in his seat, hunching his shoulders to keep his neck muscles in check.

'You might have talked to me first.'

The last thing a fellow needed was to be back among his own too soon. Nothing worse than home to remind him how far he'd strayed from innocence.

'You weren't down home yourself for a while. How's the missus? And the young lad? He must be a fine big fellow by now.'

'Are you telling me to take some time off too?'

'I am.' Gaining in sincerity as it deepened beyond the initial pretence, Gallagher's descent into mellowness infuriated Enright. 'Two years was all I got with poor Agnes and no child. I often wonder what would it be like, you know, putting a fishing rod in a young lad's hands for the first time or teaching him to swim down in Dunmore East where my own father taught me. You should take the family down there some time. A lovely place with the sea and all. I still have relations below. You can take next week off. Timmoney's going today.'

'I'm not going anywhere. Not until we sort out this stolen car.'

'That business will go on for weeks yet. The rebels have no local Liaison Officer appointed yet. There's a fellow below in Cork dealing with it and that'll take time.'

Enright assented grudgingly. No point, he decided, in giving the impression that things weren't right between himself and Mary, and tempt the bugger to poke around even more in his business.

'And, Sergeant, take the train. You're abusing that car of ours no end.'

'And make a sitting duck of myself for the rebels? Not bloody likely.'

Enright endured the last week of August bereft of drinking company. He might have joined in with some of the younger fellows but they'd be on the floor after a few shots and full of youthful bluster in the meanwhile. Except for Harvey, but he invariably maddened Enright with his secrecy over who he was and where he came from. *Been running all my life, Sergeant, but not from anything I done wrong.*

Drinking alone was something a fellow had to get used to all over again. After Marshall and Clancy and Gabriel Jack, it had been a hell of a lot tougher knowing they'd never be back. Still, it turned the whiskey sour not to have some harmless old nonsense to chat about that wasn't the wild nonsense spinning around in a fellow's head. Nothing to joke away the bitter twist inside that came after the first few shots of Jameson when the mind still floated freely like a bald eagle catching the breeze above Morning Mountain.

Timmoney and his books had always been worth a laugh and a sneer when Enright was getting tight and the young fellow had grown more amiable about his sergeant's scepticism. From time to time, Enright had even shut himself up and listened to the stories of the books, which were sometimes quite absorbing, though he knew that only a fool could take them seriously. A woman jumping under a train out of love or shame or spite, he couldn't tell. A fellow worrying himself to death over killing a lad and letting his God catch him when the police couldn't.

God had still been good for a laugh too with Timmoney and, when Enright felt really crabbed, there was always the subject of women and the young constable's embarrassed discomfort at stories of La Cheposa and other whores. He regretted that sourness now and the sneering and wished he hadn't been so hard on Timmoney but knew no other way to get a young fellow's mind off eternal damnation than to mock the preciousness of his God-bothered conscience.

A few glasses now, however, up in his paraffin-reeking room and he was stuffing the bottle back in his kit box and returning to the midnight manoeuvres through the town's back lanes he'd once delighted in.

Each night he donned his scuffed plimsolls and went down first by the river walk behind the houses on Cathedral Street to spend a while looking up the long garden at Dooley's house. He wondered which window was Bridie's and whether she dreamed of Cullinane or lay awake worrying over her brother's aversion to the smooth Kerryman's flawed pedigree. Wondered too where that brother of hers was hiding and when he'd show his face again. From there, he would make his way to the lane behind Healy's pub, watching to see if the rebels dared use the place again for their pow-wows. Sometimes, he'd check out the furniture store where the Republican Court had held its sessions before his intervention, and other buildings they'd used before his arrival in town. The Christian Brothers School, the Pipe Band Hall on New Street. But after a few more ports of call, he found himself each night at the one destination. Helen Peters's stone shed.

Four nights Enright stood there at the small high window and dreamed of avenging the wrong done to her, of emptying the Colt and the Webley into eyes, mouths, genitals. Finally, on a night devoid of stars or shadows, as he played the front rails of the Union Workhouse softly as a harp, he decided to go inside. Flakes of rusted lead paint fell in a faint, tinny rustle. An exquisite tension flooded through him, made him want to piss and he did so, through the rails. Inside, he jumped a pebbled path as though it were a stream, tiptoed along the grass margin.

The window of the girl's shed was no larger than a quarter-folded broadsheet. Its glass pane had a crack on the top left-hand corner that he didn't remember seeing before. He tested the fractured glass with the tip of a forefinger and felt a gap big enough to let the night air carry its cold inside. He pressed his face to the window but saw nothing. Reaching down to where the handle of the door should have been, he found instead a heavy sliding bolt that seemed to him an indignity too far.

As he slid back the bolt, he imagined that in some small way he was releasing Helen Peters, rather than indulging his own foolish desire to see her. The pitch of the metal's slack harmonies recalled her saving screams. He eased the door inwards and the heavy timbers gave way with an unexpected solicitude and closed behind him as noiselessly. The denser darkness took some time to adjust to and the riot inside him even longer to subside. At last, her breathing became faintly audible and her outline composed itself. He became aware of the strong perfume of sweet-pea flowers and wondered if it was Dooley's hunchbacked aunt who'd brought them.

'Who's there?'

No terror resided in the girl's voice, but rather a dreamy hopefulness and an intimacy that suggested she had been expecting a caller.

'Don't worry yourself, miss. I'm a policeman doing my rounds. I thought I heard someone poking around outside when I was passing.'

A faint glistening of teeth, of lips and eyes arose from the darkness before him like lights on a far shore.

'Is it very late or very early? I never seem to know.'

'Late enough. But I never carry a watch when I'm out or I'd always be looking at the time and wondering will I ever be finished. You didn't hear anything, by any chance, any noises or . . .'

He stanched the silly effusiveness, wondering why his face burned as violently as when the polish had been daubed all over it. Only a girl, he told himself, a poor cripple of a thing, the worst stab at a miracle any gom of a God ever made.

'No.'

Her breathing became inaudible and Enright felt the same panic of listening those first nights to the newborn child down in Listowel. Mary listening too and not a word spoken between them.

'Miss?'

The girl sighed. He heard the brush of her hair across the pillow and was startled. He had imagined she couldn't move at all. But of course she could move, move something.

'I didn't hear nothing in the night for a good while now. People used be coming to the window for a gawk at me first but they don't bother any more.'

The flame rose on his cheeks and he began to feel damp all over, only then realising how much colder it was in the stone shed than outside, cold as the sleeping porch in the Balfour San.

'They don't have much to be doing, miss.'

'I thought I heard shots one night. They told me I was dreaming. Maybe I was, because I thought I seen a ghost up at the window that night too. Would you get me a sup of water, sir? If you light the lamp, there's a jug beside me somewhere.'

Enright fingered the matchbox clumsily. The struck match flared and guttered out quickly. He prised another from the rattling box and, steadying his fingers, cupped the new light in the curve of his palm. The oil lamp stood on a súgán chair by the bed and, beside it, a tin jug covered with muslin and a rough delph mug. He removed the globe from the lamp, wound up the wick and lit it. Blue-edged flame took hold, thin spirals of black smoke spun upwards and caught him off guard with an astringent battlefield odour. When his vision cleared, it was to a light dulled and jaundiced by the scorched yellow glass of the lamp globe.

It should have been an unflattering light, shadows cast along her face the filthy grey of angry clouds. Much as she'd been in his thoughts, he hadn't remembered at all precisely the perfect symmetry of her dark eyebrows, her long-curved eyelashes, the singular perfection of the nose, the mouth, the slight pout of the upper lip, the pearls within.

'Thank you, sir. I'm a nuisance.'

She gazed up into the cobwebbed well of the ceiling with a kind of unaffected yearning that was divinely sad to Enright. He lifted the jug and set aside the square of muslin on its top.

She found Enright in the corner of her eye and her head fell
softly to the side so that she faced him. Her look bore the same
sleepy candour as her speech.

'You're Sergeant Enright, aren't you?'

Dizzied by her recognition of him, he floundered again. It
seemed even more inexplicable to him now that he'd not been
aware of the girl's existence before the day of the ambush.

'That's me. From County Kerry. Listowel, do you know it?'

'I was never outside County Tipperary. Imagine that.'

Enright filled the mug and approached her. His hand
burrowed gently through the long dark tresses, silky to the eye
but wiry to the touch. Her scent rose and so keenly vegetative
was it, so pure and unadorned, that it seemed to him more
exotic than the sweet peas or any other flower. He found the
nape of her neck and was taken aback by the heat residing
there and the slow, strong pulse that filled his palm like drops
of warm water. His arm, held stiffly at an acutely awkward
angle, ached in premonition of the pain he might cause her.

'I hope I don't hurt you.'

'I'm used to being handled rougher.'

She returned his self-conscious smile weakly as though it
were a gesture she was learning anew by imitation. Her head
felt heavy in his hand when he raised her towards the mug. The
bed sheet slipped down a few inches, revealing a threadbare
cotton smock and a bared shoulder. She drank thirstily and
from the corners of her mouth the water trickled along her
chin, over her neck and down into the depths below. He
wondered at what precise point of her long neck, or lower, the
sensation of that trickling flow ended and how strange that
must have felt.

Descending further, the disturbed bed sheet released a more
acrid odour; a stale concoction made of sleep and sweat and
urine and, underlying it, the humming fishy smell of cor-
ruption, of her wasting away. The smell of Marshall's decay.
Cursed whores, Tommy lad, damn them all and that crooked

whore in Barcelona, the worst of the lot. But passing down the
Suez Canal in that long funereal procession, hoving to every few
hours to make way until Ismailia, through Great Bitter Lake
and on to the Strait of Bab el Mandeb, Enright had turned on
the old fellow, knowing they'd shared the same whores more or
less for a year or more, Marshall leading the way from one
brothel to the next. *If I pick up whatever clap you got, I swear I'll
kill you.* And Marshall's answer, out of the first calm in the
storm of his dying. *I wish to Christ you would, Tommy lad.*

The girl coughed and gagged, setting the nerves in his arm
jangling.

'Have you enough?'

'I have. Thank you, sir.' She lay back on his hand. Her neck
moved from side to side against the flesh of his palm, her eyes
closed momentarily as though there was pleasure for her in his
touch. 'You can put me down now.'

Realising she had merely been trying to release herself back
on to the pillow, he eased her down and withdrew his hand
slowly so as not to jolt her. He closed his hand to keep the
memory of her warmth there as he chased his glance from the
bare shoulder.

'I'd better be motoring on then. Will I leave your lamp lit for
you?'

His sudden high-spiritedness rang false as she stared at the
ceiling again.

'You can quench it.'

Enright tried to compose his goodbyes and they were all
wrong or silly or downright callous. Good luck to you then.
Time I hit the road, so. I'll leave you alone then.

'Goodbye so, Miss Peters.'

'Helen. I used hear terrible things about you, Sergeant, but I
don't believe the half of it now.'

'My bark is worse than my bite, girl.'

'I suppose they used be talking about me too. At the dances
I always knew they were watching me.'

'Admiring you, I'd say.'

'No. Running me down. The only way I could forget was to dance faster and wider until I was pure dizzy. I know it must sound foolish but I miss the dancing more than anything else.'

Enright turned the wick on the lamp, drawing the gloom down upon her. He thought about adjusting the bed sheet over her shoulder but couldn't bring himself to. Blanketed in darkness, she called out more urgently as if he had already vanished with the light.

'Will you say a prayer to the bleeding statue for me if you're ever in Templemore? I never got over to see it.'

It seemed incredible to him that she knew nothing of that young chancer over in Templemore and his red-ink chicanery, in spite of the regular visits of Dooley's hunchbacked aunt and of those who came to clean and feed her. Maybe they were protecting her from the irony of her hapless pursuit of a fake divinity or protecting themselves from the memory of their own gullibility.

'You never know. You might get to see it yet.'

'I might. I might be saved, mightn't I?'

'I should be off. I've a stretch to do yet.'

'Will you call in again if you have the time, some time?'

'I will. If I get the chance. Busy times, you know.'

'Will we ever have peace do you think, Sergeant?'

Heading back towards the barracks, Enright felt himself too large and throbbing a thing for true stealth. An inexplicable panic took root in him, yet he could neither hurry nor stop to think, until he found himself breaking into the Stella Cinema. He had no idea why, even as he pulled asunder the rusting careless bit of a lock.

A series of long windows along one side of the hall offered a desultory impression of light. He padded along by the central passage through the seating, and sitting on the stool before

Bridie Dooley's piano, lifted the lid. He touched a finger to one of the keys, which felt cool and hard at first but soon had a creamy give to it that invited pressing. A book of sheet music lay open before him, the barely visible notation as incomprehensible to him as the senseless scratchings in Danny Egan's notebook. Enright hated not knowing these secret codes that others understood.

His hands were of no use to the piano and the music waiting to be released from it. Might as well be dead hands or Helen Peters's hands for all the good they were, except to punch with or pull a trigger. He thought that if by some miracle he could wrest music from out of that script and those keys he would be at once happy and tremendously sad but, either way, relieved of the cramps that beset his stomach, his chest, his neck, his very brain. He had always liked watching musicians in action. How they concentrated at first and then, note by note, their eyes easing from a gaze to a daze and away further until the music wasn't something they were making but a thing that was happening to them. All his life, he thought, he had found nothing with which to so utterly empty his mind and yet be so fully, so vividly alive.

He turned over the pages of the music book to read the cover. With a hand over the bad eye that had begun to leak like a tap, he eventually deciphered the Gothic script. *Mendelssohn – Songs Without Words*. No such a thing, he thought, unless you counted that Okanagan yelping of Gabriel Jack's. *No wonder you own that song, Gabe, who else in the name of Jaysus would want it?* His laugh threatened to volley out through the big barn as another amusing memory offered itself up. Another song without words.

Marshall the whistler. Loudest whistle he'd ever heard out of a man, plain as your ear fore to aft in a following gale. Whistling his party piece, 'Moonlight Bay', in a bar in Valletta and Enright contemplating the Barracca Superiore pink with evening. Marshall soused as a goat and swaying like the air

about him was seawater until halfway through the tune he
stopped whistling, cursed himself crimson as he explained why.
Can't remember the flaming words, Tommy lad.

Enright smiled but other memories of Marshall intruded.
*Some night when I'm sleeping, Tommy lad, do me in before I lose
my marbles with the pain in my lad.* The piano lid, as he closed
it, seemed heavier than earlier. He tried a few bars of a song in
his head as he went out on to Friary Street towards the barracks
because he felt he must be going soft or mad again breaking into
the cinema and because his legs were making such heavy work
of dragging him along. *I know my love by his way of walking/
And I know my love by his way of talking.* No use. Nothing
could distract him from the bilious emptiness within.

Maybe tomorrow, down in Listowel, Mary would have given
up trying for the moon and there'd be some peace to be had
for a few days and nights. Maybe even a bit of the other. If
she didn't mind too much. Before it was too late to bother
any more.

The cottage had been transformed. Gone were the high waves of bramble that had engulfed the front garden and clawed maddeningly at the window frames on windy nights. The high laurel hedges to each side, no longer crazily out of line, had been tamed into a neat box shape. Flowers, long covered in webs of thorny vegetation, had begun to peep through to the light. The magenta of wild English roses, the rich yellows and reds of marigolds bordering the path mere suggestions yet, a tentative spray of colour against the newly whitewashed walls, a promise of Madeira brightness. Front gate and window frames alike blazed with fresh scarlet paint.

Enright peeled the damp shirt free from his back, loosened his tie and collar, and carrying the suit coat over his shoulder, crossed the narrow road to the gate. In a patch of strawy grass by the path to the cottage door, the child sat on a grey army blanket and played with a biscuit tin. Busy hands reached out, but the bare, kicking feet pushed the tin further away. The child's hair was the same yellowy white as the spiky grass that hadn't yet greened after its disinterment from under the brambles. Swaying forward and back, as if on an invisible rocking chair, Enright's son chased the tin teetering between happiness and frustration. Then he noticed the long shadow hovering on the grass alongside him and exploded into a terrified scream as he toppled forward. Too far away to intervene, Enright watched as the child's forehead met the edge of the tin. In an instant, Mary appeared at the open door and ran to the child. Her eyes recovered from their surprise at her husband's presence, she seemed vibrant and summery again in the red-and-white dress she wore, and he wondered why.

'He fell before I . . . '

'Oh, he's always falling. Aren't you, Jerry?'

'He's not marked, is he?'

'There's a bit of a bump, isn't there, Jerry? You little scally-wag, what'll we do with you?'

Any moment now she would look up at Enright, because that was her way, fiddling about as she steeled herself. There had been a time when he liked that shy habit but he knew it wasn't about shyness any more. The child was calming down, surrendering to Mary's soft talk, letting itself be pampered into amusement by her nose rubbing against his. She turned to Enright, smiling, ready.

'It's nice to see you in the suit.'

'I was wearing it last time.'

'I mustn't have noticed. Will we show your daddy what you can do now?'

She lowered the child's kicking feet towards the blanket and when they got there they curled up to grab the cloth as if not yet sure of their true purpose. The bandy sea-legs wobbled and the child held on to whatever part of Mary it could find. A breast, an arm, a knee, and then nothing. Mary skittered backwards on her knees and the child found his balance and followed her, stamping along like a diminutive Okanagan dancing up a spirit guide until he fell excitedly into his mother's arms.

'Jimmy was over here the other day and I was in the kitchen. And the next thing he let out a shout and I ran out because I thought Jerry was hurt and all it was when I came out was Jerry walking. I was so sorry though not to see his first step.'

The child watched Enright cautiously as it pressed against Mary and was lifted upwards. A flicker of recognition emerged but quickly receded. Enright smiled tentatively, to no avail.

'The place is looking grand. I hope you weren't killing your-self working.'

She stepped onto the path and walked ahead of him. It felt like a spiritless procession.

'Jimmy did it himself. He's getting married, so he'll be wanting the place.'

'He's hardly out of short pants. When's the big day?'

'October or November. The girl's a Fitzgerald from Tarbert. She's very nice.'

All neat and tidy, Enright thought, the vague wedding plans pumped up into urgency with the renovations just to put the skids under him. Mary was inside the cottage and he lost sight of her for a moment in the cavernous dark.

'We can find some place else around here, can't we?'

Mary sat at the kitchen table looking tired, tired even of the child's clinging and climbing all over her. She shook her head dispiritedly.

'Or in the town. You'd still be near your mother.'

With the fingers of her free hand she gathered breadcrumbs, making little hillocks of them, razing them. She began to cry silently. The child looked dumbfoundedly from her tears to Enright, trying to make the connection.

'Why does everything have to be so rotten?'

'What do you mean?'

'You were right about Toussaint. Mags left him. She caught him worse this time and she won't have him back.'

In other circumstances, Enright might have delighted in the slick Frenchy's unmasking. Instead, he found himself discomfited by a dangerous precedent. He'd always expected that Toussaint would leave Mags in the lurch and not vice versa. He suspected that this was Mary's trick, twisting the story to her own ends, making a threat of it.

'He probably walked out on her, more like it.'

'Are you saying I made it up? Do you want to read the letter, Tom?'

She seemed more angry than hurt, though there was enough hurt there too to convince Enright and leave him regretful.

Losing herself in the child's needs again, she wiped its dripping nose and made it more comfortable on her shoulder.

'Just as well they've no children, I suppose.'

'Really? A child might be some consolation to her.'

'Money-wise, I mean. Since she'll have to make out on her own.'

Piled upon the tears and the dreary exhaustion, her bitterness made her repulsive to him.

'I should be grateful so, is it, for your blood money?' She wiped the tears roughly away to examine him more closely; or to confirm, perhaps, what it was she was seeing. 'Were you in that murder gang above in Tipperary, like Jimmy says you were? Tell me it's not true, Tom, make me believe it's not true.'

Not the same thing, Enright thought, and wondered if she knew it wasn't either. He held himself perfectly still, teeth clenched to keep the muscles of his face from wavering, shoulders clenched to stop his neck from twitching. He introduced a melancholic slackening in his eyes to counter her impression of his silence. Only when he saw her retreat from naked accusation did he allow himself to speak.

'Must be true if Jimmy said it. He's your brother, isn't he? I'm only your husband.'

'Can we not just go, Tom? Isn't it finished now?'

'Does Jimmy think it is? Have they thrown away their guns?'

The child wanting to rub noses again, banged its forehead in awkward haste continually against hers. Nothing the child did seemed to cause her pain.

'I don't want to talk about it now, Tom.'

'Do I come home whingeing about what they did to our lads, to our friends, to innocent young . . . Am I supposed to run off and let them away with it?'

'Not in front of Jerry. Please.'

'He hasn't a bull's notion what we're saying.'

'He knows the way we're saying it.'

Mary cuddled the child closer, infuriating Enright with a jealousy he knew was infantile even as it seized hold of him.

'You wanted us to talk and now you're hiding behind the child.'

'His name is Jerry. Can you not say it or will you not let yourself or what? I've plenty to say, Tom, plenty. When I'm good and ready.'

'Have you now?'

Enright felt his neck begin to act up and allowed one stretch of it, but one was never enough. He stood up so abruptly that the child's head snapped around and its grip on Mary tightened.

'I have. Plenty. And another thing, Mags isn't on her own, so stick that in your pipe and smoke it, Mister Enright.'

'Call me when the dinner's ready. I'll be out the back.'

Beyond the hedge at the far end of the cottage acre, Enright sat considering the downward glide of a solitary seagull all the way in from Ballybunion, he supposed, and stared at the clear sky long after the gull had gone. *The self-same sky.* Captain Big Toe one sudden morning bright and strange with birdsong behind Courcelette, telling how it was the same sky that Homer knew and that the generations to come would know. *The self-same sky we and our children roofed under once.*

We and our children? Not their first-born. An awful pity what happened to the little thing, named for Martin Fuller or not. Stripped to the waist, he'd dug through four feet of packed snow to hack out two miserable feet of frozen earth. The blanketed bundle soggy with Mary's blood. And that last petrified glance, the blanket unrolling from the purple face, anguished, simian, like Enright's dead sibling but his poxy fault this time. Afraid to go back into the shack and find her dead too and thinking, *Jesus Christ, why did I let her marry a pox-ridden old sailor and soldier the likes of me?*

For two nights and three days, Enright and his wife disregarded each other stubbornly. He refused to speak at all and Mary's cooing, nonsense talk became so emptied of emotion that the child sank into a puzzled quietude. The reach of an arm became their no-man's-land by day, the reach of a hand by night.

In bed, Mary lay rigid and clenched, while Enright came to feel strangely at ease, every muscle tingling pleasantly so that there were moments when his mind was emptied of the darker thoughts and he felt as though he were floating. He was reminded of those nights in the Balfour San when he knew he was coming right; the wounds, the constriction in his chest and neck, and the pain behind the bad eye, all sloughed off. He found himself dreaming nightly of Arrow Valley Snow, of reaching for silver trophies and raising them, until, on the third night, it was Mary he held and she was upon him before he woke, her mouth on his and her pubic hair scratching his penis from beneath her nightdress, filling him with a forgotten lust.

At first, he surrendered to the sweet, lazy surprise, letting himself grow hard against her and almost falling back to sleep on the tide of easeful delight. Then his hand chanced upon her sleek thigh and the first of the confusion came with the un-familiar silky feel of her nightdress. He became less urgent and couldn't hold on to the pretence of sleepy unselfconsciousness.

She'd never sat astride him before and he'd never wanted her to. He couldn't see her in the curtained dark of the coach bed but was unmanned by images of pendulous, wrinkled, bruised paps; the smell of semen, sweat and cheap perfume, of La Cheposa, of Helen Peters. He squeezed her buttocks too sharply and her small cry resounded in the roof of his mouth from the lips she pressed on his. He took her by the shoulders and put her down on her side of the bed, touching the silk again and an anger that began inexplicably in his fingertips. It was a question now of not letting himself down, of proving himself upon her or, the thought insinuating itself wildly, of letting his hands go at her throat. He struggled to contain the ferment in his murderous hands and the obscure fear that the touch of her nightdress induced in him. As he lowered himself between her legs, she began to wriggle and he suspected that it might not be resistance, as it sometimes had been of late, but playfulness, which it had never been. Her voice tinkled girlishly as on that long-ago summer lane.

'Maybe I don't want to.'

'What?'

'I mightn't be in the mood, Mister Enright.'

Her moist centre evaded him and he grasped his cock to direct it but she was chuckling like the whore he failed with back in Hastings, the first one after Clancy copped it. He squeezed himself hard, hurting himself to a final thrust and went down on her. His cock skidded along her pubic hair, the tip tearing painfully and sending shudders through him.

'Will you stop hopping around like a Hong Kong whore?'

His semen shot out over her belly and only the faintest tickle of pleasure was his at the release. He fell back on to the bed, muffling his neck spasms in the folds of the pillow.

'What were you at, jumping on me like that?'

'I thought you wanted to. You started it. You touched me.'

'I was asleep. I was dreaming.'

He sensed that she was getting braver, readying herself to cast off restraint.

'Why shouldn't I move? Sometimes I think you'd prefer me dead or dumb or a sack of spuds with a hole ripped in the front of it.'

He wanted to hit her. He wanted to do more than hit her and the unspeakable wish shamed and angered him.

'Shut up that talk.'

Enright sat up in the coach bed, threw his legs out over the side and became entangled in the curtain he'd forgotten hung there.

'What's that bloody thing you're wearing?'

'The kimono you sent me one time.'

'Sweet Christ, take it off you. Say whatever you have to say, it's all the same to me, all the one answer.'

He pulled at the curtain until it split like a mainsail from top to bottom. His breathing felt all wrong, fluttering in his throat and leaving him light-headed. His heart raced, the pulse pounding in his ears. Damn stupid, he knew, to be in such a funk over a kimono death-white with the black borders but he couldn't reassure himself. His whole body shook, the mattress shook, the whole world aquiver, just like in Pozières and Commotion Trench.

She spoke slowly and dejectedly as a dead bell ringing.

'You'd fight for any cause under the sun, Tom, but not for me. Not that you need a cause and that's worse. I'm not even second-best to some notion of King and Country or Mother Ireland like the rebels' wives are. But it's my own fault. I let you back without a fight after you hit me so it's no wonder you take me for granted. You think I'll cry and moan while you're here and that'll be the end of it until next time. But I don't disappear when you're gone and my mind doesn't stop turning and turning.' Hardly above a whisper now, all her strength sapped, it seemed, in the struggle to drag words to the surface, she went on. 'I've no life any more, only a purgatory.'

He lowered himself back on the bed. Tears welled in his eyes, the bad and the good. *Ah, Tommy, you'll be all right before you're twice married.* The mad aunt, when he cried on the bar floor where he slept after he'd moved in with her. Rubbing his hair and his neck, and her hand roaming down along until it nearly got to where he knew even then it shouldn't go and damn well didn't let it. *Don't be trying to take the blame for your daddy any more, Tommy. I'll mind you now and the pub'll be yours when I'm gone.*

'Are you all right, Tom?'

'Sorry I tore the curtain.'

'The curtain doesn't matter. I took off the kimono.'

'I got all tangled up.'

They lay in silence a while. He was no good to her now and never had been, he thought, only a danger, a poison.

'We're not used to being together, Tom. Every time you come we have to start all over again. Can't we just start again somewhere else before the two of us go mad?'

He wanted to be held. He wanted to pretend as she had once suggested, pretend for a little while to be something other than the half-crazed survivor of too many hells, though he knew pretending was a kind of madness too. Clancy, before the dawning of his last day, pretending he was speaking to his dead brother Ramie and not to Enright. *We might get the hay finished today, Ramie, it's a grand sky.* Ramie, the witnessing of whose decapitation in a logging accident had driven Clancy into the Male Chronic Building at Essondale. And Enright, fearful of where the game was leading, wouldn't play. So Clancy talked instead to the Hun corpse stretched across the back lip of the Jack Johnson hole. In the cottage dark, a flood of nausea rose in Enright and swept away the corpse's grotesque answer, a sight no man deserved to see or remember. He was going to be sick.

'Soon . . . '

Trying to say more drew whatever slime was coming up out of his chest closer to the spill of his throat.

'Soon won't do now, Tom.'

Enright didn't know if it was a fading away within himself or in her voice but he felt strained to his very limits to hear.

'I've tried every way I can to keep our love alive. I've forgiven the unforgivable in you, damned myself with your sins and all I get is silence or abuse.'

'If you hadn't come over to Balfour. I'd have gone back to the war where I belonged, where I should've been. Why in the name of Christ did you come? Were you afraid you'd lose your last chance of a man or what?'

Ah, les larmes d'une femme, the tears of a woman turn to ice, Thomass, when they are not smoothed away by her man. The bile overflowed into his mouth, the same vile yellow soup he'd watched coming up out of a hundred mouths after the gas at Maroc and the slime out of Marshall as he died in a misery Enright hadn't had the courage to put an end to. In it too there was the unmistakable raw warmth of blood. His breath came bull-furious and he felt her move away from him. He struggled out of the coach bed and across the kitchen. A table kicked him on the hip bone, almost knocking him over, a chair snared him briefly and he fought it off, a door flayed his knuckles until he stopped trying to punch his way through and found the two bolts and the latch.

Barefoot and in his long underclothes, Enright got himself around to the side of the cottage. By the wall, where he'd stashed the Colt, he began to vomit. The stars pitched further away into the universe above and then dipped far below him as once they'd done in a North Atlantic swell he'd been through when the whole of the fo'c'sle head was buried underwater one minute and the ship thrown back almost perpendicular the next. The coughing started up halfway through the vomiting and long outlasted it as he crouched against the gable end, finding his bearings so that the sky stayed where it belonged and the tree-tipped silhouette below settled back to equilibrium. He felt the burn of scratches on the soles of his icily cold feet.

'Tom?'

Mary stood a little way off, the coach bed quilt over her nakedness for a shawl. Her voice quivered with terror and cold. He saw that she too was in her bare feet.

'Go on in, Mary, you'll catch your death.'

'You're as sick as you ever were in Balfour, Tom, can you not see that?'

'I'm not. I was dying that time. You didn't see the half of it.'

He tried to release himself from the wall but wasn't ready yet.

'What'll we do if you die on us now, Tom?'

It seemed to Enright that there was something wrong and then many things wrong with what he heard. For a start, Mary was no longer crying. What she said too had not the ring of a question about it. Also, she stayed where she stood. On and on the reasons went burrowing into him like rats skulking through their purulent dark. He drew himself up.

'You might have more time for me if I was dead. Like Martin Fuller.'

'What kind are you to be jealous of a poor dead man?'

Mary looked up at the sky. Up, Enright thought, at the indifferent void in which fools and the God-bothered imagined the dead glowed with eternal starry life. A jaundiced quarter moon rode the swift clouds.

'So that's an end to it, is it, Tom? You found your excuse to decide against me.'

He felt too tired to argue further though he knew what he might have said, that there were no decisions, only some instinctive force like the pull of the moon on the tides, irresistible, eternally recurring, indifferent.

Next morning, alone in the coach bed, he heard the child coughing steadily in the bedroom and was immediately infected. A spinning mass of white dots before his eyes reminded him of the woozy sky from the night before. The rich aroma of baking bread and of tea on the brew filled the warm kitchen but his appreciation of it lasted no more than a single intake of breath. When he got his feet out on the floor, the flagstone was cold and he felt cheated.

The old poisoned feeling suffused itself through every pore. Four years since the poison gas. Thirteen years since his first dose of the clap. Twenty since the maggoty blood of the sheep hanging in the yard. He looked up from his purpled feet and knew that Mary had been watching him, perhaps for some time.

With the child wrapped up to twice its bulk sleeping in her arms, she stood by the bedroom door. Her face bore the same dull patina as the undusted white of the china delph arrayed on the dresser beside her. She looked smart, none the less, in the three-quarter length grey coat and matching hat Mags had bought her in Chicago for the trip home. The dance she did when she'd first modelled it for him. *Don't I look swell!* Such a different cast to her features back then, so forgiving, so glad he'd returned to her and accepting the cigar box with his letters. *I didn't mean to leave them, Tom.*

'I'm bringing Jerry into the doctor. I'm afraid of his cough again. You should come too with yours.'

He saw no bag but remained convinced once it occurred to him that she was about to leave him.

'It's only the chlorine cough I get sometimes still. But I'll drive you in.'

'I'm well used to the walk.'

Suddenly, Enright saw what it was she was hiding behind her veil of neutrality.

'You're afraid he'll catch something off me. That's it, isn't it? I get one fit of coughing and I'm a leper all of a shot.'

Mary walked by him and he felt like one of those bug-eyed Arab beggars in Tangiers, low-down on the street and getting nothing for their troubles but a disparaging look. When she got to the other side of the table, she paused. The moment of hesitation dragged on until he was left unprepared for the swiftness of her pirouette.

'Yes, I'm afraid. Afraid of opening my mouth to you for fear of what you'll do. I won't live like that any more.'

'Do you want me to pack my bags, so?'

Her common, throaty laugh shocked him because it was not her laugh and not directed at him or even at herself. He was glad not to have been standing near enough to hit her.

'What have you to pack, Tom? There's nothing here belonging to you.'

He watched from the kitchen window as she leaned down and tore some flowers from beside the path outside. It seemed to him that she plucked them as though they had, like all her other efforts, failed in their purpose of seducing him into surrender.

For the remainder of his stay, they slept apart. The child had to be watched through the night, she informed him unapologetically.

Its harsh terrier-bark of a cough went on unrelenting and could not be slept through. Enright did his own coughing out in the yard, his smoking too, though in three days he never made it past halfway on a cigarette.

In the cottage, silence might have been better than Mary's dutiful talk, the gabble of someone whose mind was busy elsewhere, perhaps on a plan. His own few contributions were delivered all the way up out of a knotted gut. Mostly they spoke of food and the weather, passengers on the same ship but bound for separate destinations. Everything he said or did made him feel like a fool. Everything she said or did made him feel loathsome. Whenever Mary spoke, she held on to something big, the table or the dresser, as if to draw the strength to overcome her revulsion of him. Or she held on to something small, the washboard or the bread knife, as if to protect herself should he pounce on her.

On the last day, when he said his goodbyes, she made no answer. He hadn't expected her to. The child slept loudly in the bedroom. His final impression as he left the cottage was that there remained something he had forgotten to do or to say but he couldn't dwell on it because that would have meant dwelling on Mary's face. She had become beautiful again. Not a trick nor a tear left in her. A brackish light prevailed in the kitchen all that overcast morning, he and Mary its ghostly creatures. Any fool could tell it was going to rain.

Half a mile from the cottage, Enright had already begun to loosen out. The weak, lemony sky was fringed to the east with banks of coal-black clouds like portents of an Indian Ocean typhoon. He didn't care. The brutish noise of acceleration felt like a cry coming from inside of him and he joined it, his voice queer and howling at first but deep-chested then as though it might roar away the pain in there that left him fearful of lighting up a cigarette. He was still shouting when Jimmy White appeared on the road up ahead.

A foot planted each side of the grass tuft that ran along its centre, Jimmy stood, arm raised like a traffic cop. Enright's first thought was to run his brother-in-law over but, already, instinct had him pressing the brake and clutch pedals. Within ten yards of his brother-in-law and down to a snail's pace, Enright let the Ford slip forward so that the young fellow had to yield and step aside before he snatched the brake lever back. He opened the door, moved sideways in his seat so that his left hand hovered casually, ready to alight on the Colt.

'I hear congratulations are in order, Jimmy boy. You're marrying into money. I always said you were a sharp one.'

There was a new sturdiness about Mary's brother, broader and heavier on the shoulders, more meat on him. Nearly a man or near enough to a man for the young lad to imagine he was one anyway.

'If I was you, I'd try riding her before you get married just to make sure you're up to it, son.'

Jimmy blushed and it was Mary's blush, the same unblemished skin dusted with the same velveteen of blood rushing to the cheeks and along the neck. *Why do you keep asking where that fucking half-breed is gone, how do I know?* The same brown eyes greened with offence. *Don't you talk to me like one of your whores, Mister Enright.* The same holy righteousness. *Oh yes, a sailor is a sailor, Tom, do you think I'm a fool?*

'I wouldn't expect anything else from a pig only a grunt, Tom.'

Enright scanned Jimmy's shirt where it was tucked into the trousers for evidence of a gun. Nothing. Around the back maybe. He reached in for the Colt and found only a rag sticking greasily to his fingers. Then he remembered that in his rush to get away he hadn't taken the gun out of the wall behind the cottage shed.

'Leave your hands out where I can see them, Jimmy.'

Jimmy smiled, slung his hands in his trouser pockets.

'We could've shot you a dozen times this week if we wanted to, Tom. We knew you were coming.'

Though the roster in the front office had been plain for all to see, he knew that it was Keane who had betrayed him. He couldn't wait to get back to the barracks. Watching him all the week, maybe even listening in, Jimmy probably knew things he'd said that he couldn't remember himself. The thought was unbearable, the disgusting peep-show exposure of it all. Enright jumped from the car but before he had time to strike, the hedgerows all around them spat out half a dozen armed men. The air became sulphurous, though no shot had yet been fired.

'You must be coming up in the ranks, son.'

Enright surveyed the faces of his brother-in-law's companions. Some familiar, none much older than Jimmy himself. That redhead, a Brosnihan; the fellow with a first stab at a soft brown *smig* on him, a Kearney. Not one among them from the barstool patriots back when he'd volunteered to shoot Vicars. All cast aside, he supposed, like the late Clem Shanahan above in Tipperary.

'I'm to give you a message from the brigade. If you come back to Listowel, you'll be shot.'

'Your brigade can go and shite.'

'You can come the once to collect Mary and Jerry. If you want to.'

Surrounded by the young faces aping cold intent, Enright wondered what these boys would be like on a front line, getting ready to go over the top, wishing they were never born and praying they'd never die. And wish or prayer, brave or gutless, it was only a toss of a coin decided whether a fellow found a space to crawl through between the wild trajectories of a thousand bullets. Luck was an illusion, a quality men ascribed to themselves to explain why they were still undeservedly alive and their best friend wasn't. Did any of these young lads know that yet?

'You were spared for their sake. For all the good you are to them.'

His calm resolve gone awry, Jimmy was a boy again, Mary's little brother. *Dear Tom, thank you very much for the penknife which is the best one I ever saw in my life.* Now that the breeze no longer puffed his shirt up, Jimmy's true dimensions became clearer. A bony bit of a lad not yet fully grown. Enright remembered with disgust, Clancy's severed torso oozing maggoty tendrils into the no-man's-land quagmire. How small it was. So miserably small it rose up a foot into the air when he'd kicked it. He felt sick again. He got himself back in the car.

'How she stays with a murdering heathen, I'll never understand.'

Jimmy held the car door so that Enright couldn't reach to close it. Too many guns lolled in inexperienced hands that were tightening like a fellow's fist did when an argument started up beside him in some grog shop and if he was drunk enough he'd take sides in a row that wasn't even his. Only one side these boys would be taking. Enright remembered the Colt.

'I left something behind at the cottage that I have to pick up before I go.'

'If it's the Peacemaker you're after, Mikey over there has it and he wouldn't think twice about using it on you. So get on your road, Tom, and don't turn back.'

Enright grinned, though it pained him to, and snatched the door from Jimmy's grasp.

'Plenty more where that came from, boy. And tell your brigade I'll be back and . . . What are you staring at? Do you think I'll wet myself or what?'

The look that undid Enright was a knowing one, a judgement made and instantly confirming itself. Mary's look when she found out about Fritzy. *I had nothing to do with Fritzy Bildheim, he's Gabe's old man not mine.* Jimmy spoke with relish and an almost disbelieving satisfaction.

'You've no intention of coming back for Mary or Jerry, have you, sailor-boy? Nothing is sacred to you. Not your wife nor your child nor even your country. What kind of rotten, godless world do you live in?'

'Same one you do, son, only I seen more of it than you ever will and I don't waste my time fooling myself that it adds up to anything much.'

'Is it any wonder Mary is still laying flowers on Martin Fuller's grave?'

A cough of such intensity exploded from Enright that he banged his forehead on the steering wheel as he doubled over.

'I'd see a doctor if I was you. Be an awful pity if you went and died in your bed before the lads above in Tipperary got at you. The peace talks might be starting soon but they won't be sitting on their hands.' Jimmy White enjoyed the spectacle of Enright coughing himself into a starry stupor. 'Or maybe you'll hang yourself like your Scottish pal did and save us the bullets.'

Enright shot the Ford away, scattering the youthful pot-luck shooters back into their ditches. The shakes broke out across him; his arms, his legs, the lunatic, spastic neck. Puddled pot-holes shook him and the howling Ford to the core. Rain turned itself on and off, sometimes a North Atlantic dark and driving, sometimes a Mediterranean light and milky, and at others, a Far East straight as bars and merciless. The bad side of his chest ached with the force of his heart trying to break out of him or burst. He drove on until he was out of Kerry and across Limerick and into Tipperary, shaking all the way. The drip out of his bad eye too all the way; enough, he imagined, to bore a hole in a stone.

Eyes closed and lying on his barracks mattress, Enright lay still though the journey continued to rush on through him. Sometimes dizzily he felt sudden plummets and not towards sleep but into some chasm that once or twice would not release him until he willed his eyes open again. He remembered swaying past Gallagher somewhere below stairs and not taking in a word he'd said. He remembered offering the excuse of tiredness or, at least, thinking the excuse. Then the stairs, the eternal ascent, trying to grab on to the wall whose embossed flowers slid from his grasp.

Much later, it seemed, he'd reached his room, which was the same as ever except for something he couldn't for a long time figure out. Not the fireplace, more flowers there, gun-metal daisies in a chain. Nor the mantelpiece; the Aladdin lamp, the bit of mirror shard for shaving at, the book he got from Timmoney but never read. Conrad. *Men that I often think are you.* Nothing different there. The bed, the pale square on the far wall where a picture once hung that was taken down before Enright arrived; some other man's life, here and gone. Then, from under the bed, his kit box screamed up at him. The wrong way round, the handle out to the front.

On his knees, he'd found that the contents had been rifled through and carelessly rearranged. Even the string around Mary's letters had been tampered with and, for that reason, they seemed not to be his any more or not his alone, which was the same thing. All lies anyway. He blamed Keane again and swore he'd corner the snooping bastard. Tomorrow. He didn't have to stand up to bring the bundle of *Dear Toms* to the fire grate and they embraced the matchstick's flame quickly as though from the very moment of their disingenuous conception they'd been meant for burning. The heat reminded him of how cold he felt after the drive, reminded him that the summer was gone and that frost and ice was all that awaited him.

After that brief conflagration he threw himself upon the bed; coat, suit, boots and all. Another dark loomed under him and he lost the struggle to keep from falling into it.

The morning after he burned Mary's letters, Enright woke in the early light, his blood still boiling and the shakes persisting inside of him though not at least in his hands. A cold-water shave helped to steady him. He took the time too, because there was plenty of it, to polish up the silver buttons of his uniform tunic and he worked up a shine on his boots though the smell of the boot polish brought a flame of memory to his cheeks. He wet his hair and slicked it straight back off his forehead instead of the usual across because it was getting long at the front.

Downstairs, he found equine-faced Harvey and his fellow Tan on duty. They played nap, regarding the cards with indifference. Enright exchanged a grunted greeting with them. In the report books at the front desk he found a series of infuriating entries.

'Five bloody complaints here about my dogs next door and not one name. Who made these complaints?'

'Who knows?'

Harvey went back to his cards. *Oo nowse.* Sounded like Thyssen, that Norwegian cook on board the *Abbot* this time.

'I'll find out who and what you are yet, Harvey. Who filled in the reports?'

The two constables shrugged in dumb unison.

Then Enright recognised the neat, miniature script as Keane's. He climbed the stairs to Keane's room and punched him awake with a right to the shoulder blade. A face pained and ancient with sleep looked up at him from under a tossed grey thatch.

'You're mad, Enright. I'll report you for assault.'

'You bastard, you told the rebels I was off to Listowel and

you rifled my kit box while I was gone. I swear to Christ I'll do away with you one of these days.'

Enright picked up Keane by the scruff of his undershirt. The fist attempting to knock away Enright's arm was unexpectedly strong but he held on tight.

'Why didn't you sign your name to those complaints about my dogs?'

'Because Mr Gallagher told me not to. And you damn well know why there's no names. Because you're a bloody lunatic is why.'

'If you ever call me a lunatic again, I'll swing for you.' The tremor in Enright's voice proved difficult to contain as he withdrew from the sudden awakening in Keane's eyes. 'Play one more trick on me and you'll end up a barracks accident.'

'Why would anyone bother going through your kit box? Have you something to hide or what?'

Gallagher, when Enright finally stole a few minutes with him after morning parade and a lecture on Public Health Nuisances, seemed perplexed.

'I told you about the dogs last night. You were in a bad way though.'

'I wasn't drunk if that's what you think.'

'You weren't well either. Should you see a doctor, maybe? You're letting yourself get all wound up.'

'And why wouldn't I? That bloody slob Keane went through my kit box. And what's worse, he – '

'Maybe you did it yourself, only you can't remember. But the dogs . . . '

Enright's neck strained against the spasm threatening to judder through him.

'You know what happened to my dogs out at Lady's Well. Who's complaining anyway?'

In Gallagher's fingering of the grey moustache there was a hint of the old nervousness but he stood firm, taking time to consider his answer.

'I'd rather not say. Just sort it out as soon as you can.'

Some shopkeeper on Friar Street, Enright speculated, or Cullinane, the Kerry paramour? Like a bad penny that lad, always turning up when he wasn't wanted.

'I hear them myself in the night sometimes and I'm a heavy sleeper.'

Or Donegan. The fellow was sneaky enough to try it and he'd never wanted the dogs there in the first place. Enright couldn't wait to get out next door to the garage and knock the truth out of him.

'By the way, Sergeant, the rector out in Barnane got his motor car back. Mint condition too. Says it's going better than before it was borrowed.'

Borrowed. Not stolen. All's well that ends well, the smile and the upraised bushes of moustache and eyebrow declared.

'And they've appointed a Liaison Officer. Some Fitzpatrick fellow below in Clonmel that we can contact through Seán Dooley. His poor father must be turning in his grave to see that young lad a rebel. I knew the father well, you know, used to have a drink with him now and again. But Seán was very helpful in the matter of the motor car, mind you.'

'His name is Johnny not Seán.'

'And speaking of motor cars. You've a wreck made of ours. You're to come to me for authorisation whenever you want to use it from now on, do you hear me?' Gallagher relented then with a shuffle of the papers on his desk. 'For the longer journeys, I mean. The damage is done on the longer journeys. Did you not notice the cogs on the throttle lever are damaged?'

Donegan's denials were despairingly uttered sighs though it wasn't the crack of Enright's whip that had him quaking.

'Kinahan was in. I think he might be on to me. What in the name of Christ am I going to do?'

Enright leaned against some shelves in the rancid den, though he knew he'd have trails like bicycle tracks across the back of his tunic from the oily timbers. His head reeled as badly as when he'd woken all those times during the night.

'When was Kinahan here?'

Donegan looked like he was shaking a bad dream out of his head.

'A few days ago. I'm not the better of it yet. You know the way you stick out your paw to shake hands with a lad and it's hanging there half an hour and he's looking at it the same as if it was a beggar's? I'd swear someone told him I was fishing for answers about Danny and the young one. Why'd you make me do that?'

'What exactly did he say?'

'He says, do you know where Enright is gone? No, says I, how would I know? Doesn't he keep his dogs here, says he? See what you landed me in now, Sergeant, and you supposed to be minding me.'

'Minding you? I wouldn't care if he sliced rashers off your arse. Did you ask him why he wanted to know?'

Donegan's neck sank down into its folds again.

'Didn't they leave their message out at Lady's Well when they burned the dog? The next dog for hell. Kinahan's not the same man since Larry Healy was shot, doesn't even trust his own now, I heard. They say he was over in Limerick at the time and blames himself and everyone else for not getting Healy out of town that night. Mother of mercy, I'm between the devil and the deep blue sea with the two of you.'

'All you have to do so is decide if you want to burn or drown.'

Cullinane wasn't around to deny he was the complainant. The mechanic hadn't shown up for three days, Donegan explained, as he sank deeper into depression. A bad cold had been the excuse but the garage owner thought otherwise.

'He won't be around much longer, especially when Cathal gets out of internment soon, like they say he will. He won't be having a policeman's brother in the family. As if things weren't bad enough already and now I'm losing my best man.'

'His name's Charlie, not Cathal.'

Out at Lady's Well with Foley and the dogs there was further cause for irritation. Even before the doggyman started up, Enright felt a disappointing lack of enthusiasm on seeing his dogs, a mucky wash off the grass caking their flanks. A bunch of ragged no-hopers they seemed. Arrow Valley Snow too went about flat-footed and dispirited. He lit up a cigarette and began to cough and seeing Foley look on worriedly, he went on the offensive.

'What's wrong with the white?'

He threw away the cigarette. Foley watched the discarded fag greedily.

'He's a flyer but I can't get him to run straight. He loses sight of the hare and buckles off to the left.'

'Are you saying he's half-blind or what?'

'No, but he only starts running because the other dogs start and he don't know what he's running after till it's too late half the time.'

'Maybe he's lame on the left, if he's buckling that way?'

'If he was lame, wouldn't I know it? He gets distracted or, I don't know, maybe he's so busy running he forgets what he's running after.'

As if for the first time, Enright noted Foley's physical ugliness. The leprous, scabby skin. The peculiarly cramped features; mouth, nose and eyes, all too close together, a face punctured with toothless age that made an unseemly joke of his continuing ambition to father yet another child. The dogs too were ugly; black soulless eyes and blue thirsty tongues thrust out to their naked utmost. Foley's gaze lingered on the cigarette in the grass as if he were memorising its exact location so that he could pick it up when Enright had left.

'There's another problem too, Sergeant. I had a couple of lads from Roscrea out here the other day. They made out some

Kerryman stole the white off their father. Lucky enough your dogs weren't here but those lads'll be back. Nothing surer. They threatened the Republican Court on me.'

'There's no Republican Court in my town.'

'But what'll I do if they come back?'

Enright made no attempt to contain the chuckle that burst out of him. Funny how a fellow could be sinking in a black boghole one minute and gliding over the turf the next with a bright, mischievous idea. If the Roscrea boys wanted a Kerryman, he'd give them a Kerryman.

'Tell them the dog wasn't stolen but bought by a Kerryman called Cullinane.'

'Cullinane? The new lad in Donegan's garage?'

'The very man.'

Stepping away from the bandy-legged doggyman, Enright found the burnt-out cigarette in the grass with his heel and made ribbons of it. Behind him, the dogs seemed to yelp for his attention but he ignored them.

'But how did you come to have the white so, Sergeant?'

The puny voice echoing across under the leaden sky became in its plaintive bevels and twists the voice of Enright's father calling after him, the last time they parted. A boy climbing the steps behind his mad aunt up out of the cellar in Tralee jail for the last time and a cry like a trapped animal's crashing along after him. *I don't care if I never get out of here. What have I to come out to anyway only more drudgery?*

'I swapped the dog with Cullinane for a woman.'

Back at the barracks in the days that followed, Gallagher made no further mention of the dogs but had another trick up his sleeve to keep Enright off the streets now that the Shinners were pouring back. *I can't keep up the files now that I'm doing the DI's work as well as my own.* Every other week, it seemed, another train pulled into a packed, festooned railway station to deliver a few more returning heroes. *We won't be going up there letting ourselves be provoked, Sergeant.*

The Quarterly Assizes fast approached and the Head Constable wanted to act as though things were back to normal. Licensing law breaches filled a file as thick as Enright's thumb. Cattle straying up at the Bullring, bicycles fecked, unlit or drunkenly steered, made up another bundle of papers. Most of the complainants Enright knew, and maybe none of the accused would show up anyway, all warned off by the rebels. But Gallagher persisted and kept him unrelentingly busy with so much paperwork that in the evenings he fell into bed and sometimes even into sleep, his mind awash with futile detail. After a week of confinement, Enright took to the Jameson again and paid a second visit to Helen Peters.

A fellow never knew how drunk he'd got until it was too late. Even as he hung precariously over back-lane walls, Enright imagined he was merely giddy with escape. Taking alleyway corners a step too soon, he blamed the clouded night sky for the crack of stone against his forehead. Once, when he tripped as he skipped across a stable yard, he cursed the cobbles and then his heavy boots and berated himself for not wearing plimsolls. When he reached the workhouse, he felt battered but undeterred from posing the questions he'd drunkenly prepared for the girl.

Such a bad, noisy fist did he make of the bolt that he knew he'd given the game away before he'd even begun. When she asked for light he refused, certain his resolve wouldn't survive the sight of her. He dropped back a shoulder blade to find the wall and misjudged the distance. The wallop of the wall knocked the breath out of him.

'I forgot my matches.'

'Are you drunk, Sergeant?'

She might have been asking him the time of day, so unaccusingly did she speak. In spite of the darkness, he closed his eyes to balance himself out.

'I'm not drunk. I'm on duty, aren't I? Anyway, I'm asking the questions.'

Helen sighed. Not the first drunk she'd put up with, Enright supposed. A father from before the orphanage? Old Sebastian Bennett? Or Dooley? No, that string of misery hadn't the frame to be a serious drinker. Or Danny Egan who'd drink a barrel of porter and lick the insides through a bunghole for an encore. Ask her, he told himself.

'Did you know Danny Egan? Fool of a lad going around these parts with half a face on him.'

He teetered forward from the wall, cocking his ear in a pantomime of listening for meaning in the silence. He heard only her breathing, weighted a little on the exhalation with tiredness. He knew he'd asked the wrong question first but couldn't remember the intended one. The logic of his proposed interrogation unravelled, its deductive progress was lost to him.

'I heard he was often above begging at Bennett's back door.'

'It's not nice to talk about Danny like that.'

'Ah, you knew him, so. How well did you know him?'

'I used fill his billycan with tea and give him some leavings from the kitchen. Sometimes we'd have a chat.'

'A chat? Is that all?'

'What more could I do? Is he all right? Is something after happening to him?'

He swayed queasily and his legs folded at the knees. He slid down along the wall.

'No, he's . . . he's gone on his travels and I was wondering if he ever mentioned any place he might be inclined to wander off to . . .'

'Castle Bennett, maybe. He told me there was something he lost one time that he thought might be out there. He used come out to try and think what it was. Are you all right, Sergeant?'

Enright wished the girl didn't sound so pleasantly naïve, so truly concerned.

'When you came in the first time. I thought it might be Danny. It'd be like him to come when no one else would bother. He's very good-natured.'

His head hurt so badly that he imagined a pair of hands in there kneading the grey matter. The filth of that slush, he thought, when it came through a hole in a man's head; slush that was all a fellow had to know the world with or know what to do or say. No wonder a fellow's thoughts turned so sour. No wonder what slimy words spilled down on to his big slavering famished greyhound tongue.

'Who was it that made you pregnant?'

His face burned and then the burn spread through him. He longed for some water, a drop to drink and the rest to douse himself cold and clean with. He heard the soft sniffle of her distress and it grieved him.

'I only want to know because whoever he was, he left you high and dry and that's not good enough.'

'Haven't I torment enough without this? Can't you mind your own business?'

'I'm drunk. I can't think only what I shouldn't be thinking.'

He pulled himself up out of the twist his body had gotten itself into and tried along the wall to the right of him for the door but then remembered it was to his left. In the way of all drunks, he couldn't resist a last excuse.

'No one deserves to be left on their own. That's all I meant to say.'

Enright craved punishment, was almost ready to pray for it but didn't need to.

'I don't know for sure who the father was. That's what I was going to the bleeding statue to ask God about. To give me a sign or help me some way or other. This is the answer I got and maybe I deserved it but the child didn't.'

The day-room table held a mess of files, reports and telegraphs. Enright had taken to using the place because he couldn't bear the company of others out in the front office. Not a friend in the place and no sign yet of Timmoney back from whatever he was up to in Tyrone. Joining the ranks of the men in black again? Or getting up the courage to hang himself off a roof beam? Hard to tell with these holy fools, though he fervently hoped it wasn't the latter.

The monthly tabulations still awaited completion and Enright had put it off for days now since his visit to Helen Peters. Under the table stood a bottle of Jameson, uncorked for the occasional quick swig by the neck. The lid of an old polish tin by his left elbow overflowed with ashes, butts and a half-smoked cigarette. A few puffs was all his aching chest allowed and even those could only be swallowed with the burn of whiskey.

Of the papers before him, only the Intelligence File offered any compensation for his confinement to the barracks. In it were noted all sightings of IRA men by patrolling constables. Some titbits too from an old retainer of Sebastian Bennett's; the mushroom field out by Loughtagalla used as a drilling ground with hurling sticks for rifles one of the many careless boasts overheard of young rebel recruits whose numbers grew steadily. Pub sightings too traded for the price of a bottle of stout. Swaggering rebels like Johnny Dooley out of hiding, dangerously embittered ones released from internment or jail like dead Martin Dwyer's brother, Eamon.

Enright viewed the file with a mixture of frustration and relief. Desk-bound, he sometimes wished he was out on patrol himself to stare down the returnees and throw a few jibes about their heroic shooting of policemen off in search of a miracle or their crippling of young whores with careless tripwires. At the same time, he knew he wasn't well enough yet to knock the smug grins or the scowls from their faces, which they would remark in the file they kept on him too, no doubt. Not, he supposed, a typed-up, clipped-together sheaf of paper but a file none the less, stored in the minds of Kinahan and his go-boys.

Tedious as the paperwork proved to be, Enright saw how a fellow could get comfortable and lazy at it. Muscles stiffened up and there grew a reluctance at times to move even a finger. He urged himself to take an occasional walk around the day room, pacing it like a deck or like a priest reciting his office in a presbytery garden. Sometimes these walks revealed an unexpectedly pleasant sense of well-being right through his body and he imagined the enforced rest was paying dividends. Those more frequent days, however, when the short walk left him breathless and cramped, he returned to his seat wearily cursing his useless body and, guzzling down more Jameson, wrote caustic letters to Mary, none of which he posted.

Too often he reached boorishly for Danny Egan's notebook and lost himself in the impossible task of deciphering the contents. A sheer peak in the scrawl an *l* perhaps, the wide backwards loop a half-formed letter *e*. The inevitable failure of finding any meaning there brought him back to imaginings of Danny's last hours. Did he know the faces of his killers, even one of them? And how did he die? Well, or on his knees pleading, or oblivious to it all, which, in the end, was the best that Enright could have hoped for? In such a melancholy mood he wandered out one Friday evening with no particular place in mind to go.

The doors of Donegan's garage beside the barracks were padlocked but he knocked anyway. For once, he bore no malicious intent towards the garage man, simply wanted to talk of unimportant things for a while. He received no answer other than the barking of his own dogs, and reminded of that unsolved problem, he moved on dejectedly. Further along Friar Street he came to the lane leading to Dooley's cinema. He might have passed by but for the printed poster glued to a square of cardboard and tied to the lamppost at the outer edge of the footpath.

STELLA CINEMA
Uncle Tom's Cabin
(Sun–Tues)
Elmo, the Mighty
(Wed–Thurs)
Cameron of the Royal Mounted
(Fri–Sat)

The Royal Mounted Police. He wondered if the film might have actually been made up in Canada. Not BC probably or not up in the wilds behind Nelson in any case. Only when he reached halfway along the lane did he consider the possibility of meeting Johnny Dooley. Instead of the young rebel, however, it was the hunchbacked aunt he found at the ticket booth in the dank, bare-blocked lobby. He couldn't be sure if it was the sight of her or the damp air in the place that induced the Arctic, arthritic cold in him. The woman looked up from counting the cash, without surprise or apparent trepidation. From behind the cinema door came a busy piano accompaniment stoking the cheers of an excited audience.

He went by the booth and slipped inside the hall, unnoticed in the general hubbub as some wide-eyed Mountie untied the rope from a fair damsel lashed to the rails before a fast-approaching train. A familiar landscape framed the scene. The rocky creek through which the rails had been cut, the vast sweep of pine high up on the surrounding slopes, the heady disproportion of scale that made tiny, crawling bugs of men. Might have been the same trees he'd got lost in half a dozen times until he'd given up looking for Gabriel Jack out beyond Morning Mountain and returned to the shack to find Mary beaming with the most extraordinary news. Some crazy guy from Penticton called Ted Randolph had owned up to shooting Fritzy Bildheim, and he'd known damn well that if anything flushed out Gabe, the charging of an innocent man would. *You don't seem too pleased, Tom.*

The music settled down, the Mountie having set off to find the culprit. Bridie Dooley fixed a lock of hair back with one hand but the tune went on uninterrupted. Neither Johnny Dooley nor the besotted Cullinane were anywhere to be seen among the pale-lit, spectral faces of the audience.

At the booth, Dooley's aunt continued to count the takings. Enright approached her, making himself bigger and broader than he felt and thinking it was all the same to someone whose line of vision couldn't be dissimilar to a fair-sized dog's.

'I hear Johnny's back ruling the roost in the Dooley household.'

Her silence invited him on.

'Saw off that smooth-talking garage mechanic mighty quick too. Is he saving Bridie for some republican hero or what?'

'Mr Cullinane is a fine young man. So is my nephew. But it's no secret they don't see eye to eye.'

Her answer caught them both off guard and she already seemed to be regretting it. Enright sensed that she didn't approve of young Dooley. *My nephew*, and no mock-patriotic insistence on the Gaelic Seán. He wondered what her hump would feel like to touch. Hard or soft, sinewy or a fatty pulp. The prospect discomposed him and he flexed the hint of numbness out of the fingers he'd imagined touching her with.

'So where is the bold Johnny now?'

'He was here earlier. Is there a message you'd like to leave, Sergeant?'

'Is he gone up to see Helen Peters, by any chance? He won't get much good of her now though, will he?'

'God forgive you for speaking like that.'

Enright drew closer to the glass frame that separated them. Only now did he notice the sickly hue of her countenance, the frightful greying of her eyes that signalled life's recession.

'He made her pregnant, didn't he? Rode her and left her to her own devices. That's why you go up there praying over her, isn't it, so your little runt of a nephew might get into heaven after all?'

Enright watched as she placed a hand on a mother of pearl rosary beads that lay beside the biscuit-tin till.

'I've always visited the sick. I know what it's like to be sick, Sergeant. So do you, by the looks of you.'

'Helen Peters isn't sick. She's crippled. There's a difference.'

'She's not long for this world, one way or the other.'

A raw sadness burrowed itself into his gut. He caught a glimpse of his own reflection in the glass. A face, open-mouthed and anguished. He pressed a fist against the glass and heard the protest at the edges where it was set in the timber. The woman heard too, and betraying concern, took a firmer hold on her rosary beads.

'And if she is, it's thanks to Johnny and his rebel pals. How do you feel about that, miss? Or about Danny Egan that they dragged out and shot in a boghole?'

Inside the hall, the cheers rising towards a crescendo again broke across the music from Bridie Dooley's piano, smashing it into meaningless ripples. The punters would soon be leaving and he knew the danger of getting caught up in a crowd like DI Hunt had the year before Constable Finnegan copped it, coming down from the races and getting plugged in the back.

'Was Johnny the father of the child or not?'

'I have no idea who took advantage of the poor girl. But to tell you the truth, I don't care to know much about what happens in this world. It's best not dwelt on.'

A loud whooping and stomping of feet from the cinema unnerved Enright and he reached into his pocket to lay claim to the Webley. It occurred to him that he could shoot her and be back down in the barracks before the crowd reached the lane outside. He was reminded of his murderous urge in the coach bed with Mary and the ugly precedent when he'd slapped her face back in the Nelson cabin. *Why don't you go looking for Gabe yourself, Mary, you miss him so much.* He'd become convinced the half-breed was going to hand himself over to the police and one slip of the tongue from Mary had him lashing out. *Yes, I do miss Gabe because at least I had a laugh now and again when he was here.* The shame of hitting a woman. Back outside among the trees, he'd held the axe over the offending hand a long time. *Never again, Tom.* And he'd let her pack up and go because he knew he deserved no better and still didn't.

'Is that why you keep Helen Peters in the dark over that farce of a bleeding statue and everything else that happened since they crippled her?'

She stood up from her seat and arched her head towards him as she worried the rosary beads, a juju charm to ward off evil.

'I don't tell her because the worst thing about being sick and dying is knowing that life goes on as if you never existed, Sergeant.'

He could tell that the film was drawing to a close because a satisfied quiet had descended upon the building. Glancing behind to ensure he wasn't reversing into a trap, he backed away to the laneway door. The woman's fixed gaze troubled him, seeming as it did to note his apprehension as keenly as his anger. Had the holy eyes on her too like Mary's, like his mother's waiting to escape into something better than a swampy farm in Bedford and howling greyhounds and a mealy-mouthed thief of a husband and a snotty-nosed young lad with claw marks all over his face and body, crying for a sign, a word, half a bloody glance. Chairs scraped the floor in the main hall, the screech of timber across timber.

'Life will go on all right, miss. But not for your two nephews.'

Her timing was so perfect as to seem deliberate. She delayed her response until the trundle of the pushing crowd had just reached the door of the main hall and Enright himself had stepped out into the lane.

'You're a very unhappy man, Sergeant Enright. I'll pray that someday you'll know peace.'

He hurried down the lane and, certain he hadn't been seen as he reached Friar Street, he crossed over and took up position at the dark entrance to Moat Lane, whose ubiquitous smell of decay was thankfully carried off behind him on the breeze. He watched from the shadows as the crowd dispersed; ambling, shambling, strutting or preening, each according to the importance or lack of it they attached to themselves. Poverty or relative wealth comprised the usual self-estimates, except in the younger men. That cock-of-the-walk pair pausing just beyond the barracks to light their cigarettes. The defective streetlamp under which they stood issued a weakly wavering light but Enright fancied they matched some of the descriptions in the sightings files though he could put names on neither the tall fair one nor the shorter one with a lazy eye on him like a permanent wink. The last of the stragglers passed them by and as the two men sauntered away down Friary Street, Enright thought his instincts had failed him because he'd been convinced Dooley would return to the cinema to collect the money.

He stepped out of Moat Lane and crossed back over towards the barracks. From the cinema lane, a couple emerged so deeply engrossed in a heated argument that they hadn't yet noticed him. At first he thought them a courting couple heading home after a quick shift in the lane. Then he recognised the man's rooster strut, the woman's poised bearing. Johnny and Bridie Dooley. Their pace slackened momentarily on seeing him but when it quickened again, it was Bridie Dooley who took the lead. She'd been crying and the soft glow from the gas globe of the streetlamp the pair now passed beneath deepened the sense of melancholy emanating from her.

Enright stood out in the middle of the footpath. Ten yards off, Bridie Dooley began to veer towards the kerb. Johnny, however, made no such concession, even if the effort played havoc with the insouciance he attempted against the will of his facial muscles. The fellow's eyes squinted desperately into the darkness beyond Enright but clearly caught no reassuring sight of his henchmen.

'How are you, Johnny? I missed you, so I did.'

Dooley halted within a few feet of Enright. His sister had advanced further and, stepping off the footpath, floated by like a stick in a stream swept wide by the ripples of a boulder.

'My name is Seán.'

'Come on home.'

Dooley dismissed his sister's plea, having found his voice, even if it had reverted to the unbroken one of a boy.

'I'm grand, Bridie. I'll wait until the dung is cleared off the path. There's two men down behind you there, Enright, and you're in their sights.'

'Can they see in the dark, son? Are they owls or what?'

'I'll report this to Gallagher. You're in breach of the Truce, harassing me like this.'

Bridie Dooley came back into view and took her brother by the arm. He let her drag him along a few steps but pulled up as Enright's smile widened into a knowing leer. He untangled his arm from his sister's and dragged himself up the last quarter inch of his height.

'Don't let him vex you. All he wants is an excuse.'

'I have all the excuse I need already, miss. Did he ever tell you about Helen Peters?'

She looked from Enright to her blushing brother. Her black-gloved fingers melded themselves together in a prayerful clench. He imagined her in the same attitude as she appealed her brother's verdict on her liaison with Cullinane and began to feel sorry for her. The half-light, Dooley's rat-in-a-corner eyes, and the musky perfume of the girl left Enright with a sense of *déjà vu*. The Chinese hawker, his first trophy but, in truth, no more than an accident. Bought three bottles of Black and White from the fellow that turned out to be water coloured with saffron. Hours later with a young whore down between the sheds at Kowloon docks, he'd turned a corner and walked straight into the swindler. Threw a punch from instinct, then another to impress the girl and got half an inch of ice pick in his neck before he could knock it away. Then a mad blind tussle amid the fading screams of the whore deserting him until the hawker suddenly stiffened up on top of him. The memory of that dead weight pressing on his chest chilled him. The wide stupefied eyes seeming to wonder who had blinded them for eternity, the last breath of a stranger icing over the sweat on his face.

'The young girl they crippled with their tripwire, miss. Your aunt is trying hard to get her into heaven because the bold Johnny here put a bun in her oven before she ended up in the workhouse. Wasn't that lucky for you, Johnny?'

'I never went near that young one, Enright. Is that what the Crown Forces are reduced to now? Poking around in a young one's business.'

'No smoke without fire, Johnny.'

'Bridie, go down to Healy's and get Cathal.'

So, Charlie the Toothless was back out of the internment camp in Ballykinlar and no one at the barracks had bothered to put it in the files or tell him. Or, more likely, the rebel sympathisers among them were banking on Charlie to come looking for revenge before Enright knew he was out.

'Bridie, go down for him. He's only waiting on the chance to meet this fellow.'

'Can he talk without the teeth, Johnny?'

Enright wrapped his lips back over his teeth and gave Dooley a gummy grin.

'Bridie!'

'And there was me thinking you wore the trousers in the Dooley house, Johnny. Maybe she'll have Cullinane in spite of you, boy.'

He was sorry he'd mentioned Cullinane when he saw Bridie Dooley's myopic eyes become glaucous with tears, her lips quivering like a plucked string as she spoke.

'Do you have nothing better to do with your time than listen to gossip like an old biddy?'

'Not at the moment, no.'

Enright didn't feel as affronted as he should have done, beset as he was by a weary longing. He missed the sound of a woman's voice, an unadmonishing voice addressing him and him alone, the music of it.

'Your aunt just told me I'm an unhappy man.'

He was the one blushing madly now and hoping it didn't show in the dim light.

Bridie stared at him a discomfortingly long time. He tried to rescue himself with a half-hearted jibe.

'But she's not a barrel of laughs herself, with her rosary beads and her gam-on miracles, is she?'

Bridie Dooley seemed genuinely engaged in an effort to understand him.

'You don't like yourself very much, do you? And you don't like being despised either, for all your bluster.'

'Wouldn't we all like to be loved, miss?'

'There's plenty wouldn't be able for love even if they got it.'

'Bridie. Go and get Cathal and the lads and don't be talking to that murderer.'

'There's no need to call anyone. We'll go home. Auntie Eily will be worried.'

Johnny Dooley's courage returned to him when they'd moved off a little. He fended off his quietly insistent sister and shouted back at his tormentor.

'If you don't get out of town soon, Enright, you'll be shot like the dog that you are and you'll be no loss to anyone.'

'Go way and make a decent woman of that young . . . that young one above in the workhouse.'

Dooley let himself be led further away, so that Enright could no longer see him when he delivered his parting shot.

'Maybe you did it yourself, Enright, only you don't want to pretend you did.'

He stared after them as they were swallowed up by the dark and then he stared at the dark.

Sometimes the only way to climb a hill was in reverse. The trick had worked before with the Ford Touring car but not today. Funny how a fellow might know nothing of the inner workings of an engine and yet know when it was about to let him down. The mysterious tapping and scraping, the high screech of a discomposure that matched Enright's own at the confrontation in prospect up at the Union Workhouse. Every last thing had its own song, according to Gabriel Jack, and that song forgot itself in the face of annihilation and became a scream. *Even a goddam rock screams when it's busted open, 'cept you can't hear it 'cos of the crack of the hammer.*

As the reversing car bucked against the railway bridge's steep incline, Enright coughed so hard and long he couldn't speak to Timmoney. Good to have him back though, even if he looked more gaunt and bone-thin than before with his shaven head and hadn't looked in on Enright on his return the previous night. Tired after the two-day journey from far Tyrone, Enright supposed.

When, halfway up the hill, the engine gave out with a cracking snap of metal, Enright felt almost relieved. He barked up the last of the phlegmy irritant and spat out onto the road. Blood again. But some of the old mustard yellow there too and that reassured him. He hoped the cough wouldn't start up again at the workhouse, especially if Paddy Kinahan showed up.

'Grand morning for a walk, Ned. And you can fill me in on your adventures above in Tyrone.'

He meant to surprise Timmoney with the mildness of his

reaction to the breakdown but the young constable stared ahead, preoccupied.

'Not a whole lot to tell. Maybe we should've brought some more men.'

Enright tapped the breast of his tunic where the Webley lay.

'Don't worry, Ned. I brought a friend with me. Anyway, Kinahan'll be well gone by now, if he was up there in the first place.'

'We're not supposed to be carrying, are we?'

'Would you trust the Shinners not to be carrying?'

They abandoned the Ford and headed over the brow of the railway bridge and across towards the workhouse. Timmoney sulked but Enright felt indulgent towards his young companion. Give him time to settle, he told himself, and they'd be the best of drinking buddies again. He thought about what lay ahead of them at the workhouse.

Three guttersnipes from up by the Bullring had been roaming the countryside near the town in recent weeks stealing hens and ducks from various farmyards in the night hours. By day, they'd spied on farmhouses and cottages, waiting for their chance to sneak in and take anything of value. A clock here, a set of silver cutlery there, a few pounds of butter when there was nothing better to take. None of these thefts had been reported, of course, except to Kinahan or some of his local minions. Enright had recognised the names of the culprits. Lynch, O'Donnell and Riordan. The lowest of the low, callow by day and wild dogs under cover of night. The beating they'd got from the rebels was the least they deserved.

All that concerned Enright was that the IRA were in breach of the Truce and he'd jumped at the chance when the word came to the barracks just ten minutes earlier that Kinahan was at the workhouse. Already, he was regretting his haste. He wished he was in better shape to face the rebel leader, not so stiff in the legs or battered in the chest or cramped in the neck. The more he walked, the more his every breath dizzied him and widened the broad abstract space inside his skull so that he felt like some faltering giant, top-heavy with vertigo.

'I thought you mightn't come back at all, you were gone that long.'

'I very near didn't. But I hadn't a whole lot of choice in the end. They wouldn't have me back in the seminary.'

'You're better off out of that game, son.'

'I could join a monastery though. There's one in Cork will take me.'

'What d'ye want doing that for? Stuck with a crowd of men and vowed to silence and not a woman in sight. Are you mad or what?'

'Like living in a police barracks?'

The grim bulk of the workhouse loomed into view with its forbidding high railings, a vast deadweight of a place even in the airy lightness of Enright's vision. He couldn't see Helen Peters's shed but from her prostrate image there seemed no escape. And no escaping either the image of Johnny Dooley above her or some ageing bachelor, tossed grey hair and red in the face fit for a heart attack from sowing the last of his wild oats in a maidservant's attic room, hot as the heights of a summer haybarn. Even as he recognised the desperation in his efforts to draw some response from his ascetic colleague, Enright laughed and jollied along like a half-wit at a funeral.

'Did you not go out to a dance or anything? The women won't come looking for you, you know.'

Except for Mary, he thought, all that way, and he wouldn't mind but he told her in the letter that he'd be dead before she got it. His patience began to wear thin.

'For Jaysus sake, Ned, did you take the vow of silence already or what?'

'The first week at home, I stayed locked inside my room. The smallest wee sound had me in a ball of sweat, I was so sure the IRA were coming for me. That and the shame of letting my family down again, and God too.'

They had reached the by-road that led to the workhouse entrance. The girl's shed could be seen clearly behind the front railings. He didn't want to have to walk by the place and be stared at by that small window. They probably hadn't even bothered to fix it though the winter would soon be settling in and would settle across her bed in the cold nights to come, on the limbs she couldn't feel and on the white face, frost along the snow.

'We'll go round by the back.'

Timmoney seemed not to have heard Enright speak.

'Then I remembered what you always said about hiding out in the open. So I dragged myself outside eventually and every day I walked the boundaries of my father's farm. I know it might sound a wee bit peculiar but I counted my steps all the way round and the strange thing was that nearly every day I got a different tally. I wrote them down, so I know.'

'You're losing me now, Ned.' ·

'I mean . . . you think you know the measure of things, some things at least, things you knew from a child, but you don't.'

Enright hated this no-man's-land talk that dragged his bones down and worsened the ache in his muscles. Captain Big Toe spouting words of wisdom through the white pipe smoke that seemed like the only light in the dugout those long minutes before zero hour, his last day, quoting another Hun philosopher whose name Enright couldn't remember. *Absent and future things are the origin of care and fear and hope.* Must have been dreaming up the last wave goodbye with his big toe even as he spoke.

A smile transformed the young constable's face, brought light and mischief to the shadowy sockets. His tall man's hump shrugged off, he raised the peak of his cap to see more of the road ahead.

'Well, isn't it grand to hear the Grim Reaper laughing for a change.'

'I was just remembering . . . My father brought Father O'Rourke out to the house to me and after I made my confession, he says, bring a missal with you to read and you won't know how long or short you're walking.'

'True enough. Long as you don't fall in a hole with your head stuck in a prayer.'

Timmoney's laughter was of the hysterical kind that tempted the listener to puncture it but Enright resisted, though the mention of confession bothered him unreasonably. He remembered all those First Fridays when the mad aunt dragged him off to the chapel for confession, and waiting in the days that followed for the heavens or something damn heavy to fall on him because all he'd ever done was invent a few venials and kept the mortal to himself until he became convinced it wasn't his.

'But it was the Devil in Heaven that saved me.'

The young constable seemed suddenly to have achieved the elevated calm of a visionary. Enright looked up at the sky that Timmoney drew wonders from.

'The Devil in Heaven? Did you go get a dose of the DTs up in Tyrone or what?'

'No, it was an old story Father O'Rourke told me from his side of the country. Donegal. See, the Devil was wandering around by Gweedore one time, searching for souls to take off to hell with him. So he came on a man called Sweeney working away at his poteen still and grabbed him by the collar. Hold on a minute, Sweeney said, we'll have a drink before we go and not have the curse of the road on us. Right, said the Devil, and they had a few and headed off. But the Devil got so drunk, he started flying in the wrong direction, thinking he was going down into hell when really he was going up into heaven. Sweeney, though, was only gamming on drunk and when they sneaked in past the Archangel Gabriel, he was delighted with himself but certain the Devil would drag him out of heaven as soon as he sobered up. But the Devil didn't and do you know why?'

'I couldn't care less why.'

'Because Sweeney saw the honey but the Devil only saw the bees and swatted at them and got stung all over. And Sweeney saw the gallons of purest milk but the Devil saw only cow dung and fell in it and ran off out of heaven after five minutes.' Timmoney thrust his eager face towards Enright. 'See, the point is that the Devil wouldn't know heaven if he got into it, only make a hell of it for himself. Same thing with men who go down evil ways. All I had to do, Father O'Rourke told me, was trust in God. And then he quoted Deuteronomy at me. "For the Lord thy God bringeth thee into a good land".'

Old Marshall, in birth and death a Presbyterian and nothing in between, thought the Catholic God the ideal one for the seafaring man. *Do what you ruddy well like, whoring, cursing, drinking, and only spit it out in the dark to a priest and you're away again for more.*

'So, it's milk and honey for Kinahan and his crew, is it, Ned? Long as they're good Catholic boys?'

'I don't know. But I suppose . . . if they repent, like.'

The rear of the grey stone block had thirty-three eyes. Thirty-four if Enright counted the glass panel in one of the back doors. He wondered if the rebels were still inside and had them both in their sights. Timmoney loped long-legged and lazily reluctant beside him and Enright realised that what had felt like a determined bustling forward was instead a leaden struggle that sucked the breath out of the bad side of his chest. Trickles of sweat found their way in by the collar of his tunic and passed through the scarred creeks on his chest and back and thighs, not hurting but reminding. *Fifty-one wounds, Lieutenant!* How they'd laughed in the Bagthorpe Military Hospital that day. *One wound short of a deck, nurse, and no jokers. Why don't we count 'em and see can we find another one and have a game of Five Card Stud?*

He'd have to cut down on the Jameson for a while. A few shots tonight to celebrate Timmoney's return and leave it at that, he thought. An early night and a new start in the morning, get back his appetite, take an interest in the dogs again. Maybe they were better than he imagined, Arrow Valley

Snow in particular. There had to be something in a dog built like that. The first outing at Knockgraffon next week would tell a lot.

The workhouse hadn't been built with light in mind. Soup and shelter, he supposed, considered luxury enough for the poor. Timmoney had dropped a pace behind.

'They'll know you're carrying, Tom. There'll be trouble if this gets back to Gallagher.'

'To hell with them. I want them to know I'm on my guard night and day in case they get a notion I'm gone soft like the rest of that shower in the barracks.'

Timmoney squinted hard at him as though the half-light had revealed some new and unwelcome aspect of his sergeant. Like Gabriel Jack staring out at him from the shade of the trees on the plot after he appeared back out of the blue yonder. Standing stock still, a squat little totem carved out of a tree stump painted the colours of fall. *You're not thinking of turning me in, are you, Gabe?*

A little way up the stairs he had taken too quickly, Enright stopped to catch his breath. His calves ached and he leaned against the *mal-de-mer* green wall pretending to wait for Timmoney, who took the steps by pairs without a break in his slouching stride. That was the great thing about being young or, at least, not rattled to the core in a war, the unappreciated because unconscious ease of movement.

The spaces above him were filled not so much with noise as with a disturbed quiet. A cough here, a moan there, all muted; the creak of a door; footsteps on hard floors with the ring hollowed out of them by the time they reached Enright's ears as though he were below deck, down maybe as far as the pit of the engine room in a docked ship. The same teetering roll across his brain too, leaving him nauseous.

Enright pushed himself off the wall and continued his climb. At the next landing, Timmoney waited for him. Enright didn't look up, fearing the strain might show on his face. His heart raced as wildly as it had done all those times in the Canadian Red Cross Hospital when some cold-hearted doctor would send him scuttling up the stairs and take his pulse to prove he was recovering. *My head is spinning, Doc, how do you measure that or the weight in my legs?* They'd pushed him too hard too soon and later, out at the plot in Nelson, he'd pushed himself too hard and too soon. Those nights out in Clonore and down the town after Healy and out chasing the hare Shanahan, pushing himself along when he wasn't right and no wonder he was dragging his body along like a corpse after him now.

Timmoney whispered breathily from above.

'Tom.'

'Don't tell me you're winded already. After all your walking up in Tyrone.'

Joining Timmoney on the second landing, Enright discovered the reason for the shell-shocked daze he'd just divined in his companion. The three men standing above seemed, at first, as tall and arrogantly self-possessed as those plane trees Enright had hacked at until he dropped over in BC. Kinahan, in the middle, was the smallest of them, though the difference was negligible from where Enright stood. He recalled what he could of Kinahan's description in the file. Five foot five. That couldn't be right and the face astonishingly youthful and softer than he'd expected, the square chin less pronounced than in the photograph, the eyes not at all so coal-black or riveting.

'Mr Kinahan. Visiting the sick, are you? Isn't that very noble, all the same, a busy man like you.'

Kinahan's answer was to begin his descent with a studied casualness. His two companions followed, aspiring in vain to a similar nonchalance. Eamon Dwyer, the dead spit of his martyred brother that Papenfus had shot and Enright wondered if the fellow had the same steel in him as his younger sibling. Charlie Dooley, the chubby mellowness of whose face before Ballykinlar camp had fallen away and left him with a look as lean and vicious as a greyhound's.

The pair's resolve being too self-conscious, the weight thrown into their swagger made jerky string puppets of them. Kinahan was different. He glided downwards, his hands slung in his trouser pockets. Funny the things about a fellow no file could tell, Enright thought. Small things, but if you didn't know them you might as well have a photo of the fellow's rear-end for all you could tell from the black-and-white face. The way a fellow held himself and moved. The rolled-up sleeves in this thick-walled building that was colder inside than out. The eyes like flitting steps across the stones at a ford, barely alight-ing before moving on but the tread sharp when it touched.

Enright felt sure that Kinahan would stand his ground a step or two above not to lose face having to stand a few inches below him, but the young rebel came all the way to the landing. Martin Dwyer's elder double and Charlie Dooley stayed on the steps while Timmoney backed down the stairs a little. Kinahan gave the impression that he was waiting for Enright to speak or step aside and that he'd prefer the choice be made quickly.

'You're awful small for a big man, Paddy. The King of the Fairies.'

Kinahan allowed the trace of a smile to appear; a finely tuned show of condescension, enough to irritate but not infuriate. The faces of his henchmen displayed no such subtlety, the same fiery blush spreading from one to the other. Enright watched their hands, the ones out in the open and those secreted in bulky trench-coat pockets.

'You washed your face, Enright. The old polish must be hard to get off, is it?'

Even as he reeled at the rebel leader's directness, Enright found himself surprised by the voice. He had expected a boy's thin volume. The indented boxer's nose too had presaged a nasal quality, a fanatical whine. Kinahan's voice was neither thin nor plaintive. Instead, Enright heard the light baritone of a man at ease in the depths of himself. Kinahan looked at Timmoney rather than Enright when he spoke.

'I won't delay you, Sergeant. You're a busy man, I'm sure, and I've a few things to do myself.'

Dwyer and Dooley together moved down a step closer to the landing but hesitated as Enright continued to block their leader's passage. The crooks of their gun arms flexed more tightly, hidden fingers burrowed after triggers. Enright reached in through the unbuttoned gap in his tunic front.

'I hear you beat the tar out of those pups from the Bullring. Fair play to you. That's all the likes of those buggers understand, isn't it?'

Kinahan slowly helped himself to a cigarette and gave all his attention to the lighting up and the savouring of the first drag. He blew the smoke with deliberate ease in Enright's general direction, as if he knew of the bad eye and that this knowledge was only the beginning of what he knew about his adversary.

'Will you be calling in to the young one you crippled while you're here? She's only dying to meet you.'

His laughter at the unintended jest burst out of him before he could stop himself. He read the same disgusted indictment in the expressions of Kinahan and his cohorts. Timmoney too, no doubt, skulking behind him.

'I might be laughing, Kinahan, but I didn't string the wire across the road.'

The little knot of gristle on the flattened bridge of Kinahan's nose showed whitely through the light flush on his face. The smoke from his cigarette seemed to be filling up the landing and going nowhere. Enright's torn tear duct overflowed and his confidence began to spill away, his body letting him down as he knew it would; the fifty-one wounds, the ache in his chest, the nerve-tingling cramps in the leg muscles, and something new, a painful itch in his penis, *the last thing to go, Tommy lad*. The disarmed curiosity of the rebels unnerved him further.

'And Danny Egan that you shot in the back of the head and dumped him in a boghole?'

'You have some nerve, Enright. My brother, you bastard, and my cousin and Larry Healy in front of his poor wife and she with child. You should be roasting in hell long ago after all you done.'

'And what about Clem Shanahan who was supposed to be minding the tripwire. You won't be sticking his name up on your monuments beside Larry and the Dwyer boys, will you, Paddy?'

Kinahan stayed Eamon Dwyer's rage with a wave of his cigarette hand but Charlie Dooley broke his silence too and the rebel leader began, at last, to display some unease.

'You know nothing, Enright. Shanahan wasn't at Clonore.'

So spontaneous and insistent was Dooley's declaration that Enright knew he spoke the truth. What then had been the gasworks mechanic's mistake? The question, the awareness of the world's utter opacity, the vague shame attaching to his ignorance; all of these things wearied Enright and he responded bitterly.

'Are you still saving up for the false teeth, Charlie? Or Cathal, I hear you're calling yourself now. *Cathal gan Fhiacail.*'

'Tom, leave it, will you?'

Timmoney turned as pale as the watery sky outside the landing window as Enright ignored his objection.

'Did your brother Johnny tell you how he poked Helen Peters, Charlie? A bun in the oven for Ireland.'

'Charlie . . . Cathal, don't be drawn.'

Realising his mistake, Kinahan attributed it to Enright with a glare suggesting malicious depths that only moments before had seemed unlikely.

'That's right, Charlie. Do what the little fellow tells you or he'll put you on shorter rations than you had up in Ballykinlar.'

In an instant, Enright found himself crashing back against the wall, his hand knocked away from inside his tunic and two guns pointed at him from the men on the steps. It seemed impossible that a man as small as Kinahan could have taken him so easily and with such force.

'Don't shoot the young lad, Kinahan. He's not carrying.'

'There'll be no shooting. Not while there's a truce.'

Kinahan reached into Enright's tunic and relieved him of the Webley. While he unloaded the gun carefully with a professional respect, he spoke almost off-handedly, as though his dealings with Enright were of little consequence.

'You mightn't believe this but I'm standing between you and the grave. Don't tempt me to step aside. I'm holding a lot of men back from finishing you off, Enright, and every one of them has damn good reason. And I have too after what you did out at my house.'

Kinahan tested the heft of the Webley admiringly before passing it back to Charlie Dooley.

'I should push you down the stairs, Enright, like you done to Larry Healy.'

Timmoney stepped out from behind Enright's shadow.

'He wasn't pushed.'

'Shut up, Timmoney, you bloody clown.'

Kinahan smiled at Enright's outburst. He tossed the butt of his cigarette on the stone floor and stamped on it.

'I hear your dogs are running at Knockgraffon next week. Mind they don't go lame or worse on you. The white especially.'

'Why? Are you going to burn it like you burned the black?'

'We know who burned your dog. What we're trying to figure out is why he burned it.'

'Who?'

'Do you really think I'd tell you, Enright?'

'It was my dog. I deserve to know.'

'You don't even deserve to keep the white you stole. But at least Foley minds it better than the fellow up in Roscrea did.'

Enright's humiliation seemed complete. He wanted Kinahan to go. He wanted to sit down and stop the world's vertiginous somersaulting. His shoulder dropped to the wall alongside and he found some relief.

'I paid a fair price for the white.'

'Three guineas? I'd say that was a steal. Is it any good?'

'No.'

'What's wrong with it?'

'Running wide and blind.'

'He must've picked up that habit from you, Enright. Remember what I told you now. No more stirring it up with me or my men.'

Dwyer and Dooley reversed down the stairs awkwardly, their guns still pointed at Enright and guarding their leader's back.

Enright waited until all three had disappeared from view before shouting down into the stairwell.

'Don't forget to call into Helen Peters, boys.'

Timmoney vaulted up three steps of stairs, across the landing and a couple more steps up the next flight. As he listened to the muffled altercation below he whispered savagely at Enright.

'Will you shut up in the name of God?'

About to spit out an answer, Enright paused. The conference in the unseen pit below had ceased but had not been followed by retreating footsteps. The young constable swallowed drily, the smack of his throat audible in the profound quiet. Enright thought of haring it up the stairs but knew his legs weren't up to a race.

Kinahan's voice came deliberately raised and clear.

'No, lads, not here. Not yet.'

Timmoney lowered himself to rest on the stairs, all the while shaking his head in disbelief. Enright sat on the windowledge at the landing. His heart stumbled and ran, stumbled and lumbered too long before racing on again. White stars fell across his inner horizon and he heard that hiss in his ears that came when the mind tried to make something of the null silence. He closed his eyes to staunch the leaking tear duct. After Clancy got himself blown to kingdom come and Enright had kicked the stuffing out of the bit of him that was left, he'd raged, roared across the lines, promised revenge under the rain, vowed a slow dismemberment of the next Hun bastard he found bleeding in a trench but never got the chance, blown halfway to kingdom come himself.

'You might have had us shot.'

'Don't be giving me the holy eyes. I've had enough of them gawking at me. *He wasn't pushed.* Are you gone mad or what, making your confession to a gunman?'

'I don't want you getting all the blame. We all deserve it. That lot too.'

Timmoney's insistence on taking the blame reminded him too vividly of Gabriel Jack back among the trees on the Nelson plot. *I ain't gonna see you hang for doing what I didn't have the guts to do, Thomas.* Maybe he wouldn't have either.

'We could do with a few scoops, Ned, the both of us.'

'I'm off the drink and I'm staying off it.'

'No drink, no women. What's left?'

'I'm on a warning from Gallagher. He won't write me a letter of commendation for the Palestine Police if I keep going the way I was. Queer in the head from the ghosts I saw when I was drunk and thinking about that poor girl and who made her pregnant.'

Enright felt the old groggy nausea of waking up from ether, his body recalling the careless poking after shrapnel of harried doctors.

'What happened to joining the monks then?'

'I haven't decided yet. I still wonder about seeing the world or seeing a bit of it, at least, before I give it up.'

'You think you can give up the world? Not unless you're lucky enough to get half your head blown off like Danny Egan and all your bloody rotten memories along with it.' Enright looked up the stairs that led to the three injured men and shook his head. 'Go on up and take some statements from those thieving pups. Kinahan'll have them well warned not to tell us anything, but do the best you can.'

Timmoney removed his cap and wiped away the sheen of sweat from his shaven head. He played with the rim of the cap for a while, turning it around, turning something around in his mind to ask. Enright thought about Helen Peters or rather gave up trying not to think about her. The God Almighty indifferent cruelty of all that suffering for a shag or two in a loft.

Still fiddling with his cap, Timmoney hazarded his question. 'How many men have you killed in your life?'

Fellow would make a damn good priest all the same, Enright thought, with that guileless, forgiving tone.

'Not half enough. And no, I don't feel guilty and I don't look for forgiveness and if I had the chance again, I'd do the same and worse.'

'But that's your problem, Tom, can't you see it? If I had the chance again, you say, and it's like the men you killed aren't dead or dead enough. Without God, there's no place for the dead to go. And they weigh on you, Tom, it shows.'

'Bullshit, Ned. And as for you and the rest of the holy rollers, you're just soldiers looking for someone else to carry your pack.'

Timmoney shook his head and gave up whatever line of mystical logic he'd had in mind.

'Wait until you're out in the world, boy, and you'll know there's those want to die and can't. And those who damn well deserve to and don't.'

Marshall. *In the name of Christ, Tommy lad, have mercy on me and do me in.* Sailor-boy Paudie too, naked under the mad aunt's bed sheet, sleeping off a feed of free drink while she served out at the bar. The boy passing by the open door on his way out the back to slice some rashers off a side of bacon, the knife in his hand, his last memento of Bedford, his one inheritance. Dawdled too long and Paudie woke up. The pig eyes in the bloated flush. *I don't care what throats you cut or didn't cut but, by Jesus, you won't cut mine, boy.* His days in Listowel numbered after that. And worse still, the hard-won belief in his own innocence thrown into doubt again.

At the next landing, Dr Brady appeared. He descended regally, his chest out, the watch chain on his waistcoat swinging in tempo with his stride. Better not start coughing, Enright told himself.

'No rest for the wicked, what, boys?'

'Nor for the rest for us either, Doc.'

Brady, almost upon them, betrayed a hint of resentment at the familiarity.

'Did I talk to you about the TB before, Sergeant?'

'You did and I haven't it. I got poisoned with the chlorine gas, remember? Bronchitis is all it is.'

Close to, the elderly doctor betrayed the signs of a new frail-ness since Enright had last seen him. A sagging of the cheeks that spoke of self-doubt instead of the previous certainty; the little telltale quake in the voice; the mist of age on the eyes. The old duffer was in decline and knew it, Enright thought, and a thousand deaths witnessed in hovels and on bloodied street corners hadn't prepared him for that knowledge. Some corner to be stuck in, a doctor on the slippery slope and nothing he could do to help himself. Worse than a policeman who couldn't find out who burned his own dog.

'Sergeant, if you're not concerned about your own health, I can't be either. What concerns me is the danger you might pose to everyone around you. Your family, the men you work with. You need to think about that.' He turned dismissively from Enright and began to descend the next flight. Holding tight on to the banister too, Enright noted. 'In the meantime, I'll be having a word with the Head Constable. And keep away from that young one over in the laundry room. She's enough on her plate without a dose of TB on top of it.'

'She's dying anyway. It'd be a bloody ease for her to go, for all the good you can do her.'

Clamped between the shocked gaze of Timmoney and Dr Brady's outrage, Enright looked away from them and saw below the window at his side, Kinahan and his two henchmen crossing the front yard towards Helen Peters's mausoleum. If only he had the Webley. Drop one of them, any of them, before it was too late and all his strength had deserted him. What good was a man if he couldn't be master of the bit of space around him, if that space was no longer expanding but shrinking inexorably?

'Helen Peters will last a damn sight longer than you, Sergeant, if you keep going the way you're going.'

'It'd be more in your line, Doc, for you and that hunch-backed holy Mary to tell Helen Peters the truth about this shithole of a world and not have her believing in miracles.'

'The lady you refer to is not in a position to visit the girl any more.'

'Why? Because her nephew took his pleasure and ran, is it? Because she realised what a bloody hypocrite she was?'

'You haven't heard the end of this, Sergeant.'

The doctor's stiffness made of his hurried descent a ridiculous spectacle. In the yard below the window, Paddy Kinahan walked by Helen Peters's shed and on towards the front gate. Behind him, Dwyer and Dooley shared a cigarette and a joke. He wondered if a shiver passed through Helen Peters as they went by, if she felt that someone had walked across her grave.

'It's for your own good he was telling you, Tom. You don't look a well man.'

'You're another of them afraid I'll poison you. I thought I had a friend in you, Timmoney, but you're just another holy-eyed craw-thumper.'

'You don't want a friend, you want a dog that'll do what it's told and jump through the hoops for you, someone who'll listen to your old guff and believe it's wisdom. I'll go up and take those statements.'

'What the hell do you know about friends? Did you ever have one die on you?'

A stony face Timmoney's was, a boulder across a cave, a plaster statue saint's face.

Ten minutes later, Enright stood at the side of Helen Peters's bed. Not since the morning of the ambush had he seen her in daylight or what passed for daylight in that room. She had aged terribly, shockingly. Her raven hair, unwashed, had fallen to greasy locks, her eyes deep hollows bruised with dejectedness. On her face a film of dust seemed to have been gathering for too long. Gabriel Jack had that same ghostly pall about him when he appeared back at the plot after Mary had left. *I'm going down to Penticton to turn myself in, Thomas. Won't let no innocent man take the rope even if he's crazy.* Back then, Enright had been convinced the half-breed would crack once he found himself in a cell but there was no dissuading him. *I'll come along with you some of the way, so, Gabe, it's the least I can do.*

At first, she wouldn't look at him beyond an initial hurt dismissal. Then she couldn't keep herself from staring at him.

'Why are you crying, Sergeant? Is it the state of me?'

She cried too. Enright shook his head, and falling to his knees, buried his head in her bedclothes. All that way Mary came, he thought, for a man with more corpses in his head than a graveyard and more whores than a Barcelona brothel. He clung to a body that couldn't feel, with hands that seemed ugly, parasitic. A terrifyingly familiar sensation gripped him. It was as if his mind had forgotten how to hold itself together and had lost its corporeal bearings. He knelt on shifting ground, the blood he'd coughed up outside the shed sour on his tongue, tasting of dissolution. His every word seemed pathetic to him but would not be left unsaid.

'I'll never be right again, Helen, never be the man I was. I'm weak as a straw and I'm afraid I might be going mad from the swill in my brain.'

'I can't help you. I can't even help myself.'

'I know that, Helen, but I'll do anything for you, everything. I'll come every day and bring you . . . bring you . . . things, nice things, good things. There might be some reason then for me to wake up in the mornings. And you too maybe.'

'The things I want I can never have now. Maybe I never had a chance of getting them even when I was alive.'

'Don't send me away, Helen love. Let me do the decent thing with these hands for once in my life.'

'Don't call me love.'

Bedford,
Listowel

Dear Tom,

Why I am bothering to break the silence between us again,
God only knows. I can assure you though that it isn't to
plead with you but to lay my cards finally upon the table.
I certainly don't feel I owe you any explanation over
Martin Fuller. On the other hand, I feel it my bounden
duty to defend his honour and my own.

How long have you been holding him against me? All
you ever had to do was ask and I would have told you what
I am going to tell you now. It would not have been easy
for me because I would have been afraid. But I would
have told you, little and all as there is to tell.

Yes, I walked out with Martin Fuller for a little while. We
held hands and one day he even kissed me on the cheek but
for a reason you would never understand. It was over a book
that the two of us read and something I said about it that I
can't even remember any more. Books and travelling the world
was all he ever talked about. France and Russia and America.
Martin was never a well man and delicate from a child, as you
must know. For that reason he could never travel and it broke
his heart to be stuck forever in a poky little office.

And the terrible thing is, considering your outburst, that
you were a hero, nearly a God to him. He used call you
Ulysses. Any word from Ulysses Enright, he used ask and

not unpleasantly but all admiration. When I'd tell him where you were, I could see the dream in his eyes. His death shook me very badly. I felt very old after it and the world was a different colour ever after until you came back into it with your letter from Balfour.

To tell you nothing but the truth, Martin Fuller was never enough for me, as innocent as I was. He was too sickly to be good-looking and, secondly, he was too ordinary or at least his life was and I was too harmless to tell the difference. I only really started walking out with him because you stopped writing to me before the war. What was I to think only that you had no further interest in me?

I will not allow you to make me think Martin Fuller a shameful secret nor will I allow you to blacken a boy whose intentions were as snow. You were the same with Gabriel Jack, when all we ever did was swap songs and a laugh that I couldn't get out of you all that time on the plot. I am more convinced than ever that there is something wrong with the way Gabriel Jack disappeared.

As for your claim that I took you because I was stuck, I am slow even to dignify it with an answer but I must. Do you think, Mister Enright, that I never got a second look off any man only you before or after Martin Fuller? Do you think I don't even now?

If I am hard in this letter, you deserve every bit of it and worse. So I will say more. Smart and all as you are with your doubts, Jimmy's wedding day is fixed. It is the end of November and I won't be there. My own brother's wedding and I am not even talking to him any more after I heard about him sticking you up. He said he was only doing as he was told and that you, a soldier, should understand that. I still won't talk to him or now too, my mother, who is all 'what did I tell you?' which I can't bear.

Now, Mags has made me a very generous offer which I must tell you of. She is in another restaurant business with the man who persuaded her to leave Toussaint. Her offer is to pay mine and Jerry's way to Chicago to live and work with them. I have told her I will make a decision very shortly but that letter probably hasn't reached her yet.

I will freely admit that there's not much of me left to give but I'm prepared to give it for all our sakes if you come away with me. I must be soft in the head or gone very hard somewhere very deep inside, knowing all I know and suspect of you and yet still willing. That is who I am now and your famous letter from Balfour is but an old dream that I often doubt you even wrote but was the work of another heart, as surely as the handwriting was. If I felt old after Martin Fuller, I feel now like someone who has been dead for an eternity. Our child is the child of two ghosts. In Chicago or some other far place of your choosing he might find himself the mother and father any child deserves.

Your wife,
Mary

Bedford,
Listowel

Tom,

Aren't you very brave all the same, Mister Enright? Up there
all these weeks, hiding away and waiting for Jerry and me
to be gone. Well, you will have your wish. I am expecting
shortly to have the money from Mags and have already
been to the booking agent. We will, please God, be setting
sail from Queenstown on the 6th of December. A winter
passage but it can be no worse than what we have been
through already.

Yesterday was Jimmy's wedding and I went after all. He
went down on his knees nearly to me. He said he would
never raise a hand to you personally whatever about the rest
of his comrades. When I told him I was going over to Mags
in Chicago, he cried like a boy. He said he might never see
me again but would I at least be at his wedding. So I went.
My heart was breaking all day to remember our own day out
in Nelson when I thought I was in heaven not knowing that
among the four of us there were two devils, a French one and
an Irish one.

Everyone was fine to me at Jimmy's do. Not a bad word
nor even a dirty look all day. No one pretended you ever
existed but how could I pretend that? You might have thrown
my love and devotion to you back in my face but there are
times and even yesterday there were times when I could feel

the sweet memory of our better days, short and all as they turned out to be. All day they were asking me to sing and in such a foolish mood and with the courage of sherry, I sang. For you I sang 'Just a Song of Twilight' and though I don't expect you to understand why, it was the saddest moment of my life so far but I shed not a single tear.

I see you getting sick in the dark of the yard here outside the cottage and I cannot seem to care. I see you bruised by war and consumption in Balfour and less do I care. I see you covered in blood all those years ago in the field beside Gun-Mahony's estate and I know that I have broken myself with care for a man who will not care even for himself. It is not from lack of pity that I say these things because I do pity your troubled nature. For such a private man, there's something very exaggerated and public about everything you do that I have never quite been able to put my finger on. Something loud about you, even when you are at your most silent.

I suppose all men have things in their lives that are more important than their women, like farmers have their farms, shopkeepers their shops, or poisoned things even, like the drunkard and his drink. I don't know what you have deep down eating away at you but I know for sure it'll be the end of you. I can't let it be the end of me or especially Jerry.

My letters in latter days always seemed to displease you. On that score, you need have no more worries. I have no further claim on your life, Tom Enright, nor have you on mine. I return to you also your letter to me from Balfour with all its promises and lies. We made such a good start of it over there. We surprised each other, we quickened each other's hearts but we were never easy together because with you it is all running, rushing and bother until you fall down flat. At the end of the day, if a man and a woman cannot lie down together in peace there is no reason for them to be in the same house never mind the same bed.

There is nothing more we can do for each other only pray, which I can assure you I will never cease to do.

Goodbye and God bless,
Mary

*T*he last thing to go, *Tommy lad* and far from gone. Enright whipped off the blanket from over Helen Peters and found her naked beneath, her legs akimbo. He felt a slight give in his penis at the unexpected because impossible sight. Climbing onto the bed he kicked wildly against the snare of his trousers but couldn't free himself.

'Look at me. Fifty-one bloody wounds. One short of a pack and no jokers.'

'You don't like yourself very much do you, Tom?'

He knelt between her legs and realised that while he'd been distracted, her arms had raised themselves above her head. He felt afraid but imagined himself still to be strong enough to succeed with her. His torn flesh salved itself upon her perfect flesh.

'*Puedo ayudarte, marinero?*'

'I'll help myself, thank you.'

He laughed and raised himself for one final thrust. The cold of the hand that touched his naked back was deathly. The girl's arms hadn't moved from their upraised gesture of submission. All desire was rent by panic. He turned and, at once, flung himself in terror from the bed, and woke, spread-eagled, on the floor of his barracks bedroom. He shivered in the dark, trying to recall whose cold hand it was that had left a mark of such fiercely imagined bloodlessness on him. Ice it felt like, a frostbite that would spread the rot of death across him.

'You had dealings with Jim Donegan, hadn't you? Apart from the trouble over the British Petroleum lorry and the petrol, I mean.'

237

Gallagher's uncustomary forthrightness caught Enright off guard. Playing for time, he feigned a difficulty with easing back the chair on his side of the Head Constable's desk.

'I'd no dealings with him beyond that.'

'What I mean is Clonore and the information he gave you about the Dwyers. I've no intention of going into all that dirty business but I'm telling you now that there's no need for you to go enquiring into his disappearance. I have it on good authority from the Sinn Féin people that no harm came to him, that he's gone to England. His brother out in Holycross confirmed it to me. No question of kidnap or the like.'

'They ran him out of the country and you're happy to leave it at that? Jesus Christ, we might as well take off the bloody uniforms altogether and give them to Kinahan and his crew to swan around in.'

Donegan's departure felt like a bad omen. Reaching back awkwardly to that unrelentingly cold spot where the hand had touched him in his dream, he wrenched his neck and set off a spasm there.

'He wasn't run out of the place. He got a summons from this court of theirs. Hadn't paid the rent on the garage for two years and gave the poor widow woman who owns it nothing only the height of abuse. Then he takes every last penny out of his bank account and high-tails it.'

Enright raged against the looming sense of finality that oppressed him. He saw, down to every last detail, Helen Peters, not as in last night's shameful dream, but dead; the high-knuckled clench of the joined hands, the Punch-and-Judy nose, white, wintry, weakly scented flowers all about her.

'Their court is back in action? For Christ's sake, I broke my bloody back putting an end to that sham and now no one lifts a finger. Is it any wonder the Quarterly Assizes last week were a farce of pub found-ons and bicycles without lamps?'

'They're well within their rights to try arbitration cases under the Truce Agreement, you know that. And as for lifting a finger, what, may I ask, have you been up to this last month because you're doing sweet damn-all here in the barracks only sleeping half the day and moping around the rest of it?'

'What do you expect, putting me out of commission like that, sticking papers in front of me until I was goggle-eyed?'

A hissing swirl spun through Enright's head and left him with the curious impression that his superior had somehow drifted further back from him and seemed to hover a little higher than before. Like God, he thought, even as the nausea threatened to undo him.

'And another thing. You still haven't handed over the gun you helped yourself to after the trouble in the workhouse. You defied me. Well, you won't any more. Give me the gun. Now.'

'You know they took a gun off me that day.'

He was gripped once again by the expanding claw of ice on his back. Gallagher's expression revealed a sinister aspect that hadn't been apparent before.

'Which you shouldn't have been carrying in the first place. You were lucky you weren't done away with and young Timmoney along with you. I'm ordering you now, Sergeant. The gun.'

'They'll kill me if they think I'm not carrying.' It seemed to Enright that he'd stumbled on the truth. Keane wasn't the spy in the camp after all or, at very least, wasn't alone in his treachery. 'That's what you want, isn't it, Gallagher?'

'They could've shot you above in the workhouse, only Paddy was a damn sight more sensible than you were.'

Gallagher was a Shinner, had been all along. Tried to take the car off him, so he'd be a soft target on the train to Listowel or on foot around the town. And where was the car now? How could it take four weeks to fix? And now he wanted to take the gun too, make it easier still for Kinahan and his pals. Gallagher's proffered hand floated before Enright, a hairy, disquieting paw.

'So it's Paddy now, is it? All pals, are we? After all he done. Helen Peters, the Clonore men, Danny Egan. I should fucking shoot you, never mind give you back the gun.'

Two fiery red spots high on his cheekbones lit Gallagher's passion. It became infuriatingly clear to Enright that the Head Constable no longer feared him nor feared to let his detestation of him show.

'He's no friend of mine but I know this much for sure, he never ordered Danny shot. He was coming under pressure from higher up because they thought he was too soft, and when he was away in Limerick, one of his men took it on himself to target Danny and get himself up the ranks. You know how Danny was about death and funerals? Well, he went up to Clonore to the wakes of those men you shot. Yes, that you and Baldwin and Papenfus shot, and they took him away to Ballytarsna but not before they got a priest . . . a priest, God forgive him, to give Danny the last rites.'

'How the hell do you know all this? Who shot him?'

'I don't know who shot him and even if I did there's nothing we could do about it. Listen to me now. The rest of those rebels will be released as soon as a settlement is made in London and it will be. And soon at that. I don't want you carrying and I don't want you next nor near the railway station when they arrive. Don't force my hand, Tom, and don't draw them on you, because if you do, you'll be on your own.'

'I'm damned if I'll march around with my hands hanging. You won't get rid of me as easy as that.'

Gallagher looked around the room as though he hoped that when he looked back across his desk, Enright might have disappeared. He sighed, picked up a letter and dropped it on Enright's side of the desk.

'I sat on this too long. I thought you'd come to your senses and realise the state you're in. It's a note from Dr Brady. He thinks you might have TB and I have to take his word. He wants you in the infirmary next Wednesday, to check you out properly. And what's more, he says you'll have to stop calling up to that young one every night of the week and let her die in peace.'

Enright's rage was a loose, dissipated, ranging thing that could find no true focus.

'Christ Almighty, I'd know if I was that sick, I was sick and dying often enough. It's a stunt is all it is, to get rid of me so your Shinner pals can have it easy.'

A rasping knock on the door came, at first as a relief to Gallagher's weariness and Enright's confusion but a further quick succession of knocks announced an urgency neither man was in the mood to respond to. Timmoney peeped in the half-open door. His hair had begun to grow again, not in lank black waves but stiff and straight as a yard-brush, giving him a permanently startled look.

'Bollocks, Timmoney.'

'What? Why?'

'What is it, Constable?'

'Judas.'

'Constable Timmoney, are you gone deaf or what? What is it you want?'

'Mr Foley to see the sergeant, sir. He says it can't wait. It's about the dogs.'

'You never made an effort to move those dogs, Enright, and all the times I asked you.'

'Someone let your dogs out on the street, Tom. What am I accused of? Judas?'

Enright felt besieged as if by gilly-gilly boys, hawkers pouring up onto a deck. *Cheapess price, Panama hat, velly cheapy Malacca canes, beeg value, jig-a-jig.* Dogs, guns, TB, rotten dreams, every bothersome thing. Nothing ever went away or stayed away forgotten.

'I'll have them forcibly removed.'

'Foley says you'll have to talk to Cullinane.'

'What? Cullinane? Why?'

Enright was standing though he couldn't remember how that had come to be. Suddenly it occurred to him to buy bull's-eyes for Helen Peters. Maybe bull's-eyes might do what rosewater, black enamel Chinese clips, perfume, lavender soaps and chocolates had failed to, lift her out of her drowning for more than a few precious minutes. Bull's-eyes. He laughed aloud.

'He has every right, Tom.'

'Who has? What?'

The floor tilted under him.

'Cullinane, he means. Did you not know he took over the garage?'

Enright got his legs moving like the child's that day below in Bedford and there would be Helen Peters's shed to fall into before they gave out. He wondered if there was a bottle of Jameson in the day room or if he'd taken it upstairs with him. A fellow would nearly pray for the drink to be in the day room, he thought, and laughed again.

'There's a turn-up for the books, Timmoney. You wanted to be Christ the Saviour and you ended up a Judas pretending to be a pal and snooping on me for Old Grey Whiskers here, carrying stories . . .'

Gallagher took imperial possession of his throne again, fingering his papers of state with a worrying aplomb.

'Do you really think you're the only one with eyes and ears on the street, Sergeant? And a damn sight more respectable and refined than your Mr Donegan at that.'

'Refined?'

'Yes, refined. My informant doesn't burn dogs for a start.'

'Donegan burned my dog? You're lying, Gallagher.'

'Sir, to you. You'll keep that appointment with Dr Brady. No ifs or buts. No more dragging the heels. I can tell you now a transfer is on the cards for you. Or if I'm pushed to it, I'll have you suspended.'

Gallagher's office had that high, manic atmosphere of ether before the sudden dark drop about it. Donegan's treachery seemed to Enright a matter of little consequence, the impossibility of ever avenging it a minor irritation.

'Suspend me from what? The rafters above in Baldwin's room?'

'Will I help you catch the dogs, Tom?'

He ducked through the gap between Timmoney and the doorjamb.

'Go way the two of you to hell. I'm off to buy some bull's-eyes.'

The quart of Jameson, his first in weeks, made a phosphorescent lightness of the overcast sky. Enright's mind had cleared and become high and wide with optimism. He was a tree, it occurred to him, that could never be felled because there was a fist-like core in him, a knot that resisted every last cut of the axe. He might shed a few leaves and even a dead branch or two but he'd survive the winter and when the cold had passed he'd be stronger than ever. The breeze along Friary Street stung his flesh but he told himself that this was Pago Pago compared to a winter's dogwatch at Cape Horn.

Neither Foley nor the dogs were anywhere to be seen and the big timber doors of the garage were closed. A few cursory kicks elicited no response. Cullinane had bolted, he supposed, after Foley reported to the barracks. From the far end of the street, which wound from sight a hundred yards off, he heard the barking of dogs. Every man should know the sound of his own animals but Enright realised he no longer did.

As he crossed the street towards Kennedy's grocery shop, he decided the two brindles and the blue would have to go. But not the white, which had made the last four in a decent stakes its first day out at Knockgraffon and almost won out in a good card down in Mallow. Maybe it would be third time lucky in Kilmallock next week. Enright still hadn't decided if he would go himself, thinking he'd put a hex on the dog like he put on everything else. He passed by the entrance to Monk's Lane, holding his breath from the stale odour of cabbage and cold smoke.

The ringing of the bell over the grocery door seemed almost celebratory to Enright as he went inside. The mean-spirited silence of the moustachioed grocer annoyed him hardly at all. When he stepped back outside, he saw that the garage doors had been opened and felt a thrill of expectation at the prospect of punishing Cullinane. A metallic tinkling rang out across the street and he saw Cullinane peering out from the deep pit under the barracks Ford.

'Jaysus, Cullinane, you're an awful man. Have you Bridie in there with you this hour of the morning?'

Enright felt the same ugly, angry stirring in his crotch, as in the dream of Helen Peters. Something heavy fell with intent to the bottom of the pit and the eyes slipped away from under the grille of the Ford. Enright fished out some loose change from his pocket and pressed the knuckles of his charged fist into the palm of the other hand. The movement in the pit became less decisive. The raw tickle of his hardening became a craving and he pressed it away with his fist. His heart began to race too quickly. Sweat trickled annoyingly inside his tunic that had already become a burden. Cullinane appeared from behind the car before Enright expected him to and he wondered where the last half-minute had gone because it seemed to have passed him by.

'Did you let my dogs out on the street?'

Clean-shaven and with not a hair out of place, the mechanic nodded and gave his attention to the cleaning of his hands on an oil rag. When he did raise his head, he tossed the oil rag brusquely to the bench beside him, making the one off-handed gesture of both acts.

'I had a visit from a couple of Roscrea lads yesterday. Why did you tell them I sold you a dog?'

'Don't tell me they roughed you up. Isn't that desperate?'

Cullinane rolled up his shirtsleeve and held out the thick forearm. A large angry bruise covered the greater part of it.

'Go way out of that, Cullinane, that's a love bite.'

'You're a vulgar man, Sergeant. How would you like if someone talked about your girl like that?'

'What girl?'

Helen Peters had come immediately to mind and the conviction that Cullinane, too, knew of his nightly visits to her. The mechanic's hand hovered by a thick spanner on the workbench.

'Your wife, if you're married.'

The fellow made no move to ready himself.

'Nobody turns my dogs loose and gets away with it.'

Like a dreaming watchman, the mechanic lolled, a lazy eye taking Enright's measure and so unruffled at the result that his arms appeared to slacken further. Cullinane blocked the first punch so easily that both men paused in surprise before Enright's loose left strayed off target and found a solid upper arm instead of the face he wanted to bloody. His right came up again but somehow lost its knuckleduster coins along its passage and met the mechanic's chin too weakly to do any more that set the teeth juddering together. Cullinane grimaced though not in pain. From the tip of his tongue that touched along the crowns of his teeth, he spat out a chip. With a look of disbelieving offendedness, he threw an unpractised but rock-like punch at Enright and put him on the oil-sloppy floor of the garage.

A long way from the undefeated dockwalloper of old, Enright raised the top half of his body and leaned against the curved fender of the Ford. He looked down at his soiled uniform. His head rolled and he snapped it back upright.

'I'll kill you for this, Cullinane.'

'Why did you take a set against me from the start?'

'I knew your game, boy. Any fellow who says he threw up everything for love has to be up to no good.'

'If you ever loved a woman you might understand.'

Enright stirred himself too hastily and the few inches he'd gained on his ascent were lost. He felt the despair of helpless rage as in those days after Marshall's death when the sores started appearing on his own body somewhere along the Red

Sea bound for Tandjungpriok and not even the old goat's corpse to kick around because it was weighed down in the depths and leaking its poison into the waters of the world.

'I have a wife. And before that, I had a hundred women from Barcelona to Singapore.'

'I should've let Johnny shoot you above at the workhouse.'

When Enright found his feet, it was like being up in the royals of a mast. A feint of soaring airiness passed through him and took him a little way with it. He held on to the side of the Ford.

'So, you're a Shinner after all. Why am I not surprised? Didn't they hand over the garage to you after they hunted Donegan away?'

'The woman who owns the place asked me if I wanted to rent it. I knew nothing about Donegan's troubles. And I'm no rebel. I pulled Johnny away from shooting you that night when the girl started screaming.'

'Why were you with him up there, if you weren't one of them?'

'I had to get him seen to after you beat him up. He started coughing up blood when we got him home and how could I let Bridie up to the infirmary in the night with him?'

Dogs barked on the street outside and were answered by a guttural yelp that Enright recognised as Foley's. A wave of melancholy washed over him, a tepid shower of self-pity that was almost comforting.

'I'm sorry. I shouldn't have hit you. I can see you're not well.'

Enright's bad eye leaked a tear. He let it fall, too tired to brush it away. The quarrelsome dogs drew closer. A rawness burned upon his skin, across all the old wounds. He was burning up. *I can feel the flames of hell, Tommy lad, if I pissed now I'd piss fire.*

'Will you not believe me, Sergeant? I saved your life. Would you not just let me live mine in peace?'

Enright spat on the garage floor by Cullinane's boot. He went back out onto the street to meet the ghost of his father and his spectral dogs.

In the lift of the girl's smile, Enright became momentarily playful in spite of his sense that he was re-entering that wild dream place. Like a vaudeville magician, he swept the brown paper bag of bull's-eyes out from behind his back.

'When was the last time you tasted a bull's-eye, Helen?'

He hoped there would be some faint trace of music left in her answering voice and not the dirge-like monotone of the last few evenings that had marked a new descent from hope in her.

'There's no need to be bringing me something every time you come, Tom.'

Her smile wavered and her music was a descending scale. Sooner than he'd hoped, Enright felt that veering off course that would leave them both floundering before evening's end.

'I'll hold you up while you're sucking them.'

Only a hint of the old odour of neglect clung to her now. She smelled of perfumed soap and rosewater. The deep yellow glow of the oil lamp flattered her.

'That's plenty high. I'll try a bull's-eye now.'

Enright opened the bag and found that the sweets had welded together into an amorphous mass. He took a tight grip on the uneven lump that had the indented feel of a Mills bomb. He cracked it against his knee and the bull's-eyes flew like bullets onto the counterpane of the bed, against the wall beside him, across the slate floor. For an instant, he felt certain that the girl's body had come alive, so electrified was she by the shock.

He opened his fist. Three bull's-eyes remained, none of them quite whole. Her lips parted to reveal the tip of a waiting tongue. His hands felt unclean as he placed the sweet between her teeth. Her tongue flicked at his fingers as she drew the bull's-eye in. He knew that he shouldn't, that it was too strange, but he placed his moistened fingers to his lips.

Helen closed her eyes, savouring the sweet, and as he wondered what memories came with the taste she began to cry. He thought he might scream. He thought that if he was a dog, he could at least howl and bark and not have to give himself or anyone else a reason and not have to think he was going soft or mad again because of the broken thing lying in his arms. The crackle and splinter as she bit into the hard sweet ricocheted along his arm.

'Don't be biting on it, girl, you'll chip a tooth.'

'I'll have one more only. When I start, I can't stop.'

Enright didn't know if she meant the sweets or the tears.

The second sweet, sticky from the sweat of his palm, stubbornly attached itself to his fingers. She licked and sucked so hard to prise it away that when she succeeded, the bull's-eye shot into the back of her throat and the convulsive panic that seized her invaded Enright too. He watched her pleading, terrified eyes begin to bulge, but before he could move to help her he wondered whether he should let her die. Let her go, he thought, like he'd let Mary go.

Her head rocked madly on his extended arm, her strangled groan resonating in him. The absurd indignity of her dying because of a boiled sweet propelled him into action. He bundled her upward and smacked his hand firmly into the middle of her back that felt oddly crusty as he did so. Blood began to seep through the flannel of her nightdress. The convulsions worsened and the thrashing movement of her entire body was no illusion now. He punched her a little further up the spine and again came the bloom of blood. *But every day our love blooms, gets, grows . . .*

Bed sores, he realised with relief, wounds she couldn't feel, though he felt the raw sundering of old scabs on her behalf. Another punch triggered the barrel of her throat and he saw the bull's-eye shoot from her mouth, hit the iron end-rail of the bed and smash into pieces. She fell back on his arm, gasping for breath, her face frozen in a grotesque rictus of humiliation and defeat.

'I'm sorry, Helen, it's my fault for bringing the damn sweets.'

She shook her head and moaned softly, unrelentingly. The damp of her blood spread along the underside of his arm. He couldn't think what to do about her wounds, whether to undress and bathe her or leave it to the attendant to do in the morning, by which time the flannel would have stuck fast to the wounds though she would feel nothing when they were peeled off.

'You should've let me die, Tom.'

A long interval passed in which the arm holding her head grew stiff and then began to tingle with a presentiment of numbness. He couldn't help thinking that he'd saved her for his own sake, to drag every last ounce of comfort he could out of her. He was no better than the ones who'd crippled her and those who took advantage of her longing to be more than a servant girl with no past or future. Both Enrights were the same, the one shivering as he held her and the one like a dog in heat of his dream.

'Go on home to bed, Tom, you're very tired.'

Amiably dismissive, a woman addressing a young boy who would never understand her needs and desires.

Enright wandered aimlessly around the outskirts of the town. A light frost lay upon the fields he crossed. His legs aching, his trembling sometimes furious, he felt drawn to the river and followed its course through the town. He heard singing and laughter from busy pubs, celebrating the return of yet another freed rebel, he supposed. He heard silence from the orchard garden of the convent, women safe among their own. Under the river bridge he rested and listened to the drag or hurry of footsteps above and caught snatches of conversations distended by the hollow lapping of the water. He hurried along the more exposed stretch of river bank beyond the bridge and soon found the cover of a tree-lined path, only then realising where his feet carried him. The Dooleys' house, whose garden backed on to the river just up ahead. He wished he'd brought the Jameson to warm himself up but he had the gun and that was more important should he chance upon either or both of the Dooley brothers.

His boots untied and cast off, the thick socks absorbed the pin-pricks of the stony path. The cap of the garden wall, quilted in an ivy slithery with frost, hastened his descent to the lawn inside. Six windows to the back of the house and three of them lit, he observed. Two downstairs, one above, and none with curtains drawn. When he had gone halfway along the garden, Webley in hand, the piano started up.

He stood beneath the wide, bare-leaved crown of a copper beech. The music was, as yet, too fragmented to make sense of. *Songs Without Words*, he thought, and remembered Gabriel Jack launching into one of his songs without words up among the pines off the road to Penticton. *Stop the humming, Gabe, and don't be looking back at me.* Ponderosa rust smeared over Enright's face after he'd steered the half-breed into the trees with the Colt Peacemaker. Hadn't known where he was going that night either, but Gabe had; the steep-sided gorge, buried in the sloping woods and impossibly deep, but of a span that with a bit of luck a man might leap across.

Enright scurried forward towards the house, his attention divided like waters parted by a mid-river island, murder and music flowing through his mind. A short clearing led to the next tree in his path. A sour apple tree, by the gnarled squat look of it, and when he reached its shelter, the music's disparate nature had been tamed and marshalled to harmonious purpose. Enright wondered whether if he stepped slowly back, he might find the precise point where the music disintegrated.

Along the foot of the rear wall lay a flowerbed whose clay had been turned for the winter. The blocks of frosted earth crumbled under his feet so that, as he approached the window from which the music emerged, he seemed to be sinking further with each step. At the edge of the fan of light before him, he paused and crouched. He saw only an empty corner of the room inside, crossed with indecipherable shadows. On his knees he drew closer to the window. The music had become rivery and soulful. Enright leaned against the wall and his heart slowed to the music's measure. His gun hand grew lazy too. He knew he couldn't shoot the Dooley boys in front of Bridie and the aunt, the virginal and respectably middle-aged La Cheposa.

He closed his eyes. The soft knell of the bass notes reverberated in some deep lonely place within him, the higher trills trickling pleasantly along the hunched curvature of his spine. Funny how a fellow roamed the night with a scream trapped in him, mad for wild relief, and found instead this music, intricate and swift in its particulars but containing within a sweeping grandeur that somehow raised his spirits without exciting them. He knew he wasn't one to judge but it seemed to him that Bridie Dooley played very beautifully and with a gravity so belying her years that she might have had as hard a time of it as Mary, driven to distraction by a madman. No more of that for Mary, he thought, nor would the child have a useless old man for a father.

He put the Webley back inside his tunic. Bridie Dooley was all right. Maybe a slicker of a lad like Cullinane really would give up everything for her. He remembered her look that night on Friary Street. Fearful perhaps but curious and brave too, wanting to know something of him so that she might understand, like Mary when he started to come right in the Balfour San. *Is it sometimes very hard for you to sleep, Tom, with all those terrible things on your mind?* He regretted having upset the girl that night with his loose talk of Cullinane and speaking so crudely of her to the fancy Dan mechanic. He felt sorry that this girl whose playing was replete with such depth of feeling should find nothing but discord in the life she had dreamed for herself.

The windowsill looming above him was the lip of the Jack Johnson hole up in front of Commotion Trench as Clancy talked to the dead Hun up on the brow, pretending the corpse was his dead brother. *Get up, Ramie, we've the milking to do.*

Then his mad eyes had widened and Enright, looking over his shoulder, saw the dead mouth opening impossibly and emitting a sound like a wet grunt that electrified them. Another grunt emerged from the corpse's mouth and the head of a rat poked up out of it, and filthy wriggling, the rat slid out and away and Clancy was on his feet. *I'm away to do the milking, Tom.* Gave the game away with his *Tom,* not mad at all, only driven demented there, where he would never have been had Enright not gone back to the Essondale asylum and talked him out with the promise of adventure.

He crept closer to the window and what he saw scraped at his every last bone. He couldn't understand why he felt so profoundly unnerved to find that it wasn't Bridie Dooley but her hunchbacked aunt who commanded the keys. Her niece's arm lay lightly across the white crocheted shawl, confirming his earlier impression of the older woman's deepening fragility. There seemed no explanation for the grief that consumed him nor for the consternation that ensued. He wanted to scream at the woman to stop playing but instead dragged himself away from the window and, abandoning caution, raced down the length of the garden, slipping and sliding on the frosted grass, scraping and scrabbling at the garden wall like a frog stuck in a shell-hole and up over the parapet and down the other side, a dead man falling.

He found his boots and set off into the night again.

God only knew where the real bleeding statue stood now. Maybe that young chancer, Walshe, had taken it with him, a souvenir of his blasphemous shenanigans. Hardly, Enright thought. More than likely the Blessed Virgin lay hidden in some old wardrobe or shed, its possessor too superstitious to dump the thing. Not that it mattered to him. Any old statue of the Blessed Virgin would serve his purpose and he knew where to find one.

For all his haste, he seemed to be walking the two miles to the Auxies' vacated HQ at old Sebastian Bennett's pile for a very long time. More than once, he stopped and tried to take his bearings lest he'd already gone by the grand pillared entrance to the house. With each delay, the cold burrowed deeper into him and he set off less certain than before, thinking that even Danny Egan for all his foolishness had known his way around in the night on the Castle Bennett Road. When, at last, the pale sentinel pillars raised themselves, the sense of reassurance galvanised Enright and he hurried through the greener dark of the yew-lined avenue.

The front door of the house refused to yield to the pummelling from his shoulder. In the window alongside, the small pane by the catch resisted his elbow twice, three times, before giving in with a crashing noise that seemed hugely disproportionate. Though he knew no cottage stood within half a mile of the place, he worried none the less while the silence emptied itself out again. He found the catch of the window among the pointed shards that remained embedded in the frame.

Inside the house, he felt jumpy among the shadows from the matches he lit. He caught a glimpse of a grand piano, the serpentine curve of a love seat, a flash of his wild self in a mantel mirror, and finally a door. From the hallway he turned left into the pitch-black passage that led to the chapel. His hand reaching forward, he moved gingerly along, but stumbling on an unanticipated downward step, he pitched forward. His forehead met some hard rounded point on the carved chapel door and he sank to his knees, stunned by the blow.

When he found himself standing again, he felt certain that several minutes and perhaps more had passed though he couldn't tell for sure. He lit one of his last matches to find the door handle. The figure carved on the timber of the door, naked but for a loincloth, stood tied to a leafless tree and had copped five or six arrows. As the door heaved itself inwards, he felt the gnawing sadness that sacred interiors always induced in him.

Some residue of superstition, he supposed, the boyhood memory of God's indifference to his prayers, a magic denied him.

He saw obscurely the statue in its alcove to the left of the altar. The prospect of lugging the thing, three foot tall and a big blocky base adding to the tonnage, two miles into town wearied him. He steered his way through the pews and at the centre of the altar found the red-globed lamp he remembered seeing inside the chapel when Papenfus had let him down. He lit the stub of thick candle inside and sat on the carpeted plinth below the altar.

In the red bordello light, the carved panelling along both walls etched itself lightly upon his vision. Scarlet and black figures trembled a flickering moment and when they came to rest Enright thought he knew what it was that Danny had lost in Castle Bennett.

He didn't imagine that all of the wooden panelling was Danny's work and, at first, there seemed no way to confirm which figures the ex-soldier had retrieved from the oak plane. He searched for resemblances to Danny in the halfpenny-sized side faces of Christs, apostles and centurions but discovered none. In Mother Marys and Mary Magdalenes he looked in vain for Danny's wife; the thick eyebrows meeting above the nose, the broad plainness of her face. He tried for some signature stamp along the edge of the panelling and again found nothing. He turned from the wall and as if by divine direction found himself face to face with Danny's handiwork.

A certain pliancy in the Virgin's features, a flatness in the colours, suggested that the paint lay not merely on the surface but had been absorbed. The statue was made not of plaster, as he'd presumed, but of wood. A touch confirmed the intuition, a subtle lithe agreement between the pads of his fingers and the material. Oak again, he thought, from the weight as he tilted the statue back and peered at the base.

Mary of the Sorrows, Montanês – Daniel Egan Jr. He felt glad that Danny had left some kind of a mark on the world, even if it was on a lump of wood hidden in the private chapel of an abandoned mansion. A hell of a lot more, Enright knew, than his own swinging of an axe through the plane trees outside Nelson and failing to get to the end of them, as he'd failed to get to the end of everything else he'd ever turned his hand to.

He took the altar globe with its sputtering, hissing flame and raised it towards the face. Nobody he knew or had ever seen and not unimpeachably beautiful. The nose a fraction too long and flat along the bridge. The mouth too wide and too great a recess in the philtrum. Yet Enright was moved by the familiarity of her expression. Hadn't he wrought that same disappointed abstraction in Mary White's face often enough, that downward glance from the ruins of affection? And in Helen Peters too, hadn't he sculpted that mildly embittered cast of the upper lip? *You should've let me die.*

The candle gave a last fluttering salute of light and died. Gripping the hard folds of the statue's drapery, he stumbled under the weight. Then he heard the shuddering bass of something falling and bouncing along to a deliberate halt elsewhere in the house. He lowered the statue to the floor and listened a long while, his Webley at the ready. He soft-shoed his way to the chapel door and along the dark passageway, mindful of the step he'd missed earlier.

For all of an hour, he crept quietly about the house, pushing in creaking doors and silent ones, watching for a stir among the shadows, checking every room on his way up through the house and again on his way back down. With the Virgin up under his arm and the free hand wielding the Webley, he listed to starboard as he ventured out from the chapel. Apprehension doused him from his dog-tiredness and he listened to the dark countryside for the skulk and brush of ambush.

Fuck it, he told himself, only two miles to go.

*Y*oung Mary White places her box in the long grass. She raises the crinkling veil of leaves from the boy's hiding place. He has retreated into what he imagines is an impenetrable darkness. But the dog barks and its whiteness is a ghostly glow and the knife in his hand seems to glisten. He has never known a silence so profound as the sibilant stream below him.

'Are you all right, Tom? Where did all the blood come from?'

'It's not all my blood. Only some of it is.'

He feels ashamed to be cowering, ashamed to be the pathetic object of this girl's holy concern. Yet her presence makes him want to cry and because he cannot understand this desire, he despises her. His sweat moistens the dried blood on his face. She is so close that her white dress brushes across his cheeks. He sees the stain on the dress though Mary White doesn't.

'Are you hurt, Tom?'

'No. Go way and leave me alone.'

His free hand scrabbles for support on the awkward incline above the stream and falls upon a rock fashioned by time and weather and chance to fit the flexed cleft of his palm.

'You should go home, Tom. It's getting dark.'

'So should you.'

The boy weighs the rock and the knife on the scales that are his hands, sensing the oddness of the lighter object being the more lethal.

'I will so if you're going to be like that about it. I only wanted to help you.'

She waits a last while before she releases the hissing swoosh of hedging. The perplexed dog whines to have lost sight of the ink-blue sky. Every moment is darker and more dangerous now.

When the boy shouts, the white leaps away into the void where the leash catches it like a wall and the dog plummets into black water that burns with unexpectedness.

'What's in the box?'

'There's nothing left in the box.'

Mary White's far-away voice is tremulous or the boy hears it tremblingly, he cannot tell and does not ask himself which.

'What used be in the box?'

He decides to use the stone first, then the knife.

'That's for me to know and you to find out.'

The white splashes itself upright in the shallow stream. It begins to piss hard into the water and barks urgently a wild warning. There is too much noise for the boy to hear the swishing grass of Mary White's retreat and measure it. So he calculates; her familiar, short deft strides, the topography of the field. He absorbs the plangent protests of the dog and makes of them a stillness within. He readies the rock, locates the dog's skull above the slavering wheeze the barking has reduced itself to.

The boy moves quickly among the dog's electrified limbs and he batters the skull until it cracks. There is pride and satisfaction in having so accurately divined the dark dimensions, but no time to savour either emotion. His wrist is briefly ensnared in the wide, toothy jaw that cannot scream because it is a dog's and cannot bark because its brain is pouring out and, with it, all instinct of what can or must be done.

The frantic machine of the dog's body is giving out. Wetness is everywhere. Blood or water, spittle or the slush of grey matter, the boy does not know or care. He plunges the blade between the dog's ribs and leaves it there. Then, with his bare hands, he throttles the dog. His own mad pulse seems born of the desperate thrashings of the animal and races on beyond its last frozen moment. The boy is holding a thing carved of ice and stone. He lets go and it tumbles heavily in upon itself. He listens to the darkness falling. The cattle in Gun-Mahony's field move like spies. He imagines their startled eyes and the vision incites him.

Above the field hovers a multitude of stars, vast as his exploding thoughts. He is huge to himself and yet invisible to the world. Visions of the slaughter to come propel him through the hedge into Gun-Mahony's landscaped pastures. Amidst the web of elder, whitethorn and barbed blackberry vines, he holds back a thick branch to ease his way through. A thorn drives itself cruelly under his fingernail and the branch snaps back and meets his temple and the queer sleep of concussion empties the boy from time.

Later, when the boy regains himself, his father is calling from a far field.

'She's gone, Tom, look what you started!'

The boy imagines his mother rising from her bed and down the narrow stairs, seeming to float in her long nightshift and out into the night and beyond that he cannot imagine.

The boy is standing among Gun-Mahony's cattle. The light is different here beyond the rude contours of peasant fields. The boy looks up because he cannot look at what lies in the field before him. He has never seen a fruit so full and ripe and unattainable as this moon. A moon coloured with a memory of the sun. The colour of Mary White's hair. But the sight of the dead cattle proves irresistible. The slick of their slit throats, the bulbous pickled eyes fearing him. He can neither remember slaughtering them nor yet believe in his own innocence. He cannot remember hearing their last cries. He thinks he has been dreaming but doesn't know if the dream has yet ended.

Small in the long grass, he runs through fields that are all eternities. Then the moon dies and is wrapped in a shroud of cloud. The black sky chases him down like a seamless flock of screaming crows. A blood-warm rain falls on the running boy and he loses his bearings. He lies down in the wet grass and cries. Even a dog, he tells himself bitterly, knows its way home.

Six days pass before they find him miles away in a cove at Ballybunion staring at the sea. When they ask him where he has been all this time, he tells them in all truth and bafflement that he has been dreaming. Then they take him back to the cottage. His mother has left for heaven with the stillborn brother. The boy cannot sleep that night with the blue-blind baby of his father's description crying in his mind.

On the seventh day, Sergeant Larkin takes his father away.

Tom Enright was a shellback. More than that, he was a golden shellback, having not only crossed the International Date Line three times but, first time around, passed through its point of convergence with the equator. Crossing westwards, he had gained one day in the calendar of his life, but crossing east, he had lost two.

Marshall it was who'd taken the part of King Neptune and presided over his initiation and that of half a dozen others. Red-robed and paper-crowned, he'd prodded the pollywogs to the deck with his wooden trident and Enright had taken the head-shaving and the ducking in good spirit. On his second crossing, his face blacked above an oakum beard, he'd played with a savage enthusiasm the role of Royal Constable and roughed up a second mate who'd pulled rank once too often. But as he lay in his barracks bed the morning after his exertions with Danny Egan's oak virgin, the feverish disarray within him found its precedent in his third, ill-starred crossing.

Somehow he'd hidden the sores and the debilitating weakness for long enough to be taken on board the *Amphitrite*, a Vancouver-bound steamer, as a workaway. Two days he'd stayed on his feet before his forehead met the deck and he woke in rabid terror of the endless plains of seawater that were poisoned with dead Marshall calling in dulcet whispers from the deep. *The last thing to go, Tommy lad.* Then, somewhere between Suva and Apia, the door of the cabin where he'd been quarantined flew open and a drunken mob of Royal Constables and Royal Barbers, some blacked, some masked, mistaking him for a pollywog, jollied him to a battered pulp before the captain and the first mate dragged them away.

The statue lying under the covers beside him, Enright sensed that the precipice over which he'd fallen after Apia and which had left him a jittering wreck in the Male Chronic Building at Essondale loomed close by again. *Two kinds of madmen, Tommy lad, the harmless ones who don't know they're mad and the dangerous ones who do.* His father had said the same of fools. All morning he lay there reining in the crazier impulses, a slipper holding back the apoplectic dogs as the hare went by. Every footstep on the landing outside his bedroom door seemed replete with stealth and malice. Every whisper joined in conspiracy. He challenged each sound with a warning shout and aimed the Webley at the door but couldn't bear the tremendous weight for very long.

Half-dreamt speculations, by turn, frightened and assuaged him. They had decided to kill him. The whispers, the comings and goings were the advancing and retreating arguments over which of them might brave the storming of his room. A sudden awareness of the blood that was everywhere deflected Enright from his speculations. In his mouth the spittle coursed raw and rank with it. Dried stains of Helen Peters's blood stiffened his shirtsleeve. The floor by his bed was a no-man's-land pocked with the dark clots he had coughed up during the night. When he lay back and closed his eyes, he found the solace of Mary's scent in the pillow and she came all dressed in white except for the green felt hat and no dark rancour. The glide of her skirt, its soft fall when she came to his bedside.

'Mary, are you not gone yet? What date is it today?'

'You're in an awful state, Tom, why did you stop writing to me?'

The sweet melancholy of her voice thrilled Enright.

'I was in a madhouse for a while but I wasn't mad, only driven demented. Will you ever start singing again, do you think?'

'Oh, I'll be fine. Who's sleeping beside you there, Tom?'

'La Cheposa. Would you not hold on to the letter and keep that much of me at least?'

'Words, don't mind words. They're only all pretend.'

Enright smiled. The warm lapping tide of a great and benevolent emotion washed further and further in upon him.

'Sergeant, what are you at in there? Why's the door locked?'

Gallagher's voice, emasculated by a heightened pitch of worriedness, suggested he had been calling Enright for some time.

'I'm due a day's leave. I'm taking it in bed. Go way and let me sleep.'

The wooden statue elbowed into his side and, startled, he pushed it away.

'We're written off, Tom. They signed a treaty in London with the gunmen and made fools of us.'

Unlikely as it seemed, Enright suspected the peerless Head Constable was drunk. He raised himself from the pillow, his movements deliberate and slow. The tickle in his throat lay a mere breath away from convulsion, his lungs a gasp away from collapse, his stomach a swallow away from retching, his spinning head a glide away from a long dark fall.

'The depths we were dragged down into.'

Gallagher's tone implied a sad camaraderie of the damned that Enright felt no part of. No doubt about it, he thought amusedly, Gallagher was three sheets in the wind.

'DI Johnstone has an awful lot to answer for, getting you to do what he wouldn't do himself. And what does it turn out, only that he's a murderer himself.'

'Go soak your head.'

Enright pictured the old policeman addressing the door, stubbornly erect in spite of the drink and his collapsed spirit. The story of the old bugger's life. The story of any man's life who imagined there was anyone or anything beyond the closed door that gave a toss for his distress.

'He's been poisoning his wife with arsenic for months. Their servant girl suspected it all along and now it's proven and it's too late because he's gone, scot-free, off to the Continent. That's the kind of man you followed.'

'I never followed any man.'

A first attempt to stand up into the ridiculous, topsy-turvy world had already gone awry before he pushed himself from the bed. Top heavy, he slumped down sideways.

'You're transferred back up to the Phoenix Park in Dublin to see out your time in the force. And you're suspended until you take a medical.'

Anger proved a mistaken motive for his second ascent. The Blessed Virgin's unyielding, slippery drapery broke his fall. Better to say nothing, Enright thought. Silence drove every last one of them away, undid their awful clinging grasp. Mary's *You never talk.* Marshall's *Talk to me while I'm dying, you heartless son-of-a-bitch.* Clancy's *If you don't talk to me, Ramie, I'll go mad.* Gabriel Jack's *Just talk, Thomas, don't matter what you say, make it easier on the both of us.*

Through the dust on the barred window, a weak purgatorial light passed indifferently. He leaned his head back to rest and the cold wood of the statue touched the nape of his neck. He remembered whose hand it was had touched him in the dream and thought himself no better than a buck savage to have been afraid of a dream statue with blood for tears and hands made of ice.

'I wish to God I'd stayed on the bit of land below in Dunmore East. There wasn't much but between that and the fishing I'd have got along grand. They'd spit in my face if I went back there now, blame me for murders I had no hand, act or part in. Murders I warned against and warned Larry Healy and Shanahan to get themselves out of town. Is it my fault they didn't go that night? Is it my fault that you . . .'

The dark began to claim Enright again and he snatched himself continually back from the brink until he drifted into wordless waters where the wind was vaguely recognisable as his own sigh and his incantatory moan was the sound of whatever vessel bore him away.

'Tom! Wake up, Tom.'

Hands clutched at his wrist, slapped his cheeks. Timmoney seemed to float before him. He wondered if this was another ghost or whatever it was the inhabitants of dreams or fevers were called. He struck out at the hands that had been molesting him but his fist fell empty to the floor, his upturned palm trembling like the underside of a small poisoned animal.

'Let me help you up.'

Enright felt himself dragged upwards to the bed and propped to an altitude he wasn't yet ready for.

'I'll get some water. You're parched.'

'Don't mind the water. Have I any Jameson left under the bed?'

His knees dodging the islands of clotted spittle, Timmoney sent a long arm blindly in beyond the kit box amid a tinkling clangour of empties as he feigned disinterest in the statue that he couldn't keep his eyes from.

'There's a wee drop in this one but it's water you should be drinking.'

'Give me the bottle. Was it you opened my box and read the letters, you little weed?'

A mere half-inch of whiskey lapped in the bottle Enright held in both hands. He drank sparely, only wetting his lips at first, rinsing his mouth, letting his gullet accustom itself gradually to the burn. Then, with one quick hard swallow, he emptied the bottle. His stomach protested wildly, sending poisoned, caustic juices up into his throat. He tossed the bottle aside.

'I searched your box for guns and whatever else you might have, like the Head Constable ordered me to. He's been going through your stuff for months now but I doubt he'd touch any of your letters, no more than I would.'

'Whatever else I might have?'

There being no place for Timmoney to sit or stand in Enright's vicinity that hadn't been marked with blood, he retreated to the other side of the cast-iron fireplace. A retreat too in the eyes, from disgust of Enright to self-disgust.

'He thought you might have . . . well, there's three grenades down in the gun-locker that were found on a rebel a few years ago and Gallagher thinks there should be four. I'm sorry. I spied on you so he'd give me a good reference for the Palestine Police. I'm not proud of myself.'

'Have you anything else to confess while you're at it, Judas?'

'I've been spying on you since I came back from Tyrone. I followed you to Dooleys' last night.'

'So that was you out in Castle Bennett then?'

'I lost you after Dooleys'. No. I didn't lose you. That's what I told Gallagher. I couldn't bear to watch any more. What in God's name were you doing there?'

'Reconnaissance, boy. You were never a soldier, you wouldn't understand. Do you think they're not reccing me?'

'Of course they are. What do you expect with your wandering around in the night and your drinking and your spoiling for a fight you haven't an earthly hope of winning and whatever you're up to with that wee girl every night of the week? I'm sick of trying to keep a watch over you. I can't believe I used to admire you. I can't believe I came to think you were the devil incarnate when all you are is a bully, a foul-mouthed, perverted empty vessel of a man. And now this lunacy.'

Timmoney pointed shakily at the prone figure of the Blessed Virgin Mary. Enright laughed.

'Don't worry, boy. I might have slept with her but she's still a virgin.'

'Close your eyes!'

Enright peered in jokily by the door of Helen Peters's shed, bursting with suppressed giddiness. Her eyes were already closed above a faint smile. He went back out and unstrapped the blanket-wrapped statue from the bicycle. Difficult to recall where this playfulness in him had originated. With the filthy shoeless waifs he'd met on the street by the entrance to Monk's

Lane, perhaps? Little old faces on them like sailors and whores as they whipped at a spinning top and at each other with tattered twines. The feet of young birds though, spare and restless. *Where did ye get the spinning top? Did ye feck it?* A little waif, with big eyes so beautiful a chestnut brown they transformed the grey of her skin in the early dusk, had answered him. *We found it, sir.* The wire waiting on the road for her, he had thought, as he proffered the change from the Jameson he'd just bought. *Here, buy yourselves some sweets. Not bull's-eyes, mind. You could choke on them, ha, ha!*

Her eyes still shut tight, Helen's smile seemed to have become anticipatory when he lugged the bundle inside.

Or perhaps the high suspended feeling had begun when he'd been struggling down the barracks stairs with his Blessed Virgin in disguise and met Constable Harvey dragging one foot up after the other and singing quietly in some language unknown to Enright. And, like Gallagher, drunk as a lord. *Where you from, Harvey, who're you pretending not to be?* He'd pinned the mystery man against the wall with his own weight and the statue's. Too drunk to lift the unrelieved pressure from his chest and close to tears, the fellow spat out the truth. *I wass born into the circus but when I come back I wass too afraid of my bears and too bloody sed to be clown. You heppy now, mate?* All the way down the rest of the stairs and out into the yard and the bicycle shed, Enright shook and guffawed, and the coughing that started up in him was a joke too and the bloody phlegm he spat up.

On his knees and untying the last of the knots that bound the statue's shroud, he chuckled to himself again at the memory. He wanted to infect Helen with his cheerfulness and dredged his old life for a story to amuse her with as she waited.

'Did I ever tell you about this old pal of mine who whistled for a party piece and one night in' – he glanced back at her and wondered if she might be asleep but that was impossible because the least of sounds woke her – 'in Panama it was, and . . . no, Valletta, and . . . '

Or maybe the giddiness had started as he'd wheeled the bicycle up along by the railway bridge, the blanketed statue propped along the bar. The song he hummed to himself was another of Mary's. 'Roses of Picardy'. *Not showering, Mary, shining and then flowering.* The steep incline tested Enright, the gathering dusk composed of some glutinous substance to be waded through. But the song helped, and when he'd reached the brow of the bridge, almost all of the mercurial words gathered in, he rewarded himself with a rest against the cut limestone wall that overlooked station buildings hewn from a similar stone and the twin set of tracks and the metal foot-bridge that rattled like ships' ladders under passing feet.

Tomorrow, Enright supposed, the bulk of the internees would be arriving back now that the Treaty had been signed. A good place this from which to lob down among the returning heroes the grenade Gallagher imagined he might have and do some real damage. Give them all a taste of the charnel house he and Danny Egan, even Baldwin and bloody Papenfus, had mullacked through, he was thinking, when a tap on his shoulder had him reaching for the Webley in the wrong pocket of his trench coat.

Foley's broad grin had disarmed him. *You're looking fierce chipper, Foley.* Having just noticed Our Lady of the Sorrows peeping out of the bundle on the crossbar of the bike, Foley stepped cautiously back. *And why wouldn't I? Nothing only good news today. For the both of us. You'll never guess.* An exaggerated wink squashed up his features. *Myself and the missus are going to make the dozen after all. She's with child. What about that? Sixty fecking two and still firing.* Enright pushed away the unsavoury spectacle of the wiry doggyman climbing the hillocks of his large wife. *So what's the good news for me?* And good news it had been. Mooncoin Shine, the favourite for the Diamond Stakes in Kilmallock on Tuesday, declared a non-starter. *You'll have to come this time, Sergeant, but I'll take him down on the train 'cause he don't travel well in a car.* Enright's spirits rose again. *I believe I will. What day is today?* Foley added the statue and Enright together and the result clearly worried him. *Sunday.* Enright had freewheeled down the bridge laughing then, one foot on the pedal as he sailed into the dusky distance.

Below the base of Helen's bed, Enright hazarded a sip of the Jameson to get the shake out of his hands and his voice. He took the razor from his pocket and opened out the blade that was still damp from the barracks kitchen whetting stone. Sharp enough to open a sheep's belly. His low angle of vision made a high-nostrilled, tight-lipped corpse of the girl and he looked away. The Blessed Virgin, big as a tree stump on the Nelson plot, rooted itself into the floor below him.

He puffed and panted loudly to fill the silence and the one unthinkable source of it that played at the edges of his consciousness. The weight of the world in her sorrowful mien, the Blessed Virgin resisted his advances with divine stubbornness. Enright bullied himself to the task. As he raised the statue, he became acutely aware of how badly he smelled. A trench-stink off him every bit as bad as Danny Egan's, so foul that he began to wonder if the smell was his at all. He deposited the statue atop the washstand. When he bent down to pick up the razor, stars burst from the floor and, instinctively dodging them, he fell back against the metal rungs of the bed end.

'Sorry, Helen. You didn't look, did you?'

The putrescent smell sharpened in intensity as he brought the blade of the razor to the tip of his index finger. A corpse in the dead house alongside maybe, he speculated. The razor sliced too deeply into his flesh. Blood welled up as though the very purpose of its long coursing back and forth below the skin had been to seek escape.

Enright raised the bloodied finger to the statue. He touched the lower lids of the Virgin's eyes. The words of a Hail Mary arose like a song in him. Asking the impossible of the improbable, as Captain Big Toe had once said of prayer, or was it the other way around? He hid away the bleeding finger in his pocket.

'You can look now, Helen.'

So relieved was he to see her alive that he could only interpret her shocked expression as one of wonder.

'I'm a hard man to convince. But there's not a shadow of a doubt. She was crying blood all the way over from Templemore.'

'Take it out of here this minute.'

'But do you not want to pray to . . . '

The flatness of her speech, the sense that she couldn't be bothered even to be angry with him, told Enright he was despised.

'I know all about the statue in Templemore. You kept me in the dark like all the rest of them did and I had to learn the truth from a no-good bastard.'

Enright sank back against the rough wall. His pocket damp with blood and growing damper; he didn't care.

'It wasn't my idea to keep you in the dark, Helen, it was the hunchbacked woman. Who told you?'

Helen laughed and her laugh was a cruel, sluttish one. He could kill her now if she still wanted it, if she said no more, only kept on laughing at him like that.

'Wouldn't you love to know, Tom. One of my old friends it was, one of the lads who took their pleasure and ran. Big fat greasy Jim Donegan. He came in to beg my forgiveness before he scooted over to England but I told him he could ask God for forgiveness and not to be expecting an answer this side of eternity. There you are now, Tom, that's what you wanted to know, wasn't it? Or would you like to know more. Or do you just want to get up on me?'

'Helen, don't be upsetting yourself.'

The Queen of Heaven with rivulets of red mascara streaming from her downcast eyes didn't know where to look, he imagined, between the harlotry of Helen's abandon and him with his damp hand in his pocket and the lobster-red blush on his stubbled face.

'Seamus Breen that works in Molloy's Hardware, Tom. Johnny Dooley who tried but couldn't and cried like a child. *Don't tell anyone, Helen, sure you won't?* And Mick Ryan Rover, who's married and should've known better. But what harm in that, Tom, aren't you married yourself, though I'd never have known if Donegan hadn't told me. Nor would I know that you're worse than any gunman, all the men you shot in their beds and in front of their poor women.'

'They shot Danny Egan and two of our boys. And they crippled you. And as for Donegan, he's the one led us to the Clonore rebels.'

She looked despairingly at the statue and then seemed to mimic its sorrowful averting of the eyes from the world. Her black hair fell, veiling her profile. When he'd found Gabriel Jack's body at the bottom of the gorge off the road to Penticton, that face too had been veiled in long dark hair. Just as Enright had begun to have second thoughts about shooting him, the half-breed, his white shirt and his black hair flowing behind, had taken off over the edge of the tree-cloaked precipice towards the other side as though he were the blue jay of his Okanagan imaginings and not just a solitary bad luck magpie, half a jackdaw and half a dove and the wrong half of each. One for sorrow.

'Why did they shoot Danny?'

'He went up to the funerals in Clonore and they jumped on him like a pack of dogs.'

Enright eased himself down by the wall and sat on the floor, sipping occasionally at the Jameson though it sickened him. The wound on his finger throbbed wildly. He pushed it into the neck of the bottle and tilted the whiskey onto the cut, enduring the burn of healing.

'You shot those men because of me, didn't you? You had no right to. Now I'm guilty of your sins as well as my own. Those names I told you, leave them alone. Promise me you'll leave those men alone. Even after I'm gone.'

'I never keep my promises.'

'You'll keep this one or I'll haunt you.'

'I'm already haunted but I promise anyway.'

'And don't come here any more. I'm sick of that hungry longing on your face. I'm looking at it all my life.'

'I don't want anything from you, Helen.'

'Yes, you do. Donegan said you got a bee in your bonnet over me after seeing me in the ditch, after going through my clothes. Do you know how that makes me feel, do you? Like the occasion of sin that Father O'Leary told me I was, one time in the orphanage. Just because I was . . . '

'Beautiful.'

'Good-looking. Is it a sin to have a face like mine or my fault that men were forever chasing, asking, promising? And you. Was I the cause of you running off on your wife and child? Because, of all things, I couldn't bear to think I broke up a family.'

'That was my own poxy fault.'

'You had everything I can't ever have and you threw it away. Is it any wonder that I sicken at the sight of you?'

'Was I any help at all, Helen? I mean to say, Jesus Christ, no one else bothered, did they?'

The quick flicking back of her hair astounded Enright with its lightness. She examined him so intensely that he dipped his head like a dog that knew it failed to impress a potential buyer. He downed a greater draught of whiskey than he was able for and dribbled most of it down into his shirt.

'Can I have a drop of that before you waste it all?'

He panicked at the thought of her drinking whiskey adulterated with his blood.

'It's strong stuff, girl.'

'I know that. How do you think I lay down with the likes of Jim Donegan?'

They drank the Jameson without once speaking or, rather, she drank while he mimed large gulps. When the bottle was three-quarters empty, he reached down to place it on the floor.

He realised that he was drunk on the little he had managed to swallow. He lay back on her pillow and floated voluptuously. Her talk was dream-talk, at once languorous and lethal.

'Touch my face. No one touches my face, only to wash the dirt off me.'

He raised a hand towards her but quickly withdrew it because of the bloodied finger. He sat up and touched her face with the good hand. Once upright, the sharp whiskey bile cut through him from stomach to throat.

'The other cheek as well. The two hands.'

He wiped what he could of the blood on his finger along his trouser leg and held her face. He couldn't tell if it was him that was shaking or her. In her flushed cheeks he found a damp intimacy that stirred him briefly.

'Now my neck all along. The two hands.'

He longed for a shot of the sulphonal or the paraldehyde they'd jabbed away his Johnny-jitters with in the Male Chronic Building.

'If I could only go now, Tom.'

Grabbing the bottle from the floor Enright fled outside, as once he had fled the horror of Marshall's depraved end. On the pebbled path his legs gave way and he slumped to his knees, wobbling like a poisoned pup trying to stay up. When they locked the old goat into isolation in his cabin, Enright had guarded the door for hours like a faithful dog as the black typhoon clouds approached and he listened while the pleas and then the screams died away and the storm was upon them, the sea blown flat, the wind roaring like a train in a tunnel, and when he opened the cabin door his howl became one with the howl of the world. Black blood everywhere and the source exposed in Marshall's desecrated loins while in his left hand lolled a knife and in the other his Bobby's baton shrunk to a God-awful sliver of grizzle.

All the cold air of the Tipperary night was useless to him because he couldn't pull the breaths through the phlegm that filled his lungs, his chest. He drank deeply and vomited, drank again and again until there was nothing left to throw up but wild laughter and the wild screech of a wordless song.

After the sea-crazed nightmares in the Male Chronic Building ended and he had Clancy for a friend – *the only sane man in Essondale barring myself* – Enright began to have a recurring dream that came and went for a few years, especially in France those days and nights of snatched sleep. Now, heading into the town, he seemed to be staggering drunkenly through that dream again.

In the dream, only the location ever changed but always it seemed that he'd just shaken off Marshall to venture alone along some night street, busy and brightly lit and high-spirited as the Main Street of this landlocked Tipperary town in its celebration of the Peace Treaty. Men fell in and out of bars, women called across to each other from high windows, children ran amok as though night had become a day that might never end. And straight-backed, tall if a little unsteady on his feet, Enright spat at and swaggered through the looks of mistrust and the muttered imprecations, fists in his pockets hard with coin, waiting to be importuned. Going nowhere in particular, just being where he wasn't wanted and not afraid. And always the dream ended in the same way. He'd stop in front of a bar or a nightclub. In Hong Kong or Barcelona or wherever. Always some place where things had gone wrong once, but wouldn't this time around. But in the dream he'd never get through the door. The waking dream through which he had just wandered differed only in this way.

He stood inside the late Larry Healy's crowded bar. Paddy Kinahan's unfamiliar companion at the open door of the snug had already drawn his gun. The resident biddies banished for the duration, Kinahan appeared to have made an office of the enclosure. Working on a neat bundle of papers, the fellow looked as anonymous as any bank teller, until he turned to Enright. Deep in the shadows, the face matched more exactly that in the photograph back in the barracks; the proud chin, the eyes like an Okanagan Indian's that never entertained surprise no matter what confronted them. Enright half-raised his empty hands like a priest at benediction and smiled, but pushed to the wall from behind and spread-eagled, his arms were swept up aloft. From behind, fists pummelled through his coat and uniform.

'He's not carrying.'

Quite certain he'd had the gun on his way to see the girl, Enright glanced enquiringly back at a red-eyed Charlie Dooley.

'Are you sure?'

A further battering search provided the answer. Dooley nodded an all-clear to his OC. His tight-lipped, gummy expression amused Enright greatly. He gained the clear impression that the fellow had very recently been crying. Suddenly diminished by self-consciousness, Dooley pushed him towards the snug. Inside, Kinahan's pen moved in short snappy bursts like a hen feeding in a farmyard.

'Did you want to see me?'

'To tell you the truth, Paddy, I haven't an iota why I came here.'

He dropped down heavily onto the unoccupied bench on the other side of the table from Kinahan, whose eyes flitted quickly across a typewritten page and satisfied themselves with what they saw. The youthful rebel leader looked up sharply then and crowded him with an appraising look that felt more invasive than Charlie Dooley's search. Fumbling after the buttons along the top half of his tunic, Enright discovered that they'd been ripped away. The rebel sat back and tossed his pen on the papers. The snug had an air of the confessional about it and Kinahan a priest tired of observing human foibles.

'I hope for your own sake you come to say your goodbyes.'

'Why? Don't tell me you're leaving, Paddy. Won't you be getting a big job for yourself now or a parcel of land?'

'We don't have mercenaries on our side, Enright.'

'You'll all be well paid for your troubles when you divide up the big estates out the country. Or will you be handing all those acres over to the mugs in Monk's Lane?'

A small window on the counter between the snug and bar slid open. The large box that filled the aperture blocked Enright's view but he recognised the voice from behind it. He drew back from the table, hoping the shadows were sufficient to hide him. Kinahan watched him too keenly.

'Another wedding present for you, Paddy. Michael Shaw dropped it in. You'll have more delph than a chainy shop.'

The girlish chime of Mrs Larry Healy's voice seemed to set off a riot of tinkling in the box that Kinahan reached for.

'Thanks, Mary. All we need now is another dresser.'

The shock of the widow's name and of her frozen stare fixed on him, confounded Enright. He couldn't move and, besides, there was no further recess into which he might retreat.

'You're getting married? Well, fair dues to you, Paddy. How did you find the time to court a young one and you running around the hills these past . . . tell her to stop looking at me.'

'Why?'

Kinahan glanced up at Mary Healy and received in return a look of hurt admonition. Somehow the frosted glass window survived the force of its abrupt closing.

'How would you like to be gawked at by Helen Peters or Danny Egan's widow? Will you be praying for them when you're up at the altar with your missus?'

Enright felt sure he'd discomposed Kinahan. Picking up the pen he'd discarded earlier, the rebel tapped at the papers before him and the quickening drum roll suggested anxiety, the weight of the watchful audience's silence at the door of the snug compounding the impression.

'I have a question, a real question, Paddy. No more of the old messing, I swear. D'you know the way in a war, after a war, there'd be things playing on your mind . . . mysteries bothering you and in the heel of the hunt a fellow'd be better off not knowing. But Helen Peters and Danny Egan, what in Christ's name had they to do with your fucking rebellion?'

The twitch started up in Enright's neck and with both hands he tried to quell the spasm. The crowd by the snug door lapped up his spastic antics, leered for more. Charlie Dooley and his pint-sized brother Johnny among them, smirks and whispered sneers starting up in the corners of their mouths.

Enright sang at Johnny Dooley in plaintive jest.

'*Don't tell anyone, Helen, sure you won't? Don't tell anyone, Helen, sure you won't?*'

Johnny Dooley looked like he'd heard a banshee before he ducked away for cover. The audience's attention was divided now, more of them observing Dooley's retreat than Enright's tic.

'All right, Helen was one of your mistakes and I know you weren't in on shooting Danny, but all I want to know, Paddy, is whether the bastard who shot Danny and the one who should have been guarding the tripwire got away with it or did you let them off for fear any more of your boys turned against you?'

Apart from the very lightest of blushes that might have been mere embarrassment at Enright's drunken debasement of himself, Kinahan remained unmoved. Enright wished he had the Mills bomb that Gallagher thought he had. Lob it on the table and make a dozen sundered Clancys of them. And himself. He leaned closer, lowered his voice to a whisper.

'Do you want to know about Martin Dwyer's last minutes? Or Larry Healy's? Fair exchange is no robbery, am I right, Paddy? Give a little, get a little.'

Kinahan leaned towards the snug door and to the consternation of those outside, closed it.

'The man who shot the ex-soldier is dead. You and your pals got to him before I did.'

'Larry? No? One of the Dwyers? Clem Shanahan. Bloody hell, I didn't even get to put a bullet in the bugger.'

'So what have you to say about Larry?'

'He wasn't pushed down the stairs, he fell making a break for it and broke his neck. I'll tell you something that might surprise you, Paddy. I was sick to the gills of killing when he landed at my feet, sick of looking into the eyes of dying men but I shot him anyway to put him out of his misery. There were men closer to me I couldn't do the same for. Women even. There you are now, cards on the table. What about Helen? Who loused up out at the ambush?'

Kinahan reached over and opened the snug door that filled to brimming with vengeful faces.

'Don't you want to hear about Martin Dwyer? We had a deal, Paddy.'

'Show him the door, Cathal, before I do something I'll be sorry for.'

'Dwyer wouldn't tell us where you were, Paddy, he gave his life for you. How does that feel? Do you think you deserve it, Paddy?'

Charlie Dooley reached in over the table to catch Enright by the collar, as if he were a stubborn dog too intent on gnawing at a bone to follow his master.

'Why were you crying, Charlie? Did you cut your gum on a crust or what?'

Enright made a barricade of the snug table, sending Kinahan's papers flying as Dooley lurched at him. The guns in the hands of the others didn't bother him because the Luger Parebellum in Paddy Kinahan's was, he knew, the only one that mattered at this moment. Even when Dooley landed the soft outer edge of a blow to the side of his face, Enright kept a watch on the rebel leader. He saw that in the youthful face, a lifelong struggle with the depths he had opened up within himself had already begun.

'It never ends, does it, Paddy, once you pull out the gun that first time? To tell you nothing but the truth, it'd be an ease to me if you pulled the trigger.'

Charlie Dooley blustered in between Enright and Kinahan's gun.

'My aunt is dying, you Kerry bastard.'

The timber-panelled wall gave out a hollow echo under the deadweight of Enright's head rebounding from Dooley's punch. A gasp of breathlessness set his heart stumbling. He felt immeasurably sad at the hunchbacked woman's plight.

'I'm sorry to hear it, I really am. I heard her playing the piano one night up at your house when I was pooching around and I swear I couldn't believe something so . . . so perfect could come out of a little . . . a little . . . She saved your life, you know. I was going to shoot you and Johnny but I couldn't with the way she played so . . . with all that pain.'

Taken aback, Dooley loosened his hold and Enright fell onto the bench. The drowning phlegm rose in his throat again.

'There was a whore in Barcelona that shape that an old goat I knew blamed for a bad dose. But wasn't she just the same as ourselves, making the best of the way life twisted her up and scratching a living out of a boggy field.'

There came a moment in the training of coursing dogs, after they'd been blooded on the easy pursuit of rabbits but before they had yet run down a hare, when they were at their greediest and meanest. A good trainer knew how to prolong that moment and drag the savagery up into the dog's every last sinew and bone. A bad trainer brought the wrath of the dogs upon himself. This, Enright sensed, was Kinahan's dilemma now as his restive charges advanced on the snug.

'Listen, Enright. I'm getting married tomorrow morning up the country and I'll be away for a week after that. Cathal here takes charge while I'm gone, so, one way or the other, I don't expect to see you when I come back.'

'You think you're some kind of God denying me answers. Well, here's one for you, boy, your fucking God won't give you any answers either and you'll never be happy all your life wondering was it worth all the blood you spilled, was it worth going down into hell for. Eh, Paddy?'

Unlike the faces of the others, Kinahan's revealed neither self-righteousness nor the self-pitying sense of grievance that justified revenge nor the cowardliness that drew men together to hunt in packs with the odds stacked on their side. What defence was left, Enright wondered, in the inner struggle that lay ahead for the young rebel leader? Love? Some priestly reassurance in the dark of a confessional? Or one day seeing Ireland *a better place entirely* than ever it was before he drew his gun?

'You're fucked, son. We both are.'

Set upon by the mob, Enright felt himself being lifted out into the night as by a wave, felt a sharp blow on the very spot behind his right ear where he'd long ago taken the rough edge of a swinging lamp in a storm-tossed cabin off Port Moresby and then a heavier blow in the stomach like he'd shipped in a score of Sailortown brawls, and then the boots came kicking like in a jail cell once under Salonika. *Roll yourself up in a ball, Tommy lad, a hand on your face and another on your lad.* But he did so too slowly and his mouth was prised open with a boot. For a moment he thought his jaw had locked askew but the boot came and straightened it up again. He spat out shards of teeth, chewed off a loose flap of skin from his lip and spat that out too and when Charlie Dooley bent over him with Kinahan's Luger, he spat whatever was left in his shattered mouth at the rebel's face.

'You don't have it in you, Charlie boy.'

As Dooley's gun hand wavered, Enright saw that he was in the lane beside Larry Healy's pub. The light from Main Street, the last gap in the darkness descending on him, seemed very far away. A boot found his groin.

'Give me the gun, Cathal, if you won't. You know what he did. You heard what he said about Martin in there.'

Enright recognised the voice of Eamon Dwyer, and knew the fellow had the necessary steel to finish him off. From among the muttering of the others, Johnny Dooley's excited whine rose.

'Give him the gun, Cathal.'

'Shut your filthy mouth, you. That young one up in the workhouse. Christ, have you no shame in you, no respect for women? If you weren't my brother, I'd put a bullet in you.'

'It isn't true. I never touched that lying whore.'

A scuffle broke out above Enright. Placatory noises intervened, but first his anger and then the pain consumed his awareness of the opportunity for escape.

'Cathal, the gun. You can deal with that little runt after.'

'Don't call me a little runt, Dwyer, she wouldn't be up in the workhouse only for the tripwire your sainted brother was supposed to be taking care of. And another thing, you're talking behind Paddy's back against the Treaty, making out he hasn't the will to fight on. Don't deny it.'

As the rebels exchanged blows, it occurred to Enright that a man chased down the truth for all he was worth and when he found it, it wasn't worth knowing and next day it wasn't even the truth any more. He muttered an incoherent protest at the futility of his obsessions. Then a roar rose from his throat before he'd summoned it and, lifted bodily by the power of his own voice, he sprang away from their feet and lashed out wildly with fist and boot at the air around him, making for the light, knowing his back offered too broad a target for even the very worst of pot-luck shooters to miss, but he fell out onto the loud, bright street and scrambled across the footpath out onto the open square. Passers-by struck differently by fright, froze or ran away. On his knees, he savoured the mutters of dissent among his attackers at the lane entrance and yelled aloud.

'Come on, Johnny. You tried before, try again. You can't shoot and you can't ride. Wouldn't make much of a cowboy, would you?'

Paddy Kinahan stood silhouetted at the pub door. The red dot of his cigarette signalled a final pull before he spun it away. Then he gestured at his men to return to the pub. Charlie Dooley was the last of the stragglers. They spoke briefly, looked across the street at Enright and went back inside.

Enright went down again and the passage of time became a bewildering muddle. When he lifted his head, the lane had emptied and the wide spaces of Main Street were his alone to scrabble through. All the way back to the barracks he told himself that tonight he might be the next best thing to a corpse but tomorrow he would be like a god answering the call of a crippled girl and visiting the fire and shrapnel of damnation on the town. And after that? After that, the Diamond Stakes in Kilmallock and Arrow Valley Snow and the lift of silver.

He stared up at the great big ugly sway of the barracks, glad to know that this would be his last night aboard the godforsaken HMS *Tipperary*. So glad that he sang aloud.

So, goodbye Mick and goodbye Pat
And goodbye Kate and Mary.
The anchor's weighed, the gangplank's up,
I'm leaving Tipperary.

'I need the car. If it's not fixed I'll have to requisition one of the others.'

Enright had filched everything else he needed from the barracks gun locker overnight. Another pistol, a Browning of dubious worth, a No. 5 Mills bomb with the shellac gone worryingly damp, its ridges badly rusted. Cullinane, dapper as ever under his tan dungarees, still hadn't got over his surprise at seeing a pulp-faced Enright climb awkwardly down over the wall between the barracks and the garage yard. Swollen lips and broken teeth made of speech an art to be learned all over again.

'They'll be watching for me on the street. Where's the car?'

'I'm still working on it.'

Dismayed but unsurprised at how dog-tired he already felt in spite of having stayed in bed until mid-afternoon, Enright rested against the wall and set down his kit box. He drew out the Browning.

'What can I do? I'm a mechanic, not a miracle worker.'

Enright laughed and the laughter provoked a spell of dizziness from which he recovered only to be shaken by a fit of coughing. He spat blood but didn't mind because somehow in the midst of his distress, inspiration had struck. Funny that.

'Do you know the girl up in the workhouse that the rebels crippled? Well, she wasn't out of that damn shed ever since and I want to take her for a spin because all she can see is a dirty little corner of the sky out of a hole of a window.'

The effect on Cullinane was encouraging but not yet decisive. He looked from the blood on the cobbles to Enright's bloated face. He held himself less tautly, his defences going slowly down. Enright noted a new ruddiness in the fellow's sallow countenance that suggested inner content.

His jaw getting used to the discomfort of speaking, Enright went on.

'I'm not coming empty-handed. I've something to trade for the car. Something for you and Bridie.'

'Leave Bridie out of it.'

'No, listen. Her brother Johnny is standing in the way of you getting married, right? Well, here's a thing. Helen . . . that's the girl in the workhouse, she told me that the brave Johnny tried to have his way with her and the little bugger couldn't raise the flag. "Don't tell anyone, sure you won't," he says to her. Whisper that in his ear and he'll back off fairly fast.'

Cullinane blushed and didn't know quite what to do with his big-knuckled hands. He turned from Enright and walked towards the garage. Enright limped after him.

'It's already settled. We'll be married next June, please God.'

'You're running away with her?'

'Bridie's aunt talked to Johnny . . . Seán. She's dying and she asked him not to stand in the way of Bridie's happiness. Cathal too.'

The Browning dragged at Enright's hand. The very least of movements caused him pain. He saw the barracks Ford washed clean and the body polished so keenly that the light adorned its curves like silver braiding. He thought that if he looked closer he might see carnival mirror images of his distorted self in the black sheen.

'Shouldn't you see a doctor?'

Enright addressed the puzzle of car parts on the shelves before him.

'It's just a beating. I'm well used to them. Has she long left to live?'

'A week at the most. Last night, she slipped into a coma.'

His flesh stiffening with fear, Enright chased away the sharp envisioning of that queer peace of mind, that absence of the spirit from the living flesh.

'Was she afraid?'

'Not a bit of it. She'd a few close calls before with the bad heart and she has a powerful faith in God. In people too. Take the car, Sergeant.'

The sense that he'd been allowed a glimpse of a forgotten world overwhelmed Enright as surely as if he'd landed in a new port. A place where ordinary people lived and died and did the decent thing for the most part. Pago Pago before the first foreign boat landed bringing trinkets and disease.

'Mr Gallagher told me to hold on to the car as long as I could. Well, I did, I can't do any more with her. Only give her plenty of oil, and make sure you grease and water her. Come here and I'll show you. This is the 1915 model. Some nice changes, the curves on the body and the like, but these leatherette seats and door panels instead of leather, I wouldn't go for at all. Same engine though.'

A mild envy stirred in Enright as the mechanic took him on a tour of those points that needed regular attention. Oil every hundred miles in the steering ball bracket and the spindle bolt, every two hundred miles in the front and rear spring hangers and the commutator. He was glad to let Cullinane ramble on and delay him from the task ahead. When the mechanic stood up from a final wipe of a cloth to the dusty glass of the head-lamps, Enright felt a forlorn admiration for the fellow. Not yet inclined to leave, he asked about the faulty throttle lever.

'I rethreaded the notches and did the same inside the steering gear. If you like, I could come and do the driving. The girl might be hard to manage in a moving car. With the bump of the road and all.'

'No need, but thanks anyway.'

The impulse to decency did more harm than good, Enright knew, its consequences insufficiently thought out. Like Cullinane, for all his noble instincts, providing him with a getaway car. Like himself hiring a boozy half-breed with trouble, past, present and to come written all over him. Or befriending a mad boy from Clare in an asylum.

'Don't drive her too hard or too far and she'll hold up a long while yet.'

'I haven't far to go. See if the street is clear, will you?'

Enright endured every last brooding moment of dusk's slow fall before he could get himself from the Ford to Helen Peters's resting place. Even then, he couldn't decide how to go about killing her. Should he speak to her first or go silently to her side in the dark? Or go back to the car and find a rag for a mask? And have her die at the hands of a stranger? No. Should he, for her sake, say aloud a prayer as he slipped the pillow from under her head and placed it over her face? Or tell her the truth in the only plangent words he could dredge up, that she was the last pebble falling?

His boots crunched heavily along the gravel path. His hands, for shame, hidden in the pockets of his Sunday suit, the suit he'd been married in. Soaped all over and his hair Valentino-slick, the rot of weeks washed off with water punishingly hot on the old wounds and the new bruises, his torn face dabbed clean with a sponge. At the door of the shed he stood, a fluster of a fool in the last grey shimmer of a frosty dusk.

Imagining her last wild instinctive struggle and doubting his strength, he opened the door and found nothing but the choke of disinfectant and dampness in the empty shed. His first demented thought was that a miracle had occurred. Then Dr Brady was behind him, articulating his second.

'She's dead, Sergeant.'

Enright began to sob. He kept his back to the doctor, not to hide his face but to refurnish the room with her presence.

'She's in the morgue if you'd like to see her. The face of a saint and all she suffered. I could almost believe she'll never decay.'

Such a lightness and optimism coloured Brady's tone that Enright believed the fellow might actually be smiling. He wondered if the old took some kind of perverse relief or some irrational intimation of immortality from the death of the young.

'Who murdered her?'

'Why would anyone want to murder her? She drowned on her own vomit. Some idiot poured whiskey into her. Damn reckless, but hardly murder.'

The elderly doctor retreated from Enright's distraught and forbiddingly pulped countenance. Veering off the path by the morgue that was no more than another stone shed, Enright crossed through the frosted grass to the Ford thinking that he'd better hurry no matter how much it hurt, planning the attack and the getaway, thinking every mad and distracting thing to spare himself from the truth worming into him that he'd poisoned her with too much Jameson and misguided caring.

Before he started to turn the crank, Dr Brady called to him.

'Come and look at her now, Sergeant, before they douse the light.'

The breeze along the narrow creek into which the rails had been cut made diabolic ululations of the crowd's murmurings on the railway station platform. Peering through the arch of the bridge, he saw that from lamppost to lamppost, green flags and bunting flapped, casting bat-like shadows over the people below. He withdrew quickly, imagining his bruised moon-face too garish a sight for the crowd to miss. In one pocket of his trench coat, the Mills bomb offered rough solace to his frozen hand. In the other, the Browning itched for the mayhem of release.

He grew colder by the minute, more faint and nauseous. A fellow could die on a night like this if he let himself drop off, he thought, once and for all below the nightmares locked in his skull. Some kind of blessing that might be, not to be killed by any man getting the better of him or, worse still, by a stranger. Even hanging from the rafters had that much to be said of it.

The train's whistle and the crowd's eruption into cheering stirred Enright into action. He freed the grenade from the mouth of his reluctant pocket, and measuring its weight against the distance from the platform, found the conclusion worrying. The train turned the bend out by the Union Workhouse and its light began to scrape the dark painfully from his eyes. The scream of metal skating along metal shuddered through him as though it were his own scream. Then a banging, like gunshots fired from the train, sliced through the shudder but he saw the scarlet bursts of sparks below the train and knew that celebratory firecrackers had been placed along the line.

He slid down through the cling of brambles as the engine went by, the driver and the fireman preening themselves in readiness for the crowd's acclaim. Within a few feet of the train and below view of the windows, he readied the clip of the grenade. At the platform, the excited throng pressed forward. He pulled the pin, drew back his hand for an under-arm bowl through the arch. He counted. *One.* Something snagged his swinging arm and the grenade shot from his grasp, *two,* and lodged itself on the running board beneath a door of the train. He lurched back on *three,* certain the grenade would go off under the bridge and the shock wave flatten him. But *four* passed through his mind and then *five,* and the end of the train gone past him, he began to scrabble up the embankment. The count of *six* saw him through the gap into the railway field and then he stopped counting.

Useless old thing, the No. 5 compared to the No. 36. Pull the clip, count to four and everything within seventy yards razed to the ground. Then the earth rumbled like Java and the sky lit startlingly up Pozières-bright and the screaming started like night in the Essondale asylum. He bowled away by the overgrown hedge bordering the field, the pain in his crotch infinitely worse after his exertions, the frosty air raw in the roots of his broken teeth. With every step, he expected the pack to descend but no one followed him.

He reached the handball alley where he'd parked the Ford and was glad of Cullinane's sure touch. The car started on the first turn of the crank, and seized by the engine's new enthusiasm, he headed for the Limerick road. The headlamps too shone more brightly than before and illuminated the finest tracery of the roadside vegetation in their beams. The mere act of seeing had never seemed so intense.

At Ballycahill, he steered the Ford off the Limerick road and on towards Dundrum and the road to Kilmallock. He coasted through the night with a swift ease that brought to mind the *Bardus*, steaming back through the Red Sea, the wind and the current of a northeast monsoon adding a knot to the speed. In Kilmallock he looked for a hotel and found a last bed in one. An attic room with too long a stairs to climb. The young red-haired boy who showed him to the room bounced upwards like a kid-goat and sneaked awestruck glances at Enright's scabbed and puffy face.

'We're packed out for the coursing, sir. Are you running something yourself?'

'I am, son. A flyer of a white called Arrow Valley Snow.'

The boy bounced away again and Enright rested against the wall. He thought that if left alone he might crawl the last few flights. All through his body, the heat of the house tingled pleasantly. He began to find sleep where he stood but the boy appeared again, slipping down past him.

'The room's ready, sir. You can pay my grandmother in the morning.'

'Did no one ever tell you it's bad luck to cross someone on a stairs?'

He regretted his sharpness when the boy turned fearfully to look up at him.

'What age are you, son?'

'Fourteen, sir. Mam says I'll take a spurt one of these days and be as big as any of them.'

When sailor-boy Paudie showed him the door from the mad aunt's pub, he hadn't been much bigger than this young fellow himself. *There's a lad called Dempsey on the Beckstone'll sign you on, so pack your bags and fuck off.* The aunt, porter-drunk and weeping in the afternoon. *I'll take you to Limerick, love.* The sun in by the smoky window, the filth of that light, the absence of warmth in it. *I'm old enough to go on my own.* Both dead now, he thought, and no loss to anyone.

'You will too grow, boy. Did you ever think of going to sea at all?'

'I seen it a few times, sir, and I don't know if I'd care for it much.'

Enright laughed and took a coin from his trouser pocket.

'You're a sensible lad. Here's a tanner to start you off. That's a tanner more than what I got.'

In his surprise, the boy misjudged the flight of the coin but descended as deftly as those olive-skinned urchins gone to pale streaks of liquid light way down in the waters of Funchal harbour to scavenge for the pennies and dimes tossed from the deck above. He wished he'd asked the boy to carry his kit box to the room as he struggled up the final short flight but he began to see the bed through the open door halfway up and the sight soon became one in his memory with his falling onto it.

The wry satisfaction he'd felt in the disguise of his swollen face and broken-toothed mouth at the coursing meeting had not survived the double blow. An overheard conversation about the railway station explosion in Tipperary. The Diamond Stakes ending in a runaway victory for the black from Newcastle West now feasting on a ball of furry guts. He blamed the slipper for Arrow Valley Snow's poor performance and watched in simmering fury as Foley and the dog straggled back up towards him with their heads bowed, their quick breaths visible on the frosty late afternoon air.

'The slipper held him back, Foley. I'll swing for him.'

Foley shrugged. The dog wheezed. Men pulled dogs back from the fifteen-yard stretch between Enright and Foley, and pretended not to listen.

'The two dogs got the one start. He was beat by a better dog.'

'A blind man could see he was held back, Foley. Did you tell him who I was? Is that why he pulled him?'

'You're Mr White, like it says on the card.'

The wizened doggyman made up the last of the ground between them in a trot, half-strangling the reluctant dog. He poked his face up into Enright's and whispered savagely.

'Will you shut up, in the name of God, or you'll have us shot.'

Enright went in search of the slipper. The pain in his groin made a clapped-out sailor's roll of his progress. Though he knew they were heading for the gate, the coursing done for the day, he was unnerved by the crowd following behind. He held on tightly to the Browning in his coat pocket.

Inside the wooden slipping shed that was no bigger than a latrine hut, he found the slipper crouching to gather up a heavy brown overcoat and a billycan. The young fellow was huge. His rolled-up shirtsleeves revealed powerful arms that contrasted oddly with the delicate, nimble movements of his hands.

'You held my fellow back, you big lug. How much did you get for cheating me? Who paid you?'

The slipper ignored him and a soft, curiously strangled hum emerged as he counted out a handful of coins he'd retrieved from the coat. Incensed, Enright went for his gun but Foley trapped his arm.

'He can't hear you nor talk to you.'

The giant with his slanted eyes and a limpid gloss on the high fat of his cheeks, rose before him. His expression, guileless but sensitive, suggested a grappling with the mystery of Enright's ugliness and anger. Out of an uncertain smile, compassion flowered and Enright felt unable to refuse it.

'But how can the fellow be a slipper if he's deaf and dumb? And how in the name of Christ can he hum a tune when he never even heard a song? Or hum at all, for that matter?'

'He don't know he's making those noises. If you've a complaint, make it to me. I'm his uncle.'

The speaker had the same Oriental cast to the eyes as the giant. Enright had seen and heard him before. Of the group whose discussion of the railway station incident he'd listened into, this fellow had been the most vocal in his condemnation. *Any man who'd kill a nineteen-year-old off back to Dunmore East after six months in Ballykinlar camp and maim a couple of innocent townspeople deserves to be hung, drawn and quartered.* A measly toll after all, Enright had thought, just another boy dispatched before his time.

'Is there something wrong . . . Sergeant?'

Unmasked, Enright tried to divine the consequences but the fellow gave nothing away as he leaned against the timber shed. Enright's mirth was unconvincing, a craven laugh that he quickly abandoned. The giant had traced Enright's descent and his compassion had become a confused sadness.

'Lieutenant, actually. I was a lieutenant in the Canadian army. Tell your nephew to stop looking at me.'

He retreated then, Foley and the dog in his wake, and saw among the last of the departing crowd faces that were alarming in their vague familiarity. That dark-haired fellow with the thick moustache might, he suspected, have been in Larry Healy's pub the night before last. And that tall young lad, pale and freckled under a rusty thatch, who was it in Listowel he reminded him of, someone over Coolagowan way? The hand gripping the Browning, so long tensed, began to grow numb as he waited by the Ford for the lane to empty of its stragglers. Except for Foley. And Arrow Valley Snow. The last thing a sailor wanted to see on a boat, that harbinger of misfortune, a white animal. Foley mounted the buckboard of the Ford and tugged at the dog's leash.

'Where you going, Foley?'

'We're going home, aren't we?'

'Go on the train like you came and take the dog with you. I don't want it.'

'Where you going to?'

He took out a few banknotes from his pocket and handed them to the doggyman

'I don't know. A better place entirely, maybe. Listen, do us a favour, will you? Buy a plot up in the cemetery for Helen Peters.'

'Helen who?'

'The girl who died above in the workhouse yesterday. I don't want her dumped in a pauper's grave. And Foley? Buy a pair of shoes for your child's first steps out of the change.'

He sat in the Ford for too long a time watching the milk leak from the wintry sky, listening to the rumble of the silence as he leafed through Danny Egan's red notebook. Page by page, he tore it into little pieces that he tossed confetti-like out of the car. He read the letter Mary had returned to him. The letter from a dying man in Balfour. *The things I have seen you could not imagine, so I will not mention them except to say that only the memory of you can erase them from my mind.* Erase? Never used the word in his life, though Martin Fuller might well have done. He shred the letter too.

Flanagan's Hotel, a modest three-storey building painted an insipid green, stood on the corner of Sarsfield Street and Water Street in Kilmallock. In a front room on the top floor the blind when it had been lifted earlier had revealed a view of Water Street, that strip illuminated by the nearest streetlamp its focal point. The yellow Post Office building; Clery's Hotel, with its granite steps up from the footpath treacherous with ice; a group of trench-coated men smoking hungrily and stamping the cold from their booted feet at the entrance to a lane between these two buildings. From the street, patches of ice could be seen glittering on all the windows of Flanagan's Hotel, except for the window of that upper room. A small room so intensely hot from the coal-fire the landlady had lit when the stranger returned from the coursing that the ice had not yet taken hold on the drenched panes, though the chill of what she had told him persisted long after she had gone. *Did this lad who wants me leave a name, missus?*

Enright sat at the end of the bed, naked but for a bed-sheet toga, his feet propped on the brass fire-rail. The taste of the gun barrel in his mouth, or rather, the metal-tainted spittle he swallowed, seemed somehow familiar. He tried to remember in which of his lives he had previously tasted that particular poison. The narrow space hummed with heat, its contents shimmering and, at times, grossly distended. The crucifix on the wall above the mantelpiece, with its stricken, dagger-thin Jesus; the washstand; his own kit box standing on end because there wasn't room on the patch of linoleum between the bed and the wall to lay it flat.

He applied some pressure to the trigger of the Browning. His sweaty hand, he knew, made a slippery risk of what had until now been an absent-minded game. Seeking out the precise mid-point between life and death quickened his pulse, though his mind was inclined to dwell upon the taste of gun metal. The joint of his crooked finger began to hurt disproportionately, which he took for a warning and relented.

The rat in his stomach began to gnaw again, feeding on the scraps of yesterday's farcical failures and on Arrow Valley Snow's failure a few hours before. The dog's defeat shouldn't have mattered. Not after Helen Peters. Nor the damp squib of his railway station escapade. The laughter of men on the street compounded his humiliation. He wondered if the caller the landlady had spoken of earlier was among them. *Oh, young like all of them, Mr White, but taller and darker.* What laughter, what gloating would be theirs to enjoy if he did away with himself in this room. The news travelling over to Listowel, up to Tipperary, out to the wilds of Clonore. Not as long as there was one man still alive who despised him would he give them that pleasure. Not here. Nor anywhere else on this godforsaken island that he was booted out of and came mistakenly back to. It was as simple as that. A fellow didn't give in to some over-educated inner debate or to disgust of the world or of himself. If the world craved his absence, Enright thought, it could damn well come and do its own dirty work.

He pulled the bed sheet more tightly in around his front and leaned over to the lamp on the mantelpiece to douse it. He found some troubled equivalent of sleep, and when he came to, thought, at first, that some unremembered nightmare accounted for his furious trembling. Then he saw that the fire had almost burned itself out and felt the lash of raw air on his flesh.

Sanguine waters swelled inside him. He knew that death was near. Perhaps not tonight nor tomorrow nor even next week but soon. Sooner than a man of thirty-two had a right to expect. He thought that if there was a God to pray to he would ask not for some miraculous cure or some absurd rescuing circumstance, but to die on his feet or, at very least, to be spared the tubercular death. At the Balfour San, they called the dead *les noyés*. The drowned. Drowning in their own blood.

The rectangular rim of jaundiced light around the blind guided his path to the window. He rolled up the blind and pulled himself up on to the deeply recessed windowsill. A web of ice had formed and begun to spread jaggedly inwards from the edges of the glass. He scraped at the ice with the stubs of his fingernails. He remembered when Mary had got back on her feet again after the dead child and taken down all the fancy lace curtains to the front of the shack facing the road, a rut of a lane really where a passer-by was an event. She'd sat there all day for weeks, as if compelled by some sainted, histrionic need to let the whole world see her grief, while he, out behind the shack, sliced the axe of his own grief into the knotted hearts of trees.

On the street below, a man neither tall nor dark staggered down the steps of Clery's Hotel and went along the footpath with his overcoat open and held out wide like wings that made a glide of his weaving walk. At the lane by the Post Office, he sailed inwards and emerged a minute or so later, talking to the half of his shadow that loitered inside. On the other side of the street a shawlie, a dark shuffling bundle of a thing, shod incongruously in bright if tattered plimsolls. He'd met her earlier, begging by the door as he came in from the coursing. *Would you have a copper to spare, sir.* Her astonishment at the heft of the half-crown in her palm before she dared look down to confirm her good fortune. Or maybe it was just the sight of his dropsical face. *A dacent man like yourself, sir, don't deserve such a hiding.* On the other side of the street, the drunkard had disappeared.

The ice on the windowpane made deep hollows and high ridges where his fingernails had scraped. He studied the contoured map, how it distorted his view of the street. A map that by mid-morning wouldn't exist.

Stiffening in his crouched perch on the windowsill, a numbness played along his spine and in the joined hands clutching his knees. He straightened himself up and lowered his feet to the floor. He saw the empty bed and his shadow lying across it, a misshapen cast-off of a thing that was tired of following him. Funny that, he mused, how a shadow could be tall and dark one moment and fold to a hunchback the next, depending on what lay in its path.

Water Street resounded with the tramp of men and their expansive voices as Enright slowly dressed. Heading up from the pubs to Clery's Hotel for tomorrow's coursing draw. A good time to get out of Kilmallock if a fellow had some place in mind to go. He came up woozily from tying his shoelaces and let the swirl pass through him. He combed his hair back again. A sailor bound for shore leave. *We'll cut through the ruddy Daisies tonight, Tommy lad.* Couldn't cut butter with a hot knife tonight.

Enright picked up the Browning from below the bed and got the trench coat over his shoulders. His passage down the unlit staircase proved remarkably easeful though it seemed to take an eternity. Three times he stopped, until the stained glass fanlight over the front door bathed him in colours; blues, reds, greens. He found after some time that the landlady stood by his raised elbow while his hand rested on the catch. A middle-aged widow, dressed in black, her dark hair not yet touched with grey, the skin of her handsome face only recently loosened below the chin. Earlier he had noted the attractiveness of her voice, gentle but not obsequious, tough but not coarse, and the accent not Limerick but the west, Galway maybe.

'That man was looking for you again, Mr White. I told him you were gone away.'

'And why would you tell him that now, Mrs Flanagan?'

He took great care not to let his broken teeth show and hoped that his face wasn't quite so grotesque any more. He touched it and winced. His groin hurt too and she looked away from him.

'I don't want any trouble in the house.'

'And I'm trouble?'

'You've had your share of it, I'd say.'

The youthful toss she gave to her hair suggested that she'd grow old eccentrically. He'd imagined that of Mary too, though he'd never know for sure now. When he opened the door that led directly onto the footpath, the woman slipped past him and looked up and down the street like a pub landlady ushering out her last customer after hours. Moves young too, he thought. She nodded and he stepped outside. The ice-laden air made light work of his trench coat and suit.

'Do you know who I really am, ma'am?'

'I'd rather not, Mr White.'

At the outer edge of the footpath and about to cross the street, he saw that the woman had not yet gone inside. He wondered if this short distance made a half-decent cut of a man of him with the worst of the limp gone and his face bandaged with shadow. Not that it mattered. Raising his hat to her, he set off. The street seemed much later than the hour and he heard no sound but the wasp-drone of men in Clery's and the crack of his studded heels on the stone of the footpath. He felt at an odd, slow remove from himself. A man pacing a room rather than a street, alone in his preoccupation.

He passed by the Post Office, its yellow bleached and blistered close up. He stepped over the narrow stream of urine that had already turned to ice all the way back to its source in the empty laneway and took great care on the glistening steps leading up to the hotel. The smell of cigarette smoke and booze checked him momentarily in the lobby but he found he could stomach it and went along past the frosted-glass panelled door with its clear glass lettering, Lounge Bar – No Ladies. An old habit. *Always find the back way in, Tommy lad, you might need it on the way out.* A double door led into the hotel proper and, beyond it, Enright found the residents' entrance to the bar.

Inside the thick fug of smoke and raucous banter, it was standing room only. The laughter of men shouting to make themselves heard above the jarring of glasses echoed volubly under a disconcertingly low ceiling. His arrival proved less remarkable than the punch lines of their jokes and their whiskeyed eagerness to be amused, and he received not a second glance from any of them. At the bar counter nearby, chance offered him a stool, with the unsteady departure of a florid Cork man in a bowler hat leaving his pals with a joke.

The mirror running the length of the counter behind the bar made Enright less wary as he sat up on the stool. But the mirror had its disadvantages too. He saw himself too clearly and when he looked elsewhere, his mirror image seemed to continue gaping at the doughy face with its imprint of Charlie Dooley's heel below the right eye. He called for a Jameson just to have a glass to nurse, some liquid to swirl about and make something playful of the light, and the noise would do the rest, because a fellow stood a fair chance of not being able to think in it. His neighbour on the next stool addressed him in the mirror.

'Did'ye have any luck today?'

'None at all.'

'Fucking dogs.'

Satisfied with the profundity of his declaration, the man went back to pondering the depths of a large bottle of stout. Sunset ripples of Jameson sparkled in Enright's glass. Behind him, the draw for the next day's coursing about to begin, order was called for amidst much mock-serious hush-hushing.

'Ah lads . . .'

'Shut up, Dorney, you blaggard.'

'*Ciúnas, no bainigh mé scealp asat.*'

Enright caught a glimpse of the Gaelic speaker at the far end of the mirror. A Kerry accent and a fist big enough to make a *scealp* hurt but he saw nothing in the ruddy-cheeked smile of merriment that threatened.

The draw began and each inaudible declaration was followed by wild cheers and backslapping. Lifted by the high spirits all around him, Enright raised the glass to his lips and wet them. He began to cough and retch at the same time. He buried his face in his folded arms on the counter and struggled to regain control of himself but the rasp of his coughing grew louder and he spat blood-clotted phlegm on to the floor. When he came up for the first time, he had already attracted too much attention. He folded in upon his spastic self again and in the throes of his retching remembered where he'd tasted that metal-tainted water. Kieler, a steward aboard the *Theytus,* an old coal barge of a thing, did a crooked deal with some fly-by-night in Piraeus over the drinking water supply. Had the fellow hose in engine water, but they found him out and beat him to a pulp before the captain threw him off at Limassol. The useless old things a fellow remembered.

Emerging from the second fit, he saw dozens of blaming faces in the mirror, their night's enjoyment spoiled. The barstool beneath him rocked forward and back, his forehead cracking harder against the teak counter each time. He planted his feet on the ground to steady himself but it felt like he was standing on sand that was being sucked out by the tide. He tried to whistle but couldn't recall one song. Something touched the ball at the top of his spine and he froze. He couldn't see his killer in the mirror.

'Tom.'

Enright tipped sidelong towards a dark release but felt himself hauled upright again. The mirror had emptied itself of faces but for his own and Timmoney's. The young constable in mufti whispered, with an eye to the last of the doggymen, a small group by the glass-panelled door squeezing the last drops out of their bottles and jokes.

'I've been searching the town for you. I heard talk in the barracks. They're saying the Shinners know you're here in Kilmallock.'

''Course they know. Who sent you, Ned?'

'Nobody sent me. Nobody gives a damn what happens to you. If you're shot they'll rest easy in their beds, is what Gallagher said when he warned me not to come down here. I never saw the man in such a rage as he was after the explosion. The young lad that died is from his own hometown. I'd swear he sent the word to the Shinners where to find you.'

A fierce gratitude welled up in Enright.

'You're a damn fool coming down here, son. Any friend I ever had is in the grave on my account.'

'I didn't come as a friend. I came because I owe you my life. And my sanity, mad as you are.'

The men by the door knocked back their drinks and began to banter playfully. They jostled each other from the door handle, their rough companionship a touching sight to Enright. *The dust before the broom. The calm before the storm. The what? The horse before the cart.*

When the men had finally left, Timmoney sat on the edge of the barstool next to Enright's, so tired he seemed just to hang there. Not a lad any more. That needy look gone from his face, the puppy-dog look of one being judged by God and other men.

'Why did you bomb the station, Tom?'

'Leaving my mark on the town, son, the only way I can.'

'That's just more of your bluff and bluster. You're acting the hard man a long time but I don't know is it your nature.'

'I know only too well my own nature, the mean streak in it. Same as it was in my father's. Not my fault nor his nor even my great-grandfather's that betrayed a Whiteboy for a pub and a wet field.'

'Look, Tom, I know you did terrible things in your time and that business at the railway station that was . . . unforgivable of any mortal man, but if you gave yourself some credit, that might be the start you need to steady your thinking. You pulled me away from a bullet and from under Baldwin's corpse. You minded that young one like a child. You were the only friend Danny Egan had. It all adds up to something . . . something more than a mean streak anyway.'

'If a man gets up every morning and does the first daft thing that comes into his head, isn't he bound to get it right now and again? That doesn't mean he ever intends to. No, I've the father's malicious guile. I was down the Gold Coast one time and a fellow told me about this tribe there where the women ran the show. See, they believed the child gets the mother's blood and the father's spirit and the blood always wins out. Chances are I'd have taken after the mother if I was born there. I'd be a buck naked savage but I'd be decent. An accident of birth is what I am, Ned, what we all are.'

'Without God, it's all accidental.'

The heat left behind by the departed crowd hadn't dallied long. On the cold draught, the ice waiting to form itself found Enright and his bones. Timmoney wasn't looking at the mirror image or even the real Enright as he stood up from the barstool. He drew a Webley from inside his black clerical overcoat and checked the breach. He went across to the front window, making a gap between the drawn curtains with the barrel of the gun, and peeped out.

'We'll make a break for the car, Tom. And there's a monastery below in Cork will give you sanctuary. I've it all arranged. Whenever it's safe, you can take the boat out of Queenstown.'

Even as he laughed, Enright raised an apologetic hand.

'I can't drink, I can't smoke and my lad's gone for a Burton. No wonder you want to stick me in a monastery.'

'Tom, I can't help you if you won't help yourself.'

'You're a damn decent man, Ned. Mind yourself in the world, won't you? Put all that happened out of your mind. Me and all.'

The man in the mirror couldn't bear to look at the gom crying. From the bad eye and the good, tears big and warm as monsoon globules fell on the backs of Enright's hands.

'If I could find the place in my brain where the memories are and if I had the knife my father gutted the sheep with, I swear to Christ, I'd cut them out.'

'I didn't come down here to get myself shot. Where's the car?'

'When I was a young lad down at home, Ned, there was a spot by the gap into the potato field and every summer a little cloud of midges used gather there. Back in the Famine times a woman died on that very spot on her way to the burial ground at Teampallín Bán and wasn't found for months. Rotted away a whole summer before they got her and every class of a maggot and insect fed off her. If a thing isn't buried, my father said, the midges come back year after year because the memory of the place is bred into them. That's memories for you. Every last filthy thing. Swarming. Even the things you can't rightly remember.'

Torn between the spectacle of Enright's tears and the empty reassurance of whatever it was he saw by the gap in the curtains, Timmoney searched out the spaces in between for inspiration.

'It's not natural the quiet out there. I don't like it.'

Enright ignored him. His was a different sense of urgency. Speaking aloud the old shrapnel of despair that had festered too long beneath his skin offered neither clarity nor hope but a kind of pained relief like the day the lump of bomb casing big as a crab-apple burst out through the skin of his shoulder on the Nelson plot. *Oh God, Tom, look at the blood pumping out of you.*

'Helen's dead, did you know that? I was going to kill her myself but I poisoned her with drink by mistake and she choked on her own vomit. Everything I touch goes rotten, Ned.'

'I should've listened to Gallagher. You're beyond redemption.'

'The Redemption of Tom Enright, wouldn't that make a grand book for you now? Wouldn't it suit you all grand that even the likes of me fitted into your tall tales, that there was somebody up there with the power and the pity to make it all work out. Well, there isn't. That's the terrible thing. Not that there isn't somebody, but that we can't help thinking there should be, no matter how fucking godless we are.'

The tickle of bile at the back of his throat set Enright coughing again, wearily, painfully. Bent double, he heard himself hum but could not recognise the tune. A sudden flurry of shouting and breaking glass jolted him dizzily upright. The mirror behind the counter fell apart, taking his and Timmoney's reflection with it. He panicked, got his hands in a tangle as he went for his gun and his legs in a tangle dismounting the barstool. He keeled over backwards and something hard and sharp kicked viciously in around his spine and he hit the floorboards long before he was ready for the impact. The breath gusted out of him and even as he lay still his fall seemed to

continue. In the suddenly blinding light he could see nothing
of the barroom nor Timmoney nor the barstool that seemed to
hit the floor just then with such reverberating force that his
body rose an inch and fell again. He tried to move his fingers.
He laughed, making fists, pounding the boards with them.
How many hundred times had he fallen off barstools, from
Funchal to Tandjungpriok? He laughed again in spite of the
arrow of pain in the middle of his back.

'I'm hit, Tom, my leg is open.'

Timmoney sat on the floor beside him, leaning against the
foot of the bar counter. His face was white and moist as fresh
bone, his palsied hands hovering over but afraid to touch the
bloodied hole in his right thigh where the cloth of his trouser
leg had burned away and still smouldered.

'Jesus, Tom, look at you.'

Enright started up, using his elbows for a prop and fell
down again when he saw the blood thick on his shirtfront.
Timmoney's, he told himself, even as he ripped the shirt from
his chest and found a raw quarry of sundered flesh filled with
a stew of pulsing innards. A dumdum bullet. He knew he was
done for. He shouted to make himself heard above the clatter
and buzz in his brain and saw the swinging bar door.

'Who shot us, Ned? Give me strength. Jesus, give me
strength.'

He lifted himself up, the weight on his chest immense, the
pain remote but advancing. Twice he fell down onto his knees
and all the while he scrabbled after the memory of where his
gun lay.

'Don't move, Tom, don't be trying to move.'

They screamed at each other, floundering across the barroom
like castaways near a shore, waves of pain and faintness knocking them sideways and back, holding on to each other because
there was nothing else to hold on to.

'Sweet Christ, there's wee bits of you falling out, Tom.'

'They'd no right to shoot you. Who the hell was it, Ned?'

'I don't know. I didn't see. Tom, I can't follow you. My leg . . .'

Enright plunged through the doorway, the Browning finally in his hand. He staggered out through the lobby and passed the face of a woman whose screams he couldn't hear over his own scream.

'Get a doctor for the young lad inside!'

At the front door of the hotel, the ice clutched at his chest and tried to push him back. He fired a shot at it, kicked on through and skidded down the frosted steps, somehow staying upright. The street and all its houses were etched coppery-vivid by the yellow light and at the far end, by Flanagan's Hotel, four men raced for the junction. He fired once, twice. He pulled the flaps of his trench coat together and clamped the fistful of canvas to his torn chest. As he ran, the blood froze to grit in the clenched palm of his hand. His attackers turned right, off Water Street, and he urged himself on, roared to hear his voice in the world.

'Face me, you bastards. Face me!'

Something bilious and bloody spilled from his mouth and put an end to the screaming that continued inside. Enright reached the corner at Flanagan's Hotel. He wanted to stop running. He wanted the middle-aged landlady to be at the door and to touch the glass of the lighted window over there for warmth. He wanted just to see the face of one of his killers under that last gaslamp on the next street that led into the dark of the countryside.

He moved more slowly, though he pushed himself harder than ever he had done in his life and a vague pride stirred in him. The house fronts on his right held him aloft as he went on, and catching sight of a moving shadow by an open gate beyond the streetlamp, he fired off another round. He heard a cry above the pounding in his head and crossed the dark of a cobbled street to the gateway. The silvery glare of the frosted field under a big moon hurt his eyes. A trench coat lay belted wrongly with brown serge on the grass like a scarecrow's cast-off and a column of footprints bisected the field until it branched out into three narrower trails. A force greater but more gently insistent than gravity called his body down and he resisted it, firing another shot at the far ditch. The kickback knocked the gun from his hand.

The white field before him rolled softly as a calm, as he plunged forward. He raced, free of fear and memory, unburdened, unleashed, hot with joyful purposelessness. Across the whites of his astonished eyes, which would not close because there was so much one last time to see, a first crystal of ice formed itself.